Praise for
Kris Longknife
REDOUBTABLE

"Readers have come to depend on Mike Shepherd for fast-paced military science fiction bound to compelling story lines and adrenaline-pumping battles. This eighth [book] in the Kris Longknife series does not disappoint. Kris Longknife is a hero to the core, with plenty of juice left for future installments."
—*Fresh Fiction*

"A rousing space opera that has extremely entertaining characters . . . an enjoyable addition to the series." —*Night Owl Sci-Fi*

Praise for
Kris Longknife
UNDAUNTED

"An exciting, action-packed adventure . . . Mr. Shepherd has injected the same humor into this book as he did in the rest of the series . . . I really love these books and *Undaunted* is a great addition to the series."
—*Fresh Fiction*

Praise for
Kris Longknife
INTREPID

"[Kris Longknife] will remind readers of David Weber's Honor Harrington with her strength and intelligence. Mike Shepherd provides an exciting military science fiction thriller."
—*Genre Go Round Reviews*

"A good read for fans of the series and of military science fiction."
—*Romantic Times*

Ace Books by Mike Shepherd

KRIS LONGKNIFE: MUTINEER
KRIS LONGKNIFE: DESERTER
KRIS LONGKNIFE: DEFIANT
KRIS LONGKNIFE: RESOLUTE
KRIS LONGKNIFE: AUDACIOUS
KRIS LONGKNIFE: INTREPID
KRIS LONGKNIFE: UNDAUNTED
KRIS LONGKNIFE: REDOUBTABLE
KRIS LONGKNIFE: DARING

eSpecials

KRIS LONGKNIFE: TRAINING DAZE

Kris Longknife
DARING

Mike Shepherd

ACE BOOKS, NEW YORK

THE BERKLEY PUBLISHING GROUP
Published by the Penguin Group
Penguin Group (USA) Inc.
375 Hudson Street, New York, New York 10014, USA
Penguin Group (Canada), 90 Eglinton Avenue East, Suite 700, Toronto, Ontario M4P 2Y3, Canada
(a division of Pearson Penguin Canada Inc.)
Penguin Books Ltd., 80 Strand, London WC2R 0RL, England
Penguin Group Ireland, 25 St. Stephen's Green, Dublin 2, Ireland (a division of Penguin Books Ltd.)
Penguin Group (Australia), 250 Camberwell Road, Camberwell, Victoria 3124, Australia
(a division of Pearson Australia Group Pty. Ltd.)
Penguin Books India Pvt. Ltd., 11 Community Centre, Panchsheel Park, New Delhi—110 017, India
Penguin Group (NZ), 67 Apollo Drive, Rosedale, Auckland 0632, New Zealand
(a division of Pearson New Zealand Ltd.)
Penguin Books (South Africa) (Pty.) Ltd., 24 Sturdee Avenue, Rosebank, Johannesburg 2196,
South Africa

Penguin Books Ltd., Registered Offices: 80 Strand, London WC2R 0RL, England

This is a work of fiction. Names, characters, places, and incidents either are the product of the author's
imagination or are used fictitiously, and any resemblance to actual persons, living or dead, business
establishments, events, or locales is entirely coincidental. The publisher does not have any control over
and does not assume any responsibility for author or third-party websites or their content.

KRIS LONGKNIFE: DARING

An Ace Book / published by arrangement with the author

PRINTING HISTORY
Ace mass-market edition / November 2011

Copyright © 2011 by Mike Moscoe.
Cover art by Scott Grimando.
Interior text design by Kristin del Rosario.

ISBN: 978-1-937007-03-4

ACE
Ace Books are published by The Berkley Publishing Group,
a division of Penguin Group (USA) Inc.,
375 Hudson Street, New York, New York 10014.
ACE and the "A" design are trademarks of Penguin Group (USA) Inc.

PRINTED IN THE UNITED STATES OF AMERICA

10 9 8 7 6 5 4 3 2 1

Acknowledgments

As so often is the case, Sir Winston Churchill said it best. "Now, this is not the end. It is not even the beginning of the end. But it is, perhaps, the end of the beginning."

Eight books ago, we began the saga of a young boot ensign from a well-connected family who chose to run off and join the Navy. Her folks were sure there was no need for heroes in their day and age, thus no need for soldiers or sailors or Marines.

Boy, were they wrong!

But with this book, *Kris Longknife: Daring*, everything changes.

And at a time like this in Kris's life, it's appropriate that her writer acknowledge a few important things as well.

Without the support of an editor like Ginjer Buchanan, these stories would have never been told. A writer couldn't ask for a better editor than I have with Ginjer. Few writers get as long a run with the same editor as I have gotten with Ginjer, and I treasure every minute of it.

Jenn Jackson is the best sort of agent that a writer could hope for. She's always there when I need her and kind enough to keep out of my way when I have a head of steam up and just want to run with it. Thanks to her and the Donald Maass Literary Agency, Kris's story is now being translated into Japanese and Spanish as well as available at www.audible.com.

The list of other folks who've been a part of bringing Kris to life for the readers goes long and includes way too many for me to name. However, I'd like to highlight the gang at the Historic Anchor Inn in Lincoln City, Oregon. I twisted my back during one of my writing weeks at the coast. For four days I was in a drug fog as my back did horrible things to the rest of me. They were the home away from home that I could only hope for, bringing food up to my room and finding ice for my back. Thank you, Kip, Candi, Misty, and all.

Special thanks go to Edee Lemonier, one of those people born with an eagle's eye for spotting typos and nits that escape me. After all, once I've written the story, I know what's supposed to be there. Seeing what's not there is a special blessing Edee gives me.

Last, but hardly least, I'd like to thank my wife, who has held my hand and encouraged me from the first day to find the writer inside me I was afraid to let loose. Thanks, Love.

1

Lieutenant Commander Kris Longknife fought the shot-up controls of the Greenfeld Ground Assault Craft. It seemed bent on smashing itself into the rocky ground below. She would much rather stay in the air, putting more miles between her and the whoever it was who'd put so many holes so quickly in her borrowed air vehicle.

"Jack, get me some more controls."

"I've already flipped on the backup stabilization and directional controls, Kris."

"Then find the backup to the backup!"

"I don't think Greenfeld puts more than one in any craft."

"What kind of cheapskate, death-happy crazies only put one backup system in a fighting vehicle?" cried Nelly, Kris's personal computer and no help at the moment.

"Our newest ally," Jack muttered.

The air vehicle fought Kris, flipping right, then left, but it put more rock-strewn ground between Kris and the apparent mining concern that had been the target of what was supposed to be a quick snatch-and-grab raid.

"Where did all that firepower come from?" Kris asked no one in particular.

"I think who- or whatever we're dealing with is very, very trigger-happy. And really paranoid, to boot," Jack answered.

"You can say that again," Nelly said.

A flash came from behind Kris. Her air rig chose to zig at that moment, giving her a fairly good view out of the left corner of her eye at the target they were now fleeing. A laser beam winked out, to be replaced by several more.

"Oh, oh," Kris muttered. "Admiral Krätz just got tired of messing with the problem and lased it from orbit."

"God help us," Jack said. And very likely meant it for a prayer. The shock waves coming off the target were only seconds away from ripping their damaged ride to pieces.

"There's a swamp up ahead," Nelly said.

"I see it," Kris said. "I'm aiming for it." As much as she could aim that riddled bucket of lowest-bid bolts.

She managed to pancake the craft into what looked like the softest mud bank in sight. They bounced, settled again, slid for a bit, then slowly turned sideways.

Then the shock wave from 18-inch lasers pommeling a mine head hit them.

The Greenfeld assault boat flipped and lost its stubby wings as it rolled and started coming apart.

As the cockpit was ripped from the rest of the craft, Kris grayed out but fought not to lose consciousness. As she struggled to avoid the looming darkness, one question kept running over and over in her mind.

What am I doing here? What am I doing here?

Then she remembered.

Oh, right, I insisted on being here.

2

"YOU will not," thundered King Raymond the First, Hammerer of the Iteeche, Killer of the Tyrant Urm and Ender of the Unity War (it was in all the papers), and presently Sovereign of the 173 planets in the United Society (or Societies, depending on your political persuasion). That royal claim was circumscribed by a brand-new, if as yet not very tested, constitution.

A recognized legend for the last eighty years, what Ray Longknife bellowed, he expected to have done.

"Yes, I will," said Lieutenant Commander, Her Royal Highness Kristine Anne Longknife, Defender of the Peace at Paris (even if it did involve mutiny), she who commanded at Wardhaven, and presently Commander, Patrol Squadron 10. She'd had enough of her grampa Ray running her around on a short leash and was ready to take her squadron and do what *she* thought necessary to save humanity . . . this time.

The space between them and the room around them took on a noticeable chill. Those forced to witness this intrafamily squabble, which, like everything the Longknifes did, was of near-biblical proportions, did their best to gaze at the ceiling, desk, carpet . . . anywhere but at the two so committed to disagreement.

Kris locked eyes with her grampa Ray. He scowled back, a scowl he'd been practicing for a hundred years. Kris didn't try to match him, scowl for scowl, but met his gaze with a rock-solid blank stare that promised no flexibility on her part.

Neither one blinked.

It got kind of boring.

So Kris checked out General Mac McMorrison's new digs. He'd been promoted from Wardhaven Chief of Staff to Chief of the Royal U.S. General Staff. The republican blue rug and frayed blue curtains were gone, replaced by a royal red. The new curtains even had gold tassels. The couches that held Kris's staff had also been reupholstered in red and gold stripes.

Kris would never have guessed Grampa Ray was so into red.

The king himself sat in a large visitor's chair next to Mac's desk. Why did Kris suspect that chair was only brought out from against the wall when the king came to call. Mac sat at his desk. To his left, in a normal-sized visitor's chair, was Admiral Crossenshield, the head of Wardhaven Intelligence.

Or maybe U.S. Intelligence, now.

Royal Intelligence?

It was hard to tell what to call anything in this changing world.

What hadn't changed was the unholy trinity, as Kris had taken to calling them. Today, they'd hollered for backup. Kris's other legendary great-grampa leaned comfortably on a bookcase to the king's right.

Oh! Kris almost broke eye lock with her royal grampa. Atop the bookcase was a fancy something-or-other. Was that a field marshal's baton? Had Mac gotten a promotion for taking on the new royal pains of commanding 173 different planets' military as they somehow merged into a unified command?

Kris would have to ask Mac . . . but not now. Not while she and her grampa were locked in a battle to see who could avoid blinking the longest.

Retired General Tordon cleared his throat in his place by the bookcase. The king glanced his way, and so did Kris. Trouble to his enemies. Trouble to his friends. Double trouble to his superiors. Whenever one spoke of the Longknife legend, it was rare that Ray and Trouble were not mentioned in the same breath.

He was Grampa Trouble to Kris. She'd learned the hard way to expect trouble when she saw him coming.

"You know," Trouble began almost diffidently, "it's an ancient and respected custom that when a superior expresses a preference, it's treated as an order."

Kris greeted that gambit with thoughtfully pursed lips . . . and a glower of her own.

The retired general soldiered on in the face of Kris's rejection. "When a king gives an order to a lieutenant commander, the officer's response normally is 'Yes, sir, Your Majesty.' "

"Yes, sir, yes, sir, three bags full, sir," Kris said under her breath, for the entire room to hear. When it was clear her message was received by all, she added, "Just like you always did, Grampa Trouble?"

Grampa's lips showed just the hint of a smile as he turned to his king and shrugged. "She's our kid, Ray."

"She's an undisciplined brat," came back in a royal growl that any old lion would be proud of.

Kris locked eyes with her royal grampa and prepared to renew their unblinking war. To keep from being too bored, she used her peripheral vision to check out how her own team was taking this little family unmeeting of the minds.

Abby, Kris's maid and occasional spy, seemed unbothered by it all. She studied the coffee table/comm display between their couches as if she might somehow decant whatever secret it had lately displayed.

Across from her, Lieutenant Penny Lien Pasley likewise eyed the table. She was Kris's intelligence analyst, interrogator, and, by right of her upbringing by two cops, usual contact with the police, a frequent and inevitable part of any visit Kris paid to a planet. Right now, her eyes were also fixed on the low table between the couches.

Beside Penny sat Colonel Cortez. As a result of having led a hostile planetary takedown that Kris had defeated, he was her prisoner. Since she'd put him on her personal payroll, he was her tactical advisor and principal ground logistician. He'd last begged to be returned to prison . . . any prison . . . rather than risk the cross fire at another Longknife family confab. Today, he calmly studied the ceiling.

Closest to Kris, and in the direct line of fire between her and her royal grampa, sat Jack. As her Secret Service agent, he'd sworn to take a bullet for her. With her spending more and more time away from home, Grampa Trouble's suggestion that she draft him into a Marine captain's uniform and head of her security had sounded like a good idea. Only after he was in uniform did Grampa Trouble let drop that, as the security chief for a serving member of the blood, Jack now had authority to countermand any order of Kris's that he considered a risk to her safety.

And Jack had a pretty broad definition of what constituted Kris's safety.

They were still working out their differences.

And Kris was now a lot more careful about any suggestion coming from Grampa Trouble.

Today, even in the holy of holies, Jack's head swiveled slowly, eyes searching for anything that might physically harm Kris.

Grampa Trouble cleared his throat again. And again, that got his king's and Kris's attention.

"You know, Commander, when one is given a mission a couple of hundred light-years out in space, normally, you don't show up at home with your whole squadron."

Kris nodded. "You have a good point," she admitted to Grampa Trouble, before rounding on Grampa Ray.

"I completed your mission," she spat.

"Already?" came from the king in what sounded like a royal yelp.

Have I really surprised him?

"Done, completed, finished," Kris said. "You ordered me to take care of the budding pirate problem out on the Rim of Peterwald space without getting any complaints from the newly crowned Emperor Harry."

The newly officialized King Raymond nodded.

"I captured three pirate schooners, one freighter, and a skiff. I liberated one potential pirate refuge and took down a main base. I also put out of business fifteen thousand hectares of drug plantations and liberated twenty-five thousand slaves. Oh, and you didn't get one whimper from your new, neighboring emperor, did you?"

Kris eyed Field Marshal Mac.

"Not a word from him," he said.

"I'm just guessing on this, but I think we'll split the two planets. Kaskatos will likely apply for membership in United Society. The Greenfeld Empire will get Port Royal, and they are welcome to it," Kris said.

"All that in three months?" Grampa Trouble whispered. There might have even been a touch of respectful awe hidden in there.

Kris kept her eyes locked on Grampa Ray. "I'm sick and tired of draining swamps and dodging alligators. I want to get on to something important."

"Um," the king said. Exactly what Kris considered "important" was too classified to discuss among even this small group. From the glance around that Field Marshal Mac gave the others, even he apparently hadn't been read into this one.

Mac opened his mouth to say something, then froze.

He struggled for a long moment to keep a look of horror off his face. When he finally got words out, they were full of horror. "Two. No three. Make that four super battleships just jumped into our system, using Jump Point Gamma."

The last time six super dreadnoughts jumped in system using that jump point, they'd threatened to blast Wardhaven down to bedrock if it didn't surrender.

"What are they squawking?" Grampa Trouble asked, standing bolt upright like an old fire horse who heard the alarm bell and couldn't stay out to pasture.

"They're Greenfeld," Mac said.

King Ray and Grampa Trouble paled. There was much bad blood between the Longknifes and the Peterwalds. Neither one breathed, waiting for the next shoe to drop.

"Oh, good," Kris said, clapping her hands with all the joy of any four-year-old presented with a tall stack of birthday presents. "Vicky Peterwald talked her dad into letting her come, too."

All four of Kris's team now rolled their eyes at the ceiling.

Four sets of very senior eyes locked onto Kris as their mouths dropped open.

3

King Raymond, being the legend that he was, recovered first. He was half out of his seat as he shouted, "You told Vicky Peterwald about our meeting with the Iteeche!"

"What?" said Mac. The field marshal apparently *was* the only one in the room who didn't know about that very secret meeting.

He turned to Crossie, the intel chief, who whispered, "I'll explain it later."

Kris didn't dare wait to defend herself but jumped right in, talking over them. "I did not," she snapped, keeping her seat.

"Then what's Henry Peterwald's daughter doing riding four battleships into Wardhaven space?" the king demanded. Half-up, half-down, he was clearly torn between his options.

With reservations, he settled back in his chair.

"She wants to come with me to find out what's gobbling up Iteeche scout ships and not spitting back so much as an atom," Kris said.

"You *told* her!" Grampa Ray repeated the accusation.

"I did *not*." Kris repeated the denial.

"Then how does she know?" Grampa Trouble asked, kindly breaking Kris and her other grampa out of an endless do-loop of accusations and denials.

"*He* told her," Kris said, and pointed at Admiral Crossenshield, the chief of Wardhaven, or maybe all U.S. Intelligence.

"I did not," he snapped, with sincerity so refined and polished it might actually pass muster of, say, a kindergartener.

Both of Kris's grampas scowled as they eyed the man who was supposed to find out other people's secrets and keep their own. From the looks of them, Crossie's sincerity had not passed *their* smell test.

"I didn't tell her about the meeting," Crossie insisted.

"No, you just sent her a video of the whole get-together," Kris snapped.

"You've seen it?" Grampa Trouble asked.

"Vicky showed it to me," Kris admitted. "I let my team view it after she did."

"What makes you so sure it came from me?" Crossie demanded.

From the glowers around the room, including her own staff's, that was considered a valid question.

"I'm in it," Kris said. "The king and Grampa Trouble are in it." They nodded agreement. "Jack's in it." At her request, the king had allowed Jack to remain when everyone else had been ushered out.

"The Iteeche are in it." Humanity and the Iteeche Empire had fought a six-year war that almost made humanity extinct. Just ask any veteran. Kris had only recently discovered that Iteeche vets of that war felt the same way. That the humans had almost made the Iteeche extinct! After twenty-five years of being told one story, Kris was still struggling to absorb the other viewpoint.

"The only person who was in the meeting that wasn't in the vid that Vicky had was you, Crossie. Methinks you did edit things a bit too much."

Now it was the admiral's turn to frown. "I might have outthought myself on that one," he admitted, and admitting to the edit, he allowed that he was the guilty party.

"So, Crossie," the king said with a tired sigh, "why isn't my most important secret a secret anymore?"

The head of black ops, white ops, and all the rest in between didn't seem at all embarrassed to be caught red-handed going against his king and luring the daughter of his strongest opposition in human space into some sort of game.

And probably gaming Kris as well.

She hated being played by Crossie.

Usually, she refused to get involved in his dirty tricks.

Problem was, today, the two of them seemed headed in the same direction.

Which left Kris wondering if she needed to make a hard right turn.

Oh bother.

While Kris spun those thoughts through her own head, Crossie was doing his best to spin his own defense.

"You and I both know this is the worst-kept secret in human space," Crossie said. "Walk into any pub in the capital here, and I'll bet you money that half the tables in the place are discussing whether or not you met with an Imperial Representative."

"They're arguing the case," Trouble pointed out. "They don't know. Big difference."

"The difference was big enough that your pet project of naming us United Sentients fell through," Crossie countered.

That got a wince from the king.

"You and I agree, we can't bring up the problem of Iteeche scouts disappearing without a trace while all we have is their own word. Your granddaughter here wanted to go do some exploring. You sent her to chase pirates instead. Sorry to say, the pirates didn't provide her all that much of a distraction." He gave her a respectful nod.

Kris returned a proud grin . . . showing plenty of teeth.

"Now she wants to take a swing at whatever is going bump in the night under the Iteeche beds. If a Longknife goes out there hunting bug-eyed monsters and finds something, how much of human space will believe her? Her word alone. If Kris Longknife and Vicky Peterwald come back saying they found something . . . ?"

"Assuming whatever they find doesn't follow them home, nipping at their heels," Grampa Trouble said darkly.

The king shook his head. "Last time I checked, I was the king, and nobody has asked me if I want my granddaughter rummaging around under the galactic inner springs to see if anything bites her," he grumbled.

That took Kris aback. Then again, Grampa Ray, seventy years ago, when he was the President of the Society of Humanity, had pushed through the Treaty of Wardhaven. Under that rule, humanity had slowed down its expansion to a more reasonable pace, colonizing most of its known sphere before pressing on to explore and people a new layer.

The argument for that kind of measured pace had seemed logical after humans' first wild exploration brought them up against the Iteeche . . . and a bloody war.

Did Grampa Ray want to keep at that measured pace?

Or did Grampa just not want a certain Kris to be the one putting her head in the potential lion's maw.

The room fell silent. She suspected everyone there was trying to draw out the unusual meaning of the king's revelation that blood might actually be thicker than water.

Kris was still struggling to manufacture a reply when the field marshal once again put his hand to his ear. "Two Swiftsure-class battle cruisers just came through Jump Point Beta. They say they're from the Helvitican Confederacy and on official business. They want to know if Princess Kristine is still here?"

"Crossie, how many copies of that damn meeting did you send out?" the king demanded.

"Several," the admiral admitted. "I didn't think I'd get many responses."

"I think you just got another one," Mac said.

"Who?" came from several of the seniors in the room.

"Two Haruna-class battleships have jumped into the system. I don't remember the last time we had a visit from Musashi."

"Not since the war," Grampa Trouble said.

"I take it you sent them a copy," the king said, dryly.

"I just wanted them to know what was going on. I didn't actually expect them to come all this way."

"Your Highness, I have an incoming message for you," Kris's personal computer spoke from where she rode just above Kris's collarbone. Nelly, very upgraded, very expensive, and very much no longer a compliant, obedient computer, was being nice today.

"Who's it from, Nelly?" Kris asked.

"Rear Admiral Ichiro Kōta aboard the IMS *Haruna*. He would appreciate an appointment, at your convenience, to meet with you concerning certain matters. Oh, ma'lady, Rear

Admiral Max Channing sends his compliments and also requests a meeting with you at your convenience. And Vice Admiral Krätz sends his compliments and says Her Royal Highness, Grand Duchess Vicky is dying to dish the dirt with you on how she got permission to charge off on this Mad Hatter idea."

"He didn't say that," Kris said.

"He did. His very words. Cross my heart," Nelly answered.

"What have we done?" King Ray asked the overhead.

Grampa Trouble scratched his right ear while not struggling very hard to suppress a grin. "You two families have been at each other's throats for years. Maybe these two girls . . ." left all sorts of possibilities unsaid.

Kris herself wondered what kind of bridges she and Vicky, two Navy officers, might build between two families that had been hating each other's guts for almost a century. She was pretty sure that Vicky's dad had paid the kidnappers who killed Kris's six-year-old little brother when Kris herself was ten. She was also fairly sure several of the recent attempts on her life could be traced, if not to the old man's door, then at least to his next-door neighbor's.

Was it possible for Kris and Vicky to bury the hatchet between their two families?

And survive the experience?

Kris was willing to give it a try.

While keeping a careful eye on her back.

To her two great-grandfathers, Kris gave a noncommittal shrug. "Nelly, send my regards and compliments to all three flags, and tell them . . ." Now it was Kris's turn to do some quick math. "It would take a good three days for all the different squadrons to finish their approaches to High Wardhaven station. Crossie, you invited them. Can you arrange to have them all docked somewhere close to the *Wasp*?"

"I can do that," he assured her.

"Then, Nelly, tell them that they should feel free to call on me one hour after the last of them ties up."

"I'm doing that, ma'lady,"

"Ma'lady?" the king said.

"Yes. Nelly is studying etiquette and protocol," Kris said.

"A gal's got to know how to fit into polite society," Nelly announced for herself.

"A polite computer," Crossie observed. "I wonder how that works."

Kris was glad that none of the black-hearted seniors present extended that observation to the logical conclusion. The line between tactful diplomacy and bald-faced lying was often a thin one. Kris now had to watch that line very carefully with Nelly.

Not for the first time, Kris wondered if Nelly's latest upgrade had been all that good an idea.

And not for the last time, she told herself that Nelly was Nelly, and her life would be a whole lot less fun without her pet computer/BFF.

Maybe if she kept telling herself that, it would get easier to believe it.

With a regal, if a bit limp, wave of the hand, King Raymond I dismissed Kris.

By Kris's own count, there were still a whole lot of issues hanging fire between them. Still, she took the dismissal and moved out.

With luck, he'd be in a better mood the next time they butted heads.

4

With three days of hurry up and wait ahead of her, Kris found she had a little time on her hands.

The *Wasp* had already been moved into space dock before Kris got back from her little confab with her great-grandfathers. With dockworkers crawling all over the ship, Kris moved herself and her staff down to Wardhaven. Nuu House was waiting for her.

It was also empty except for the old family retainers. Harvey, her driver since first grade, and his wife, Loddy, the cook, made Kris and her staff feel right at home.

For a change, Kris did the dutiful-daughter things. She called to see if she could have supper with Father . . . the Prime Minister . . . and Mother.

Unfortunately, both of their schedules were too full to make room for the prodigal daughter.

No surprise there.

She did call her brother, Honovi. She was dutifully invited over to hold the new baby. Brenda, named for Kris's mother, allowed her newly minted aunt to hold her, then promptly spit up on Kris's blues and was removed by a nanny for cleaning.

Honovi was on a slow burn; he had not forgiven Kris for being included in the meeting with the Iteeche while he was given the bum's rush by Grampa Ray. What with a small fleet of ships headed for Wardhaven, he and the prime minister had finally been brought fully up to speed. Still, he was not happy to be so late to the party.

Kris left after barely fifteen minutes.

"Oh, sis, I hear you're leaving to explore the very heart of the galaxy," Kris muttered to herself in her brother's voice as Harvey drove her back to Nuu House. "I hope it won't be too dangerous. Do take care of yourself, little sister," she finished with a sigh.

Brother had mentioned that Father had been forced to call for new elections. The opposition insisted the present Parliament could not ratify the constitution the old Parliament had negotiated.

To Kris, that seemed quite reasonable, but somehow Brother made it all sound like it was Kris's fault.

Given a choice between helping Brother and Father run for reelection and hunting the galaxy for bug-eyed monsters, Kris found BEMs winning by a nose.

Chasing pirates was a runaway favorite.

Family duties fulfilled, Kris looked for other fun. Taking a now-thirteen-year-old shopping sounded like just the ticket. Besides, Kris had been promising Cara a trip to the malls. Kris remembered what it was like to be young and have a credit chit burning a hole in your pocket.

Somehow it didn't come up in conversation until Cara was attacking several rows of very-cool-looking dresses that her credit chit was now zero. Nada. Empty.

"Auntie Teresa took me shopping while you were meeting with those old guys," Cara admitted. "We got the most gad dress. It flashes lights, and you can have it send out messages. Dada can make them flash real fast."

Kris raised an eyebrow to her maid, Cara's only flesh-and-blood aunt.

Abby shrugged. "Which of those unspoken questions do you want me to answer first. Nelly, it's your kid that has my niece flashing 'those' words."

"And I am not happy at all. At all at all," Nelly said, sounding more like a granny than a proud mother. "I am trying to explain to Dada that humans have 'things' that are not at all logical. She is learning."

"Mighty slowly for a supercomputer," Abby said, dryly.

Kris wanted the other half of her questioning eyebrow answered. "About her zero credit balance? For a spy, you're letting your boss get strangely surprised."

"Oh, that," Abby said. "Doctors shouldn't operate on their own families, and you can't expect me to be all that good of a spy where my own flesh and blood is concerned. Besides, that girl is learning from the best of us."

"Worst of you," Nelly put in.

"Whatever. She got in her shopping run with Teresa de Alva while I was biting my tongue and sitting on my hands listening to you and your family not communicate. Then we had to move down here, and when we got things all settled, somehow it didn't come up. She didn't lie to me. It just never came up."

"Until we walked in here," Kris said with a half smile teasing at her lips.

Cara was back with a surprisingly colorful and traditional peasant dress. The bustline highlighted that the twirling sprite wearing it was not a little girl anymore, but Cara didn't seem to notice.

What Kris was delighted to notice was that Cara's smile had come out to play once more.

After Kris and her Marines had liberated Cara and flattened Port Royal, Cara had been painfully quiet. Now she walked where before she skipped or ran. Worst, that infectious smile that played on her lips had gone away.

Kids have to grow up. Inevitably, they learn that the world is not as safe as the adults around them try to make it. Somewhere in the process, that childish laugh, the innocent smile, get lost.

Kris could only imagine what Cara had gone through as a slave on a drug plantation. Kris had feared Cara's smile was gone forever.

Today, for this bangle or that glam, it came back out.

So Kris paid for the dress. And the skirt and blouse. And both pairs of shoes.

"Shopping therapy," Nelly said, as they waited for Cara to try on "One, last dress. No more."

"Where'd you hear that?" Abby asked the computer.

"I read it somewhere. Mind you, with this princess lady, I've never actually seen it in operation, but, hey, I can recognize it when I see it."

The three of them fell silent. Somewhere back in the dressing room, Cara was singing. Kris tried to remember when she'd ever been so happy she just had to sing.

She couldn't.

"Are you going to send us away now?" Abby asked.

"Send you away?" Kris started at the abrupt change of topic.

"There are not going to be many dress balls where you're heading. And not a lot of snooping that a maid can do." Abby swallowed something hard. "I figure you'll want to leave me and Cara behind."

Kris shook her head. "I don't think I could afford to break your contract. You had a good lawyer draw it up, and my mom never did have a head for legalese."

Abby snorted. "What paperwork have you been reading?"

"Maybe it wasn't paper I was reading. Maybe it had something to do with a human heart. If you want to come, you'll always have a berth by my side."

"And Cara?"

"Do you really want to take her out on the limb I'll no doubt be sawing off?" Kris asked.

Abby didn't answer for a long minute. Her eyes were on the door to the dressing room, but Kris suspected, from the distant look, that she was seeing something else.

"Cara told me that when she was captured she kept going because she remembered Bruce saying 'Marines never leave anyone behind.' Poor kid, Cara was none too sure she qualified for that promise, but she kept holding to it, no matter what happened."

Kris nodded. She'd found Cara a major pain in the neck . . . but there had been no question that the *Wasp* was going after the kid. Cara was one of their own.

"You should have seen the look on her face when Sergeant Steve and his team came charging into that drug field where they had her. She'd done her best to keep her head down and be good, but she'd just done something I would have done, and her luck was all run out. Then a Marine stomps in, and all bets are canceled."

"I was kind of busy elsewhere," Kris pointed out.

"You've got to change your scheduling priorities, Kris. You miss too much of the fun stuff."

"Tell me about it," Kris said with a sigh.

"Anyway, for the last two, three weeks, Cara has been kind of sinking into this idea that she *does* have a home. She *does* have people who won't leave her behind. You know what I mean."

"Sort of," Kris said. "But Abby, this is not my usual kind of mess. If it's a choice of leading monsters back to human space and not coming back at all, well . . ."

Abby snorted. "You done gone and changed on me, kid?"

"Changed?"

"Yeah. I've followed your sorry ass through all kinds of smelly hell. I've seen people do their absolute best to put an end to your breathing. And you refuse their kind offers and just keep right on taking in air and letting it out."

"A habit of mine," Kris admitted.

"Well," said Abby. "You're mighty good at it, and I don't expect you to fail to keep on keeping on."

"That's very definitely my plan." Kris admitted.

"So, there are billions of kids Cara's age. Billions more that ain't been born yet. I don't see that we'll be any less careful of their futures if we have one of them edging around the door, looking in on us while we decide if she and they will ever have a chance to grow up."

"Now that you put it that way," Kris said, "I don't see any problem with you sharing your room with Cara.

Cara bounced out of the dressing room, wearing an ankle-length skirt that chimed like a mad carillon when she spun in it.

"I'll have it put on our tab," Nelly said without being told.

5

"I brought along three replenishment ships and a repair ship to accompany the four battlewagons," Vicky said proudly, as Kris greeted her on the USS *Wasp*'s quarterdeck.

"I watched that parade the *Fury* led in," Kris said. "Between the big guns and the big cargo capacity, you look ready for anything."

"Her father, my Emperor, requires it," said Vice Admiral Georg Krätz, commander of BatRon 12, all its supporting elements, and one Victoria Smythe-Peterwald, now a lieutenant in her father, the emperor's, Navy.

"I think Dad was afraid I'd starve to death or run out of oxygen or maybe break a nail and not have a file," Vicky said, dismissively.

"I think he's more worried about why Iteeche scouts are not coming back at the end of their voyages," the admiral said darkly, "and very much wants his daughter back after this voyage."

Vicky gave him a sideways glance. "I wish I really believed that. I'm not at all sure his new wife wants me back. And her already preggers with a boy, not that she doesn't mention that every five minutes.

"And it's going to be a body birth. No auto-jug for my new brother. Dad is just always checking in on her. He has Brother's heart monitor forwarded to his personal computer. Old men should not be fathers!" Vicky said in exasperation.

Kris had been delighted to have a younger brother. But then she'd been four and already being bossed around by a big brother. To her, Eddy looked like a chance for Kris to even up the bossing. Vicky's experience of her big brother, now deceased thanks to Kris, had not been a topic for much conversation.

At fifteen, Kris had made the discovery that her family met most of the requirements for dysfunctional. Poor Vicky had only recently come to that conclusion.

From the sound of things, the Peterwalds were about to plumb new depths on the dysfunctional scale. In the back of Kris's head, a small alarm went off. People died in the games Peterwalds played.

So how could Kris keep her distance?

Funny thing, people died around those damn Longknifes. Now it was Kris's turn to watch her back around someone else.

"How'd your father take to us digging the dirt on the economic wool that's being pulled over his eyes?"

Vicky snorted. "He didn't. He didn't believe me. Didn't want to do anything about it. Didn't want to hear another word about it. If you ask me, between my stepmom's not liking the sight of me and Dad's not wanting to hear about the way he's being snookered on the economy, he's glad to be rid of me."

Kris shook her head. As much as she wanted to hear more about this, she said, "You'll have to bring me up to date on all the gossip later."

"You girls do that on your own time," Admiral Krätz said, "but I have some official business to perform." He pulled a flat box from his pocket.

The form of the box was familiar. They usually held a military decoration of some level, but Kris was more than surprised when he flipped the lid up.

A blue Maltese cross was surrounded by golden eagles. Kris would have mistaken it for finely crafted jewelry except for the words written on the decoration.

Pour le Mérite

"Dad, being emperor and all, decided he should start doing emperor stuff, like having a greatest and highest award. The

Order of Merit. Or *Mé-rite* as he insists it be pronounced. Anyway, you're the first to get it. That oak leaf at the top, that's for valor. Only people who earn it in combat get the oak-leaf version."

"What am I getting this for?" Kris asked. "Is there a citation to go with that?"

"Everyone else got a citation on parchment suitable for framing," Vicky said. "Somehow you got skipped. You can decide whether it's for surviving the admiral here lasing you from orbit on Port Royal, or liberating Kaskatos from our rogue state-security nut, or for saving Dad's neck on Birridas. Your call."

"Ah, no citation to read at my award ceremony, huh?"

"Award ceremony? What award ceremony?" the admiral said, looking around blandly. "You've got the medal. You can explain it the same way you do that Order of the Wounded Lion."

"I don't explain it," Kris said sourly.

"Just so."

Kris pocketed the award; one more thing to add to her growing collection of stuff she rarely wore because of the problem of explaining it all. It was time to get down to business.

"Admirals Channing and Kōta are already waiting in the Forward Lounge with their command teams. I see you brought yours." Kris eyed the large collection of Greenfeld Navy and Marine officers who followed behind Vicky and the admiral as they went through the ceremony of crossing the *Wasp*'s quarterdeck.

Most looked familiar.

"You bringing everyone who was with you at Port Royal?" Kris asked.

"In truth, we have orders to make ourselves scarce," the admiral said. "After the slaughter at Port Royal, there was never any doubt my battle squadron was to be exiled with you. While the Greenfeld Navy, er, I mean Imperial Navy is happy to have Port Royal as a Navy colony, no one wants me running into any stockholders of N. S. Holding Group. The only question was whether or not the young grand duchess here got to come along for the ride."

"Dad took some persuading."

"I can imagine. Grampa Ray is making noises like he doesn't want me doing this either."

"I thought your gramps considered you so totally expendable," Vicky said.

"I sure did," Kris agreed.

"One would think so after perusing your file," the admiral said.

"Grampa Ray had me to dinner last night," Kris said. "He spent half the meal trying to convince me that my different assignments had been intended for my development."

"Development!" Vicky said. "Did he read the same file I did?"

"Selfsame," Kris said. "The other half of the meal he tried to talk me out of leading this scouting mission."

"Did he?" the admiral asked.

"Not bleeding likely," Kris said.

They reached the Forward Lounge. A Marine guard held the door open for them, then closed it behind them.

"You're keeping this meeting quite secure," the admiral observed.

"Yes," Kris said. "I didn't invite Crossie. There will be no leaks from *my* meeting."

"Did King Raymond's Chief of Intelligence admit to being the source of the leaks?" the admiral asked.

"Yes, and no, and maybe. The man is pathologically incapable of telling the truth. At least Grampa Ray is no longer holding me responsible for the leaks."

No one announced "Attention on Deck" when Admiral Krätz entered. The Forward Lounge already had two other admirals present. Adding complications to the etiquette challenge were the princess and grand duchess. A consensus had apparently formed that the Forward Lounge was a private restaurant, owned and operated by its own contractor, even if the containers were presently attached to the USS *Wasp*. When Kris introduced Krätz to Channing and Kōta, they all kept it informal although Kōta did give both Kris and Vicky a very stiff bow from the waist.

NELLY, DOES MUSASHI HAVE AN EMPEROR? I FORGOT.

YES AND NO, KRIS. MUSASHI PROFESSES TO OWE AFFECTION TO THE EMPEROR ON YAMATO. HOWEVER, FOR THE LAST TWO HUNDRED YEARS SINCE ITS FOUNDING, THEY HAVE KIND OF GROWN THEIR OWN EMPEROR. A PRINCE OF THE IMPERIAL

BLOOD, THE EMPEROR'S KID BROTHER, STARTED OUT BEING A
KIND OF VICEROY BUT AFTER TWO OR THREE GENERATIONS,
THE BIRD IN THE HAND WAS A LOT MORE REVERED THAN THE
BIRD FIFTY LIGHT-YEARS AWAY.

ISN'T THAT CONFUSING?

ONLY TO OUR WAY OF THINKING, KRIS. I UNDERSTAND
THAT THE JAPANESE ARE MUCH BETTER THAN YOU AT HOLD-
ING TWO CONTRADICTORY OPINIONS AT THE SAME TIME AND
NOT BEING BOTHERED BY IT.

Kris did her best to not let her internal discussion with
Nelly reach her face as she returned a half bow to the admiral.
The highest introductions done, Kris glanced around the room.
The captain, XO, and Marine detachment skipper for her ships
held down the left-hand side of the room, closest to the bar,
though that watering hole seemed decidedly unbusy tonight.
The representatives from Musashi and Helvetica occupied the
middle, while the Imperial Greenfeld contingent took up
nearly half the room on the right.

"Let's get started," Kris said, and went to stand with her
back to the forward viewing screen. In space, that usually
showed a lovely view of stars. At the moment, all it showed
was the ugly underside of a working space station.

"Admirals, ladies, and gentlemen, good afternoon," Kris
said. The room fell silent as all heads turned to her. Captain
Jack Montoya, the skipper of the *Wasp*'s Marine detachment
and chief of Kris's security detail, came to stand a bit behind
her and off to one side. Even here, on her ship, he didn't relax
the alertness he'd acquired as her Secret Service agent. Some
might say his devotion was excessive.

Kris had survived enough assassination attempts to appreciate it.

In the silence, Kris continued, "I suspect we all know why
we're here. In order to make sure we all understand it the same
way, I'd like to lead you through a short review."

Kris turned to the screen behind her. From a view of pipes
and cabling, it changed to a star map. "This is human space.
Over seven hundred colonized planets stretching across several hundred light-years. Linked by jump points bequeathed to
us by aliens who built them a couple of million years ago, our
migration from Mother Earth has been relatively quick over
the last not quite four hundred years."

Kris paused for people to take in the view and her words. "You might notice that, from a certain outside perspective, human space looks very much like a sausage." She waited to get a few nods and smiles, before adding dryly, "Only one species has tried to take a bite out of us, and they haven't been heard from for eighty years."

That got a few chuckles.

NELLY, EXPAND TO VIEW TWO.

"Which brings us to the Iteeche Empire." Kris used a laser pointer to draw an oval around a much larger expanse of space that now showed. "Over two thousand worlds, but growing slower than us. They, too, kind of resemble a sausage, larger and lumpier. One of its ends kind of bumping up against the middle of us."

Kris let the image of the Iteeche Empire, covering nearly four times the space of humanity, sink in to her audience.

"I can say, from personal experience, that we've been expanding human space away from the Empire." NELLY, LIGHT UP RECENTLY COLONIZED PLANETS.

Quite a few planets on the edge of human space began to flash. None of them were close to the Empire.

"I can now say that I have it on good report that the Iteeche have taken the same approach." NELLY, HIGHLIGHT THEIR RECENT COLONIES.

A large number of planets began to flash, not as many as those in human space, but still a major number. However, all of them were well away from human-occupied planets.

This brought a murmur from Kris's watchers, but no one voiced the question that should have been on all their minds.

How did Kris know where the new Iteeche colonies were?

Well, Crossie had leaked them the original meeting's video. Kris waited for her audience to process that.

NELLY, VIEW THREE.

Slowly, the view of human and Iteeche space shrank as the star map expanded to a view of the entire Milky Way galaxy.

"Humbling, isn't it?" Kris said, once the view settled. Human space and the related Iteeche area were two tiny eggs in a vast expanse of stars.

"We've got a big backyard. Unexplored. Unknown. The last time we went charging off into the unknown with wild abandon, we bumped heads with the Iteeche. I believe the Treaty of

Wardhaven that my great-grandfather rammed through the Society of Humanity's senate passed unanimously. Since that time, we've been more careful about sticking our noses into the unknown. I understand the Iteeche have gone about their exploration with a similar caution," she added dryly.

Again, heads nodded. No one seemed to doubt she was humanity's greatest living expert on the Iteeche.

She was. Still, it surprised her that no one demanded to examine her credentials.

"As some of you have heard, the Iteeche Exploration Bureau has suffered some losses lately. Three jump points to certain stars have been eating up any ships that drop in and not spitting up so much as an atom. Anything the Iteeche send there do not come back. We have been asked if our high technology might allow us to slip something in without drawing fire. Could one of our probes make it back?"

Her audience leaned forward. What she said next could easily have a life-or-death impact on them.

"I've refused to dangle our highest technology in the dark where it can be snapped up by unknown forces with us none the wiser as to what we face. So far, that has been adopted as Wardhaven, ah, excuse me, U.S. policy. If we're going there, we're taking the human eyeball along with us. Which brings us to the next options.

"I spent much of my dinner last night listening to King Raymond, Grampa to me, telling me in great detail why we should not duplicate the same search that the Iteeche have already done and lost a small squadron of ships while doing it. If Grampa had let me get a word in edgewise sooner, we could have saved a lot of time for some other topic to argue over."

Kris went on quickly without waiting for a reaction.

"I do not propose this Fleet of Discovery go anywhere near those stars. They are hot datum for somebody, drawing attention to this edge of the galaxy, and I would just as soon not attract their interest any closer to my dad, brother, nieces, and nephews.

"Are we clear on that?" Kris said firmly.

"I'm glad to hear it," Admiral Krätz said for all.

"You might not be so glad to hear what comes next," Kris said, putting her hands on her hips. "I've already heard mention of the fear, even if it is said as a joke, that I or we will come back with something mean and ugly snapping at our heels." Kris's eyes roved the room. From the looks of things, most of them had heard, or made, the same crack.

"None of our ships return unless and until we are sure that there is nothing behind us but empty space."

"How very Japanese of you," Admiral Kōta said into the silence.

"So far, all you've told us is what we won't do," Admiral Channing said. "When do we find out what we will do?"

"Right now," Kris said, turning back to the star map. "All of the Iteeche and just about all of humanity are hanging out here on this arm of the Milky Way. Humanity does have one exception. Santa Maria."

Kris swung her laser pointer to a tiny light Nelly had blinking a third of the way around the galaxy. "Founded by the hopelessly lost and desperate crew of one of Earth's first exploration ships nearly four hundred years ago, it hangs alone out here. There's been some exploration around it, but the Santa Marians are still busy colonizing their own system. Few people looking for fertile ground want to start out with the long jump it takes to get to Santa Maria."

Kris turned back to her listeners. "However, for a voyage of discovery, it looks like a great place to begin. Gentlemen, I hope your ship's power plants and stabilization systems are in good shape. I intend to lead this fleet on some fast jumps with very high and very precise spins on our ships. If you don't think you can do it, drop out now. I'd hate to lose your ship in a bad jump."

If possible, the room fell even more silent.

Somewhere, someone broke it. "I told you we were crazy to follow one of those damn Longknifes."

Kris let a wry chuckle sweep the room before going on.

"I would draw your attention to the U.S. contingent. PatRon 10. They are converted and armed merchant ships. Corvettes, folks. Small, fast, and loaded with sensors. They're good at poking their noses into things and getting out fast.

"That, folks, is our mission. We will scout far, scout well, and run like bats out of hell. Our job is to see and report back. Nothing else."

Kris paused to let that sink in. "I can't help but notice that for some reason, you have brought battleships. I know it feels good to be backed up by muscle and they are good in a fight."

That brought proud smiles from the battleship sailors among them.

"But you Big Boys are slow and very conspicuous. I do not intend to start or allow myself to get involved in a fight," Kris snapped, and the smiles got swallowed.

"We are going out there to see, identify, and run back. You remember that old saying. 'I came, I saw, I conquered.' Forget it. Our goal is, We came, we saw, we ran like hell away."

That got a laugh, which grew louder when some wag was heard to exclaim, "Who is this strange woman, and what have they done with Kris Longknife?"

Kris waited a moment for things to quiet down to a dull roar before saying, "Just so long as we understand ourselves." Then she began to outline all the boring details that needed to be covered before they departed on their voyage of discovery.

6

"That's Santa Maria's star field. We made it," Nelly announced. Only then did Kris and everyone in her Tac Center start breathing again.

Grampa Ray had strongly encouraged Kris to take the two-week-long, dozen-jump route to Santa Maria. Since he didn't actually make it an order, she'd chosen to lead her fleet through the wild, two-jump route that had first accidentally taken Grampa Ray to the lost colony of Santa Maria. That sabotaged jump had been intended to kill him and everyone on the ship carrying him.

Instead, he'd discovered a couple of million lost humans and the first map of the jump-point system.

"Longknifes aren't easy to kill" was Grampa's usual ending to that story.

Kris watched as the jump point rapidly coughed out more ships. Once through, each ship dampened its spin to a steady course but did not slow down. When the count reached twenty-two ships, Kris finally relaxed. For a recon mission best done by a scurrying mouse, this fleet was rapidly becoming very much like an elephant.

Just how much of a zoo it would end up remained to be seen.

A day's trip sunward was Santa Maria's inhabited planet.

On any normal cruise, Kris should go there, if for no other reason than to pay her respects to Tommy Lien's folks. Tommy had been her first friend in the Navy. She hadn't seen his parents since his wedding to Penny.

Or his funeral three days later.

Kris glanced at Penny; she was busy taking reports from each ship as it came through the jump. Penny had not mentioned Tommy in months.

Kris would respect her silence.

"Where to next, Princess?" Captain Drago, the contract skipper of the *Wasp*, asked.

"Jump Point Beta," Kris ordered. "See that we get there with the same velocity on the boat. Please have maintenance take a good look at the ship's stabilization system."

"Already doing it. Nothing wrong with it and I want it to stay that way."

The jump points built by the aliens two million years ago had opened space to humanity. Well, the Iteeche, too, and maybe someone else.

That didn't mean the jump-point system was without its problems. The jumps connected several stars, all of which could be accessed if you knew how and were willing to take the risks. What this meant was that the orbit that any particular jump point took around any individual star tended to be a bit erratic as the impact of the other star system's accumulated gravity had its effect as well.

In addition to the tendency to wander, there was also the question of which star system your ship jumped to. If you entered the jump at a safe, dead-slow pace and with your ship stabilized rock-solid steady, you exited into a star system not too far from the one you left. Always the same one.

That was nice and dependable. Insurance companies liked that.

Enter a jump at high speed, or under acceleration, or with a spin on your hull, and the results could be spectacularly different.

For the last four hundred years it had been human practice to do the nice and slow and steady thing at jump points. Owners, shippers, and high commands like the dependable results.

Ship captains who took chances were frequently never heard from again. Grampa Ray's ship was one of the first to recover from a bad jump. The *Sheffield* had been outfitted as an exploration ship, and instruments had recorded all the motion on the ship. That allowed them to double back.

The news of the *Sheffield*'s return had been greeted wildly, not the least by Great-gramma Rita, eight months pregnant with Kris's grandfather Al.

Other folks had also been excited about exploration prospects. Ships were quickly fitted out.

And they bumped right into the Iteeche.

One thing about a war, it concentrates the mind. It also sucks up all available cash. Exploration funds vanished from the budget.

Once peace came, Grampa Ray made sure human exploration of space was measured and careful.

Now Kris Longknife, Ray's great-granddaughter, was wadding up the restrictions of his beloved Treaty of Wardhaven and tossing them in the trash can.

And taking a small battle fleet with her.

How was that for the new generation trashing its elders?

In a few weeks . . . maybe months . . . Kris would know whether all Grampa Ray's caution had been a good idea.

Kris's Fleet of Discovery stayed well out; few people on Santa Maria would even know they passed that way. And those few had been sworn to secrecy. With any luck, this secret would last long enough for Kris to go and come back.

Kris suspected that whatever information they brought back could be kept secret for, oh, maybe twelve seconds.

Following behind the *Wasp*, PatRon 10 accelerated at one gee in echelon with Kris's flagship: the *Fearless*, and *Intrepid* in close, the resupply ships *Surprise* and *Surplus* . . . already rechristened by the fleet Misplaced and Misfiled, formed a square with the messenger packets *Hermes* and *Mercury*. Kris had no intentions of leaving a trail of communication buoys behind her at every jump point she used. Once the fleet took leave of Santa Maria, communications back to human space would be by ship.

The rest of the fleet trailed behind PatRon 10. The four battleships of Greenfeld's BatRon 12 followed in a fighting square, their four auxiliaries trailing them in a square of their own. The Musashi and Helvitican warships formed another fighting square, the *Haruna* and *Chikuma* to the right, the

Swiftsure and the *Triumph* to the left. Behind them came the two supply ships they had contracted for at Wardhaven once they'd realized what they were getting into.

Lieutenant Commander Taussig's *Hornet* pulled up the rear with a message packet that was also a last-minute addition, the *Kestrel*. This rear guard was responsible for riding herd on any of the trailing ships. If their jump point did a last-second juggle, and the large, lumbering battleships couldn't find where the jump had gotten to, the *Hornet* would see that they got through.

All of the battleship admirals assured Kris this really wasn't necessary. The sensor suites on all their ships were just as up-to-date as anything Wardhaven had.

Maybe that was true. Still, Taussig was back there with the *Hornet* just in case.

Matters went well as the fleet quickly crossed Santa Marian space. They accelerated for the first half of the trip, then flipped and decelerated for the rest. They were making fifty thousand kilometers an hour, with twenty clockwise revolutions a minute down the long axis of the ship as they sped toward Jump Point Beta.

With thirty seconds to go, the navigator goosed the *Wasp* up to three gees acceleration.

One after another, twenty-three ships vanished into the unknown.

7

"HOW far did we go?" Kris asked expectantly.

"I'll tell you when we find out," Nelly answered.

"What's the new system look like? Any sign of life?" Kris added, eyeing the blank screen of her Tac Center.

"You will know when we all know," Nelly snapped. "Now, will you quit juggling my elbow and let me process what's coming in?"

"Nelly's in a bad mood," Kris said, glancing around at her team.

"Kris, things take time, even for a Longknife," Jack said. His eyes were on the screen as it slowly filled up with a sun and three huge gas giants. It took a minute more for a half dozen small rock planets to blink onto the screen.

"The *Kestrel* is through," Penny said, her breath coming out in a sigh. "Everyone made the jump."

That was a relief to all. The *Wasp* had dropped its acceleration to half a gee. Until they spotted a jump point, there was no course for the fleet to follow. Throughout the ship, on the bridge and in boffin country, sensor teams pored over a whole raft of instruments. Slowly, the products of all that effort flowed onto the four screens that covered the bulkheads of Kris's Tac Room.

They had jumped over 750 light-years.

None of the planets orbiting the soft yellow sun was in the life zone, where water could survive in all three of its life-giving options: gas, liquid, and solid. Life as we knew it was unlikely here.

The usual telecommunication frequencies were silent. No one was transmitting radio or TV messages. Laser communications also seemed absent. The boffins would continue monitoring for a sudden change, but, for the moment, technology showed no evidence of ever having touched this system of cold rocks and colder gases.

Per the jump-point map Grampa Ray had found on Santa Maria, two jump points were supposed to be in this system. After ten minutes of searching, the bridge reported they had located both of them.

Kris reviewed the two options they offered. Some of the best astronomers and astrophysicists had been called in to develop a list for Kris to choose from. One jump led to an old red dwarf, slowly moldering away into a quiet death. The other led to a giant star, a prime candidate for something explosive like a nova ending its life. Not the thing Kris wanted her ships to find at the end of their next jump. The red dwarf also offered several jump choices that should be equally safe.

Or at least had been two million years ago, when the aliens blazed this trail across the stars.

To get long leaps between stars, you had to leap before you looked.

On Kris's orders, the fleet set a course for the jump that led to the red dwarf. As luck would have it, it was the closer of the two.

As before, they accelerated until midcourse, then began the deceleration. Once again, they flipped at the last minute and hit the jump at what at any other time would have been considered a suicidal speed, with ships accelerating and spinning like delicately balanced tops.

In two weeks, they'd made ten nail-biting jumps, and were over fifteen thousand light-years from Santa Maria. They'd trotted through ten lifeless and uninteresting systems. For a Fleet of Discovery that had launched with such great expectations, they had very little to show for all their effort.

Then the eleventh jump changed everything.

8

"Your Highness, we need to spend a couple of days refueling in this system," Captain Drago said as they shot into their eleventh new star system.

"You think so?" Kris answered.

"That last jump dropped the *Wasp*'s reaction tanks to below half-full, Kris," the captain said. "I'd like to orbit a gas planet and have the courier ships do some cloud dancing."

This was no surprise; they'd done it a week ago after the fifth jump. Every ship in the fleet needed reaction mass for acceleration and deceleration. Ships like the *Wasp* and the battleships, even the freighters, weren't designed for the knocking around that came while trawling for fuel in the upper atmosphere of gas giants.

"Pick a big one and make it happen, Skipper. Once we've refueled the fleet, I want to dispatch one of the couriers back home to bring them up to date. All we've got to tell so far is a lot of nothing, but I suspect they'd like to know that."

"We were lucky last time and only took two days, Princess. It could take longer this time."

"I don't have a problem, Captain. Whatever is out there will still be out there when we're ready."

A gas giant wasn't too far from their jump point. The fleet decelerated toward it at 1.3 gees.

Kris was on the bridge as they approached orbit. The *Mercury* had already deployed a balloot and was dropping away for its first run at skimming the outer atmosphere of the planet.

At Sensors, Chief Beni shook his head. "There's something wrong with my instruments," he muttered.

"That would be unusual," Kris said.

"Yes, and I've checked them. I can't find anything wrong with them, but this can't be right?"

"What can't be right?" The chief now had Captain Drago's attention.

"There are eleven decent-sized moons around this puppy. According to my readouts, they have wobbled a smidge farther away from the planet than they were just after we came through the jump."

"They are in unstable orbits?" the captain said.

"If what I'm reading is right, they sure are. It's not a lot, but then, we've only been observing them for a few hours. Let me check with the boffins. Just a minute."

Kris was at her usual station, Weapons. She'd brought it up more out of habit than any expectation of a shoot. She double-checked her board; all four of the *Wasp*'s 24-inch pulse lasers were locked and loaded.

"Hey," the chief looked up in surprise. "One of the moons has a hot spot."

"A volcano?" Kris asked.

"Maybe," the chief muttered, his eyes studying his board. "What's this? A bit of electromagnetic activity as well?"

"Talk to me, Chief," the captain said.

"It just showed up as the moon's rotation brought it into view. I'm on it, sir."

"Stay on it, Chief."

"I've got Professor mFumbo calling me. Could someone else take the call?" the chief said, not breaking concentration.

"I've got it," Kris said. "Bridge here, Professor. We're kind of busy just now."

"I am answering Chief Beni's call about these damnable orbits. Yes, all the moons orbiting this gas giant are dancing a very strange polka."

"Any ideas why?" Kris asked.

"No idea. I've never heard of this happening before. It's as if this giant used to have a lot more mass and lost it, and now

its gravitational hold on its moons is adjusting to the sudden
weight loss.

Captain Drago scowled at the forward screen. The *Mercury*
was about to take away some more of the planet's mass as it
filled its balloot with gases that would be transferred to the
ships of the fleet to use as reaction mass for their fusion reactors. The fleet would need a lot of mass to refuel.

Still, what they removed would hardly matter to something
as big as this gas giant and its moons. Kris took a deep breath
as she considered what kind of force could make such a difference.

"Chief, talk to me about that hot spot," Captain Drago said.

"Nelly, pass all that we've gotten to the fleet," Kris told her
computer.

"Kris, I've been doing that. The other ships of the fleet have
a lot of science aboard, too. Our data is just verifying what the
other are concluding, as well. The *Haruna* has gone to General
Quarters."

"Pass the word to PatRon 10. General Quarters, Guns. Unknown cause."

"Done, Kris."

On the *Wasp*, the General Quarters' Klaxon began to sound.

"We're the closest to that moon, Captain Drago," Kris said.
"Would you close on it, please."

Of all the ships in PatRon 10, only the *Wasp* had a contractor for a captain. He was older, more experienced, more
mature. He drew his check from Admiral Crossenshield's
black-ops funds. He was here, Kris didn't doubt, at King Raymond's specific order to see that Kris didn't do any of the
damn fool stunts that he and Grampa Trouble had done before
they reached old age.

Someday, she expected he would countermand one of her
orders. She waited to see if today would be that day.

"Sulwan, put us closer to that unknown event," he ordered.

"Aye, aye, sir," the navigator replied.

So, not today, huh.

"Your Highness, the *Intrepid* is nearby," Captain Drago observed.

"Yes, right," Kris said, properly instructed. "Nelly, invite
the *Intrepid* to join us in this little side trip."

"Done, Kris."

On the screen, two dots broke from the strung-out line of ships still decelerating, aiming for a lower orbit of the giant. The *Wasp* and *Intrepid*, however, stretched their vectors to match the high orbit of the moon in question.

"Can somebody give me an idea of what we're heading into before we actually ram that damn moon?" the captain snapped.

"It's a rocky planetoid with no iron core. Its surface is a cold mix of vapors, some water, some methane, lots of crud," the chief said. "Liquid, not gas. I don't think there are any lakes; the moon's surface looks pretty rough."

"We boffins concur," Professor mFumbo said.

"One small spot is showing hot," the chief went on after a hasty breath. "I'm trying to get a visual, but that heat seems to be steaming off the volatiles. Radar . . ." He paused. "Radar isn't coming back. Something's driving our radar nuts."

"Active or passive?" Kris and Captain Drago said at the same time.

"I can't tell. I've got some sort of electromagnetic crap coming from there, but it's not organized like anything I've ever seen."

"Can you laser range it, get a picture that way?" Kris asked.

"I'm lasing it."

"Nope, nothing," he said a moment later. "Laser can't get through the vapors."

"Is there a gravity well?" Kris asked.

Every mass sets up its own gravity well. The very sensitive atom laser on the *Wasp*, designed to track twitchy jump points, was the most sensitive instrument for measuring variations in that weakest of the four natural forces. Weakest, but most important. Just ask any two-year-old trying to defy gravity with each step.

"Checking," the chief said. A long moment later, he nodded. "There's something solid there. There's definitely more mass under that hot spot than there is in the rest of the moon."

For fifteen long minutes, the rest of the fleet decelerated into lower orbit and went about beginning the process of refueling. Meanwhile, the *Wasp* and *Intrepid* cut back on their deceleration and swept toward a much higher orbit, one that would take them on a quick flyby of the mystery-shrouded moon.

Sulwan, good navigator that she was, guessed before Kris

asked her that she'd like to know if they could transform their present course into an orbit around the moon. "Even decelerating at 3.5 gee, that option is already gone. We'll need at least one orbit to match that moon. Maybe two if I miss a window."

They were halfway to the moon when the chief announced, "Something is lifting off from our target moon. Whoever they are, they're coming straight at us."

9

"Raise defenses," Kris ordered.

"Shields up," said Sulwan as an umbrella of Smart Metal™ spread out in front of the *Wasp*. Battleships and cruisers were encased in ice, some of it meters thick, to ablate away the blazing sting of lasers and even kinetic weapons. Small ships like the *Wasp*, especially when it was wrapped in shipping containers full of scientists, Marines, and other gear could hardly use the ice defense.

The rotating umbrella of Smart Metal™, especially if it was angled to the threat axis, not only provided protection but also gave the *Wasp* a chance to hide behind it.

Where, exactly, was the *Wasp* with respect to the spinning parasol?

Guess.

Meanwhile, Kris's ship had four 24-inch pulse lasers ready to strike out with a sting of her own.

Slipping out farther to the left of the *Wasp*, the *Intrepid* deployed her own protection.

Ahead of them, the unknown continued to close.

"How fast is that sucker accelerating?" Captain Drago asked.

"Three-point-five, no three-point-eight gees, sir," the chief reported.

"Can you get us a picture of it?" the captain asked.

"I got one as it launched, but the thing is spraying something into the space all around it now." The chief tapped his board, and a small window opened on the main screen. It showed a series of spheres balanced on rocket fire.

"Fusion rockets?" Kris asked.

"I would guess so, from their temperature," the chief said. "But I'm getting next to nothing from my electronic readouts.

"Nelly, hail it. Try every language we know," Kris said. "Say 'We come in peace,' for starts."

"Doing it, Kris."

While Nelly tried to open a conversation, the ship continued to close the distance, eating up the kilometers.

"Is it going to try to ram us?" Sulwan asked.

"Get ready to take evasive action," Captain Drago ordered. "Don't do anything yet. It's on a steady course. Let's not juggle its elbow."

The three ships closed. Nelly tried sending numbers to see if they would talk math back to her.

Then the thing hit them with a laser.

The spinning parasol did its job, rotating more Smart Metal™ into the vacancy as fast as the laser could make the hole. When the power hit ended, the parasol was still there. Nelly quickly patched it up, but the shield out there spinning was several meters smaller across.

"Ouch," the chief said.

"That was not nice," the captain agreed.

"Locked and loaded," Kris said. "I think Nelly and I can graze it through all the gunk it's pumping into the space around it."

"Do it," the captain said.

"Nelly, let's open the largest sphere to space. Just a quick cut," Kris said, moving the crosshairs on her board to show exactly where she wanted to hit the stranger.

Nelly put a red dot on Kris's target. With sincere regrets for starting the next alien war, Kris closed the firing switch for Laser 1.

On the screen, a laser reached out for the alien.

On Kris's board, an outside camera followed the shot. There, at least, the crud around the ship gave them something for the laser to relate to. A red beam cut right where Kris wanted.

One sphere took the hit along the top of its curve.

The alien didn't slow. It just kept coming.

"Hit it again," Captain Drago said. "Aim for the engines."

"Already setting up for it," Kris said, and moved her cross-hairs aft.

Before Nelly could cover the target with a dot, the alien shot a second time.

Once again, the shield did its job.

"We can't take many more like that," Sulwan reported.

"Let's see how good they are at damage control," Kris said as she punched Laser 2.

On the main screen, and on Kris's view, a red beam reached out for the aft end of the alien ship—and sliced right through it.

Behind it, the glow of the rocket motors sputtered, the ship wobbled on its tower of fire.

"I got 'em," Kris said.

Then the spheres of the ship rippled as an explosion ran its full length, from bow to stern. Huge chunks of the different spheres flew in all directions.

Kris had seen ships die violent deaths. It was not something she ever wanted to get used to. But this explosion looked very different from any of the other ones.

"Chief, talk to me about what just happened. Professor mFumbo, what can your experts report? Was that a reactor-containment failure?"

"I don't think so, Kris," the professor reported. "My experts here say that was some kind of chemical explosion. We're running our high-speed cameras back over it. I can tell you more in a few minutes, but the explosion doesn't appear to have been initiated in the last sphere where you hit it. Rather, it started at the opposite end of the ship and moved aft."

Kris nodded. "That was what it looked like to me, as well. Let me know as much as you can as soon as you can."

"This is interesting," the chief said.

"Everything is interesting," Kris said. "What's making your bunny jump?"

"The moon. That hot spot where the ship just launched

from. It just got very hot. Explosive hot. Whatever they were doing there, I think someone just blew up all the evidence. And unless I'm very mistaken, they used the exact same sort of explosives on the moon as they did on the ship."

"Yes," Kris said. "How very interesting."

10

Lieutenant Commander, Her Royal Highness, Kris Longknife, leaned back in her chair, reviewing in her mind what had just happened. Had she just become the one of those damn Longknifes who shot up the first alien contact humanity made in the last eighty years?

Lately, she'd spent some time wondering how her great-grandfather's generation could have made such a hash of its encounter with the Iteeche. No "Hi. How are you?" Just shoot, shoot, shoot.

It looks like I owe Grampas Ray and Trouble apologies.

Kris tapped her commlink. "Professor mFumbo, have your boffins spotted anything else in this system that we need to shoot, dodge, or otherwise be aware of?"

"I'm afraid we have found nothing of interest. Or maybe the more proper answer is that I am glad to report we have not."

"Captain Drago, I'm going to withdraw to my Tac Center. Please feed all ship data to that location after first making copies of that data and copying them out to several backup locations. Those of you on the bridge, you may want to make an extra copy of your board's data and hide it in your sock drawer. It may come in handy when you write your memoirs of today, if you don't need it earlier at my court-martial to prove that there were no changes to your data by me or anyone else."

"Ain't it great to be a part of history," Sulwan observed dryly, but the navigator was already downloading her board to a memory chip . . . and had several more on her board ready to be filled.

Captain Drago looked around. "I'll order a crate brought up from supply."

"Thank you," Kris said. "Nelly, have my staff meet in my Tac Center."

"They are already headed there."

"Ask the galley to bring around coffee and sandwiches. I'm hungry, and I think it's going to be a long night."

"Cookie is already putting together a tray for us, Kris," Nelly reported.

With a sigh, Kris stood and began to make her way off the bridge. Behind her, a gunnery mate second class slipped into her vacant station and began to download Kris's data.

Her team was waiting for Kris by the time she reached her private retreat. Captain Jack Montoya, Royal USMC and head of her security detail, had taken the seat to her left. There he had a clear view of the door and anyone trying to enter. Professor mFumbo held down the other end of the table. He'd come alone.

Abby, officially Kris's maid, was to Jack's left, fiddling with the tray of goodies . . . and also where she had a good line of sight on the door. Abby was a crack shot who even the Marine detachment's Gunny Sergeant could only match shots with.

Penny, the staff's intel expert, had taken the seat to Kris's right, which put her back to the door. If something evil got as far as that without her knowing it was coming, she'd consider her job a failure and the mess something for the Marines to clean up.

To Penny's right was Colonel Cortez, Kris's defeated foe and ground-tactics advisor. Right now, he pursed his lips in reflection. "I've never been around when a galactic war got started, but that sucker didn't leave you any choice but to shoot. Very aggressive behavior."

"I'm glad to hear that somebody else feels the way I do," Kris said. "But I need to know what actually happened back there and who was doing what to whom. There are too many unknowns and unthinkable things that leave me scratching my head. I do not like that. Not at all. Penny, will you take the lead on forensics?"

"I expected you'd want me to. I've had Mimzy capturing some of the raw feed off the boffins' video take. The wreckage is in much bigger chunks than I would expect had a reactor failure been involved. With luck, we'll have something bigger than atoms to examine. Professor, I hope you'll excuse me for having my computer do what one of Nelly's kids can do so well."

The professor scowled at the request for forgiveness. He had been offered one of Nelly's "children" when Kris's computer got the biological urge to gestate. His initial experience had been something less than sterling, and he'd returned the gift.

He and Captain Drago, both.

The boffin could not be happy to have Penny using the same secret weapon that he had declined in order to steal a march on his people.

"Do what you will. But remember, what might look like something at first blush to an amateur may have a totally different meaning when examined patiently by a trained expert."

"A good point that we will keep in mind," Kris said. "So, Penny, what are your first observations?"

"Give me a minute," Penny said, her unfocused gaze aimed in the general direction of the overhead. Penny's ivory skin seemed to pale almost to translucent as her breath slowed.

Usually, this kind of first glance would have been done on one of the wall screens for all to see and comment on. Instead, Penny held whatever output she was getting to just herself and her pet computer, Mimzy. The computer feed colored the contacts of Penny's eyes but was private to her.

The minute Penny had asked for stretched into two. Then three.

Kris began to get edgy; this was her first initial alien contact. This was humanity's first new alien contact in eighty years. The last one had gone horribly wrong.

This one looked to be going along the same downward path.

Kris didn't much like the trip. Worse, Kris didn't like that this one was her responsibility.

Just as Kris was about to open her mouth, Penny's gaze

dropped from the overhead. She took a deep breath. "Okay, I think I can see how to brief this."

"We're ready," Kris said.

"Nobody will ever be ready for this one," Penny said, half under her breath.

Across from her, the wall screen lit up. Abby turned to face it. Jack pushed his chair away from the table so he could see, without losing sight of the door.

The screen opened on a view of the moon as a large explosive blew out in a gale of expanding gases. Some of the debris cloud achieved at least orbital speed, maybe escape velocity.

"First things first. The explosion on the moon. It was a chemical explosive, conventional. Not something we use. That stuff is corrosive and dirty. It's in our books, but it hasn't met environmental standards since before we broke loose from Earth. I'll leave it to the boffins to give you all the gory details if you want more."

"Was it done intentionally?" Kris asked.

"No doubt in my mind," Penny said. "Both because of the type of explosives and the timing. It blew within five seconds of the ship destroying itself."

"Isn't that an opinion?" Abby shot at Penny.

"A well-founded one, I think," Penny countered. "When you have the same explosives letting go within seconds of each other, coincidence must take a backseat to facts. Once can be an accident. Twice, we should start looking for hostile activity. Three, and only a fool doesn't assume enemy actions."

Spoken like a true paranoid, Kris thought, raising an eyebrow to Penny's other listeners. The rest of the room took a moment to mull her viewpoint. No one chose to express a dissenting opinion.

"Go on," Kris said.

The view on the screen changed to show the unknown ship charging up to meet them. In slow motion, Kris's laser beam shot into the aft-most sphere of the ship.

"I put it right where you wanted it," Nelly said.

"Exactly," Kris agreed, and watched as the fusion engines sputtered, throwing the ship off its steady course.

"Oh, and for what it's worth," Penny said, "the hostile was on a collision course with the *Wasp* until Kris's hit in the engine room knocked it off track."

"Nasty little beggar," the colonel observed dryly. "Shooting first and hell-bent on ramming. I'm developing a serious doubt that they ever intended to ask questions."

"It's too early to start applying salve to our souls, Colonel," Kris said. "But thanks anyway."

"It wasn't a cheap Band-Aid I was offering, Princess, but a quite serious observation. I'm starting not to like these bad actors."

"Here's one to look at," Penny offered, to bring them back on topic.

A body appeared, whirling out of the explosion. Two arms, two legs. A head. The face was hard to make out, but there was a most prominent jaw. Even hair.

"They look almost human," Jack said.

"We've identified the Three alien species who built the jump points," Kris said. "All had their own evolutionary trails and look nothing like us. Or the Iteeche. Now we run into these bug-eyed monsters. They come out shooting and look amazingly like us!"

"Very much like us," Penny said, and a section of the explosion filled the view screen. Several bodies were clearly visible. Two looked to have a pair of large mammary glands on their chests. The screen cycled through the next few frames slowly, letting the bodies rotate. They certainly looked female.

"What's that other one holding to her breast?" Kris asked.

A third "woman" held on to a small bundle. In the next couple of frames she lost her grasp. The wrappings around the bundle also came undone.

"I think that's a child," Penny said.

"Dear Mother of God," the colonel said. "They blew up their ship with their women and children on board! What kind of monsters are we dealing with?"

Kris turned away from the screen, not that she could ignore it. She focused on Penny. "You're sure they blew up the ship themselves."

"The explosion started in the forward sphere," she said, and the screen's view changed to show the entire ship, again. It began to come apart, starting, as Penny said, with the forward-most of the spheres, then the second, then the third. The aft sphere, Engineering from all appearances, was the last to go, and seemed to fly into the least number of pieces.

"I think they expected their destruction to involve the reactor," Penny said. "That's just a guess, but if the reactor had blown, it would have taken the fragmentation and dispersal of debris to a whole new level."

Kris nodded. She had already done a postmortem on a ship where the reactor finished off its destruction. The wreckage had been little more than atoms and molecules. Her ongoing nightmares, however, were much more substantial.

"So, Princess," the professor said, "your hit on the power plant seems to have resulted in our having wreckage to examine that they did not intend for us to have."

"It looks that way," Kris said.

"Look at those bodies. No space suits," Abby said, pointing at the picture still on the wall screen. "No survival pods. They all were in a shirtsleeve environment, then some bastard opened that ship to vacuum for all of them."

"I don't think survival was ever the intention," the colonel said. "I've heard of 'Victory or Death' as a battle cry, but in all my study of human history, I've never encountered anything like this."

Kris could only shake her head. "This is our first human encounter with someone else's history. I know we humans have had our nasty and desperate times. I think we've found someone or something willing to take nasty and desperate to a whole new level. God help us."

Those who shared her room seemed unable to expand upon that observation. Kris looked at her options and found only one to start with.

"Nelly, tell Captain Drago that I would like for the *Wasp* to make orbit around that moon so that we can examine both what our alien was doing down there and recover as much of the wreckage as possible. I'll want to ship as much of the wreckage and bodies back to human space as we can."

"That will involve unloading one of the cargo ships," the captain answered Kris immediately.

"I figured as much. You said it would take two or three days to refuel."

"Refuel and resupply the ships from the replenishment ships, yes, Kris."

"We might as well put our time to multiple uses. Penny, put together a short report on what just happened and flash it to the rest of the fleet whenever we get a line of sight on one of them."

Most of the fleet was on the other side of the gas giant. With the *Wasp* trying to make orbit around the target moon, the two elements of Kris's fleet were likely to make "ships passing in the night" seem downright familiar. "I'm sure they're curious."

"I bet they are," Penny said, and went silent as she began to arrange her data drop.

11

Kris would have preferred that the other ships of the fleet had stayed in low orbit around the gas giant while they took on reaction mass. However, she was discovering the difference between leading a fleet and commanding one.

Where she led, they followed.

What she wanted, they considered.

And frequently ignored.

The admirals flipped to see whose flag got refueled first. As it happened, the order came out *Fury*, *Haruna*, *Swiftsure*. And, in that order, they all refueled, then climbed out of the gas giant's gravity well to join the *Wasp* orbiting the small moon.

And hunting for the odd bits of wreckage.

Since the battleships had large crew-transfer boats . . . some even looked like planetary assault craft . . . they did make a major contribution to the hunt for chunks of the alien wreckage.

Maybe it was the very ad hoc nature of the fleet, but it seemed to gain more structure . . . and pay more credence to her suggestions . . . as they assimilated the full impact that they had met an alien—and Kris Longknife had blown it to bits.

The different nationalities of her fleet had made their own arrangements for their supply needs. Most were containerships, good for passing a container from freighter to warships and quick resupply. Kris, however, needed a huge, enclosed space for collecting and organizing a messy jigsaw puzzle that had once been a truly alien ship. She drafted the *Constant Star*; its large Number 2 hold was just the place to do the postmortem on humanity's latest encounter with an alien race.

The *Constant Star* had been leased in haste by Admiral Channing when it became clear that this little jaunt of Kris's might not be over in a few weeks. The *Star* was an older, breakbulk freighter, capable of handling containers, but still with huge cargo holds for storing this and that, and more of both. However, even after both Helvitican battle cruisers had stuffed themselves to the gills, there were still supplies piled high in the *Constant Star*.

Over protests all around, Kris ordered the other supply ships to take on the balance of the *Star*'s cargo and empty her totally out. The skipper of the *Star* wasn't very happy to be losing his paying cargo. He only perked up at the hint from Kris that he would be going home first . . . and could return with another load of supplies.

Kris, herself, was changing her own plans. She'd intended to send the *Mercury* home immediately with a negative report. Instead, the *Mercury* hung around to help refuel the fleet and wait for Kris's team to complete its initial analysis of this first alien encounter. Then the *Mercury* would escort the *Constant Star* back to human space so the rest of humanity could meet their new neighbor.

Kris could well imagine the political firestorm that would follow.

There were definite advantages to being several thousand light-years away from home.

Kris waited until the *Swiftsure* made orbit, then invited all three admirals to bring whomever they chose to tour the growing collection of twisted metal tied down in the *Constant Star*'s forward holds. Admirals Krätz, Kōta, and Channing immediately replied that they'd be there in an hour.

So Kris found herself, escorted by her own staff, drifting weightless through a collection of blackened and torn metal, plastic, and ceramics.

"Any of this new to us?" Vicky asked.

"There's a lot of machinery," Kris said. "Some of it's pretty obvious what it does. Other chunks are so fragmentary that no one has any idea what they're supposed to do," Kris pointed at write-ups that were attached to some pieces of metal. "These explained what can be explained. Other sheets of paper have only a big question mark.

"Our problem is we can't decide if our ignorance is because of the damage it suffered in the explosion or whether it really is something new. It could be just a different take on what we already have that works. Their air-reprocessing system is very different from ours. I'm not sure it's better."

"And they didn't say anything. Just started shooting, huh," Admiral Krätz said.

"I'd prefer to discuss that when we've got some weight on, if you don't mind," Kris said.

"So you like my idea." The admiral grinned like a proud papa.

"Was it yours?" Kris asked.

"Close enough," Vicky said, like she was in on a secret that she wasn't about to share with Kris.

"I hate weightlessness," the admiral said. "When it was clear we were headed out where there were no spaceports, I offered a prize for the best idea. It was a seaman recruit's notion. Have you ever seen a yo-yo?"

Kris admitted that she had once played with one as a girl. "I couldn't make it do anything."

"Well, Seaman Welt can do anything with one of those spinning things. He can do it with two at the same time. That got me thinking," the admiral said, beaming.

Kris could see no reason why two spinning yo-yos should give anyone an idea to spin two ships around the same point, connected by a long beam or, in the case of the *Wasp* and the *Intrepid*, a long spun bar of Smart Metal™. Still, while the ships swung around, there was at least half a gee of fake gravity.

And no barfing.

This idea had been floated before the fleet left Wardhaven space. Admiral Kōta tried it with the *Haruna* and *Chikuma* using a cable. They were sister ships and supposed to displace the same tonnage. Still, there was enough difference in weight and the distribution of that weight to cause the ships to do a little dance around each other and the point that was supposed to be their mutual center of gravity. The line tended to go very taut, then limp, then taut again.

What would happen if, no, when it snapped was not something to contemplate. Nuu Yards got a quick contract to knock together several harnesses, and each of the ships adopted a "dance" partner. For the warships, it wasn't too bad. Each of them had a sister ship close to its tonnage at hand.

For the auxiliaries, it was a completely different story. They were exiled to the far end of the fleet-line anchorage as they orbited the small moon . . . and given wide berths. To which several of the merchant captains had added double the planned distance.

Still, no one was complaining about the problem. No sailor really liked microgravity.

The grim tour got worse. Most of the technicians were left behind in the forward holds when the admirals and their chief doctors headed aft. The last hold was still open to space. One hundred and twelve bodies floated in frozen preservation there.

"Damn, they look so much like us," Vicky said.

"Yeah. We run into the first alien that really looks like our brother," Kris said, "and all it wants to do is kill us."

"So we killed them," Admiral Krätz said.

"They didn't leave me much of a choice," Kris said.

"Yes, yes," Admiral Kōta said. "Still, it would be nice to be able to talk to them. Have you recovered any computers? Any books?"

"We'll cover that in more depth on the *Wasp*," Kris said. "It is possible that all the computers were located right by the explosives. That would expose them to a lot of heat and force and leave them in very tiny pieces."

"Almost as if someone didn't want us to have anything to look at," said Admiral Krätz.

"If that wasn't their intention, they sure achieved it," Kris said.

"What would lie at the root of that kind of behavior?" whispered Admiral Channing.

"That is something that we can only guess at," Kris said. "I'd like to give everyone a chance to do some of that guessing before I put the finishing touches on my report. I suspect you are all writing reports of your own?"

The admirals nodded in various shades of noncommittal.

"How many of them were there?" Vicky asked.

"So far we've recovered all or major portions of 132 bodies," Kris said. "Men, women, children. Elderly and babes in arms. There might be a few more out there. We're still hunting."

"How big was that ship?" Vicky asked. From the open mouths, she'd only beaten the admirals to the question by a moment.

"About the size of one of our courier ships," Kris said.

"What have you got, ten people on those?" Admiral Krätz asked.

"Yes. When they were pirate schooners they used to cram twenty-five or thirty into them."

"For a couple of weeks. Have you found any living quarters down on the moon?"

"Nothing," Kris said. "All that's down there are some digging and smelter gear. They were blown individually. But there's nothing that looks like housing."

"So they were living crammed into that ship," Vicky said.

"Having babies and growing old together," Kris added.

"Aliens," Admiral Krätz said, shaking his head. "They are aliens even if they do look the most like us of any aliens we've found."

"Will the contents of this ship be shared with our home governments?" Admiral Kōta asked.

The politician in Kris's upbringing spotted the hot button in that question, but the fleet leader in her just shrugged. "I'm sending this cargo back to human space. Then I plan to continue my voyage of discovery. I expect to have more on my mind than who gets what of this mess."

The Navy officers drifted up to a window that looked into an isolated room organized like an operating center. On one table a lone body was strapped down and laid out. Its chest had been opened and its organs removed. They now floated in glass jars.

"They've got everything we've got," Kris said. "Different arrangement. Our guess is that they started walking upright about six million years ago, too. Give or take a few months," she half joked.

"Can we go in?" Admiral Krätz's head doctor asked.

Kris nodded. "We're using level-three biohazard suits."

The three doctors who had accompanied their admirals so far took their leave and headed into the operating room.

"Have you run a DNA check?" Admiral Channing asked.

"Yes," Kris said. "They have DNA, but their base molecules are different from ours. My biologists are very excited. And no, they doubt there can ever be any interbreeding. Even if our plumbing can be made to rendezvous, the genetics just aren't going to let it happen."

"Kris, we need to talk," Admiral Krätz said, waving his hand, "about all of this. Who gets what? Where do we go from here?"

"Yes, we need to talk," the other two admirals agreed.

"Well, sirs, we have gravity on the *Wasp*. May I invite you to the Forward Lounge?"

12

Kris was halfway back to the *Wasp* before she noticed that it wasn't alone. A new courier ship hung just off where it swung in space with the *Intrepid*. A large shuttle from the *Wasp* was just departing from the stranger and heading back to Kris's ship.

"Nelly, get me Captain Drago."

"I got him, Kris."

"Hello, Your Highness," he said cheerfully. "I was expecting a call from you."

"What's a strange ship doing off our bow?"

"There's nothing strange about the *Sandpiper*. She's here to replace the *Mercury*. The king thought we might need another courier boat.

"What'd it bring?"

"Who said it brought anything?"

"Admiral Crossie would not pay for a fourth courier ship if it didn't carry something twisted and sneaky and, I don't know, special for him."

"See for yourself. Longboat 2 will be reeled in right after you."

Kris was seated right behind the two bosun's mates running the show. She watched over their shoulders as they attempted the new maneuver it took to land on the *Wasp*. Usually when a ship was in orbit, a longboat just nestled into a docking bay. But a ship wasn't usually doing flips with another ship while both of them zipped along in orbit.

Now they did.

As it turned out, it wasn't all that hard.

To watch.

The *Wasp* let out a long line with a loop at the end.

The longboat snagged the loop with a hook it now dropped from its nose. The hook was retracted once it had the loop solidly in hand.

Then the *Wasp* reeled in the longboat.

Easy.

If you didn't have to do it yourself. Though neither of the youngsters piloting the boat said a word of complaint, Kris noticed both of them wiping sweat from their brows.

"Well done," she told them.

"Piece of cake, Commander," the senior of them said.

Kris waited while the admirals exited her launch. They were admirals, and she was a lieutenant commander, so seniors go first even if it is your flagship and you are a princess. Once aboard, she had Penny lead them to the Forward Lounge while she waited to see what surprise the unholy trinity had popped on her.

The next longboat docked with no more difficulty than the last. Some people were spending a lot of time in the simulator, no doubt. It took a while for the hatch to open, but when it did, who should clop out but Ron, Kris's favorite Iteeche.

"What are you doing here?" she demanded, unsure whether to offer a hand to shake or see if she could actually manage a hug for something with four arms, four legs, and a whole lot of elbows and knees.

She did get both her arms around the trunk of her friend though it was a bit of a problem bending over his four-jointed pelvis. An Iteeche was not like the human's mythological centaur. His body trunk rose from somewhere closer to his center of gravity, as befits a creature that swam for a lot longer in the sea and owed its ancestry more to something like a squid than to a quadrupedal land critter.

Ron hugged back, doing something that almost sounded like a human laugh.

"I could ask what you are doing here," he said through the

translator Kris had given him the last time he'd dropped by human space.

"I'm hunting for whatever's eating up your scout ships," Kris said.

"You are a far distance from where they went and did not return."

"Well, yes. We call incidents like exploding scout ships a hot datum. They draw attention. We don't want to draw any more attention to those spots. Anyone who comes nosing around them might keep nosing and bump into you. I want to come at them from the other way around and draw their attention this way."

"You humans are very twisty in your minds. I think I like that."

"Well, you arrived just as I and some of the fellow voyagers were about to hash over something that happened to us in this system."

"Nothing bad I hope."

"It's me you're talking to, Ron. I'm a Longknife. Bad things happen around Longknifes."

"The way they do around Chap'sum'We," he said, giving the ancient name of those who chose his chooser.

He paused to introduce Kris to those who had come with him. Teddon'sum'Lee Kris already knew. He still wore the gray and gold of the Imperial Iteeche Navy. The other wore black and red. Kris missed his name on the first fly, but Nelly promised that she caught it. He was from the Imperial Iteeche Army.

"No green-and-white advisors this time?" Kris asked.

"I do not speak for the Emperor," Ron said. "Officially, I and my associates are still on an Iteeche scout ship. Depending on the outcome of this voyage, we will be welcomed with praise, or the Cup of Apology."

Kris knew more about the Iteeche than any human alive, which was not saying a lot. However, after spending a long two months hiding Ron in human space, she did know that the Cup of Apology was filled with a slow-acting and painful poison.

Apparently, the aliens Kris had just witnessed blowing themselves to bits weren't the only ones operating in the "do or die" mode.

"We are meeting in the Forward Lounge. You should feel right at home."

Ron and Ted nodded agreement in their strange, four-armed way. The Army officer was busy using all four of his eyes in an effort to catch everything going on within sight. He'd get over that in time.

Kris led off.

She was halfway to the lounge when Captain Drago fell in with her party.

"Ron, we have your quarters waiting for you. I see there are only three of you now. They should be more roomy this trip."

"Thank you, Captain," Ron said.

"I thought you off-loaded the Iteeche's containers," Kris said.

"No. Admiral Crossenshield suggested that I shouldn't. He also suggested that I not mention that fact to you. He said something about surprises being good for Longknifes. Every once in a while."

"I thought you were the captain of *my* ship."

"Ninety-nine times out of a hundred I am. You must allow me that other one in a hundred, Princess. It is not easy to serve two masters."

"Or three or four," Kris added, darkly.

"I am just a humble ship captain. You are the damn Longknife, Your Highness."

Since they were at the hatch to the Forward Lounge, Kris let the captain get the last word in.

With three admirals already in the Forward Lounge, Kris didn't rate an "Attention on Deck." Still, as she and her Iteeche friend entered the lounge, all conversation came to a roaring halt. The room had pretty much arranged itself as it had the first meeting. Kris's PatRon 10 officers held the ground nearest the bar . . . which was doing a fair business tonight. The Imperials were as far from the Royals as they could be, and the Helviticans and Musashi occupied the neutral middle. Jack had saved her the table nearest to the forward screen.

Kris headed for it, the Iteeche right behind her.

All hands, of the human variety, took this first opportunity in eighty years to get an eyeful of their previous mortal enemy. While Ron and Ted kept their eyes straight ahead, the poor Army officer looked like he wanted to bolt. His head swiveled through the full 270 that it could. What with his four eyes, that pretty much covered everything from front to back.

Halfway to her table, Kris chose to have mercy on her fellow sailors. "Admirals, ladies, gentlemen, may I introduce the Imperial Representative Ron'sum'Pin'sum'We qu Chap'sum'We. He's kind enough to answer to Ron. He is the reason we are making this voyage of discovery. I'm glad he could join us."

The admirals came forward to be formally introduced. All of them managed not to wince as they shook the hand Ron offered them. Vicky also presented herself. She did a bit of a curtsy and winked at Kris.

"Kris insisted she had not met you or anyone of your species. I'm glad you've made her an honest woman."

"I can understand her, ah, subterfuge," Ron said with a bit of a bow. "The powers that be make great demands on their messengers."

"Does he have a sense of humor?" Vicky asked.

"Oh, yes," Kris said. "It just takes a while for it to come out."

Vicky pursed her lips in some doubt.

Kris got to the front of the room where Jack, Penny, Abby, and the colonel awaited her. Three of the barkeeps arrived, pushing the heavily carpeted arrangements that had served the tall Iteeche as chairs during their last visits to the Forward Lounge. Kris gave the thoughtful help a thankful smile.

The amenities finished, Kris turned to face a roomful of officers, most of whom outranked her and the majority of whom came from associations that wanted nothing to do with Grampa Ray's United whatever until Crossie sent them his little home video of that recent family get-together between Grampa Ray, Trouble, and the "boy" Kris had brought home to dinner.

Kris cleared her throat. "I wasn't sure how to start this briefing. Most of you have seen the report of what happened. I doubt you want me to go over it again. However, now that we have been joined by Ron, the Iteeche who first brought us the news that there was something powerful out here in the galaxy that was shooting first and not bothering to ask questions, I think we should start with a review of what I did on my summer vacation."

That drew a dry chuckle from the humans. Ron gave her a blank stare. Since he gave it to her with four eyes, it was something to behold.

"Nelly, roll the video take," Kris said.

The screen behind her changed. The sight of the *Intrepid*, hooked to a pole a couple of thousand meters long, swinging against a star field with a moon and gas giant occasionally coming into view vanished. Filling the screen in its place was a view centered on the moon's hot spot, a ship rising from it.

It took five minutes to go through the executive summary. Now it had Penny's voice-over to explain what was happening to anyone whose eyes balked at admitting what they saw.

"I am sorry, Kris," Ron said into the silence at the end of it. "I know you do not enjoy violence."

"She didn't have any choice," Admiral Kōta said before Kris could.

"I find myself wondering," Kris said. "While, admittedly, everyone may not be as big a fan of talking as I am. Still, it's hard to believe anyone would prefer a knock-down, drag-out firefight to a bit of calm, quiet conversation. The actions of the captain of this ship leave me groping for an explanation." She paused before going on.

"We've completed a biological scan of all the bodies. Every one of them shares similar genetic material. It appears that this ship was crewed by a family or clan. What would cause a grandfather/captain to consign his own children and grandkids to the cold vacuum of space?"

Around Kris, several in the room groaned. Lots of heads shook.

"I've got to file some kind of report on this encounter. I'm struggling to get my mind around it. To have something to say. My first guess is that whoever we are dealing with here really hates or is terrified of the strange. They could be the most xenophobic population of conquer-or-die types we've ever dreamed of. Worse than our worst fictional imaginings. There is, of course, a second possibility."

"What worse option could a Longknife come up with?" Admiral Channing of the businesslike Helviticans asked.

"We've never seen a ship like the one they had," Kris said, having Nelly flash back on the screen the best picture they had of the alien ship. "I'm unaware of any ships in human or Iteeche space that are strung together from conjoined spheres."

Many in the room nodded.

"Could there be someone else out here? Someone who

builds spaceships very much similar to the way we build ours? Could that someone be so nasty that our grandfather here did not hesitate for a moment to kill his beloved kids and grand-kids rather than risk the chance of them falling under their control?"

Once again, Kris had succeeded in bringing the room to absolute silence.

She let it stay that way, so the two options could sink in, before opening her arms in a question. "Does anyone see a third option?"

The question hung in the air for a very long minute. No one came up with another way of looking at the data.

After a long pause, Admiral Krätz stood. "I hope you'll excuse me if I change the topic. But what will you do with the *Constant Star*'s load of wreckage and bodies?"

"I'm sending it back to Santa Maria with the *Mercury*. Santa Maria has a major research center devoted to trying to unravel the mystery of the Three alien races who built the star jumps. That looks like a good place to handle the further examination of what we have here."

The newly Imperial admiral from Greenfeld glowered at Kris. "And what is to keep those ships and their cargo from vanishing before they ever get to Santa Maria? How will we know that they have not been hijacked off to some secret U.S. base where no one but Royal experts ever look at them and never tell us a word about what they find?"

At that, the room exploded with words.

13

Kris allowed herself a deep sigh; she hadn't seen that one coming.

This voyage had its problems, but everyone had stayed focused on why they were there. The alien encounter had thrown them a wild twist. They had come looking for surprises and had, up until a second ago, been doing a fairly good job of juggling the strange.

Then again. The Fleet of Discovery hadn't had anything to fight over.

Silly me.

Now we've got our familiar baggage on the table, and it's back to business as usual.

The Greenfeld admiral stayed on his feet as the room boiled around him, then he raised his voice to boom above the racket. "I intend to detach my battleship, the *Terror*, to escort the *Constant Star*. That will make sure some 'pirate' doesn't make off with it and its cargo."

At that, the room really got noisy.

Admiral Channing shot to his feet. "So it can vanish into one of Emperor Harry's secret bases. No you don't. I'm going with it."

The Helvitican Confederacy had held a vote to see if they should join King Raymond's United whatever. Grampa Ray had lost resoundingly. Kris figured the Confederacy didn't much like what Grampa Ray was doing.

Then again, they hadn't even bothered to vote on joining the Greenfeld Alliance. That was understandable since Chance, the last planet to join the Confederacy, had just barely avoided being violently taken over by a Peterwald.

Kris's help and a lot of spilled blood had left Chance free to choose its own way in human space. They'd chosen the Helvitican Confederacy and, it seemed, the Confederacy remembered why.

Kris held up her hands to try to gain some quiet to think. "Hold it. Hold it. HOLD IT." The volume of her voice jumped as Nelly jacked it up artificially.

The room quieted down though it was nowhere close to silent.

"Okay. I see we humans have a trust problem. Admiral Krätz, I can understand your wanting to make sure the *Constant Star* gets where it's going. *I* want to make sure it gets where it's going."

Admiral Kōta jumped in. "And where might that be?"

"Santa Maria," Kris snapped. "Specifically, the Institute for Alien Research." Kris knew of the place. It had been established almost as soon as Grampa Ray got back from that lost colony. For the last ninety years, it had been humanity's cutting edge at researching exactly who and what were the Three alien species who had built the jump points across the galaxy. Two million years ago, they had vanished.

On Santa Maria, the Three had built some sort of adult learning center. When they left, they forgot to turn it off. Apparently, the artificial intelligence running the place had gone senescent in the two million years during which it had no students. What it would have done to the several million peaceful citizens of Santa Maria when it discovered them was something Kris didn't want to contemplate.

Grampa Ray and a handful of veterans from the recent Unity War had been there, thank heavens, when the AI and the Santa Marians discovered each other. As Grampa Ray liked to say: "One supercomputer. One company of Marines. Better-than-even odds for my side."

"The Institute for Alien Research has the best human minds available for unraveling aliens," Kris said. "Most of your governments have universities with visiting professors at the Institute."

"Isn't it run by a Longknife? Ray's sister?" Vicky said.

"Aunt Alnaba transferred to the efforts on Alien 1," Kris said. "I think a professor from Earth has taken her place."

"Dr. Ernst Kanaka," Professor mFumbo put in. "A very good man. Wrote the paper about what we think we know about the Three's power system."

"And what happens after the wreckage reaches Santa Maria?" Admiral Kōta asked.

"I honestly don't know, Admiral. But it has been my experience," Kris went on, "that once scientists get to chewing on a problem, they fight like wolves to keep it."

"I wouldn't say that," the professor said in clear disapproval of Kris's analogy. "However, I do think the Institute would be open for visits from a large collection of scientists. That is the way it has operated."

"Isn't Santa Maria kind of vulnerable, hanging out there alone, halfway around the galaxy?" Vicky asked.

"A third of the way around from human and Iteeche space," Kris corrected. "And fifteen thousand light-years from here. Looks to me like it's the safest place to be right now."

From the way heads nodded and shook, it was clear Kris was not going to get any consensus on that. Then again, she didn't need any consensus. She just needed to get the *Constant Star*'s load of wreckage off her hands and her fleet back to doing what it was out there to do. Discover.

"Let's see, Admiral Krätz, you want to send the *Terror* back to Santa Maria."

"Yes." *You're not going to change my mind* hung there with the single-word answer.

"Admiral Channing, you would like to have one of your battle cruisers in the escort. What about you, Admiral Kōta?"

"Admiral Channing and I only have two ships each. We can't both afford to send separate escorts."

The two admirals flipped for the privilege of sending a ship along with the *Terror*. Channing lost. Or won. Anyway, the *Triumph* would fly wing on the *Constant Star*.

Which left Kris's royals the least represented.

The *Constant Star* was a late addition to the Helvitican Fleet. Even though it was leased at Wardhaven, Kris knew nothing of the captain and crew. Just as bad, the *Mercury* was a recently captured pirate schooner crewed from the Wardhaven, er U.S. Navy. Still, the captain and crew were a blank to her.

"Commander Taussig," Kris said.

"Right here, Your Highness," Phil said, standing from where the other skippers of PatRon 10 were over near the bar. The other ships of the squadron were dry, just like the rest of the fleet.

The *Wasp*, however, was different. With its mixed crew of civilians and service personnel, there were several contractor-managed restaurants and public rooms. Kris had never felt the need to place those watering holes off-limits to any of her crew. Indeed, she'd often used the Forward Lounge for semi-official purposes, just like now.

Most of the visiting Navy folks had taken advantage of the bar already; her skippers were no exception.

"Phil, I got a job for you."

"Mother of God help me."

Kris smiled at his reply but went ahead with her orders. "Please form a detail from the *Hornet* and establish a Royal presence on the *Constant Star.* I'm holding you personally responsible for seeing that everything on that tub is turned over to the Institute for Alien Studies."

Phil nodded. "You got an inventory for me?"

"Yes, we do, Kris," Nelly reported, "though it's kind of vague in several places."

"Understood. Pass it to Phil."

"I've got it, Commander," he said in a moment.

That settled one set of problems. Phil Taussig came from a long line of Navy admirals in both Wardhaven and several other Rim world Navies. He would not be allowed to go missing. If he disappeared, there would be hell to pay until a full explanation was made.

Kris didn't want a posthumous accounting for Phil's family, she wanted to reduce the temptation for anyone to even try.

"Lieutenant Song," she called.

A startled young woman jumped to her feet and braced. She'd been an ensign on one of the fast patrol boats that defended Wardhaven when six unidentified battleships showed up and demanded Wardhaven's surrender. On one of the few that survived. If Kris couldn't trust someone who'd fought with her at the Battle of Wardhaven, whom could she trust?

"I want the *Hermes* to take over as the courier ship back to Santa Maria. You will place your ship at Commander Taussig's disposal."

"Yes, ma'am, Your Highness," she said, snapping a salute. Indoors. Uncovered. And sat down.

Kris often had that impact on the young. The ensign would get over it in time. People who served with a Longknife did.

If they survived the experience.

"You have any questions, Phil?"

"No, ma'am," he said easily. "Get the wreckage back to Santa Maria. Turn it over to the Institute. Leave the hassling to the civilians. May I suggest that I contract for any ships and supplies that I can find in Santa Maria orbit and get them moving out here with me and the *Hermes*?"

"Logistics is always the first order of business," Kris said.

Beside her, Colonel Cortez mouthed the same words himself and smiled. Kris was learning.

A glance around the room showed a lot of Navy officers who'd gnawed enough on this bone and were ready to get gone. Kris asked the usual final question of a meeting. "Anything further to discuss?"

Most everyone shook their heads. In the back of the room, Professor mFumbo stood up.

"Professor. Do you have something to add?"

"Not to what has been said, Your Highness. But I would like to draw the attention of everyone present to certain portions of the reports my scientists have put together. It might be unnecessary. All of you may have read every deathless word of prose we men and women of science have laid before you. Then again, you might not have."

Kris noticed eyes around the room already glazing over.

"Please go on, Professor." *Quickly.*

He must have read her mind. "Something or someone stripped away ten to fifteen percent of the mass of this gas giant. They did it in the last fifty to a hundred years."

Glazed eyes suddenly opened wide. The room got very quiet.

"Those are our findings based on the strange situation of this gas giant and its moons. I should hedge that statement with careful scientific nuances. It might have lost eight percent. It could have lost twenty percent. It could have suffered this strange reduction as recently as forty years ago or it might have happened one hundred and fifty years ago."

"What you are saying," Kris said, "is that something took very big bites out of that gas giant within my grampa Ray's lifetime."

The professor nodded. "Bites the size of three to seven Earths. Yes, that is what I and my boffins are trying to tell you."

Kris let that sink in. She let the silence stretch for a while because, at least in her head, it was not sinking in. It floated, like a yellow ducky in her bathtub when she was a kid. Only this yellow ducky was huge, and there was no way she could shove it under the water.

Her thoughts spun. What finally came out was *No. Not possible. It can't be happening to me and my world.*

With effort, she limited her gibbering to the inside of her own skull.

KRIS, THIS IS APPALLING.

ME HAVING TROUBLE BELIEVING IT?

NO, KRIS. WHAT HE JUST SAID.

YES, NELLY, THIS IS APPALLING, Kris agreed, accepting her computer's understatement and failing to find anything better, or was it worse, to offer Nelly.

Kris had no idea when the full impact of this would be absorbed. Probably, it was best to end this meeting and let people go their own ways to digest this new lump of knowledge.

"Is there anything else in your report you want to make sure we notice?" Kris said. *Say no. Say no. Please say no.*

"Yes, there is one more thing."

Stupid me. Ask a question, and you'll get the answer you don't want.

"Go on, Professor."

"We have established that there were 132 people on the alien ship. We think we have drawn up an accurate schematic of its design." The professor aimed his wrist unit at the main screen and it switched away from where it was frozen on the final frame of the explosion.

Suddenly, the ship was whole again. Quickly, the skin of the ship peeled back, showing the insides: living quarters, work spaces, storage rooms, the bridge. Most of those areas were left empty in the drawing, but their purposes were written in.

"On that ship, there were about twelve cubic meters of pressurized living space for each of the men, women, and children aboard."

"Sleeping quarters two meters by three meters by two meters tall," Kris said. It was about a quarter of her own living quarters. "Ugh."

"Pardon me for correcting you, Your Highness," the professor said. "I did not say sleeping quarters. That allotment is the total room for their sleeping and wash space. It includes their contribution to their work spaces, public rooms, and hallways. We're still debating whether or not they even had hallways. Even in the command center.

"The only space not included in this allotment was a small hold full of rare-earth ores recently extracted from the moon. That hold and Engineering. That would include the reactors and the pressurized tanks for reaction mass. I should point out that we found several bunks in Engineering in what we think was the control room."

"Oh. My. God." Vicky said.

Around Kris, the room bubbled at a low boil as, once again, people struggled to come to terms with what any rational human being would consider impossible.

It was Penny who slowly rose to her feet. She went to touch the ship on the screen. The Navy officer whispered something that Kris didn't get, but apparently Mimzy, Penny's computer, did.

An image of the gas giant appeared on the screen with the alien ship. On the screen, the giant regained ten percent of its mass, swelling noticeably.

"What kind of species could suck up ten percent of a gas giant? Then, having that kind of reaction mass to move themselves and their creation, would cram their population into a ship, allowing only twelve cubic meters to an individual?"

The room fell silent as Penny spoke.

When she finished, there was a pause. A brief one. Then the room exploded as a number of people made off quickly for the restrooms.

Others headed for the bar, giving loud voice to their need for a drink.

14

Kris sat in her chair, staring off into space. Literally. The forward screen was back to the view from the external monitors. Stars flew by. The moon occasionally came into view. More often, the gas giant that had caused this struggle with cognitive dissonance made its own appearance.

It had been a long time since Kris had been tempted, really tempted, to order a drink. So far she was winning.

Still, she wouldn't take a bet that she would be sober come midnight.

The senior NCOs aboard the *Wasp* made sure that none of the junior enlisted abused the privilege of the ship's pubs. The problem was, there were only officers in the Forward Lounge at the moment, officers from four different Navies. From the looks of empties piling up on some tables, adult supervision was desperately needed.

"Jack, inform the barkeep the limit tonight is three drinks."

"That sounds like a good idea. We're a long way from a brewery, and it doesn't look like we'll be getting a new supply anytime soon." He shoved off for the bar.

Kris wouldn't take any bets that there weren't several stills in her fleet. She also wouldn't recommend that any of the captains in her Fleet of Discovery do a serious shakedown of chief's country. Still, it was clear she needed to limit how people responded to the shock they'd all just taken to their system.

Vicky came over to Kris's table. She cast a worried glance over her shoulder toward Admiral Krätz but said nothing.

The admiral was one of those with several empties in front of him. Kris was a bit surprised at that. Still, the man had a family. He was looking forward to grandkids. He had talked of retirement.

What kind of enemy had they just stumbled into? How large a fleet and army could they muster? Kris's mind still boggled at trying to answer those questions.

"Is it as bad as it seems?" Vicky asked.

Kris ran a worried hand through her hair. "I don't know. Maybe we should turn around, run back to human space, pull in the welcome mat, and hide under the bed. Who knows how long it would be before whatever it is out here stumbles across us?"

"That is one option," Ron said. In a fashion, the three of them were seated at Kris's table. The two that Kris was familiar with took in the scene with some equilibrium. The Army fellow was showing red alarms around his residual gill slits. Occasionally, Ted would lean over and say something to him in Iteeche.

Nelly told Kris that the Iteeche Navy officer was telling the Army officer that it was all right. Things would work out.

It didn't seem to be working for the Army guy. It sure wasn't working for Kris.

The urge to run away and hide under a bed was very attractive. The thirst to crawl into a bottle and forget the future had new allure.

"You damn Longknifes have murdered us all." Like a bloody meat cleaver, that bellow cut through the noise of the room.

Kris and Vicky swung around in their seats to face Admiral Krätz. He stood at his table, swaying like a drunken bear. He swept the table with one large hand; empties flew off in the lazy arc of half a gee. Some shattered as they hit the deck. Most just landed and rolled.

The admiral pointed at Kris's table. "You damn Peterwalds and double-damned Longknifes can't mind your own business. What is it with you? You damn near got us wiped out with your

bleeding Iteeches. Now you just had to go and find something
bigger, meaner, badder."

For a long moment, the admiral just snarled at Kris and
Vicky. Then a shudder went through him. "And my girls will
never hold their babies. My grand little ones will never see the
light of day."

A wracking sob escaped the admiral.

Kris rose from her seat and took two steps toward the drunk
officer. With a glance, she caught the attention of the *Fury*'s
captain.

"Captain, I think you need to take your admiral home."

The captain reached for the arm of his commander. Admiral
Krätz shook him off.

"Don't you go giving my officers orders."

"Then you give them," Kris snapped. "We've got problems
enough. You're not going to find any answers to them in the
bottoms of those glasses. Go to your ship. Sleep it off. Tomorrow, we'll put our sober heads together."

"Come, Admiral. Let's go," the captain said.

The large contingent from the Greenfeld fleet made a hole
for their admiral, then followed him out the door.

"I've never seen him like that," Vicky said, coming up to
stand beside Kris.

"He likely has never had a night this bad," Colonel Cortez
said, joining them. "It is one thing to face battle against odds
you can gauge, maneuvers you can counter. It's something else
entirely to face the unknown and know that you can't protect
those you love and hold dear."

The colonel paused for a moment. "I'm none too sure how
I feel about all this."

"I don't think any of us are," Kris admitted. She caught the
eye of the senior bartender. "Let's close down for the night."

"Last call?" someone asked hopefully.

"No, honey. Drink up. We're rolling up the floor," the barkeep answered.

Vicky hurried off to catch the last launch from the *Wasp* to
the *Fury*. Kris turned to Ron. "Shall I take you to your quarters? I understand nothing's changed."

"That would be very gracious of you," Ron said. "Though
I should point out, I well remember the path from your Forward Lounge to my quarters. I suspect I could even find my

way without all your scientists marking the path, waiting in line to pose questions for me."

"Was it that bad?" Kris asked.

The press at the door was almost gridlock. Kris and her team waited for others to file out. Since the admirals hadn't demanded that sailors of different fleets make a hole for them, Kris didn't think she should.

Penny nudged Kris. "We're not moving all that much. Any chance we could grab a chair, sit down, and talk a bit about what all this means?"

Kris shook her head. "Penny, this is just too much for me. I've got to sleep on it. Tomorrow will be soon enough."

Penny didn't seem happy with Kris's decision, but she said nothing more.

Ron was interested in how Kris had spent her time since he left. It took her mind off the present to describe the fun of chasing pirates and claiming new territory . . . for the hostile Peterwald Empire.

He considered that funny . . . and time better spent than his own. He'd been locked down in the Imperial Palace. He was required to be available on five-minute notice to meet with several very important committees. He was required to wait upon them . . . but in the end they never called him for a personal report.

He brought his hands together and moved his four thumbs in circles around each other. "Do you have a saying like that?"

"Twiddling your thumbs?" Kris said with a laugh, as she and her team finally passed through the doors from the Forward Lounge into the passageway that led aft.

The next moment an explosion threw Kris against Ron.

Jack crashed into her back and they all ended up in a heap on the deck.

Behind them, the swinging doors of the Forward Lounge blew out. Immediately, the airtight doors slammed shut and clanged as they locked down.

"Hull Breach," the public-address system announced. "Hull Breach in the Forward Lounge."

15

Kris scrambled back to her feet. Jack tried to push her aft, but the passageway was a solid mass of people, all trying to regain their feet and move in the same direction.

Preferably at the same time.

Kris edged her way around Jack so she could get a better view through one of the small vision plates in the airtight doors.

All she saw was smoke. Something had exploded. Some of the furniture had caught fire. The smoke didn't last long as both air and smoke were sucked out through several rents in the hull.

One body, Kris hoped he was already dead, went with the smoke.

The checkered tabletops, however, were also doing their job. Some had caught fire. But others held their circular form and rode on the blasting air currents toward the rents in the ship's structure. On the ceiling, valves opened, releasing globs of sealant that also rode the wind torrents to help the deforming tabletops shore up the holes.

All this was done quickly enough that the other bar crew were able to keep their holds on whatever they had grabbed and avoid being sucked out into the cold vacuum.

"Pressure has been stabilized in the Forward Lounge. Make way for damage control parties. Clear the passageways for damage-control parties," the ship's computer repeated.

"Kris," Jack said.

"Yes, yes," Kris said, backing up and taking the first turn off the main passageway so that a dozen sailors in space suits carrying gear could pass her.

"Penny. Penny," Kris called.

The cop's daughter was at her elbow in a moment.

"That was no accident," Kris said. "Get a forensic team together from Jack's Marines. By breakfast tomorrow morning, I want to know what went down in there."

"No sleep for the wicked," Abby said with a smile for the Navy officer who'd just been ordered to do an all-nighter.

"Abby," Kris said.

"I was just headed for bed," her maid replied.

"You've been getting lazy, what with no one trying to kill me," Kris said, reaching for her maid's elbow. "Looks like someone just did. Or maybe they were aiming for Vicky. Or someone else. You're the spy. You tell me what the game is this time and who's calling the shots."

"Aye, aye, bossy princess," Abby said.

Which left Kris with nothing better to do than provide an unnecessary guide for Ron back to his quarters.

She paused at the hatch that led into Iteeche country.

"You want to come inside?" Ron asked her.

Kris shook her head, then she added, "No." In cross-evolutionary-track discussions, body language was more open to mistakes than a simple word.

"I've got some tough decisions to make, tomorrow. And they just keep getting harder."

"I do not think that bomb will help," Ron said.

"Not likely," Kris agreed. "I need to do some thinking inside my own skull."

"Then I will tell you here what I would have told you inside. I was in much trouble after my last visit to human space."

"What kind of trouble?" Kris asked.

"Many different kinds. My Emperor was not happy that I brought back no promises of help from your people."

"I'm sorry about that," Kris said. "I tried."

"I know that you did. What is written is written. However, my chooser was also very unhappy with me."

That took Kris aback. "How come?"

"He was not happy to learn what you and I had concluded about how the war was fought."

"Oh," Kris said. "Neither was my grampa Ray. I don't think any of the people who made the tough decisions were happy about us figuring out what they really did during the war."

"No. He was most unhappy. Before he let me join you on this voyage of search and discovery, he made me swear on my hope of being a chooser myself that I would not spend much time with you."

"It was that bad, huh," Kris said.

"Yes. I have sworn to go with you. To see what you see and to report back to my Emperor and chooser what you find. I am afraid that our quiet times of conversation will not be a part of this trip."

Kris nodded, risking a tight smile. Just when she thought she might be getting to know a guy, wouldn't you know his mom would tell him she wasn't the kind of girl a nice guy like him brought home.

"I understand," she said.

Ron stood aside for his Army officer to open the hatch and peer inside. Once he concluded the humans had no deviltry waiting for them, he waved the Imperial Representative into his rooms. In a moment, the hatch closed and was dogged down solidly.

Jack came up beside her as the door closed. "You want to talk?"

"About what?" Kris said with a sigh. "That another boy has been told he can't play with me or that all human existence might depend on what I do tomorrow? And at the moment, I have no idea which side I should be on when I start playing one hell of a game of Ping-Pong tomorrow."

Jack nodded, then went on. "For what it's worth, this mess is way too complicated for me to figure out. Whatever you decide, I'll support you."

"Thank you, Jack. That's about the nicest thing I've heard since we set out on this cockamamie trip."

"I wouldn't call it cockamamie," Jack said. He gave the

matter a serious moment of consideration. "Crazy. Yes. Wild. Maybe. Possibly even unusual. But not cockamamie."

His lopsided smile came out to play as he finished giving her his opinion.

"Thank you for your unconditional vote of support," Kris said, with a chuckle, and headed for her quarters.

16

Kris ordered a light breakfast brought to her Tac Center and told Nelly to invite all her key staff to report there by 0730. From the way they dragged in, it didn't look like any of them had had a good night's sleep . . . even the ones she hadn't ordered to pull all-nighters.

"Okay, folks," Kris said, as they gathered around the breakfast tray or filled cups of steaming coffee from the urn, "I need answers to a few simple questions. Who, what, why, how, and, most important, was that bomb last night aimed at me or at someone else?"

"It looks like our little girl just might be growing up," Abby drawled as she sipped her coffee. "Finally, it's got through her pretty little head that it isn't always about her."

"That last bomb hit me up beside the head pretty hard," Kris said dryly. "It would be kind of hard not to be open to the idea that the world isn't just one big gun aimed at my own little head."

"I noticed that our little princess was kind enough to leave out 'when,'" Penny said, warming up the cup of coffee she'd carried into the meeting. "That leaves all of the rest of them in my lap, thank you oh so much."

The Navy officer took a seat at the table, yawned, then began crisply. "The what was a bomb. It was in a glass similar to those used in the Forward Lounge but not one of ours. We've recovered a lot of tiny glass globules. Most came from the Forward Lounge's stock. Some didn't. We expect those are from the bomb. The glass was not manufactured on Wardhaven. At the moment, we are not able to identify just where it did come from."

"That would be nice to know," Jack said.

"Of that I am most aware," Penny said. "Forensics is chasing that down, but don't hold your breath. There are a lot of glassmakers in human space, and this particular glass got remade but good in the explosion."

"The glass was disguised to look like an empty and planted in the middle of a whole slew of other empties. The detonator was hidden in something that looked like an olive. Everything was perfectly machined to fit unobserved into a bar."

"Do we have that on camera?" Kris asked.

"Nope," Jack said. "Forward Lounge does not have any security cameras. The operator doesn't want them. 'Folks are there to relax. If there's a problem, we'll handle it the old-fashioned way.' Besides, we liked that there were no cameras in there, remember. The king met the Iteeche Rep in there. No record. We also did all that history review with the Iteeche in there. Again, nothing we wanted on the record."

"Right," Kris said. "Remind me to review our security system."

"I already am, Kris," Jack said. "We'd always considered the *Wasp* above the fray where attacks on you were concerned. It looks like we're getting a whole new grade of visitors these days. We're rigging the boat to meet level-one security standards."

"Do I need to smile when I take a shower?" Abby asked, giving Jack a most unhappy kind of smile.

"I'd never tell you when to smile, Abby," Jack said right back.

"Are we locking the barn door after it's burned to the ground?" Colonel Cortez asked.

"She's still alive," Jack said. "The barn ain't burned all that far down, as I see it."

"Enough, boys," Kris cut in. "Penny, do we have any idea who or why or what the target was?"

"Sorry, Kris, all I've got is how and when," Penny said.

"The really fun stuff is still more guesswork than hard evidence."

"Try some of your guesses on me," Kris said.

"The bomb glass was on a table in the Peterwald area of the lounge. That hints at this being a Peterwald problem."

"But if it had gone off while the lounge was full . . ." Jack started.

"There'd be a whole lot of us breathing space," Kris finished.

"No way we could have evacuated the lounge," Penny said. "And with a lot of people in the way, the sealants would have had a lot more problems closing the holes than they did."

Kris had a sudden picture of bodies and sealant half-blocking the holes in the hull. The lucky people had their legs out in space. The unlucky ones had their heads out there. It was not pretty.

With a shiver, Kris turned to Abby. "Okay, my favorite spy, what kind of threat picture were you able to put together?"

"Me, I turned it over to Mata Hari and went to sleep."

"Mata Hari?" Jack said.

"Yes. Nelly's been after me to use her computer more. To name her kid."

"And not turn her off," Nelly put in.

"So I named her Mata Hari and gave her the data dump I'd been ignoring. What'd you find, girl?"

"It was very interesting," a dusky alto voice said from Abby's neckline. Apparently, the name change from Trixi to Mata Hari had included a number of changes in attitude.

"Mata Hari," the colonel said. "Didn't she get shot?"

"Yes," Abby agreed. "But they issued the firing squad the blindfolds, not her."

"I've heard that story," Kris said.

"It isn't true," Mata Hari said.

"So, what have you got for us?" Kris asked.

"I am sorry to say it, but I think Abby was right to save her important time for other things," her computer said. "There are a lot of interesting things going on in human space, but most of it is just dishing the dirt on this or that person."

Abby grinned widely.

"Tell me some of it," Kris said. "It's not like I'm pushed for time here."

"There is the matter of the recent remarriage of his Imperial Highness Henry I of Greenfeld. His bride was announcing her pregnancy almost immediately, and her insistence on carrying the baby in her own body. 'No tin can for *our* baby,' as she put it. The court gossip has him eating out of her hand . . . and checking in on her every five minutes."

"So much for big bad Harry, uh," Penny said.

"Tell her, Mattie," Abby said, dryly.

"What I find interesting," the computer said as she went on, "is that she is from the Hollenzoller family, and major players in N.S. Holdings."

"And we took down their little slave empire at Port Royal," Kris said.

"Yes, there is that," Mattie said. "And that the lovely Imperial Empress has already had the baby tested. It's a boy!"

"Oh, and it's definitely Harry's," Mattie added.

"I wonder how Vicky feels about this," Kris said.

"Do you think there are several reasons why she's taking this little vacation from court?" Penny said.

"And as far away from court as she could get?" the colonel offered.

"Not far enough, apparently," Jack concluded.

"So, one empty glass bomb," Kris said, "takes care of one of those damn Longknife troublemakers and clears the path to the throne for a poor kid that ain't even taken a suck of his mother's milk."

"If I was that kid, I'd have that milk tested for poison," Abby put in.

"I doubt if the milk has to be poisoned," the colonel said. "It's likely poisoned direct from the source."

"That may not be all the answer as to who and why," Penny said, when the chuckles died down.

"Don't you just hate it when a good answer to our problem gets wet water thrown on it," Abby said dryly.

"Is there any other kind of water but wet?" Mattie asked.

"It's a figure of human speech, child," Nelly said. "You'll have to get used to such things. And you will if a certain human doesn't keep turning you off."

Kris cleared her throat. "I believe Penny has the floor. You were suggesting there was more to our problem than just what Abby and Mata Hari had turned up, I think."

"Yes. My forensic folks are puzzling over a bit of a problem. That olive detonator or what is left of it. We lost a lot of it to space, but the damage-control system kept enough of the detonator inside for us to discover a problem. It went off five minutes late."

"For which I am very happy," Kris said.

"No. I didn't say that right," Penny said. "It wasn't that it was set for five minutes later. It was set to explode while the room was overflowing with officers and good cheer. It counted down to just that moment. Then, instead of going boom, it waited for five minutes."

"Where'd that extra five minutes come from?" Jack asked.

"We have no idea," Penny said.

"Could there have been a second detonator? One that responded to a remote detonation order?" the colonel asked.

"We've found no evidence of a second one," Penny said. "It's not like we have a lot of bomb residue, but we found enough of the olive to know what it was and what it wasn't doing. We should have found enough of a remote detonator to know that it was there."

That left the room in a puzzled silence.

Kris spoke her thoughts as they came to her. "What are the chances that the Hollenzoller family has its own set of opposition? Someone who bought a five-minute delay for their kaboom machine." Kris shook her head, that was just guesswork.

Then she went on. "Is there any idea who might have done this?" Kris asked. "Has anyone up and suddenly vanished?

"The *Wasp* has no one missing," Penny said, "except for the poor fellow who went out the hole in the hull. He's been recovered. None of the other ships report anyone missing. It's not like we can do a lot of questioning aboard the other fleets' ships."

"So we are once again at a dead end," Kris said.

"There seems to be no lack of them in supply," Abby said.

"Kris, do you want to take a call from Phil Taussig?" Nelly asked.

"Of course. How's it going, Phil?"

"Likely better for me than it is for you," came from a smiling face now featured on one of the Tac Center's wall screens.

"To what do I owe this early call?"

"I'm ready to get out of here, Princess, before anything more interesting happens around you."

"So soon?" Kris said, and really meant it.

"I didn't have anything better to do with my night," he said, with a chuckle. "And opening more space between you and my vulnerable body seemed like a good idea. I've got the *Constant Star* ready to move out. Lieutenant Song has the *Hermes* equally ready to get under way."

"What about your heavy escorts?"

"The *Terror* and *Triumph* took some encouragement, but I think that bomb got a lot of people interested in being anywhere else but at your side, dear lovely princess, so they're moving. Oh, I did kind of bribe them. I've shipped five of the bodies from the *Constant* to each of them."

"Any of the other wreckage?" Kris asked, not sure how she was going to like his next answer.

"No, ma'am. No other pieces of the puzzle. As I see it, we're missing enough of that dang ship. No need to encourage chunks of it to go missing."

Kris breathed a sigh of relief. Phil was good. Give him an order, and you didn't have to ask twice to see if it was well done.

"Very well, Commander. You are authorized to depart. When do you expect to be back?"

The young officer shrugged. "Look for me when you see me coming."

"Most of the fleet will be here, waiting for you."

"Most of it?" Taussig asked, though Kris could see the question in every eye around her Tac Center.

"I think it's time for the scouts to start scouting," Kris said.

"Have fun," Phil said, and the screen went blank.

There was a brief pause while everyone around Kris caught their breath, then Jack asked, "Just what do you have in mind?"

Kris had Nelly open a map of the local star systems on-screen.

"The alien ship, of such shattered memory, might have come from somewhere around here," Kris said, pointing at the star map on the screen. "We ought to do a recon of local space to see if there is anything to see."

She let that sink in for a few seconds. "The nice part about this is that we don't have to go blasting off into the jumps at high speed, spins, and accelerations. We can take the jumps at a slow pace. We can even use the boffins' latest toy to take a look before we leap. While the scouts do their snooping, we can leave the battleships swinging around themselves here. Who knows, maybe they'll find the mad bomber. Or decide it's too boring and go home."

"That sounds like a plan," Jack agreed.

A second thought crossed Kris's mind. "Nelly, send to Pat-Ron 10. While we're doing this walk-around, have all ships set their reactors to produce as much antimatter as they can safely make." Antimatter powered the launches and auxiliary power units on the ships. It also could be used in some of the weapons on the corvettes. The *Wasp* had acquired eight high-acceleration, 12-inch torpedoes since her last yard period. Usually they were loaded with high-explosives warheads. However, if you really wanted to make things go boom, an alternate antimatter warhead could replace the standard issue.

That idea had come to several different people after the Battle of Wardhaven. Humanity had enjoyed a long peace. Some of her children were just starting to study war again. The 12-inch high-acceleration torpedoes were the first fruit of that attitude.

Kris doubted they would be the last.

"You really want to go loaded for bear," Jack said.

"Maybe it will be unnecessary. Then again, it's nice to have a few extra aces up your sleeve if life doesn't come at you like you planned."

Jack nodded, and Kris had Nelly call the admirals. She had a plan. Hopefully, they didn't have ones of their own.

17

Eight star systems in seven days.

Eight times the *Wasp* tiptoed up to a roiling tear in space and cautiously slipped a diminutive periscope through the jump point.

It was all very careful. All very safe. And somehow, Kris found it all very boring.

The boffins were depressed and delighted. Depressed because, try as they might, they could not broaden the instrumentation on the video view of the system before they jumped into it. All you got was a black-and-white picture. No color.

To their delight, they had developed a second instrument. This tiny sensor gave them a full report on the electromagnetic spectrum. If there was radio or TV in use somewhere around the next sun, the *Wasp* would know it before it jumped.

Each sensor had to be sent through the jump one at a time. That was fine by Kris and Captain Drago. To the boffins, it was abject failure.

While the scientists promised to do better, Kris stood by on the bridge as Captain Drago took the *Wasp* safely into eight new systems.

It was nice to enter eight new systems knowing that there wasn't a nova on the other side. Or a battle station waiting to gun you down.

Eight systems in seven days and not a nerve gone taut once.

Of course, it was also eight systems in seven days and nothing to show for it. Not a scrap of metal. Not a hint of a passage. All the gas giants had a steady hold on their moons. All the rocky planets were rocky, dead, and silent.

The boffins had gotten excited about one star. It was huge, weighing in at over three hundred times the weight of Mother Earth's Sol. And it put out enough radiation, visual and otherwise, to fry them if they got too close. Apparently, the alien Three had made accommodations for that. Their jump was way out from the star . . . and the next jump was very close by.

The scientists were quite upset with the star chart. If it had just told them the weight of this sun a couple of million years ago, they could have verified just how much the huge star had shed in the meantime. They seemed to hold Kris personally responsible for that failure of the chart her grampa Ray found on Santa Maria.

Kris didn't bother issuing an apology.

So, after eight star systems and seven days, Kris sat quietly, enjoying a lone supper in the wardroom. She was dining alone because her staff had taken to avoiding her. She hadn't hunted any of them up to ask why, and no one had come close enough to Kris to let her pose the question.

It was quiet, and boring, and she was kind of enjoying it.

Of course, it would be nice if Jack dropped by. Even if it was to argue about something.

No threats to her. No reason for Jack to argue with her. No Jack.

Such was Kris's life.

Judge Francine approached Kris with a dinner tray. "May I join you?"

Immediately, Kris found herself doing an examination of her latest high crimes and misdemeanors. All she could think of were the usual mortal and venial sins. "Of course," Kris managed to stammer without sounding excessively guilty.

The elderly lady had been a giant on the bench before she retired. In real life, settling herself across from Kris was a woman barely five feet tall. Still, she took her chair with all the gravity of a judge taking her place at the bench.

Kris didn't need to ask Nelly about Justice Francine. In high school, she'd learned of the legendary Judge Francine. She'd spent most of her life on one high court or another.

When the old jurist applied to join the boffin crew of the *Wasp*, Professor mFumbo had been ready to reject her out of hand. Kris had stepped in personally to grant her a berth. Father always said that one of the few things about his job that made it worth having was being able to make a dream come true for someone who had done their part for the people.

And that good deed had allowed Kris to draft the experienced jurist into helping her with a legal problem . . . or twelve.

"Are you enjoying your stay on the *Wasp*?" Kris asked. She didn't usually have to hunt for an ice breaker. Most everyone who approached her had a hidden agenda they couldn't wait to broach. Being the one tongue-tied was unusual for Kris.

"Matters are certainly better than they had been," the gray-haired woman answered darkly. "Those cases you had me handling on Kaskatos were nothing short of brutal. Those poor local jurists were totally unprepared to hear crimes of such depravity."

"Ah, yes," Kris said, trying not to feel guilty for making the demands the situation had required. *So much for breaking the ice.*

"This last week, however, has been nothing short of magnificent," the judge said as her old eyes filled with young wonder . . . and she settled a linen napkin in her lap. "We have long had images of this end of the galaxy. But no observatory can hope to capture what we are seeing up close. That is well worth the price of admission for these old eyes."

The judicial legend sampled her chicken pasta before she went on. "The scientists in boffin country are bubbling every morning with new discoveries. New conclusions. New ideas to test. I should think you must be bombarded with suggestions. Nay, demands to change course and get closer to this or that phenomenon."

"Nelly fields them for me."

"But it's nice to hear from someone who has an inkling of just what I'm having to wade through . . . and some respect," Nelly said. "Kris takes me way too much for granted."

"I'm sure it must seem that way from your perspective," the judge said, clearly reserving judgment.

"The captain makes the final decision," Kris said. "He has a very keen sense that the safety of the *Wasp* and its crew has first call on our course."

"Ah, yes, the safety of the ship and crew," Francine said, with a nuanced twist to the words. "That is nice to know."

For a while they ate in silent companionship.

"So," Francine said, laying down her fork. "How long are you going to continue putzing around and dodging your duty?"

"Dodging my duty?" Kris almost yelped in surprise.

"Young lady, I've sat on enough benches listening to lawyers lay out the history of how this or that crime came to be committed that these old eyes can't miss a crime in progress."

Again, all Kris could do was echo, "Crime in progress?"

"Yes, young woman. We didn't come halfway around the galaxy to loaf around, dawdling from one star system to the next. You are avoiding your duty."

"You want to tell me what duty I'm avoiding?" Kris asked. Everyone Kris had ever met either hated Longknifes . . . or expected them to save their bacon. It wasn't unusual for people to hold both views. Apparently, legendary judicial minds were no different.

"No, young woman, I have no idea what you should be doing. I'm a judge. I look at what people *have* done and tell them if it is right or wrong, or, more often, legal or illegal. You're just dithering. Get off your duff and do something."

"So you can convict me."

"Or find you innocent. I'm sure some Longknife in your long family history has been found innocent. Can't think of any cases at the moment, but there must have been one or two."

"I seem to recall that Grampa Al had some very nasty things to say about your decision that corporations should no longer have the full status of people before the court."

The gray-haired woman had the courtesy to chuckle at that. "Yes, I can imagine that my name was taken in vain several times after that decision," she said. "That doesn't matter in the present instant, however, and you know it."

"Yes, I do. Still, you must have some ideas about the matter I'm dithering over. Everywhere I go on this ship of late, people look right at me. Right through me. And don't say a word to me."

The former jurist shook her head. "The day after I retired from the bench, I rose early as I usually do. But instead of going to my chambers, I took a walk in the park. It was a lovely spring day. I took a deep breath of fresh air, and it hit me. Someone else would have to make the hard choices. I could watch the news and get just as mad as anyone else at the bone-headed things people did to each other. Nobody would ever again come to me years later and ask me to decide who was right and who was in the wrong. It felt so wonderful to feel again. I hadn't done it in years. Wonderful feeling.

"Sorry, young lady, I am retired, and I do not have to make the hard decisions anymore. With luck, you might make it to retirement someday. May your first breath of fresh, free air be as sweet as mine was. Until then, back to the salt mines, Princess."

With that, the amateur astronomer picked up her fork and continued her dinner in silence.

After a moment or two of reflection, Kris found that she was no longer hungry and left the table. It took her a few minutes longer to decide who she wanted to talk to. It took Nelly very little time to collect Jack and Ron the Iteeche in her Tac Center.

"I just had the strangest supper partner," Kris told them, then filled them in on Judge Francine's thoughts.

Jack greeted the story with a chuckle. "The word on the law-enforcement circuit was that no lawyer wanted to present before her. Didn't matter whether they were prosecuting or defending, she was not the judge they wanted to be in front of."

"I think I can understand their attitude now," Kris said. Ron was standing rather still through this. "You do have judges in the Empire, don't you?"

"We have judges. People might bring what I think you call criminal and civil cases before them. I do not understand this case brought against him whom you call your grandfather Al. The law means what the Emperor says it means. How could a judge know the heart of the Emperor?"

"I don't think we should go there, tonight," Kris said. "Nelly, get Captain Drago on the line."

"Got him," Nelly said.

"You have a question, Princess?"

"Yes, Captain. I understand we've done a lot of wondrous stargazing this last week but haven't found anything relating to aliens."

"That is correct, Your Highness."

"Any hints that we might?"

"My best guess is that we could keep this up until the cows come home, and all we'd have to show for it is a lot of cow manure."

"I was kind of expecting that answer, Captain. Would you stand by for a few minutes; I think I'll have fresh orders for you."

"I'm glad to hear you've had enough of this messing around."

"Thank you for your opinion, Captain," Kris said, and cut the link.

Kris turned to the two people whose opinion she most valued on the matter at hand. "So. What do you think we do now?"

"This is a waste of time," Jack said. "That alien ship could have come from here. But it could just as easily have come from a thousand light-years from where we found it. Heaven knows, if it was them gazing at our entrails and searching for our base, they wouldn't be finding anything of interest in these systems."

"Thank you, Jack. Ron, what does the Iteeche Empire have to say?"

"Very little. I am just along for the ride. Is that the way you say it?"

"Yes, but you're here for some reason?"

"But you are halfway around the galaxy from that reason. Our ships are not disappearing here."

"We are going to get there. I'm just taking the indirect approach."

"Very indirect," the Iteeche agreed.

"So it is agreed that we should get ourselves closer to where we might find some hostile aliens," Kris said.

"If we're hunting hostiles," Jack said, "it seems only natural to get closer to where they've found us before."

"Nelly, have Captain Drago set a course to return us to

where we parked the battleships. Also have him send the message 'Z' to those squadrons."

"It's done, Kris."

"Good. It's ice-cream sundae night in the wardroom. Jack, would you like one?"

"Don't mind if I do."

18

The letter "Z" was part of a small code sheet that Nelly and Kris had developed before leaving the battle squadrons. In that code, the single letter "Z" told the recipient quite a bit. We have found nothing. We are returning to base. Recall the other scouts.

As a code went, it was simple, brief . . . and unbreakable.

For the jaunt around the local systems, Kris had amended her policy not to leave any traces of their passage. Each scout had left buoys at the jump points they went through. They were tiny devices, just radio relays and maneuvering jets.

If a bug-eyed monster chanced across one of these bread crumbs, it might lead them to a scout ship or the battleships. It could not lead them to human space.

Now the *Wasp* collected those she'd dropped as she retraced her track.

On the second day, while crossing a system, a buoy popped through the jump point ahead and transmitted the single letter "Q."

Thus was Kris informed that the other scouts were returning.

Forewarned, Kris didn't expect any surprises waiting for her at the battleships as the next few days and familiar systems passed quickly.

Of course, Kris was wrong.

A simple code could only carry the messages that were preplanned for it. For example, "I love you," had not been included as an option in the code. Similarly, "We've all voted to go home and we expect you to come along peacefully with us," was also not available.

Yet that was the first thing Admiral Krätz announced to Kris when she jumped back into the system that had caused them so much trouble.

The Greenfeld admiral had set the situation up to present his case as forcefully as possible. He had the other admirals on net with him. Upon first seeing them, Kris had not offered to have them come aboard the *Wasp*.

None had suggested that they gather on one of their ships.

Apparently, the last blowout on the *Wasp* had ended any party inclinations among the gathered fleet.

Isn't the net wonderful?

Kris listened as Admiral Krätz made his case. The other admirals nodded along. The argument boiled down to a few simple points. Things have changed since we left human space. The present situation is not what was intended when our governments sent us. We must return to our capitals and receive new orders.

Kris nodded. "If you feel that way, then I suppose you must return. My government's orders, however, give me full authority to conduct a reconnaissance."

Actually, Kris didn't have any written orders. Never had a collection of Navy ships gotten under way with less paperwork to back them up.

Once this voyage was over, the Judge Francines of the world would have a field day for years to come.

But, until Kris docked her squadron once more at High Wardhaven, what PatRon 10 did was pretty much up to Kris.

"We're going back," Admiral Channing said. "Certainly your small ships can't go on with no backup."

"Admiral, before you arrived at Wardhaven, my intent was to sail my small ships with no backup. You might not have noticed, but the only U.S. ships here are scouts."

"How could we help but notice," Admiral Krätz grumbled.

"You have your orders. I have mine. My squadron sails on," Kris said with finality, and had Nelly cut the link.

"Vicky is on the line. Do you want to talk to her?" Nelly asked next.

"Put her through, but if all she does is try to talk me into following her admiral, we might have communication difficulty."

"Hi, Kris," Vicky said. "You find anything interesting?"

"My astronomers are in ecstasy, but of bug-eyed monsters, not so much as a hair. How have things been here?"

Vicky snorted. "A lot of scared people telling each other how scared they are and how much more scared they ought to be."

"Really?"

"Well, in the senior wardrooms that's all I hear. Among the junior officers and the younger enlisted ranks, I think there's a lot more excitement. Then again, being the grand duchess, they might just be telling me what they think I want to hear."

"There is that problem. Have there been any more bombs going off?"

"None since you left, but then we've been taking serious precautions. I think the bomber might have slipped aboard the *Terror* and beat it for home."

"Is that just a guess, or is there any meat on that bone?" Kris asked, before Jack and Penny climbed all over her to get to the commlink.

"We did find a problem. I don't like the fact that our security still hasn't gotten to the bottom of it, but there appear to have been six or seven people aboard the ships of BatRon 12 who were never here."

"Never here?" Kris said.

"Some *one* was here using any of the six sets of papers whenever it served his purpose. None of those people has been sighted since that bomb went off on the *Wasp*, so we're thinking your Commander Taussig wasn't the only one who was in a hurry to shove off for Santa Maria."

Kris glanced at Jack. He and Penny were using their new computers to go down the list of the *Wasp*'s crew. From the looks of it, they'd be busy for a while.

"Have you heard about Admiral Krätz's wanting everyone to go home?" Kris asked.

"Yeah. It took him quite a while to get the other two admirals to agree to that 'unanimous' decision. Admiral Kōta really doesn't want to leave."

"He didn't have anything to say when Krätz told me they were going home, and they expected me to follow along behind them like a lonely puppy."

"I told them you wouldn't call it quits. Kris, could I ask a favor?"

Kris had a strong hunch she knew where this was going. "You can ask. I can't promise that I'll do it."

"If Admiral Krätz bugs out, can I stay with you on the *Wasp*?"

Jack's head came up so fast from what he was looking at that Kris hoped he didn't suffer whiplash or brain damage. He was shaking his head a mile a minute.

Kris gave him a smile. One with plenty of teeth. "Vicky, I'll have to think about that. You know how risky what we're doing is. If I got you killed . . ." Kris left that thought hanging in the air.

"Kris, you know my dad has a new wife. And I'm going to have a new brother. I figure that bomb was from her family and meant for me. It's been fun while it lasted, being the main heir to the Peterwald empire, but let's face it. I'd be safer chasing after a bug-eyed monster to put my head in its mouth than I'm going to be back home."

"Vicky, I really have to think about this. I don't see anyone going anywhere real soon. We've got time to decide this."

"Okay," Vicky said. "But you will get back to me. You promise."

"I promise," Kris said.

Vicky cut the commlink at that, saving Kris from having to do it herself.

"Kris, you have another call coming in," Nelly said.

"Good Lord, I was never this popular in high school." Kris sighed. "Who is it this time?"

"Commander Phil Taussig," Nelly announced. "The *Hermes* just jumped back into the system. Oh, and there are two, no, three. Make that four big freighters following the courier ship. Oh, and the two battleships are also back."

"Put him through," Kris said.

The screen filled with the happy face of one handsome young Navy officer. "Hello, Commodore, I bring greetings and gifts from your grampa, our king."

"Does he know about the situation we have here?"

"Ah, no. They're way behind the information cycle," the commander said with a large grin. "The local government on Santa Maria was none too happy with the gift you sent them. They passed a resolution that I should tell you to come back. And they sent off a fast courier to Wardhaven to get the king to support them."

"And?" Kris said, when her subordinate wasn't immediately forthcoming with what happened next.

"These supply ships were already in orbit with orders to join you at the earliest opportunity. So, being a harebrained young officer with way too much initiative, I grabbed them and ran."

"I think I'm glad to see you," Kris said.

"Oh, you're glad to see me. You don't know how glad you are to see me."

"Tell me why I am more glad to see you than I realize," Kris said cautiously.

"Did you recently broach the subject with your grampa as to why the Iteeche War was not fought with nukes?"

"I did. Why?"

"Because three of these merchant ships following me have Marine guards locking down a special weapons magazine."

"Nukes?" Kris said.

"Nope, something better. You know what a neutron star is, don't you?"

"I think so," Kris said.

"Well, your grampa, our king, has sent you a couple of neutron torpedoes."

"What?"

"I'll explain it when I can report to the *Wasp*. Better yet, I'll bring along a scientist who can explain it all better than I can."

"I hope you will," Kris said.

19

Kris didn't invite the admirals over, but their barges showed up right behind the gig that brought Commander Taussig aboard the *Wasp*. She invited Taussig and the woman who accompanied him to her Tac Center and had the admirals directed toward the refurbished Forward Lounge.

"Is anyone refusing to go to the lounge?" Kris asked Nelly.

"No. But they brought a lot fewer people. And all three of them have their own security details. They're patting down each other and doing a first-class security sweep of the place."

Kris could only chuckle at the visual that brought to mind. "Have Gunny Brown post a security detail at the hatch of the Forward Lounge. Also have Chief Beni join them and do a security sweep to his own high standards," she told Nelly, as Jack looked on approvingly.

"I already suggested that to the chief. He likes to have a drink or two in the lounge after work. He wasn't very happy while it was out of commission. He's already got three senior Marines helping him make sure their watering hole does not end up in the body and fender shop again."

"Good," Kris said with the first real laugh she'd had in a long while.

Kris found her usual team had filed into her Tac Center as she and Nelly talked. It was not unusual for Professor mFumbo to absent himself half the time when she called. Science has its own schedule, he was quick to point out. Today, he sat eagerly in his place at the foot of the table.

Captain Drago was also there.

Kris let everyone settle in, then asked, "So, what is this gift my great-grandfather has sent our way? A neutron torpedo?"

"I'll leave it to the doctor to explain the contraption," Lieutenant Commander Phil Taussig said. "All your grandfather asks is that you not start a war with the dang contraption 'if she could avoid it.' His words, not mine."

"It is not a dang contraption," the young woman said, standing. "I am Nikki Mulroney. Some of you might have heard the story of my grandmother, Your Highness. She found the 'vanishing box' on Santa Maria that your great-grandfather, King Raymond, used in the war between humanity and the Control Computer there, eighty years ago."

"So it really happened," Penny said.

"Oh yes. It has been allowed to become little more than a legend, but my grandmother pointed the box at mountains and made them vanish."

"And you have the vanishing box working again?" Kris said. That the box existed might or might not be a legend. Every story agreed that the power supply had been exhausted in the final battle with the rampaging rogue computer.

"Ah no. We do not have the vanishing box working," the scientist said. She licked her lips before going on. "We do have something working that might be something like that instrument."

"How something like it?" Kris asked. *And how many bushes are we going to beat around to get a straight nonscientific answer out of you?*

"We can *not* make matter vanish. However, we can manipulate matter at an ever-increasing distance."

Which told Kris everything . . . and nothing . . . all at the same time.

"What kind of matter can you manipulate?" Penny asked before Kris could say something like it.

"Initially, all we could lift was a feather."

"Excuse me if I say that's not all that exciting," Jack said. "What can you lift now?"

"Only a few cubic millimeters."

"That doesn't seem like much," Kris said.

"You are correct," the scientist agreed, with precision. "However, there was a second project being funded on Santa Maria. It involved a nearby neutron star. When we used the one project to see what we could do with the other one, we got surprising results. We succeeded in chipping a half cubic millimeter off the surface of that neutron star."

"Half a cubic millimeter," Kris finally said, when no one else would risk saying anything.

"Close to 150 tons of matter went flying off into space," the boffin said.

That got a low whistle from the audience.

"What happened to it?" Professor mFumbo asked. "How did being free of the gravitational pull of the neutron star impact that mass?"

"It departed at nearly a third the speed of light. When it hit a cinder of a planet destroyed when the star went nova, it made quite an impact."

That got low whistles from Jack and the colonel. Half a millimeter was tiny. At one-third the speed of light, even something that small was bound to leave a mark.

"No, I mean did the matter. No," Professor mFumbo sputtered to a halt. Kris had never seen him at such a loss for words. He took two breaths and started again.

"What was it made of?" the professor said slowly.

"Ions and electrons," the newly arrived self-proclaimed weapons expert answered quickly and simply.

He nodded. "Okay, did this half cubic millimeter of ions and electrons expand once it was free of that gravity well?"

"No," the woman said. "As best as our instrumentation could tell, it departed the star in a compact, half-millimeter bullet, and it was the same size ten minutes later, when it impacted the planet."

"Have you run further tests?" Kris asked. She had finally gotten what Professor mFumbo was getting at. The neutron star's gravity crammed down the ions and electrons on its surface until there was really no space between them. That made for quite a dense solid. What happened to that matter after the heavy impact of the gravity was removed was a very good question.

At three, Kris had once lifted a pound of dried apricots

from the kitchen at Nuu House. She'd split them with several friends. They scarfed them down with no trouble.

But in their little stomachs, they soaked up liquids. Suddenly, they needed much more space, and the only way to get it was up and out.

Kris and her little friends had spent a miserable night giving back the apricots she'd stolen.

The idea of a warhead that suddenly needed a lot more room struck her with more than the usual appalling force.

The weapons developer gave the head of Kris's boffins an acid look.

"Sir, that question did *not* escape our concern. We have instrumentation maintaining constant observations of all extracted neutron material. We have identified no expansion. This includes the instruments observing the warheads on the torpedoes aboard each of the three transports that came out with me."

"Three transports. How many torpedoes did you bring?" Kris asked.

"Three."

Kris considered that for a moment, then went on. "I know I shouldn't ask this, but how big are these torpedoes?"

"Each of the warheads contains approximately 2.5 cubic millimeters of neutron-star material," the scientist said. "Say about fifteen thousand tons of mass per weapon."

Several people in the room whistled at that.

Kris held up her hand, two fingers a few millimeters apart. "Fifteen thousand tons in that tiny space?"

"Actually, we've spun it out into a concave lens sixty-six centimeters in diameter. That's the same size as the torpedo. We think that might have the effect of reflecting back any lasers fired at it. We didn't have time to test that hypothesis before we were ordered to pack up our test items and get them out here to you."

Fifteen thousand tons in anything like that small a space. The thought boggled Kris's mind. Her mind was getting way too familiar with the boggles.

"Pardon me," Penny said. "But if you've got this wonderful device that can reach down into this huge gravity well around a neutron star and pinch out a BB-gun-size chunk with fifteen thousand tons of mass, what am I missing? Why don't you have that doohickey out here? Think of what that can do!"

"Yes," Dr. Malroney said, stuffing her hands into the pockets of her coat. "I do imagine the primary device has significant military possibilities. However, it takes a large asteroid to hold it and requires the power plants of several large cities to power it."

"Mobility it ain't got," Abby said.

The room took a minute to absorb that.

"Let's talk about that torpedo," Captain Drago said. "With a fifteen-thousand-ton warhead, just how fast can you get it going?"

"The torpedo's propulsion machinery is simplicity itself," the woman boffin said. "Reaction mass heated with antimatter. We store the antimatter separate from the torpedo and only load it just before we launch. The containment field is of light construction. It will hold long enough to get the job done, say ten minutes to an hour."

"How *fast* can you get the torpedo going?" the captain said, cutting in.

"Two seconds after launch, it will be accelerating at ten gees," the woman scientist said. "Our initial reaction mass is water. But that's just intended to get the rocket motors started and the torpedo away from the ship that launched it. After that, we're using iron filings for the reaction mass. Iron and antimatter plasma has a very high specific impulse."

Kris swallowed. "I imagine it does."

"How many of these infernal machines did you bring out, again?" Captain Drago asked.

"Three."

"We have four scout corvettes here," Kris pointed out.

"Actually, I think your grandfather, our king, knew what he was doing," said Captain Drago. "The *Wasp* is already some twenty thousand tons heavier than the other three scouts. That's the price we pay to carry the extra Marines and boffins and their gear. I'm not sure how the *Wasp* would take to another . . . What? How large do these torpedoes mass out?"

"They come in at eighteen thousand tons—warhead, fuel, and engines," Commander Taussig put in.

"So you've given this problem some thought," Captain Drago said.

"Quite a bit on the way out." Phil tapped his wrist unit, and a schematic of the *Hornet* appeared on one of Kris's walls. "We'll have to lock one of these puppies down right at the ship's center of gravity. Otherwise, you put momentum on the boat, and it's going to go in all kinds of directions. One thing I've liked about the *Hornet* is how nimble she is. If we don't do this right, they'll all wallow like pigs."

"I'll thank you not to refer to my *Wasp* as a pig," Captain Drago said.

At that, the two ship drivers dropped out of the English language for the next several minutes, losing themselves in technical talk.

It was interesting to Kris to see both Professor mFumbo and Dr. Mulroney left to stare dumbly as the conversation went over their heads. Kris relaxed and enjoyed it.

At her father's knee, she'd gotten comfortable with people knowing more than she did about this or that technical specialization. As the great Billy Longknife said, "You don't have to know how to make it happen. Just who . . . and when." He was also quick to point out that his military was a spear he decided who to point at and when and where to stick them.

Kris let that thought roll around her skull for a few minutes while the two ship captains kept everyone else entertained.

When they paused for breath, Kris raised her hand for silence. It came quickly.

"Pardon me," Kris said, "but did I miss something?"

That brought her blank stares.

"As I recall, our mission was something like 'We come. We see. We run real fast home and report.' Wasn't that in all the papers?" Kris asked.

"I seem to remember hearing that rumor from someone who thought she was running the show," Abby drawled.

Around the table, all she got was sober looks.

"If that's the mission, how come Grampa just sent me three of the most gi-hugical and nasty weapons in human history?"

Kris let the question hang there. She had no intention of being the first to take a crack at an answer.

When the silence stretched, Colonel Cortez pursed his lips and ventured slowly. "Your great-grandfather, our king, has spent some time on the tip of the spear, Your Highness. I trust he's developed some seriously reliable gut instincts, or he'd be dead by now even if he did only half of what they say he did."

He paused, polled the room with his eyes, and went on. "The seriously nasty behavior of the one ship we encountered might have seriously bothered him. Commander, I understand that these weapons came with an injunction not to start a war . . . if she could avoid it."

"Something like that. I've got the message here if you want to read it." He tapped his wrist unit, and Nelly projected a picture of the transmittal form. It was like any other supply chit, except at the bottom, in his own hand, the king had handwritten the injunction, "Try not to start a war with these."

Kris glanced around the room, suspecting what everyone else was thinking but no one wanted to say. King Ray was handing Kris a loaded gun, then resorting to the most crass of bureaucratic techniques by adding a "not order" to cover his ass.

Kris scowled as the poisoned silence grew long. Then, with a shake of her head, she went back to the practical problems at hand.

"I take it from what you two captains were saying, we're going to need to stay put for a long while to make all of this happen."

"Actually, not," Captain Drago said.

"It's a pretty standard set of mods that we'll have to make to the *Hornet*, *Fearless*, and *Intrepid*," Phil said. "The *Vulcan* has the machine shops and gear to make the bomb harnesses. Once their specialists take the measurements off each of the ships, our scouts can go about their business. A couple of weeks later, we can get the installation done in no time at all. You weren't planning on our hanging around here for all that time, were you, Princess?"

"No," Kris said, mentally taking the bull she wanted to by the horns and ignoring the stampeding elephant in the room. "Professor mFumbo, I need your astronomers and astrophysicists to earn their keep. I know they've enjoyed stargazing. Now I need them to help us plot a course that's both fast and safe. Four courses."

Kris paused to let the full impact hit all present. With their focused attention, she went on. "I want each of the four corvettes to make its own fast, long-range reconnaissance swing.

Five planets out. Four different planets back if we can manage it. One jump from here, the *Wasp* came across a system with six jumps. Let's move the fleet there. At least as many as will follow us. We can leave the battleships swinging around there while the scouts take a gander at what things look like three to five thousand light-years from here along a wide search pattern."

That got a few low whistles.

"You're not going for halfway measures," Jack said.

"Someone asked me why we were out here, and I was dithering. The admirals want to pull up their skirts and run for home. Now Grampa has sent me the best three weapons in his quiver with the hope I won't use them.

"I admit the idea of running into something that drains gas giants for its reaction fuel took some of the wind out of my sails for a while. But running home with nothing more to report than what we've seen? No. That's not why I came out here. I'm not sure how I feel about Grampa's latest contribution to our mission, any more than I was all that excited about the big old battlewagons everyone else thought to send along with us. What I do know is that we came out here to see, so let's go see what there is to see."

Kris paused. Faces that had been locked down lit up with smiles. Clearly, she'd just given them the pep talk they wanted to hear. She knew she should leave it at that, but, being a Longknife, she let her mouth add one more thought.

"And, while we're zooming from star to star, we can set our reactors to capturing all the antimatter we put out. Then, if we find we need it, we will have it."

Jack snorted. "Spoken like a true Longknife."

Kris gave him the best shrug she could manage, then flipped her face into a smile. "Shall we now go see what our friends in the Forward Lounge have to say about where they're going?"

20

There were no surprises in the Forward Lounge. Admiral Krätz was waiting for her like a panicked nanny eager to tell his young charge the error of her ways.

Kris took a deep breath as the words washed over her. The ship's repair crews had done their usual efficient job. There was no evidence of the explosion except for the smell of fresh paint.

Admiral Krätz's verbal assault began the moment Kris walked in the door. He didn't even take a deep breath before launching into the topic at hand. The admirals had voted, and all three were for going home. Kris must follow their lead.

Kris waited patiently and respectfully until he ran down . . . not something that happened quickly. Nobody reached his level of power without developing a great love for his own voice.

Once Kris got a word in, she explained that she had no intention of going back. In fact, she had just decided to expand her scouting mission. "Even as I speak, my boffins are looking for low-risk solar systems so the four scouts can do a high-speed recon."

Admiral Krätz shook his head and pointed out that the vote was three to one to go home. Being a reasonable person, she should conform to the majority.

Kris admitted that their opinions were all valid. However, no one had ever accused a Longknife of being reasonable. As a fine point, she was not in their chain of command. Therefore, their opinions, right or wrong, had no impact on her actions.

Much discussion followed, with a plentitude of references to "those damn Longknifes" and "getting us all killed."

In the end, in an effort to present a unanimous front to exactly whom it was not clear, they all voted to follow Kris.

Kris then told them that she had found a solar system with six jump points that was only one easy jump from where they were at the moment. She suggested that the entire fleet move there. The battleships could wait there while the scouts each took a different jump out as the first of their long-range scouting missions.

Admiral Krätz demanded that they leave behind a small, silent jump buoy in this system so that anyone who came looking for them would know where they were.

Since Kris figured she could get her scouts away before any courier ship got here from human space with orders she didn't want to read, she agreed.

Six hours later, the Fleet of Reluctant Discovery accelerated toward the one jump it had agreed to make. Construction personnel from the *Vulcan* were aboard the scouts as they did their jumps, measuring them for the new weapon. The time was well spent.

Once in the new base system, the courier ships broke out their balloots and quickly topped off the scouts' supplies of reaction mass from a nearby gas giant. While they went about a second session of cloud dancing for the battleships, Kris got PatRon 10 moving toward their separate jumps. All were making 50,000 kph as they hit the jump with three gees kicked in at the last moment and 20 rpms on the hull.

As expected, the *Wasp* jumped over seven hundred light-years into a system centered on an old red dwarf. There were no gas giants around the star, only dead, airless rocks.

The *Wasp* headed for the farther of the two other jumps in the system. The closest one might be safe, but it led to a large white sun that might or might not have gone nova in the seven hundred years it took the light to get from there to here. The next jump found them in a twin system. A warm orange star had somehow managed to pick up a neutron star in a wide elliptical orbit.

The *Wasp* analyzed the double star system as they crossed to the next jump. Neither Chief Beni nor the boffins reported anything of interest. They departed that system twelve hours after they entered it, with much data but no hint that they shared this galaxy with life, benign or otherwise.

The third jump yielded an unexpected surprise. They found themselves popping into a system with a huge blue giant.

"That's not supposed to be there," Captain Drago said. "What are we doing in a system with a potential giant nova?"

A call to boffin country brought a blended flood of both surprise and apologies. "That was not on the map Ray Longknife discovered on Santa Maria." "We'd never tell you to jump to a blue giant." And lastly, "Did you do the jump right?"

The navigator, Sulwan Kann, was adamant that the *Wasp* had taken the jump exactly the way it had taken all others.

Kris interrupted the various parties in full defensive mode to slip a question in sideways. "Folks, is there any chance that big blue hot thing in the sky might go nova on us while we're debating how we got here?"

That brought a pause. It grew, but before anyone got to full panic, Professor mFumbo's calm bass voice boomed over the net. "No chance of that, Your Highness. This particular solar time bomb has a lot of ticking to do."

"How far did we come?" Kris asked next.

That question also took a while to answer. After several minutes of pregnant absence, Professor mFumbo came back on net. "This jump also took us over seven hundred lightyears. By our best estimates, we are now over twenty-two hundred light-years from where we started."

"Thank you," Captain Drago said. "That's nice to know." So saying, he slipped out of his command chair and came to stand beside Kris's offensive-weapons station. With his hand over his mouth, he said softly, "Those strange new jumps we've been talking about."

"You mean the fuzzy ones?" Kris asked.

"Whatever you call them. Is there any chance this was one of them? One of the new ones that wasn't on the Santa Maria map your great-grandfather stumbled upon?"

"Nelly?"

"No chance, Captain. That was a standard, old-fashioned jump."

"But it didn't take us where Ray's map said it would."

"No, Captain," Nelly said firmly. "I've done a double check. We are not in the system Ray's map says we should be in. I don't know how or why. I just know that we are where we are, sir."

"Any suggestion how that might have happened?" the captain asked.

"None that I want to speculate on," Kris said.

Humans had been studying the jump points for nearly four hundred years. So far, they were as much a mystery as they had been the first time three ships from Earth attempted the one jump point they had discovered orbiting out around Jupiter.

The thought that who- or whatever was out here had mastered the ability to either make new ones or redirect the old ones was a terror Kris really didn't want to give voice to. Certainly not until she and Professor mFumbo had spent a lot of brain sweat on it.

"I don't like this one bit," the captain said, letting a momentary scowl cross his face. He was his usually intent but neutral self by the time he turned back to his chair.

"Has anyone found us some jump points?" he demanded.

"One, sir," Sulwan reported.

Only one?" the captain asked. There should have been three.

"One, sir. It's within nine hours of here if we go at two gee."

The captain glanced back at Kris.

She gave him a slight nod.

"Make it so, Nav."

Nine hours later, they crossed from one surprising star system to an even more troubling one.

21

"That wasn't what I expected," Captain Drago said softly as the forward screen filled with four stars.

If a star mariner was a poet, this would be the star system for him or her. Four stars, red, blue, yellow, and white hung in the sky. It took the boffins ten minutes to figure out the dance they did.

The yellow and red ones swung around each other. The white and blue ones did the same. Somehow, the two pairs then did a jig around the center of gravity among the four. Since the blue and white pair greatly outweighed the other two, it must get very interesting.

If they had still been on the course they'd plotted initially for the jaunt, they should have been staring at a single white dwarf, sister to humanity's home star, Sol.

Clearly, we aren't in Kansas anymore, Toto, Kris thought to herself.

"Talk to me, folks," the captain said softly. "Tell me about this system."

One thing Kris had come to count on from Captain Drago was a cool head when all hell broke loose. His voice was calm, but under it was clear agitation. Agitation in a tight grip.

"There are planets around the stars," Chief Beni said from his station at Sensors. "Some small rocks orbiting each pair."

He paused, then went on. "A couple of more rocky planets orbiting the four of them."

"Jump points? Do we have any jump points?" Captain Drago demanded.

The white dwarf they were supposed to have jumped to should have had three.

"None that I've found so far," Sulwan Kann said. "There are a couple of large gas giants well away from the stars. They could be concealing a jump point. One or two might be playing hide-and-seek with us down close to the suns. Captain, I'll need a couple of hours before I can make a definitive statement, but for now, no, sir. There is no visible way out of this system other than the way we came in."

The captain leaned back in his chair, probably thinking the same thing Kris was. It wasn't unheard of for there to be only one jump into a system. Earth herself had been at a dead end. Certainly, the wild dance these four suns did would make for a berserk jig for any jump point caught among them . . . even before you added in other star systems to the confusion.

But there was no way this system could have been patched together in just two million years from the simple one-star system on the map Ray Longknife had discovered.

"Sulwan, keep one gee on the ship." He paused for a moment. That gee would give the crew weight. Still, the navigator needed a course. "Aim us in the general direction of the nearest gas giant. If we have to turn around and head back, that will help."

"Aye, aye, sir," Sulwan said.

"Chief Beni, Professor mFumbo," Kris said. "It sure would be nice to know something about this system."

"There is no activity on the radio spectrum," the chief said immediately.

A bit later, the professor added, "The second planet out from the yellow and red suns appears to have an atmosphere and water. I have no idea how much solar energy it gets during the course of a year, but the water is in liquid form, at present."

"Is that interesting enough for us to change our course and head in that direction?" the captain asked.

"I don't know," the professor said.

"I think I do," Chief Beni said, looking up from his board.

"Your Highness, I'm getting something that I've never seen before."

"Spit it out, Chief."

"That planet has a high radioactive background. It's hot all over, but certain spots are a whole lot hotter."

He paused for a long moment. "Ma'am, this isn't in any of our training, but if I had to guess what a planet looked like after it was bombarded with nukes, I'd say that it should look a lot like this."

"Sulwan, change course for that planet."

"Aye, aye, Captain."

"How long to make orbit?"

The navigator studied her board, tapped it several times. "Eighteen hours if we go to 1.73 gees, Captain."

"Make it so," the captain said.

"All hands, we will be going to 1.73 gees in ten seconds. Prepare for moderate gees," the navigator announced.

A quick countdown later, the ship put on acceleration. Kris found her weight going up, but not more than she could handle.

"Chief, Professor," Kris said. "I'd like to know a whole lot more about this system before we make orbit around that hot rock."

"I can think of at least one thing you might like to know in advance," the professor announced on net.

"What would that be?" Kris hated it when people played Twenty Questions with her. Didn't anyone spit anything out?

"We're concentrating most of our sensors on the hot rock, as you call it. However we are looking at that large gas giant, Your Highness. It is too soon to tell for sure, but the moons around that planet appear to be in unstable orbits. We may have another gas giant that has recently lost a lot of weight."

"You think so?" was all Kris managed to get out.

"It is too early to be sure, but it's possible, ma'am. We'll know more in a few hours."

Kris shared a glance with Captain Drago. It never rained but it poured.

"Chief, I really need to know," the captain said with an admirable calm. "Are there any ships in this system?"

"I'm not getting any signatures from any fusion engines. From any reactors of any kind that are in my databases."

"We may not be looking for any that we're familiar with, Chief," Captain Drago said.

"I know that, sir," Chief Beni said. "I'm as scared as you are, sir, to have a planet that's hot on the atomic scale. Probably more so. I'm bypassing my filters and taking the raw feed from the sensors. Still, sir, I'm getting a whole lot of nothing. I don't have anything giving off an electromagnetic signature. Anything making noise like a nuclear or fusion reactor. Trust me, sir. I have no desire to get popped by whatever this bug-eyed monster is that the princess here is chasing. I intend to die in bed."

"You and me both," Captain Drago said, and pushed the commlink on his command station.

"All hands, this is the captain speaking. We have an unknown situation developing here. Look smart. I may be ordering you to battle stations with very little notice. Keep that in mind as you go about your duties. Be assured that as soon as I know something, I will pass it along to you. Captain out."

Finished, he turned to Kris. "Okay, Princess. We've been lugging around those boffins for you. Would you please see that they earn their pay today."

"Yes, sir," Kris said. "Nelly, have my staff report to my Tac Center. Advise Chief Beni and Professor mFumbo that they may report or stay at their stations, depending on where they think they can be the most productive."

"Doing it, Kris."

"Oh, and Nelly, have Cookie bring around some lunch to my Tac Center. I'm past hungry."

"I already advised him. He said to tell you that he don't do 1.7 gees all that well. But he'll have one of the youngsters get your lunch."

"Thank the cook for me," Kris said, and heaved herself to her feet. Her knee complained of the extra weight . . . the one that had taken the brunt of that last nearly successful assassination attempt. She walked carefully from the bridge. It wouldn't do to have herself laid up in sick bay just when things were starting to get interesting.

22

As the hours passed, the picture grew more grim.

The gas giant had indeed recently lost a lot of weight. Say ten percent. Say in the last two hundred years.

Chief Beni chose to keep his eyes on his board, regularly having Da Vinci dig down with him beyond the standard human/computer interface to make sense of the raw feed coming in from the antennas.

The one bit of good news was that no reactors showed up anywhere in the system. The bad news was that no other jump point was identified, either.

Kris interrupted the chief's work once for a question.

"When that alien ship came charging off that moon intent on killing us all, you said your sensors couldn't get anything off the ship. Are you sure that your sensors can pick up anything off these aliens?"

"Ma'am, there is a difference between something being a big black hole of nothing in space and it being a charging bull of a ship that is doing its best to keep me from digging out interesting intel on it.

"Yes, they were masking a lot of what was going on inside their boat. But there was no question in any of our minds that there was a big houseboat down there powered by a reactor of unknown design. I could also tell you it had lasers and was shooting at us.

"Don't worry, ma'am. I may not be able to give you a read-out of their captain's battle board on one of these alien starships, but you can bet your last dollar that I'll be able to tell you that they are there."

"That's good to hear," Kris said.

Both the chief and the professor chose to stay at their posts. Kris's main staff reported to the Tac Center; Jack walked in, followed by a high-gee station, which, now that Kris had been introduced to one, looked very much like a wheelchair.

"I don't need a wheelchair," Kris snapped.

"It's not a wheelchair," Jack shot back, "it's a high-gee station."

"I don't need a high-gee station. We aren't even making two gees."

"It will support your knee. Kris, you don't want to twist that knee and end up back in sick bay."

"You're sounding more like a mother hen than a security chief."

"I'll cluck, cluck as much as I have to if it keeps you from doing something stupid," Jack said, doggedly.

"Humor him, Kris," Abby said.

"I do *not* need a high-gee station, thank you very much."

The station maneuvered itself up next to Kris's elbow and showed no evidence of going away.

"You are a stubborn old pig," Kris said.

"Oink, cluck, oink, cluck," was all Jack said.

Kris switched from chair to station. The staff gave Jack, or Kris, it was hard to tell, a ragged round of applause.

Jack took the bow, one of his silly grins all over his face. Kris spread her hands like a reigning monarch and took a bit of a bow herself.

"Now can we get down to business?" she said.

Though once she was seated in the high-gee station, Kris did find that she was a lot more comfortable than she'd been in her usual chair. The station gave her bum knee support the chair didn't.

The hint that she might not be as young as she used to be was painful to contemplate.

Before the team finished their light lunch, Kris rapped the

table for their attention. "What does a planet look like that has been nuked from space?" she asked. "And can we tell the difference between that and a planet that just got nuked in the course of its own folks being disagreeable to each other?"

Colonel Cortez cleared his throat. "One of the few agonies we humans have spared the human race is that of global nuclear war. Simply put, I don't think there's any way to tell at a distance whether the nuclear bombs came from some alien in orbit or from your neighbor's bombers and rockets from across the way, so to speak."

"You're no help. It sounds like you're saying all we can do is guess," Kris said.

"And very glad I am that there is insufficient data to go on so that we must guess," the colonel said, showing no shame.

As it turned out, the closer they got to the planet, the less they needed to guess.

"We've identified at least twenty-six nuclear strikes," the chief said. "That number may be low. Some targets might have taken several hits, and what we're identifying as a single strike may be two or three hits that have run together over time."

Later, Chief Beni expanded on that. "Kris, I've got what look like cities. Dead cities. Besides the two dozen or so that are radioactive hot, there are a whole lot more that seem to have taken very large hits that gutted their centers."

"What kind of hits?"

"It's hard to tell, but from the craters I'd say that someone threw some pretty big rocks at them at awfully high speeds."

The colonel leaned forward. "Any chance, Chief, that these are natural meteorite strikes?"

"Sir, as I said, these are smack-dab in the middle of what look to be major urban centers. Somebody built them, and somebody knocked them down. Big rocks came in fast and hit right in the bull's-eye of the town. Once, maybe. Twice, possible. But Da Vinci and I are past a thousand and still counting."

"That's hostile action," the colonel said, leaning back into his chair.

A half hour later, the boffins made their initial report.

"We think we have found something interesting," Professor mFumbo said on net. "Very little of this planet is covered in water. There are no oceans. Just some large lakes. However, all the nuclear explosions and rock craters as well as what looks

like a major road network that connects them are on high plateaus that definitely look like continental plates to our observation."

A large picture of the planet appeared on the wall in Kris's
room. Her crew gathered around it.

"You will notice what some of my team are calling
beaches," the professor said, highlighting what looked like
sandy areas along the edge of the plateaus.

"But they're a long way from any water?" Jack said.

"There's also a major difference in vegetation from the continental plates to what look like dried-up ocean beds. Oh, this
is interesting."

A second wall filled up with a new picture. "There are several places where there are these vast scrub wastelands. However, our early radar returns show knobs scattered over the
landscape."

"Knobs?" Kris said.

"Think stumps from where huge trees had been cut down
and removed. On any of our planets, there would be laws re-
quiring replanting and restoration management of the second
growth. Our reference point is to a time in Earth's past when
uncontrolled harvesting and no subsequent effort to care for
the land resulted in limited new growth."

For the next several hours, more dismal information flowed
into Kris's Tac Center.

It became painfully clear that the planet had once had
nearly seventy percent of its surface covered by water. Now it
was less than fifteen percent.

The planet had once been home to a budding civilization. It
was hard to take the measure of what those people had built,
what with over two thousand of their larger urban centers
blackened, some flattened, others radioactive.

The radioactive decay did help to time the event that had
caused all this. Two hundred years ago.

As they came closer to their target, more pictures showed
even more puzzling things. Mountains had had their tops removed. It hadn't occurred in the razor-sharp manner of the
vanishing box from Santa Maria. No, you could see the residue
of the mountaintops. They had been shoved off the mountains
and slid into the valleys below.

"Somebody strip-mined this planet as if there were no to-morrow," Abby said. "Strip-mined it real ugly-like."

The professor got back to Kris as they were decelerating two hours out from orbit.

"Our biologists are not at all happy about the level of growth on the planet. Assuming this ... event ... occurred two hundred years ago, nature should have done more to re-store the biosphere."

"Could the loss of water have led to desertification?"

"It seems worse," the professor said.

"What about nuclear winter?" Nelly said.

"Nuclear what?" the professor asked.

"Kris had me do major research recently concerning nuclear weapons," Nelly said vaguely. Professor mFumbo had not been involved in the talks between Kris and Ron the Iteeche concern-ing how the late Iteeche War had been waged and the lack of either side going to the long-forbidden use of atomic weapons.

"What's a nuclear winter?" Kris asked. Nelly had briefed her about her research, but whatever this kind of winter was, it had not come up.

"Some people, back when nuclear weapons were available, feared that if they used them, the resulting clouds of debris and smoke might hurl particles high into the atmosphere. Enough particles and high enough that they could block out so much of the sun that there would not be enough solar energy arriving at the surface to permit plants to get in a full growing season. Nuclear weapons, volcanoes, or large asteroid hits might throw up so much gunk into the atmosphere that it brought on a multiyear-long winter."

"I don't understand," the colonel said.

Nelly seemed to take a deep breath, and even sigh, before going into a deeper explanation. "If you go several years with no plants having a successful growth season, plant-eating ani-mals die. Meat-eating animals may be able to scavenge their dead bodies, but sooner or later, all that food is gone and the carnivores die along with them. And plants can exhaust them-selves sprouting, then being frozen, sprouting again and again but being hit time after time with a killing frost. In ancient Earth history, civilizations fell when volcanoes half a world away blew their top. The scientists on old Earth thought that a blend of asteroid hits and major volcanic action wiped out at least sixty to eighty percent of all life on Earth not once but twice."

Kris shivered. "So whoever these people are, they were hit by nukes and high-speed rocks. Then their planet was strip-mined, their water stolen, and those still alive left to starve and freeze in the wreckage."

"It looks that way," the professor said. "Although they might not have lived very long. We can't prove it yet, but the air pressure is about half of what would be needed to support our kind of life."

"They stole their air as well!" Penny said.

"It looks that way."

Abby whistled through her teeth. "I do not like whoever did this to these people. They are not nice at all, and I do not, for one, like them at all."

The *Wasp* made orbit. The boffins and crew began a methodical and intense examination of what there was to see.

Low-flying drones sent back photographs. Some covered wide swaths of territory. Other robotic probes focused on specific sites. They hovered over the surviving towns and sought answers about the life that died there.

The local architecture was full of soaring lines and high-rises. Many had been knocked down, but some still stood, defiant in their beauty. The undamaged towns were smaller; if they were human urban centers, none would have held more than five thousand people.

In the towns were murals and statues of their inhabitants. Apparently they'd been a population of intelligent insects, with an opposable thumb and a strong hive bent. Their architecture was soaring on the outside, but inside it was totally claustrophobic from a human perspective.

The general story that slowly grew told of desperate events. It fell to the colonel to put flesh on what they found.

"The nuclear strikes were aimed at decapitating the political infrastructure," he said coldly. "No way to tell if they had one central government with various subdistricts or if they had several independent local governments. I think the attackers smashed the command and control centers with a lightning nuclear strike. This left the survivors headless and struggling to form a response."

He paused for a moment to let that sink in.

"Likely, the attackers had only so many nukes. The rocks were cheaper, and they used them to flatten all the other large urban centers. This also disrupted the food-distribution network. The rock bombardment left people with a horrible choice. They could stay in their homes, among the familiar, and risk being blown to bits, or they could flee out into the countryside. With no food, shelter, or services, the outlook for survival wasn't all that much better than staying put."

"What a fate," Penny said.

"It doesn't look like they took it lying down. Where the attackers landed and set about plundering their planet, there are huge fields of bodies, carapaces spread over acres and acres where the defenders attacked and were mowed down."

The colonel coughed to clear his throat. "I'd like to examine some of those killing fields. It would be helpful to know how the attackers murdered the locals."

"Those are loaded words," Kris said. She wasn't getting much physical exercise these days, but jumping to conclusions was something she really intended to avoid.

"Holy Mother of God, Commander. I've looked at the data. You tell me words that do it justice," the colonel snapped, then his gaze fell to the table in front of him as he struggled to regain his composure.

Kris said nothing. There were no other words she could think of. Still, she struggled to keep a tight rein on her emotions. She might have to open negotiations with the people who'd done this sometime soon.

At the moment, she'd rather negotiate with the devil himself than whoever murdered this planet.

"Do we have any physical evidence of who did this?" Penny asked.

"That's been my job," Abby said. "We've identified several sites that do not match the local construction. Wrong design. Wrong materials. Most of them are close to sites of major resource extractions. Say where several mountains were flattened or huge expanses of trees removed."

A series of pictures flashed on the wall. They showed several villages. The alien construction used local material like mud bricks or wooden poles to make squat, one-story buildings that sprawled with little or no apparent planning close to the extraction sites.

"Are there any bodies other than the local insects left here?" Kris asked.

Both Abby and the colonel shook their heads. Abby went on. "We haven't identified anything but the carapaces strewn about. There don't appear to be any graves left around the aliens' campsites."

"They're taking everything this planet has," Kris said. "I guess that means they're also taking back their own dead."

"That may not be totally true," Chief Beni said, interrupting.

"I had Da Vinci running a pattern recognition on all the killing fields. He spotted a skeleton among all those carapaces. One endoskeleton among all those exoskeletons. A vertebrate from the looks of it."

"Please put that on-screen," Kris said.

The wall opposite the one Abby was using came to life. Its picture was of death. A ridge was covered with the dried carapaces of thousands upon thousands. They were tossed and tumbled together. How much of that was postdeath and how much had happened as they died, only a weeping God could tell.

The picture zoomed in, fleeing from the full scope of the slaughter to concentrate on a smaller tragedy. Two or three carapaces had become disassociated in death. Barely visible under them was a skull.

Two empty eyes and a nose hole stared at Kris. The jaws had fallen open in a silent scream. There were long bones for arms and legs, and a collection of vertebrae where a backbone should be.

"It almost looks human," Kris said in a whisper.

"It looks like the bastards who tried to kill us," the colonel said.

"I'm going down there. I need to see this place up close and personal," Kris said.

"Kris," Jack said.

"Jack, I don't want to read a report. I want to be there. See this the way it is. I've got a report to make to my great-grandfather and, I suspect, all of human space. Of this, I must bear witness," she said, jerking a thumb at the view.

Jack gnawed his lower lip but said no more.

"Colonel, you want to come?"

"Definitely. Captain," he said to Jack, "I hope you will provide us the assistance of your full forensic team. "

"I suspect we'll land all four longboats, what with the Marines and the boffins."

"Can I come, too?" came in a small voice from where the door to the Tac Center had edged open a crack.

"Cara, what are you doing here?" Kris asked.

"Dada told me that you were going dirtside, and I ran down here to ask if I could go, too."

"Dada?" Kris echoed the name of Cara's computer, one of Nelly's kids.

"I knew we'd made orbit around an interesting planet, from what the boffins were saying, so I asked Dada to listen in on her mom's net for anything that looked like fun."

"Nelly?" Kris now said. "Do we have a security breach?"

"Ah, yes, Kris, it does appear so." It was funny to hear a computer so embarrassed and searching for words. "I have all my other children on a shared net. I, ah, didn't notice that Dada had been lurking there, too."

"It seemed like a good idea," came in a different voice from Cara's. "You grown-ups are always ignoring us kids and never tell us anything."

"Little pitchers have big ears," Penny said, not making much of an effort to suppress a smile.

"Can I go? Please," the thirteen-year-old pleaded.

"We could really use a field trip," Dada added. "Professor Lynch is teaching us science, and he says videos can't capture the real feel of nature."

Kris noticed that all the so-called grown-ups in the room were looking around at each other, none willing to make the call. She considered the subject of this landing, fields of dead bodies, and wondered if a kid belonged there.

Kris dodged that and tried another thought. "This field trip will be in space suits," Kris said. "Do you have a suit?"

"Of course I do," Cara said. "It was a little snug the last emergency drill, but it still fits. It should."

Like most kids, Cara needed new everything at alarming frequencies. But the comment also reminded Kris that the kid *was* growing up. If memory served, Kris hadn't much liked it when adults remembered her smaller and didn't notice as she got bigger.

"Well," Kris said, taking the bull, if not by the horns, then at least by something. "You'll have to ask your aunt."

"Oh, you're tossing this my way?" Kris's maid snapped.

"Seems like a good idea," Kris said. "She is asking for permission to leave the ship this time. I'd call that an improvement."

The young subject of their consideration turned pink at the reference to her previous antic . . . and disaster. "I am asking this time. Please, can I go with you?"

Abby looked clearly torn. The kid was safe on the ship. As safe as any of them were. On the surface of a murdered planet . . . ?

"Is this Professor Lynch going down with the boffins?"

"He has asked to be included," Professor mFumbo said.

"Do you have space for him?" Jack asked.

"That depends," the professor said. "At present, I've got enough scientists to fill two launches. How many Marines are you taking down?"

Jack ran a worried hand through his hair. "I guess I'm taking two launches full of Marines, less the space taken up by these rubberneckers."

Kris did a quick survey of the room. Penny raised her hand. So did the colonel and Abby. "Chief, you want to be included in this jaunt dirtside?"

"No way. That place looks cold and miserable, and I don't see anything down there that you can't bring up here for me to examine in the comfort of my own shop."

Kris was none too sure of that, but for now, she'd let the devout coward worship at his personal altar.

"With Cara and Jack, you'll have five rubberneckers."

"Hurray!" Cara shouted and headed off to get ready. She failed to close the door, so Kris could hear her skipping down the passageway, the very image of innocent joy.

Kris shook her head. "If we could bottle that, I'd buy a case."

"It's our own damn fault that we lose it when we get old and grumpy," Abby said, the picture of a grump herself.

"Okay, folks," Kris said, standing up. "There's a planet down there. What happened to it is a crime screaming for whatever justice this universe can give. Let's go investigate the crime scene."

23

The loaded launch flew across what had once been a sea. That fact was emphasized when Kris spotted something and got permission from the boson flying to use the third backup camera.

Nelly pointed it back to what had caught Kris's eye. There, in the middle of what was now a desert, were over a hundred calcified exoskeletons.

"Any guess what those are?" Kris asked.

"They look huge," Jack said. "If this was ocean, then they must have filled the econiche held by the whale on old Earth."

"That lobster would take quite a bit of melted butter," the colonel said, smacking his lips.

"They look like a pod of beached whales," Penny said, thoughtfully. "The receding water must have caught them there and left them high and dry."

"That would be horrible," Cara said, from where she sat beside Abby.

"I suspect we're going to be hearing that a lot," Kris said, and had Nelly switch off the screen.

They were coming up on what some guessed to be the coastline. Kris had Nelly use the spare camera again to capture their landfall. There had been a city there, once. It hadn't been nuked but had been flattened by several rocks. The actual shore area was on the periphery of the zone of destruction.

The camera caught a long pier jutting out from the shore. Kris had gone fishing from just such a pier several times in different resorts around Wardhaven. What Kris would have taken for an amusement park, complete with roller coaster and Ferris wheel, passed quickly under them.

The Ferris wheel was over on its side, and the upper reaches of the roller coaster had been knocked loose. The cars from the coaster now spread along the ground beneath that break. They and the Ferris wheel still showed evidence of smashed and scattered exoskeletons.

"That's horrible," escaped Cara in a whisper.

Nelly changed the picture. One of the vanished forests came into view. The scrub brush that had tried to rise in its place showed dead itself.

"Regrowth never had a chance," Penny said.

"No," Kris agreed.

Cara just stared at the pictures, her mouth open in a silent *Oh*. Apparently, there was a limit to how much horror one thirteen-year-old girl could respond to.

The 1/c bosun's mate piloting the launch was aiming for one of the cutoff mountains. Jack had seen to it that the first launch that got away from the *Wasp* was combat-loaded with Marines. They had come down there the orbit before.

Jack held Kris's launch on the *Wasp* until the skipper of first platoon reported, "Nothing hostile here bigger than an ant, Skipper. And even the bugs are skittering away from the noise the launch made."

Still, the two launches with boffins were ahead of Kris's lander. Jack took Kris's security seriously, even when there was nothing much alive on a raped planet.

The landing was an experience; wind and what little rain there had been had done what it could to smooth the plain of the scraped-off mountain. Still, those who had done this did not have a shuttle landing field in mind as they did it.

Ron the Iteeche had wanted to join Kris on this drop, but his advisors had looked the landing zone over and talked him out of risking himself in the harness the humans would use to strap him into one of their landers. As knocked around as the landing was for Kris, she found herself glad that Ron had agreed to follow them on net and read the reports later.

The aft hatch of the launch opened slowly. With a whoosh, the residual air inside fled into the lower pressure outside.

"This planet has about one-quarter the air pressure of Earth," Professor mFumbo reported. "The atmosphere's content is about what Mother Earth gave us, seventy-seven percent nitrogen and twenty-two percent oxygen, with minor contributions from other gases. What we have here is Earth atmosphere at thirty thousand feet. Please don't open your suit masks," he added.

Kris led her team out of the lander, right behind Jack. At least he didn't have his automatic out.

The scene that met Kris's eyes brought her to a halt. Her mouth went tight, and her stomach flipped. "Desolation" was the only word that came to mind.

Death and desolation. As far as the eye could see was a dusty emptiness. Off to her right, a boffin from one of the other landers kicked over a stone and reached down. Protected from the blistering wind and sun, some sort of life clung to its underside.

"We're finding some lichens, a few mosses, and two kinds of fungi," Professor mFumbo reported. "There are also some bugs that eke out a bare survival on them. Not much alive here, though."

"Where are the bodies?" Kris asked.

"The Marines have the killing field staked out," Jack said. "No one has entered it, yet. However, I think we have an answer to the colonel's question as to how they died."

"What have they found?" the colonel asked.

"Residue of Sarin gas," Jack said.

"Ugh," was all the colonel said.

"What's Sarin gas?" Cara asked.

"Nasty stuff," the colonel said.

"Illegal stuff," Penny added.

"It's illegal for humans to use it on humans," Kris explained. "Against the laws of war and reason."

"Think of it as a jacked-up insecticide," the colonel said. "Especially if they mixed it with a bit of oil, it sticks to the skin, gets inside, and destroys your nervous system in as little as one minute. It makes it so you can't breathe."

Through her bubble helmet, the girl's face again showed pain at what she heard, but words failed her.

"Want to go back to the lander?" Abby asked.

"No. No. I can take this," Cara insisted.

"Do you have any idea how they delivered the gas?" the colonel asked Jack.

"No. The Marine guard has cordoned off the killing field. All they've done is a preliminary chemical check of the soil. That turned up the Sarin residue. The actual gas, thank God, broke down a long time ago."

"Broke down?" Kris asked.

"Sarin is not very persistent," Nelly said. "It degrades in the sun and rain."

"Did we have enough rain here?" Kris asked.

From the looks of it, Jack tried to shrug. That's hard to do in a fully armored space suit. He finally said, "Your guess is as good as mine."

"I've checked with the Marines doing the chemical check," Nelly reported in a moment. "They are finding Sarin residue. No Sarin. I'd suggest that we wash down our suits after this, but I don't think you humans have anything to worry about."

"Thank you, Nelly," Kris said.

While they talked, they'd been walking toward two Marine guards standing at the edge of the flattened mountain. If the look of the scraped mountain was shocking, the sight along the rising ground below was beyond words.

Kris's experience with bugs had been limited. Loddy, the cook at Nuu House, kept a spotless kitchen. There had been one infestation of cockroaches when Kris was about Cara's age. Kris had helped the cook spread out the roach hotels and emptied them a few days later.

She remembered one other time when she'd helped the gardener with a particularly bad summer crop of some kind of bugs. She'd been three at the time and didn't want him to hurt the bugs. She'd spent as much time as her small attention span allowed picking bugs off the flowers and toddling over to the gate to send them flying free.

If she remembered right, she hadn't been allowed to play in the garden for several days after that. Once she'd scampered off to other interests, no doubt the gardener had done his job.

Someone had certainly done a job here.

The escarpment was covered with portions of shells or complete exoskeletons. Thousand and thousands of them. You could see where others had crawled off to die at the foot of the hill.

These weren't garden nuisances, sanitary challenges to a spick-and-span kitchen. These were intelligent creatures who built towns and roads that had lasted long beyond them.

One of the boffins, his suit said Dr. Lynch, made his way carefully down the hill. He stopped at the first complete body he found and stooped to examine it.

"There's no soft tissue left," he reported. He lifted up the skull to examine it. "No teeth, just a ridge of chitin. I doubt there's anything left from which we could get DNA. Still, I'll collect a number of these more intact bodies and see if there isn't something they can tell us."

"You do that," Kris said. "Chief, can you direct us to that other skeleton you found?"

"It's off to your right, where the ground is steeper."

Kris and her group moved that way. A number of Marines came and hammered in spikes with ropes attached. Dr. Lynch joined them, along with three Marines with CSI stenciled on their packs. The four of them roped up and began a careful descent.

Kris turned on the outside mic on her suit. The wind, weak but constant, made a whispering noise as it slipped over bones and through empty eye sockets. The thin dust moved constantly, eroding what it could. Even in so much death, the planet lived its own quiet life.

Careful as the Marines and scientist were, they added their own sound as carapaces cracked and broke. Dirt and bones broke loose and slid down the ridge. A place that had changed very little in two hundred years took this chance to slide away.

Kris waited silently while the descent team made its way down half the embankment.

"I've got something that looks like foot tracks," a Marine announced, and started snapping pictures.

"Yeah, I think someone came down this hill before us and went back up," he added as he finished his recording.

"We've got a real live skull, here," Dr. Lynch announced as he reached their goal. "Several of the locals on top of him. As a guess, I'd say that before nature did its dust-to-dust thing here, the bodies hid this other body."

"Any idea of cause of death?" Kris asked.

"I think it's pretty clear," the doctor said, reaching down and raising the skull for all to see. "This skull shows evidence of our old friend, blunt force trauma. Somebody bashed his brains out."

"Murder," Kris said.

"That the murderer tried to hide," Jack added.

"Quite successfully," Penny said, and went on like the cop's daughter she was. "Look around. Whoever slaughtered this planet left none of their own behind. Normal morbidity says that some people would keel over from a heart attack, old age, occupational accidents. Yet we have no sign of any bodies. Somebody busted this poor soul's skull, hid him among the 'trash,' and so we have a body to examine."

"Sounds plausible to me," the colonel said.

The doctor examined the skull. "I think we may be able to get some DNA out of those teeth, assuming this alien had teeth like us and DNA in them."

He and the Marines began filling the body bag they'd brought down with the bones of the murdered alien. They had several bags and looked ready to fill the others with some of the local bodies.

"You might want to come over where I am," Professor mFumbo called on net. "I'm in what we think is the invaders' village."

That involved a long hike across the scraped mountain. The village was nestled in a hollow between the hill they were on and the next hill over, which had also been leveled. As they made their way down into the protection of the valley, they took in what the planet had to show of its flora and fauna.

Lots of trees, bushes, and other brush had lived on this land once.

They were dead now.

It was easy to tell the attackers' constructions from the locals'. They were made of mud bricks with wooden roofs. All were squat, one-story buildings that sprawled across the hill with no sense of urban planning. If there had been any kind of rainfall, the mud bricks would have flowed back to the ground the mud was dug from; but since someone had taken the water, the buildings survived.

Professor mFumbo waved them toward a hut he and several other boffins were coming out of. The other scientists headed for another hut to examine. The professor stayed to give Kris and her team the fruits of their initial examination.

"The rooms were tiny," he said. "There is not much furniture, and what there is is hacked out of local wood." He pointed at several rough-hewn bunk beds, stacked three high.

"They crammed them in, didn't they?" Kris said.

"It was tight quarters," the professor agreed. "And one thing more. There are no amenities. I mean that. None. Not running water. Not indoor plumbing."

"They had to have something," Kris said.

The professor pointed down the hill. "The water was apparently drawn from the nearby river even though an entire mountaintop was being shoved into it."

"That's rude," Cara said.

"The pollution must have been horrible, but that's what they apparently did," the professor said.

Cara ducked into the hut, looked around for a moment, then came back with a question. "Where did they go to the bathroom?"

"That puzzled us for a while," the professor admitted. "We'd examined several of the sites, looking for means of sewage disposal. We didn't find any. No slit trench. No pit latrine. Once we started searching this place, a couple of the folks spotted lumps of scat scattered indiscriminately around the site."

"Ew," Cara said.

"They couldn't have done that," Penny said. "That would have left them open to all kinds of epidemics."

"Apparently, they did it, anyway. Right out in the middle of everything," the professor insisted. "My guess is they didn't intend to stay long, and it's possible that the folks who got assigned to dirtside duty weren't the highest in their caste system or social structure. Here, your guess is as good as mine."

Kris had to hunt for a word. "This boggles the mind?"

"Yes, it does," Professor mFumbo agreed. "But then, so does working in an environment loaded with residual radioactivity from when you nuked them from orbit."

"Somebody doesn't care much for occupational safety," Kris said.

"More likely they never heard of occupational safety," Abby said. "Something tells me that these little hellions didn't spend a lot of time on the ground. And when they did, it was years and years apart. They might regularly build new ships, but building huts on a mud ball? Not something Great-great-grandpa liked to talk about."

"You may have it right," the professor said.

"Is there anything we can learn from their scat?" Penny asked.

"No," the professor said. "I'm afraid it is a bit too old for us to get any DNA or other useful stuff from it. We have analyzed it. No surprise, their digestive system is very effective, and their food was very well processed. We couldn't identify any specific foods from the resultant dung. We do know they ate pretty much the same minerals that we need and excreted very much what we do ourselves."

Jack shook his head. "If their concept of personal hygiene was nothing better than what you think, we ought to find a lot of dead bodies."

"Sorry, Captain, that doesn't seem to be true. They slaughtered the local folks and left their bodies to rot in the air. But of their own, nothing."

"Nothing but what appears to be a murdered and hidden one," Kris said. "I very much want to see what information that body yields."

"One body that we *think* might be one of the attackers. Not much to go on," Jack pointed out.

"Too true," Kris agreed, looking slowly around the wreckage. "All too true."

"I may be able to change that," came from Chief Beni on net.

"Please do," Kris said.

"Since I spotted that one body, I've had every drone I could get loose doing low passes around alien villages. I think I've spotted two more endoskeletons. I'll need permission to send Marines to pick them up, and we'll need time on the longboats."

"That you will have," Kris said; she turned to Cara. "Have you seen enough?"

The girl merely nodded within her bubble helmet.

"Let's go topside, folks. Professor, you and your boffins can study this place until you run out of air. I'll be waiting for your report. Me, I've seen enough. Somebody committed a crime here of biblical proportions. I don't know if we can do anything about it, but I think the human race needs to know what we've seen."

The ride up was silent. Everyone was lost in their own thoughts.

24

Back on board, Kris found that the very air of the *Wasp* seemed full of depression. The word of what the ground team found quickly spread to all hands. But helplessness and hopelessness quickly made way for grim determination as the boffins squeezed more information from their findings.

"We were able to extract DNA from the teeth of those skulls we found," Professor mFumbo reported to Kris and her team after supper. They were meeting in a corner of the Forward Lounge. There, Ron could join them.

Jack, Abby, and the colonel were also there, availing themselves of what the bar had to offer.

Everyone turned toward the professor. When he didn't go on immediately, Kris said "And?"

"All three are female, and they appear to share the same complex DNA of those folks who tried to laser us when we disturbed their mining operation a few weeks back."

"Women?" said Penny. "So dating can be dangerous anywhere in the galaxy."

"They are the same species?" Jack said.

"Yes and yes," said the professor, unusually direct with his answer. "They are all females. It's impossible to use a rape kit at this late date, but you are free to speculate as to how women ended up with their skulls bashed in, Lieutenant.

"As for you, Captain, I would add that there is significant genetic drift in this set of DNA. Those others were so alike they had to be a family; though some of the women showed sufficiently different DNA from the main family root, the others were quite close. The three women here are quite distant from that family grouping and show much diversity among themselves. I'd say they come from a much larger population."

"How distant and how much larger?" Kris asked.

"Specifically, quite a bit. If you mean how long has it been since they shared an ancestor, I can't say for sure. Not enough information to develop a timescale for genetic drift. Sorry, Your Highness. Several of my people are very intrigued by these findings. I assure you much work is going into this, but there is little to base a conclusion on."

Kris leaned back in her chair. "So, let's see what we have here. Nelly, open a small window on the forward screen and record this."

"Yes, Kris."

"What have we got?" Kris asked herself. "One, a homicidal maniac who charged out to kill us even though he had no idea who we were and what our strength was."

"And he did it," Abby added, "with a boatload of his kith and kin."

"A very crammed boatload of kith and kin," the colonel said.

Behind Kris, a first point appeared on the screen with additional points appearing below it as the team added their thoughts.

"Second," Kris went on, "we've got a huge bunch of homicidal maniacs who slaughtered a planetwide civilization, then plundered that planet of its water, air, and anything else they could walk off with."

"Including their own dead," Abby said, "except for the three women that some homicidal maniacs actually committed homicide on."

"Does anyone else find it interesting," Penny said thoughtfully, "that they had no sanitation facilities for their camp on that planet?"

"Ew, to use Cara's word," Abby said. "Disgusting but hardly interesting."

"Professor, that boatload of people who attacked us," Penny

went on quickly, "did they have the normal sanitation facilities?"

"It would be impossible to run a spaceship otherwise," the professor said. "Yes, we did find what looked like bathrooms. Not at all private. One of our engineers was very interested in finding their recycling and water-reclamation system, but we could not identify it in the wreckage."

"I see what you're getting at," the colonel said. "They have shipboard sanitation, if only by rote, but they so rarely go dirtside that they've forgotten how to do it there."

"Yes," Penny said.

"Space raiders who only make landfall to pillage and don't do that often enough to remember the basics," Ron the Iteeche said in conclusion.

"It's not like they gave the locals a fighting chance," the colonel went on. "Flatten them with nukes or rocks, then gas those that are still raising objections. Viciously effective, though."

"I think there's one more thing we need to highlight," Kris said. Her team waited as she took a deep breath. "We've called them homicidal maniacs, because, from our perspective, that's what they look like. However, to them, I suspect their actions are quite logical. The question is, logical to what?"

"We'll only be guessing," the professor said.

"But I think we need to have some guesses," Ron said. "I certainly will need to put some in my report."

"The individual doesn't seem to matter much," Kris went on. "They cram themselves into ships far beyond what we would put up with. Even when they get a chance to go dirtside, their huts are small and they load six people into a tiny room."

"That worries me," the colonel said. "Quantity has a quality all its own, someone brilliant once observed."

"Yes," Kris said. "They attack without warning. Without reflection. They come in large numbers, and they can strip a planet and even a solar system."

"Ladies and gentlemen," Kris said, "I don't think humanity has much of a choice. We have met the enemy, and it's going to be a bitch."

Kris tapped her commlink. "Captain, set course for where we left the battleships. I think we've got enough to make our report to the king."

25

"So good to see you, Your Highness," Admiral Krätz said, as soon as the *Wasp* jumped back into the system where the battleships waited. "A messenger packet has arrived from your king. You are ordered home immediately."

The admiral made no effort to suppress his glee.

"Fine," Kris said. "I'm ready to report to him."

The admiral's grin vanished. "You're not going to argue?"

"Nope. I've already drafted my report. One that I think all human space needs to see. Would you like a copy?"

"Of your report?"

"Yes, Admiral, my report."

"I guess I should look at it."

"After you read the report, you might want to crank up your battleships and go take a look at what we found."

"I doubt it," the Greenfeld admiral said, but his eyes were on something offscreen. He was quiet for a long moment, then frowned. "They strip-mined an entire planet!"

"Down to its water and air. Massacred the intelligent civilization that had grown up on the planet. We're debating whether they attacked the planet despite the civilization present or because of it. Hard to tell from the evidence."

The admiral seemed torn for a moment, but then he shook his head. "We admirals voted for all of us to go home. Even your king has issued you orders to go home. We should go home. Right now!"

"Not yet, Admiral. Have any other ships of PatRon 10 reported in?"

"No."

"Then I intend to wait for them."

"Your orders are to return immediately!"

"Admiral, may I remind you that I have not yet seen my orders. Will you kindly give me a chance to read them and decide for myself what they say."

The Greenfeld admiral slammed his fist down on his comm-link, ending a flood of language very unfit for a princess's ears.

"Kris, Vicky is holding for you," Nelly said.

"Put her through, and while we're talking, could you please find this set of orders I'm supposed to have from Grampa Ray."

"Yes, Kris," Nelly said.

"Hi, Kris. Did you have fun gallivanting around the galaxy?" Vicky asked, not even trying to sound like she meant it.

"It wasn't my idea of fun. Have you seen our report? I just sent your admiral a copy of it. I think copies are going to all the admirals."

"Haven't seen a thing. Admiral Krätz is charging around the flag bridge like a man back from a six-month cruise who found a five-month-pregnant wife. I decided to make myself scarce and see if I could get the skinny straight from the horse's mouth."

"I'd say neigh except I want my report distributed as far and wide in human space as I can get it."

"That sounds bad."

"Take a look."

The Grand Duchess of Greenfeld read from a different screen, her face going from puzzlement to a frown. She ended in a scowl.

"That looks bad."

"Huge population. Not willing to talk. Ready to kill anything in its way. Yeah, I think we need a whole new definition of bad for this."

"So you're going to take this report to your king."

"I'm going to send a report to my king just as soon as I can order up a courier ship and transfer some of the bodies we found. I'm told I have some orders around here, but Nelly hasn't found them yet. Once I read them, I'll decide if I have to go running back to Wardhaven, like your admiral insists, or can wait for my squadron to re-form, then go back looking like a decent Navy formation. I hate leaving anyone behind."

Kris thought for a moment, "Especially now that I've seen what I've seen."

Nelly interrupted their girl talk.

"Kris, I've got a copy of your orders."

"Let me look at them," and a copy appeared on the screen under Vicky's image.

To: CO, PatRon 10
From: Chairman, Joint Staff
You will report here at your earliest convenience.

"Well, that certainly comes from the top," Kris said.

"And it doesn't leave much doubt as to what they want from you," Vicky said.

Kris pulled at her right ear. "I'm not so sure. If they'd wanted me to drop everything and run to Papa, or rather Great-grandpapa, they would have addressed it to my Highnessness or my Longknifeship. Something personal. This is to the Commander, Patrol Squadron 10. That's the *Wasp*, *Hornet*, *Fearless*, and *Intrepid*, methinks.

"So," Kris said, letting a big grin out to play, "I'll wait here to get all my ducks in a row, then we'll all go home together."

"On your head be it," Vicky said. "I think this is one of those things they don't want me to learn from you."

"Sister, some things we just have to learn on our own," Kris said.

"You want to tell my admiral, or shall I?" Vicky said.

"I think I'll give him some time to calm down," Kris said. "We have to refuel the *Wasp*, anyway. I want my boffins to put together a set of physical remains to go with my report. I *do* want to get that off as soon as I can. Anything exciting while I was gone?"

"One explosion on the *Fury*. Missed me by five minutes," Vicky said, casually. "They're still trying to decide if it was an accident or something else."

"What do you think?" Kris asked.

"I think somebody doesn't like me and really takes offense that I keep on breathing. Any chance your Chief Beni could meet with one or two of my guards? Ones I trust."

"Let's arrange that today. You want to come on board for a visit? Ron the Iteeche is a fun guy to hang with."

"I just *knew* you'd been doing things with the Iteeche. How's he hung?"

"They are not hung, Vicky. Nothing. Nada in that area. Haven't you read the autopsy reports from the war?"

"I read them. I didn't believe them."

"Sorry, girl. Believe them."

Vicky seemed to think the matter over for a while. "Okay, I'll come over. Say in three hours. Have your chief standing by to talk to my bomb sniffers. I'll have them bring all their gear. If I'm going to stay alive, I'll need all the help I can get. Oh, and you will have your pet Iteeche out for me to see."

"Vicky, I keep telling you. He's nobody's pet."

"And I'm supposed to believe you Longknifes," Vicky said, and rung off.

26

The *Fearless* came in only a short time after the *Wasp*. She had visited nine systems. All of them were full of profound scientific data but not a scrap of life that her crew could spot. Also, as best they could tell, no life had visited the systems since the Three aliens first installed, built, or hatched the jump points into them.

The good news was that this allowed Captain Drago to throw a Smart Metal™ yard over to the other corvette and put a spin on the two ships. By the time Vicky arrived, the *Wasp* had a good half gee of imitation gravity to offer people's stomachs.

"You're alone," Kris observed with a raised eyebrow, as Vicky exited the admiral's barge. "No admiral?"

"He's not talking to you. I hope that doesn't break your heart. I told him I was coming over to the *Wasp*. He grumbled something about 'don't get killed,' and went back to whatever he was doing. I've noticed lately that he keeps his distance from me. You know, I don't think he wants to be around when I get blown up."

"How rude of him," Kris said. "Though I've also noticed that it takes a real friend to hang close with me."

"I like to think that my work helps in that area, Princess," Chief Beni said.

"No doubt," both Kris and Vicky said in the same breath.

That gave the two young women a chance to share a laugh.

A Greenfeld Navy lieutenant and a Marine sergeant followed Vicky off the barge. Between them, they lugged a large footlocker. Vicky introduced them to Chief Beni.

Before the three technical experts headed off on their own, Kris felt she should explain the rules. "The chief here will help you with your own equipment. After you get it working, he may give you suggestions on how to get the most out of it. Fine-tune it. He may also share some of the software workarounds that he's developed. What I will not let him do is share any Wardhaven technology that you don't have."

"Do you have to keep that last restriction?" Vicky asked. "We already know that mainstream Greenfeld technology has a ways to go to catch up with Wardhaven. We also know that some people back home have tech that's just about as good as you have."

"In some cases better," Kris grumbled. "I know. I've had to dodge it."

Kris worried her lip. "Vicky, my government has restrictions on tech transfer to Greenfeld."

"After the report you just shared with us, you think two different human families should be building walls between them?" Vicky asked.

"No, I don't," Kris said. "But until your dad and my grampa agree to bury the hatchet someplace other than in each other's skulls, I feel I have to live by those rules."

"Let's hope I can live by them, too."

Kris sighed. "Okay. I'll tell you what I'll do. Chief, you go over the gear these folks have. Tell them what you can under the limits I've placed on you. Then, when you're done, give me a call. We'll talk then. That enough for you?" she asked Vicky.

"It's a start," the young woman agreed.

The technicians left.

"Now we head for the Forward Lounge to meet Ron the Iteeche."

"I'm going to get to meet your Iteeche!"

"I keep telling you, he's not *my* Iteeche. He's very much the Emperor's Iteeche. Oh, and his chooser's."

"Chooser?"

"Think of your dad, only worse."

"That's not possible."

"Is it getting that bad?" Kris asked.

"It was getting pretty bad when I left. He's really all goo-goo eyes over his new woman. And the baby boy. I figured things were going to get bad, even before the bombs started dogging my footsteps. Now I don't know what to think."

"Nelly, will you invite Ron to join us in the Forward Lounge? I'd like to introduce him to Vicky, ah, the Grand Duchess of the Greenfeld Empire, and we can talk about the report I sent him."

"He says he will be honored to meet with you two, and yes, he wants to talk about your report," Nelly said, formally.

"So I'm going to meet an Iteeche. In the flesh."

"And he's got a lot of it," Kris said.

"Heavy?"

"Oh no. Actually, he's rather good-looking, I think. But there's eight feet of him and a whole lot of elbows and knees."

"And you think he's cute," Vicky said, with a giggle. "Have you kissed him yet?"

"Do you think a Longknife would tell a Peterwald?" Kris snapped back. "Would you believe anything I told you?"

"No and no. So don't tell me. I'll have more fun making up stories."

Kris threw her hands up in the air.

Ron was waiting for them outside the Forward Lounge. Kris did the introductions.

"Ron, this is the Grand Duchess Victoria of the Greenfeld Empire. She's the daughter of Emperor Henry I. Vicky, this is Ron, an Imperial Representative, though I don't think he's carrying a full portfolio this trip out. Oh, and his full name goes on for half a mile, but he's willing to let me call him Ron. And he calls me Kris."

"I am happy to be on a first-name basis with Princess Kristine," Ron said through his interpreting computer.

Vicky did a lovely curtsy, and said, "I'm honored to meet you. Call me Vicky, please."

Ron offered each of the women an elbow, and they entered the lounge.

Vicky giggled. "I've never had a guy with so many elbows. This is neat."

"I didn't know that you humans had empires," Ron said,

quickly switching his four eyes from Kris to Vicky. "The last time I was in human space, there was no mention of such things except in the history books."

"It was kind of my dad's idea," Vicky said. "When Kris's great-grampa got officially recognized as a constitutional monarch, Dad decided to go him one up. Be a full power emperor. The old geezers in our families have had this thing for years. Kris and I are hoping to skip that foolishness in our generation. Who knows, maybe we will."

"It would be nice," Kris said.

Ron mulled that over for a moment. "I remember an article in one of the news magazines about how Kris saved your father. The reporter thought that was a very strange thing to do, considering all the stories about Peterwald's attempting to have Kris killed."

"None of those stories were ever proven," Kris pointed out.

"There must have been something behind all of them. What is your saying? Where there is smoke, there must be fire."

"All that didn't matter. At the time of the attempt on her dad's life, it seemed like a good idea that those trying to kill him not succeed."

"Fortunately for my dad, Kris was there. So, what brings you here? I saw the video of your meeting with King Raymond. Was that all true? Are you losing ships?"

Ron glanced down at Kris, and the color of his residual gill slits did not show happy. "I thought that meeting was private. Not to be recorded. The way your king ushered everyone out of the room. I heard him say there should be no recordings. I testified so to my Emperor. Did you make my word false, Kris Longknife?"

"It wasn't me," Kris said. With Nelly laughing in the back of her skull, she went on. "I mean, my king did order that no recordings be made. And you yourself saw the room emptied out. It turned out that our chief spy didn't follow my grampa's orders very well. He made copies of his recording and sent it around to I don't know how many governments. The fleet you see around us is the result of that leak."

Ron halted beside an empty table in the front of the lounge. Two of the bar folks brought one of the things he could sit on, and they settled down before Ron went on.

"You humans are very strange. Your chooser could not or

would not order a scout force out, even though he is king. Yet his subordinate violates his orders and because of that, a search fleet goes out. Very strange behavior."

"You've got to give Kris credit for the scout fleet," Vicky said. "The battleships showed up to go where she went. If Kris hadn't insisted her next mission was to do some snooping around the far end of the galaxy, I don't think anything would have happened. Really, Kris, do you?"

Kris shrugged. "I made up my mind that I was going out here once we cured the pirate problem out beyond the rim of your empire, Vicky. All the rest just kind of followed after me like a speckled giraffe on wheels that I had when I was a little kid."

"Though it took a lot more pull," Vicky said, grinning.

"I didn't pull anything. I went. They followed. Kind of like you Ron. I didn't do anything to have you here, but here you are."

"I think my chooser and the Emperor did not want me at the court. No one wanted to talk *to* me, but the drift of the current was clear. People were talking *about* me a lot."

"Boy, we girls can really relate to that," Vicky said, with just the hint of a giggle.

"So, can we talk about what you found?" Ron asked.

Kris nodded. "I don't have a lot to add to it. What's in my report is pretty grim. What I wrote was just an effort to document what I saw on the ground."

"Will I be allowed to take some of the bodies back to the Empire?" Ron asked.

"I'll let you take a complete set of bodies from the ship that attacked us," Kris said. "If you want, you can have a complete exoskeleton from the murdered planet."

"What about the other skeletons you found? Our scientists will want to make their own determination about who those people are."

"That's a problem. There are only three of them. We've already found DNA in the pulp of some teeth. If you have the technology to identify DNA, I guess we could probably spare a few teeth for your Empire."

"Yes, we can do the thing that makes the DNA tell its story," the Iteeche said. "A tooth from each of the bodies would be a generous gift."

"I imagine all the other governments who sent representatives to the Fleet of Discovery will also want teeth," Kris said.

On the screen, a star lit up.

"There goes the *Mercury*," Nelly told them. "It has Kris's report and some of the artifacts from the planet, including teeth."

"Whoever those poor murdered girls were," Kris said, "they're going to end up with their teeth scattered all across the galaxy."

"They may be murdered souls, Kris," Nelly said, "but they were murdering souls as well."

"Too true," Kris agreed.

"Kris, the *Hornet* just jumped into the system," Nelly reported. "Phil Taussig has an urgent message for you."

"Put him on."

"Commodore, we have a problem," Phil Taussig started without preamble. "I have seen the bug-eyed monsters, and they are even more huge than we feared."

27

For a moment, Kris heard the words, but her brain refused to make sense of them. That state of affairs lasted for maybe two seconds. Then Kris jumped to her feet and pitched her voice to carry.

"People, I need this room. Please take your drinks and go elsewhere. Barkeep, this pub is closed."

The folks on the *Wasp* were used to strange demands coming from their princess. With hardly a word, the place emptied.

"Nelly, tell my staff to get down here on the double."

"They're already running," her computer reported. "All except the chief. I figured you'd want to let him keep working with Vicky's people."

"Good call, Nelly. Yes."

"Should I return to my quarters?" the Iteeche asked.

"Ron, you're the reason we're here. I don't see why you should get this report secondhand. Vicky, same goes for you."

"I wish I'd brought Maggie with me," Vicky said. "Would you mind if I sent the admiral's barge back to the *Fury* and picked her up?"

"Assuming your admiral doesn't confiscate his barge, do what you want," Kris snapped, totally in combat mode. She thought for a second. "Nelly, you want to give all the admirals a heads-up? They can join us online if they want to."

"Aye, aye, Commodore," Nelly said. "I'll make it so. I like that phrase."

Jack arrived at a full run, with Penny and the colonel on his heels. Abby, Kris's maid and spy, shuffled in a few seconds later, her hair up in curlers and wearing a housecoat and fuzzy slippers.

"This better be good," she complained.

"Phil is back. The *Hornet* caught a glimpse of the bug-eyed monsters," Kris said.

"How much of *him* did *they* catch?" the colonel asked darkly.

"I got a one-line brief," Kris said. "I've only had time to sound officer call."

"Should you sound 'Boots and Saddles'?" Jack asked. "Now might not be a bad time to beat all hands to battle stations."

"Phil didn't holler for it, but, yeah, there's no telling if he knows what's on his tail or not. Nelly, order PatRon 10 to battle stations. Tell the admirals that we are going to high alert, and I would advise them to all do the same."

The Klaxon on the *Wasp* went off. "Battle stations. Battle stations. All hands to battle stations. This is no drill," blared from the public address.

"Kris, Captain Drago for you," Nelly reported.

Oops, Kris thought. "Put him on."

"Would you mind telling me why *you've* ordered battle stations for *our* ship. I may or may not be complaining, but when the captain's the last to know about something like this, it bothers me."

"The *Hornet* just returned. Commander Taussig reports that they have seen the bug-eyed monsters, and they are huge. Until I know what all that means, we are at battle stations."

"A very good idea, Your Highness. Thank you," said the captain, and rung off.

Once again, the convoluted chain of command on the *Wasp* had gotten tangled and survived the experience. With any luck, and the goodwill of all involved, it would continue that way.

Kris eyed the screen, waiting for everyone to appear on it for the upcoming conference. It still showed the *Mercury* accelerating toward the jump point for home. Its report was still valid. However, it was now a touch out of date.

"Nelly, recall the *Mercury*. I think we'll need to add to her report."

"Aye, aye, Kris, I've ordered the *Mercury* to return to the fleet area."

"Kris, I don't mean to juggle your elbow," Jack said, "but if we might have bug-eyed monsters charging though the jump point after the *Hornet* any second, wouldn't it be a good idea to have some report headed for home right now."

Kris scowled at the screen. "Order, counterorder, disorder," she muttered.

"But there's an exception to every rule," the colonel whispered.

"Nelly, ask the skipper of the *Mercury* how long until they take the jump."

"She says eight hours at their previous acceleration. She's just about to start decelerating to return to the fleet."

"Tell her to maintain her course for the jump, but stay alert. Keep an eye out for fighting in the anchorage and record all message traffic. We may have an additional report for her."

"Aye, aye, Commodore," the computer said. A moment later, she added, "The *Mercury* is back to accelerating for the jump."

The screen flickered and changed to show three admirals and Lieutenant Commander Taussig. Admiral Krätz was already talking. Maybe bellowing was more accurate.

"By what authority have you ordered my ships to battle stations?" he demanded.

"I ordered PatRon 10 to battle stations. I suggested you might want to follow our lead," Kris said. "The *Hornet* is back, and Commander Taussig reports contact with the bug-eyed monsters."

"You have found them," Admiral Kōta said. "Did they follow you?"

"I think I gave them the slip," Phil answered. "At least I didn't see anything of my pursuers in the last two systems I crossed."

"But whether or not you shook them depends on their tracking skills," Admiral Channing pointed out.

"There is that problem," the skipper of the *Hornet* admitted.

"You want to tell us about the bug-eyed monsters?" Kris said.

"Not really," Phil answered with a sigh. "Truth be told, I didn't spend any more time observing them than I had to."

"Fill us in, Commander," Kris ordered.

"We'd done our five jumps out and had nothing to show for it. We started back, following the new route the boffins said would bring us home. The second jump, three jumps out from here, we got a surprise."

He took a deep breath before going on. "We came through the jump and headed for the next one. It was only three hours away. Thank God. Because our Sensor board started lighting up like it was Christmas. Reactors, thousands of them, all well down in the system, and headed for a different jump."

"Thousands of reactors?" Kris said.

"I'll pass along our data. Maybe your boffins can make sense of it. There must have been three or four thousand reactors humming away at full power. There were even more trickling at minimum power. We finally located the source and got a fairly decent picture of it."

The screen opened a separate window. It filled with something that looked like an elongated egg. An egg with a very bumpy skin.

"How big is that mother?" Admiral Krätz asked.

"We estimate it at over four thousand kilometers along its longitudinal axis. Not quite two thousand klicks at its widest. It's hard to tell because we don't know what is the main body and what are the ships docked to it."

"Those knobby things come off?" Kris asked.

"Three of them took off after us."

The pictures shifted to show three elongated dots detaching themselves from the main egg and making a straight line for the *Hornet*.

"How long did it take them to react to you?" the colonel asked.

"About an hour. Less, if you make allowances for the speed-of-light delay for them to spot us."

"Did they try to communicate with you?" Kris asked.

"There was a lot of activity on the radio frequencies, but none was aimed at us, and we didn't identify anything as an effort to raise us. Once it was clear the ships were headed our way with a bone in their teeth, we did make an effort to open communications with them. If there was a reply, we couldn't identify it in the clutter."

"You said a bone in their teeth," Kris said. "How hot was their pursuit?"

"Three gees. I jacked the *Hornet* up to 3.5 gees and got out of there just as fast as I could."

"Did you see any evidence of them in your next system?" Kris asked.

"Kris, when I got into the next system, I was very tempted to point the *Hornet* at the closest jump and see where it led me." He swallowed hard at the thought. Only time would tell if it would have been better for the *Hornet* to disappear like the lost Flying Dutchman rather than come home with her report.

That decision might yet have to be made.

"Instead, I kept the boat at 3.5 gees and headed for the second jump like I was supposed to. We jumped out of there before we spotted any activity at the last jump point."

He took a deep breath. "I don't know if they didn't pursue us or what. What I do know is that we didn't see hide nor hair of them in any of the systems we crossed to get here."

"We've got to leave immediately," Admiral Krätz snapped.

"I've still got a ship out there," Kris said. From her point of view, there was now even more reason not to leave the *Intrepid* out here alone.

"We need to get this information back to our governments," Admiral Channing said.

"Nelly, has the *Mercury* been taping this report?"

"Yes, Your Highness. She has been recording this and adding it to the report you filed with her."

"Good," Kris said. That took care of home as much as she could. She wasn't finished with Phil. "Commander, tell me more about this huge base ship. Did you get anything more on it?"

"It's dense. More dense than either of Wardhaven's moons. Much more dense than old Earth's moon. Almost as dense as, say, a planet."

"And they needed thousands of reactors to power it."

"Power it and propel it. It was leaving a plasma stream behind it that had to be seen to be believed."

"How fast?" Kris asked.

"It was doing about half a gee acceleration away from one jump point and headed for another."

"So it was going somewhere," Kris said.

"Definitely."

"Space rovers," Penny said.

"But we don't have a picture of who or what is at the helm of this ship. Ships," Kris corrected herself.

"Nothing, Commander. I've got recordings of what they were transmitting, but no one aboard the *Hornet* could make any sense of them."

"Pass them to us," Kris ordered. "Nelly, tell Professor mFumbo that he doesn't have any higher priority than extracting something useful from this data stream. I very much want to watch any video they have. Very much."

"Kris, we're getting the *Hornet*'s take," Nelly reported. "The boffins are already working on it. I've got my kids on it as well."

"All of them?" Kris said. "Even Dada?"

"Yes, Kris. And Cara knows about our situation. She's been peeking through the front door of the Forward Lounge for the last ten minutes."

Sure enough, the two swinging doors into the lounge were showing a crack. Cara was lying on her belly, furtively watching them.

"We *have* to get that child a battle station." Kris sighed.

"Really!" Cara said, jumping to her feet.

"In the scullery," the colonel grumbled.

"I can do more than that," Cara insisted.

Kris stared at the overhead; to the best of her knowledge, there were no standard operating procedures for getting into a war with space aliens. The Navy had a standard answer to almost everything else imaginable, but not this.

A hasty review of her actions did not make her proud. She'd bobbled her start out of the gate. She should have thought to go to General Quarters immediately, and not needed Jack to remind her. The order and counterorder to the *Mercury* were more of an embarrassment than a mistake. Still, what she'd done since felt right.

"Okay, folks, let's get organized. Phil, bring the *Hornet* down to join the fleet. *Hermes*, come alongside the *Wasp* and take aboard our gizmo for peeking into the next system. No, hold it. That won't work," Kris caught herself. "The *Hornet* was doing fifty thousand klicks per hour, and the periscope only shows you what's in the closest system.

"*Hermes*, get the coordinates from Commander Taussig and jack yourself up to maximum gees and duck back into his last system. I'd like a report on whether anything is behind him."

"Do you think that's smart?" Admiral Krätz asked.

"We can either sit here wondering if hostiles are going to come charging through that jump point or we can go look," Kris snapped.

"Or we can get up speed and get out of here ourselves," the Greenfeld officer suggested.

Kris did a quick and silent survey of the people whose opinion she valued. None of them looked interested in hiding under the bed.

"As I've said many times before, Admiral, you are free to do what you wish with your battle squadron. I reserve the right to do with PatRon 10 what I choose. Nelly, see that *Hermes* gets under way for a fast run into *Hornet*'s last system of call and return."

"Could you at least see that the *Hermes*'s computers are rigged for destruction," Admiral Channing said. "I would suggest that we all prepare our navigational systems to assure that if we fall in battle, our enemy will be unable to extract navigational information from our wreckage. That ship that attacked the *Wasp* certainly made sure that we could draw nothing from its databases."

"That sounds defeatist," was Admiral Krätz's observation.

"It's only defeatist until somebody defeats us. Then it sounds pretty smart," Admiral Kōta said. "I'll have my division heads draw up a list of what should be rigged for complete destruction. We'll also put it on a fail-safe to make sure we don't have any accidents."

"I'll also have the remaining two courier ships see that all reaction tanks are topped off," Kris said. "We may need to run for it in a hurry."

KRIS, SHOULD WE TELL THE OTHER ADMIRALS WHAT WE KNOW ABOUT THE FUZZY JUMPS? IF WE HAVE TO LEAD THEM INTO ONE OF THEM TO GET AWAY FROM THE ALIENS, IT MIGHT HELP IF THEY KNEW WHAT WE WERE DOING BEFOREHAND.

THAT COULD WELL BE A SMART MOVE, NELLY, BUT IT ALSO MEANS GIVING AWAY SOMETHING I'M NOT SURE I WANT TO GIVE. I'D RATHER KEEP THAT ACE UP MY SLEEVE FOR A WHILE LONGER.

WE MAY NEED THOSE FUZZY JUMPS, KRIS, TO GET OUT OF A BIG MESS.

NELLY, WE DON'T KNOW IF THE ALIENS ALREADY KNOW ABOUT THE FUZZY JUMPS. AND IF THEY DON'T, I DON'T WANT TO LET THEM SEE US VANISH INTO SPACE THAT HOLDS NO SUCH OPTION TO THEM.

I FEAR THAT WE WILL HAVE SOME REALLY TOUGH DECISIONS AHEAD OF US, KRIS.

TRUST ME, NELLY, I KNOW THAT WE DO.

Jack cleared his throat. "Could I ask you, Commander, to rethink one of your recent orders?"

"Jack, you're going all formal on me," Kris said.

He shook his head. "I don't think we should send the *Hermes* out."

"I'm afraid that I agree with your Marine," Colonel Cortez said.

"Both of you don't think we need to know what's coming this way?" Kris said.

"We need to be able to kill anything that jumps through after the *Hornet*," Jack said, "but no, Kris, I don't think we need to leave a bigger trail pointing at that jump point."

"It would be nice to know if something is following him," Kris said.

"Certainly," the colonel agreed. "Is there any chance that your boffins might be able to get their jump-point periscope working so we could peek through?"

"Nelly, get Professor mFumbo," Kris said.

"I'm busy," he snapped a second later. "There are several approaches that might crack these images, but right now, none of them have worked."

"Quick question, Professor," Kris said. "So far the jump-point periscope has only succeeded in showing us the closest other side of the jump point. Any chance we could dial it around to show us some of the other systems connecting through the jump point?"

"Like the seven-hundred-light-year-away system that the *Hornet* just left?"

"Exactly, Professor."

"Sorry. Not a chance. Our grasp on what we're doing is very tenuous, Your Highness. I see why you would want some selection in your view, but we can't offer it at this time. I don't know if we'll ever be able to give you that."

"Thank you, Professor. You can get back to your other assignment."

The link clicked dead.

"Okay, if we can't do that, could we bushwhack them as they enter our system at speed?" Jack asked.

"Like we think they have been doing our scout ships," Ron said.

The admirals were still on-screen, but all had turned away to consult with their staffs.

"Admiral Krätz, you said that during the last war no one ever thought of stationing ships at the jump point and shooting up anything that came out."

The Greenfeld officer turned away from his officers to face Kris. "Yes. You could never tell when a jump point might take it into its head to zig or zag. Far too dangerous for the ship. And much too exhausting to the crew of the ship to be floating in microgee for weeks at a time. The health of the crew requires that we tie up to a station for some gravity at regular intervals. That's also why we usually accelerate at one gee, young lady."

"Admiral, I believe that the 18-inch lasers on your battleships now have triple the range of the guns we used back then. So you don't have to get real close to the jump point to clobber anything coming out of it. Your battle squadron is also not tied up to a space station pier just now, but . . ." Kris said, and waited for a light to dawn.

The admiral said several phrases in a language Kris didn't understand.

You want me to translate, Kris?

No, Nelly. I suspect I have a pretty good idea what he's saying.

The admiral fell quiet, fixing Kris with a scowl. "And I imagine that you want me to take my battle squadron over to that jump point and take station to engage anything that exits it."

"It strikes me as a brilliant use of your invention."

"I would rather evacuate this system."

"I am not ready to leave."

"Young woman, you have no respect for rank, or your elders."

"I'm sorry you feel that way, sir, but I must represent the interests of the United Society as it is given me to see them. I have a ship not yet in from what is turning out to be a very hostile neighborhood of the galaxy. You are free to leave, sir. However, if you choose to stay, may I suggest that you take your four battleships over to where you may apply your 18-inch lasers to anything that exits Jump Point Delta."

"That will take me farther away from the exit jump, Longknife."

"For God's sakes, Georg," Admiral Channing snapped. "If you don't want to do what needs doing, Kōta and I will take our ships over there. Though, Lord knows, you've got the biggest guns in the fleet."

"I go. I go. Captain, send to BatRon 12, to keep the little Longknife girl happy, we will set up a prepared defense thirty thousand kilometers from Jump Point Dora. There. Are you happy?"

"Thank you very much," Kris said, taking care to keep her tone as sincere as the law allowed.

Kris leaned back in her seat and thought seriously about ordering a drink. Clearly, it had been one of those days. She sighed and fought down the temptation, consoling herself with the thought that it couldn't get any worse than this.

"Ah, Kris."

"Yes, Nelly."

"The *Intrepid* just jumped in system. He says you really want to hear what he has to say.

Kris groaned, and just managed to avoid giving voice to something that would not have been very princesslike.

"Put him on. Admirals, you might want to hear this."

28

"We found a new alien civilization," the skipper of the *Intrepid* announced, breathless with joy. "I think we were there when they sent up their very first artificial satellite. I mean, there was nothing up in orbit, then there was this little thing going beep, beep, beep."

"Did you get any pictures of these aliens?" Kris asked.

"Yes. They had radio and TV. Primitive sets. We had no trouble translating the pictures, but we have no idea what they were saying. Well, some. What passed for news had a lot on it about the satellite launch. At least, we think it did."

"Please pass your data capture to the *Wasp*," Kris said, keeping her voice even, but she sounded tired even to herself.

The captain seemed startled to have his news taken in with no more excitement than they were giving it. "Is something wrong?"

"The *Hornet* found what we think is a bug-eyed monster's mother ship. It's huge, and they look to be totally nasty."

"Oh. Well, this *was* a voyage of discovery. Looks like we made quite a few good ones."

"Excuse me, Captain," Nelly put in. "Did you follow the course laid in by the boffins for your round-trip?"

"Yep. No surprises there. Five out, then four back. The bird people, that's what we're calling them. Their TV had an advertisement that seemed aimed at keeping eggs at just the right temperature for a perfect hatching, or that's what it looked like. Anyway, the bird people were on the third system out from here. They sure looked like the nicest people you could ask to meet."

"Third system out," Kris said. She'd heard that number before.

"Kris, we have a problem," Nelly said softly.

On-screen, Admirals Kōta and Channing turned back from whatever they'd been doing to give the screen their full attention. A Greenfeld commander who had stayed attentive to the screen took a while to get Admiral Krätz's attention. He was none too happy to be disturbed.

"What now, Longknife?" he demanded.

"Nelly, please explain yourself," Kris said.

A new window opened on the screen. It showed a huge swath of the Milky Way, five thousand by five thousand light-years square. Each of the four search sweeps showed as a long white loop. The *Wasp* had taken the rightmost sweep and showed the murdered planet as a flashing yellow datum. The *Fearless* had taken the left sweep and had nothing exciting to show for the trip.

The *Hornet* and *Intrepid* had the inside sectors. As luck would have it, they'd both started on the outside legs, farthest from each other. As they returned back, they swung inward.

Three jumps out, the *Hornet*'s hot datum showed a flashing red. A short distance from it, in galactic terms, the *Intrepid*'s datum showed a flashing green.

Nelly zoomed in on the two flashing star systems. Three short jumps connected them.

"I think we have a problem," Kris said.

29

There are moments in your life when you know, even as you live and breathe them, that you will never be the same again. Kris had survived several such moments.

She knew about moments in the lives of her family members when they must have known that the future of their planet would never be the same. Grampa Al's decision to abandon politics after Eddy died was one of them. Father's decision to throw his hat in the ring for Prime Minister was another, despite Grampa Al's rage against it.

Kris had listened to their furious argument from her hiding place on the stairs. She'd seen these things done, if somewhat messily.

Kris had read of moments in Great-grampa Ray's and Trouble's lives when they must have known that the future of the entire human race would never be the same, depending on what they decided next.

As a teenager, Kris had dreamed of living just such a moment.

As a young woman, Kris was starting to get an idea of just how foolish her younger self had been.

A tiny voice inside Kris was laughing hysterically. *You got what you wished for, kid. God help you!*

It was at moments like this that Kris wished she'd been raised to believe in the power of prayer.

Kris shook off the musings that must have tied up a whole five seconds. On the screens, admirals were still giving the star map a puzzled look, so she must not have taken too much time.

"Nelly, do I have this right? The assumed hostile and the assumed friendly aliens are only three slow, easy jumps away from each other."

"Yes, Kris. And the jump Commander Taussig reports seeing the hostile alien headed for at half a gee acceleration is the one that will take them to within two jumps of the other civilization's system. They appear to be headed straight for the star system of the bird people."

"Oh sweet Jesus," someone said.

So this was it. The moment Kris had been born for. This was the decision for which history would either praise or pillory her.

"Nelly, get me the skipper of the *Vulcan.*"

"Online, Commodore."

"*Vulcan*, how soon can you begin rigging the corvettes of PatRon 10 with the neutron torpedoes?"

"We are ready now, ma'am. We have finished the prework. Give us twelve hours alongside the ships, and we'll be ready to load the torpedoes. Say no more than twenty-four from your word to start to them being armed and ready."

Admiral Krätz might not have figured out the meaning of the star-map display, but he knew what Kris was talking about. "Longknife, you aren't seriously thinking about taking on that huge alien mother ship," he bellowed.

"Admiral Krätz, I was not thinking about taking on the mother ship. I was looking at my options. Now that I find I have options, yes, I am *now* thinking about what three chunks of neutron stars might do to that ship."

"It would be a hell of a fight," Phil Taussig said, a feral grin on his face.

"You can't do that," the Greenfeld admiral sputtered. "Not even a Longknife can declare war on an alien race all by herself. No. You can't do it. I won't let you do it. And don't you go telling me that you're not in my chain of command."

He pointed a finger right at the camera so close that it looked wider than the rest of his body. "You have your orders. Go home. All your ships are here. You must go home."

He paused, took in a deep breath, and finished. "If you do not follow your orders, so help me God, I will declare you rogue. A pirate to your own allegiance. I, and I would hope all of my associates, would be duty-bound to shoot you down like the dog you are."

The pause after that grew quite pregnant. Pregnant enough to spawn an elephant. Kris let it grow for quite a while before she took a sledgehammer to it.

"Thank you, Admiral, for letting us know so clearly your opinion on this matter. As you suspect, I am coming to the conclusion that I must disagree with you."

"Captain, power up the main battery," the Greenfeld admiral ordered.

"Georg," Admiral Channing of the Helvitican Confederacy interjected, "don't you think we ought to give Her Highness a chance to explain herself?"

"No!" the Greenfeld officer snapped. "Once she starts talking, she'll run you around in circles until you don't know what you're doing, and before you know it, you'll be following her. She's one of those damn Longknifes."

"But I'm just a little one, remember," Kris said, holding up two fingers just a centimeter apart. Not too long ago, that had been Admiral Krätz's opinion of her.

He did not see the humor.

"Commander, this is Chief Beni. The Greenfeld battleships are powering up their lasers."

"Thank you, Chief. I thought you were helping Vicky's people."

"I am, ma'am, but there's no way I can be in a system with powering-up 18-inch lasers and not notice it. I'd have to be dead, dumb, and blind."

"Thank you, Chief. Nelly, send to all PatRon 10. Do not power up lasers. Take no hostile actions. I see no reason why we can't talk this thing through."

"Admiral," Vicky said at Kris's elbow, "just a reminder. I'm on the *Wasp*. Please don't shoot at me."

"Get the hell off that ship."

"Ah, Admiral," Vicky said, "weren't we talking about the chance that hostile ships might come charging into this system at any time. Do you really want me in a launch when they do?"

"You are learning too damn much from that Longknife pain in the neck."

"Can we all please slow down and take a deep breath," Admiral Kōta said. "I think we are faced with an important matter, and I, for one, would like to think it through very carefully."

"Thank you, Admiral," Admiral Channing said. "I'd really prefer that none of us went off half-cocked. In either direction, Commander Longknife, Admiral Krätz."

"I warn you, if you let her talk, she'll have you all wrapped around her little finger before you know it," Krätz grumbled.

"Gosh," Vicky said coyly, "and I thought I was the one that usually had a couple of guys wrapped around my little finger."

"Down, girl," Kris said. "Can we take a look at our options without anyone getting killed?" she asked everyone on-screen.

"I think it's pretty clear," Krätz snapped. "We can go home, or we can follow this little hellion and attack the bug-eyed monsters, starting a war between humanity and God only knows what."

"Georg, I have a fairly good idea of what that is," Admiral Kōta said. "From the looks of it, the monster is headed for a budding civilization. If we do nothing, they will strip the planet of everything needed to support life. I, for one, do not like the idea of standing idly by while that happens. I put on this uniform to stop such atrocities, not watch them happen."

"But what will be the price for humanity?" Admiral Channing asked.

"They came for them, and it was not my problem," Kris quoted. "And when they came for me, there was no one else left to stand with me."

"So you want to shoot first," Krätz snapped.

"I'm not sure I'll have a chance to shoot second," Kris said. "But hold it, hold it. I don't want to go off hunting until I have some idea of who it is I'm hunting."

"What?" "Huh," and "I thought you'd made up your mind already," came in answer to that.

"Folks, all I did was see if I had some weapons that might be able to make a dent in something the size of what Phil reported. By the way, *Vulcan*, lie alongside the corvettes and begin installation. Your twenty-four hours started five minutes ago."

"Aye, aye, ma'am."

"There you go," Krätz snapped.

"Admiral, please don't shoot up the *Vulcan*. Let's look at what we're facing. A ship attacked the *Wasp* with no defiances given, no warning at all. I don't take that for a declaration of war, but it does tell me that there is stuff out here that shoots first and doesn't care about asking questions later."

"Yes," Admiral Kōta said.

"Secondly, we found a planet stripped. Its civilized species wiped out. We found the remains of a few of the people we think did it. The connection to the ship that shot at us is tenuous, but it is there."

"I can follow you," said Admiral Channing.

"The *Hornet* came back with a report of one huge ship. We have audio and video from that ship that we have not yet been able to decode. I'd really like to see who or what is on that ship before I make any decision about what we do here."

"I agree with you on that," Admiral Kōta said. "I would prefer not to start shooting only to find out that, say, the planet we're worried about has an unstable star and the ship approaching it is on a rescue mission."

"I'm glad someone is thinking about that," Krätz grumbled.

"Nelly, would you please get me Professor mFumbo," Kris said.

"Kris, he says he's busy. Go away."

That brought a chuckle from the admirals on-screen . . . and from Kris's staff around her.

"Can they do that?" Vicky asked.

"They can get away with anything they can get away with. Nelly, put me through to the very busy professor."

"You got him."

"Professor, we need your input."

"I'm busy," he snapped, then seemed to reconsider the question. "What kind of input?"

"On taking all humanity to war," Kris said.

"Oh my God, what are you talking about, woman?"

"I think you have his attention," Vicky said.

"I think I do, too. Professor, we think the ship you got that video from is about to attack and destroy an entire civilization. We need to have a peek at what the people inside it look like. We'd love it if you could match some DNA off that video to some that we have on file, but I doubt even our boffin team can do that. In its place, I'd really need to see the video the *Hornet* recorded Real Soon Now. Time is of the essence."

The professor came on-screen in a new window. "And this may determine if we go to war with them?"

"Pretty much, Professor. I don't mean to make you feel pressured or anything."

"Don't be ridiculous, young woman. You're telling me if the video take from the big ship shows people like we found on the ship that attacked us and the bodies on that murdered planet, you plan to attack them."

"Let's say that if there is a match, we'll have to seriously consider what we do next."

The professor ran a worried hand through his hair, the first time Kris ever remembered him showing any sign of stress. "The data is in a format that we have never seen before. It doesn't fit any logical structure. I've cracked coded video, but this goes far beyond a coding."

"Could it be they don't want strangers reading their stuff?" Kris said.

"Most definitely," the professor said.

"Nelly, have you got any suggestions?"

"Kris, my kids and I have been doing everything we can think of to crack those videos. Nothing elegant works. Nothing brute force works. It is very frustrating for us computers to find such limits to our abilities."

"Have you asked the chief to look at it?" Kris asked.

"No. He's busy," Nelly answered stiffly.

And besides, Nelly, you don't want to get him involved, Kris added to herself.

"Nelly, interrupt the chief. Maybe he and the Greenfeld tech types might have a different twist on it."

"Yes, ma'am."

Nelly didn't sound very happy, but she obeyed. Kris glanced around her team. "So, ladies, gentlemen, and alien, until we have something from the ship to look at, I suggest we go about our business. Admiral Krätz, weren't you about to move your squadron over to Jump Point Dora so they could shoot up any bug-eyed monster that edged its nose through the jump?"

"Yes. I guess I can move over there."

"Kris, do you mind if I stay aboard the *Wasp*?" Vicky said.

"You aren't seriously worried about being in a launch, are you?"

"No. I can hardly be, since I had my best friend, Maggie, ride the barge back over here while all this was going on. But I have this serious concern about my admiral taking a potshot at you. My being here just might make him have second thoughts before he does something you'd regret."

"Come to think about it, I do have a spare bunk you can use."

"Thanks."

"Are we really just going to sit on our hands?" Jack asked.

"Consider yourself lucky, old boy," the colonel said. "The poor working stiffs of the *Vulcan* will be slaving away in a few moments, out to arm your little corvettes with monster killers. And the Greenfeld battleships will soon be tracking that jump point, their itching trigger fingers eager to blast anything that comes through the jump. Me, I'm curious, Your Highness."

He paused while everyone turned to give him their full attention. "Does that monstrous mother ship punch through the jump point with all her little monsters tucked in tight, or do they go charging through the jump ahead of her?"

"A very interesting question," Kris said. "It might make for a very disappointing ambush if the little monsters were out front. Phil, any idea how big the little ones that chased you were?"

"Several million tons, according to our measurements of their gravity distortions. Their mass per cubic meter was not shabby either."

"Each one as big as a couple of the admiral's battleships, huh."

"From what I saw, they don't do anything small," the *Hornet*'s skipper said. "But I can say this. They were all tied up alongside. They had no patrols out when I came across them. Admittedly, they were thirty-two hours away from their last jump and a good fifty hours away from their next one."

"Is it possible," Kris said, "that they are hungry? If they're heading for their next feeding frenzy, it may have been quite a

while since they last gobbled up a planet. They may be con-
serving resources."

"You're guessing," Jack said.

"I'm examining possibilities," Kris said. "That's all we can
do until we get a look at who's running that monster ship."

"Dear Lord," Abby kind of prayed, "I hope the picture we
get of those cusses are of little green ladies with twelve fingers."

"Amen," said Penny.

"We can hope," Kris agreed.

"Until then, we wait," the colonel said.

"I am good at twiddling my thumbs," Ron said, and proceeded to do that with four hands and a whole lot of fingers
and thumbs.

"How do I top that?" Vicky asked.

"You can't," Kris said. "Care for a bit of chow? I understand the wardroom is serving steaks tonight. It's the last of the
fresh meat, so we better get it while it's good."

So, like old friends, the team decamped for chow. Even
Ron. Jack and the colonel got behind his kind of chair and
pushed it along to the wardroom.

That left Kris to contemplate her fate. Could she really order an unprovoked attack on the huge mother ship? Would she
have a second chance if she didn't? Could she stand to live
with herself if she stood by and let them massacre the avian
people?

A gal could go crazy letting her mind race through those
questions time after time.

But she had friends.

And waiting out the possible countdown to war with good
friends almost made it endurable.

30

The hurry up and wait lasted for eighteen hours.

Which is to say that nothing horrible happened for that length of time although quite a few working people spent the time sweating bullets.

Midway through her meal, in the middle of a long line of puns being bounced around the table like Ping-Pong balls, Kris sat bolt upright.

"Something wrong?" Jack asked.

"No, but I think I just figured how we can know whether the mother ship is coming through the jump with all her little monster ships tucked in or instead is sending out a swarm of monster ships to check things out first."

"How?" the colonel asked.

Kris bopped herself on the forehead. "They are taking the jumps slow and easy. That means we can send through the periscope. Say we have one of the courier boats stand out up there, monitoring the view to the other solar system. We use the radio monitor first to let us know they're coming. Then the visual one to see how they're deployed."

"We might want to trade off," the colonel said. "We don't know if they'll go to some kind of EmCon blackout." At the blank stare he got from Vicky and Ron, the colonel translated himself. "Emission Control. A smart cookie goes silent on the radio and radar as you get closer to your target."

"We can balance using the radio and the light-frequencies spy," Kris said.

"Do we know if they can tell that the jump is in use, even a little bit?" Ron asked. "I know that we usually know something has jumped into the system by the roar of their reactors, but does the jump itself give off a clue?"

That turned out to be a very interesting question. Several busy boffins said so when Kris interrupted them with it. Unfortunately, even the two scientists who had come up with the idea of the periscope had no idea if someone could know the jump was in use. Apparently, no one in the human race had yet succeeded in answering that question.

Yes, it had been asked, but getting anyone with money to pay for the lengthy research to maybe get an answer had never been made to happen. Was one of the Longknife foundations interested in correcting that oversight?

Kris allowed that it might be. "Write up a grant proposal when we get back."

Once the boffins were back to their work, her team got back to their guessing.

"I hope no bug-eyed monsters ever asked that question, either," the colonel concluded.

"Even BEMs that have spent their whole existence bouncing around in space, hardly ever touching down?" Jack said.

Kris's crew fell silent.

"Okay," Penny said. "I've got to say this even if no one wants to hear it. I don't have the moral certainty that you have, Kris. Maybe the rest of you see nothing wrong with dragging the whole human race . . ."

"And the Iteeche race," Ron interjected.

"Into a war with God only knows who or what or how many of these BEMs." Penny shivered. "I've got a problem with it. And doing it without a word exchanged between us! We're firing the first shot in what could be a long hell of a war. Maybe worse, I think we're all hoping that those neutron torpedoes will wipe the mother ship out. Doesn't that kind of sound like genocide?"

Done, Penny let out a long Irish sigh, one her late husband would have been proud of. For a moment, her words just hung in the air above the table.

Kris reflected on them. Did she feel the moral certainty that Penny had accused her of?

"Young lady," the colonel said, "I respect both your words and the feelings from which they come. But I'm not sure it's fair to accuse us of doing what we're contemplating out of a feeling of moral superiority and certainty. There is the matter of what these people appear to have done to at least one other planet and its civilization and what they appear ready to do to another whole planetful of people. That also is genocide."

"Oh Lord," Abby said, "I am so hoping for the professor to come galloping in here to show us home movies of that little green grandmother with twelve thumbs. I do dearly want to shake her hand."

"I, too," Ron said, reaching out with all four hands and wiggling his fingers.

"Can I go on record, with what looks to be the majority?" Kris said. "I'll kiss the green cheeks of this proverbial little green lady."

Kris paused to take a deep breath. "Listen, folks, we all sat in the Forward Lounge for days, dissecting how my great-grandfathers and Ron's chooser got us into the mess of the Iteeche War and kept it going even after it could have burned itself out."

The crew nodded, except for Vicky. She looked really puzzled, which even on her face, came across quite beautifully.

"I'll explain it later," Kris said to her. "What I mean is that we really raked them over the coals in our hindsight."

"I was thinking about that," Penny put in.

"And now, here we are with a hot potato of nova temperature in our laps, and no one handy to toss it off to."

"More's the pity," Abby said.

"And we don't have a lot of time to decide what to do about it," Kris said.

"Shame that the universe won't allow for a time-out so that we can call home and get advice," Jack said.

"Do you really think that endless debate from the dunderheads would give us a better answer?" Kris asked.

"There is that," the colonel agreed.

"Aren't we being a little arrogant?" Penny asked.

That hung in the air for quite a while before Kris broke the silence.

"Our cook at Nuu House had a saying. 'Spit in one hand, wish in the other, and see which you get the most out of,'" Kris said. "We can think of a thousand reasons why we shouldn't make a decision. We can wish all we want for the problem to go away."

Kris leaned forward and looked each of her friends in the eyes. "The fact still remains that we have a horrible choice to make. Stand aside and let genocide happen or do something about it and, by doing that, commit the whole of our species to a fight until someone can somehow convince all of those involved to stop the killing."

"Or we all end up dead," Penny said.

That silenced the discussion for a while.

"You want to know one thing that really pisses me off," Kris said into the silence.

"Just one thing, baby ducks?" Abby said.

"Well, the biggest thing from today."

"I'm all ears," Jack said.

"That neither I nor Phil Taussig was able to get these BEMs to talk to us."

"And for that, we may well have a war," Colonel Cortez said, with a sigh any Irishman would have respected.

After a respectful pause, Kris turned to Penny. "Would you mind if I went back to examining our options?"

"You might as well. I'm pretty sure the hand I'm looking at only has hope in it. Your hand, at least, has something substantial."

That got a laugh.

"Nelly, if we find that a whole swarm of huge warships are heading for us ahead of the mother ship, can we break off and duck through another jump point before they get to us?"

"I don't think so, Kris."

"What's the problem?" the colonel asked.

"I assume that you intend to establish your roadblock in either the system with the bird folk or the next system out," the computer said.

"That's my thinking," Kris said. "We need time to prepare, then time to get there. I doubt we could get there any sooner."

"Your problem," Nelly said, "Your Highness, is that the jump point that the hostile aliens will be using is a dozen hours or more from any other way out."

"That long, huh," the colonel said.

"Yes," the computer said.

"So if we station the three corvettes say ten thousand kilometers out from the jump and the battleships at thirty thousand, there's no place to run to if things go bad."

"It looks like that to me, Kris."

NELLY, ARE THERE ANY OF THE NEW FUZZY JUMP POINTS IN EITHER OF THOSE TWO SYSTEMS?

KRIS, NO FUZZY POINTS IN THEM OR THE NEXT SYSTEM OUT. THERE ARE A FEW TWO JUMPS OUT, BUT YOU WON'T GET ANY HELP THERE.

"So," the colonel summed it up. "If we go, we're pretty much committed. I know if I was in charge of that mother ship, I'd never go through a jump point without ordering a couple of scouts through first and wait until at least one of them comes back to report all clear."

The rumblings around the table pretty much agreed with him.

"Of course, I'm a human," the colonel went on. "I've been raised on wars. I wonder how long it's been since any of those BEMs met any real resistance?"

"I don't think that's a question we can answer," Kris said, "but from what we've seen both in the ship that attacked us and the planet that somebody, person or persons unknown, I admit, Penny, massacred, it didn't look like anyone was breaking a sweat."

"An army gets slipshod if it doesn't go up against a first-class fighting force every once in a while. At least human armies do. Lots of ways to get sloppy," the colonel said.

"But that's not something we'll find out anytime soon," Penny said. "Not before it's too late."

With that, they adjourned to the sundae bar. The Mess President had laid out all the trimmings to go with the steaks.

That brought a series of jokes about fattening the calf and last meals. Which ended when Kris noticed the looks her team was getting from the other officers dining in the mess.

Eighteen hours passed like eighteen endless days.

31

Kris continued to use the Forward Lounge for her Tac Center. It had room for Ron and his two advisors as well as Vicky and Maggie. The doctor was shocked to discover the topic of conversation and tended to sit one table away from them and look on with only slightly controlled horror. She would join in when Penny said something against the idea of going to war. Mostly, she just watched.

The Iteeche took over a corner and had their own long and occasionally loud argument. Nelly offered to eavesdrop, but Kris told her not to. They needed their privacy. When Ron was ready, he'd tell them what he and his advisors had agreed upon.

When the Iteeche meeting was done, the Army officer stomped out of the room, and Ron and Ted, his Navy officer, rejoined Kris's team.

"You don't have to tell us what that was about if you don't want to," Kris said.

"We swam in the same waters you muddied up during your feeding," Ron said. "The Army advisor does not see that we have the will of the Emperor in what you are thinking to do. He is opposed to our riding along with you and insists that I either command you in the name of the Emperor to halt this plan or that we at least leave in one of your courier boats and return to the Empire."

"Do you want to?" Kris asked.

"No. I do not like the choice of fish swimming upstream any more than you do, but it is the choice that has been given to us. We cannot turn away from it. Besides, these bird folk may be a helpful ally in the war ahead. Are we so plentiful that we can allow those who may swim with us to be eaten already?"

"A good thought," Kris said.

"So we have a very unhappy Iteeche aboard," Jack said. "Kris, would you mind if I check in on him?"

"Please do."

"Captain Drago, an Iteeche just left the Forward Lounge."

"Yes, our security team noticed him stomp out. We don't have any experts at alien body language, but the betting up here is that he is not a happy camper."

"Sad but true," Jack said. "You know how our princess affects some people. Could you keep an eye on him?"

"Already doing it, Marine. Our disaffected Iteeche just locked himself in Iteeche country. If you'll post some Marines as an honor guard there, we can make sure he stays there."

"Done, and thank you, Captain."

Jack's next call was to his Marine duty officer. A watch was quickly posted.

An hour later, Captain Drago dropped down to check with Kris on the load for the 12-inch high-acceleration torpedoes.

"Load antimatter," Kris said.

"How much?" the captain asked.

"How much?"

"I've been talking with some of the professor's boffins, and they think we can double-load them. Maybe even quadruple-load them."

"Is that safe?" Jack asked.

"Not for any length of time, no," the captain said. "The containment systems in the warheads are lightweight, and that means limited strength and duration. However, if we load the antimatter just before we fire the warheads, they should be good for fifteen minutes. Maybe double that."

"You're taking a great risk," Jack said.

"If Your Highness here has us hunting BEMs, I think anti-matter warheads popping off early may be the least of our worries."

"Do you disagree with us taking on the bug-eyed monsters, Captain Drago?" Kris asked. He was the contractor captain hired by her king. While Admiral Krätz's threat to shoot the *Wasp* out of space seemed unlikely, Captain Drago could put an end to any of Kris's plans by simply locking her in her stateroom and heading the *Wasp* off in any direction that pleased him.

So long as the captain didn't do Kris any bodily harm, she sincerely doubted Jack would do anything to stop the *Wasp*'s skipper from doing something that probably would cut down on her likelihood of ending up suddenly dead.

The captain took in a long breath and let it out slowly. "I suspect your grampa may have me keelhauled for following you on this mission if you order us to take on the bug-eyed monsters. However, there are times when people do what they have to do. If you say it is war, I and my crew will follow you. If you say go home, I think we will all breathe a long sigh of relief and go home. However, if we abandon that planet of bird people to the tender mercies of those space raiders, I don't think any of us will sleep all that well. Probably for the rest of our lives. Hell of a choice you have there, Your Highness. Glad I don't have to make it myself."

He snapped to and saluted her. He didn't wait for her to return the honor but turned for the door of the lounge. "Let me know when you make your final decision," he called over his shoulder.

"I wondered how he'd take to it all," Penny said. "I guess that settled whether or not you find yourself locked in your room tomorrow and the *Wasp* headed for home."

"I was wondering about that, myself," Kris said, her voice not rising above a whisper.

Actually, she'd been wondering about it for several years. When would this governor sent by her great-grandfather rise up to take her down? At first, that was what she expected, someone to cut her off and substitute his mature judgment for her youthful exuberance.

Of late, as Captain Drago followed her orders more and more, she began to wonder if there ever would be a time when he would cut her off, or had she come into herself? Come to her command?

That time had come, and, for better or worse, the crew of the *Wasp* would follow her through hell and, with any luck, back out again.

She shivered. That was a heavy burden to bear. If she'd followed a normal Navy career, at some point the Navy would have assigned her a ship, and she would have had orders promoting her to god for that ship and its crew.

Nothing about Kris's life had gone normal.

She smiled to herself. She had a ship, and they were her crew.

And after that wonderful moment, Kris found herself with time on her hands, where each minute seemed like an hour, and each hour flew like a second.

She was already familiar with the irony of time in these situations. In a few days, lives might be lost for the lack of a few seconds. However, for now, they had to wait. Wait for others to do their job.

And waiting took forever.

Kris checked in with Nelly every hour to see how things were going on the translation effort. Every hour Nelly told Kris to hold her horses and not juggle their elbows.

The first time it was funny. By the twelfth time it was starting to bother her. Checks with the *Vulcan* showed the usual problems, none a showstopper. Those who had work were lost in it. Those who had duties went about them, checking and rechecking systems, weapons, defenses.

Kris would make the final decision whether many of them would live or die, but for now, she waited. Waited to verify that the mother ship shared a common ancestry with the space raiders. Waited to see if they had weapons that could make a difference.

Waited. Waited. Waited.

Reports came in from the other ships of PatRon 10; they had also built up their supply of antimatter during their walkaround. How should they distribute the antimatter?

Kris ordered them to load antimatter warheads for their 12-inch high-acceleration torpedoes, but not a double load. The torpedoes would help the corvettes fight their way out of the close quarters she was about to order them into.

All their other extra antimatter would juice up the neutron torpedoes. Those were her only hope of crippling the mother ship. If they could pull that off, they all just might live to tell their tales.

The captains accepted her orders without question.

To have such godlike power over other people's lives sent a shiver up Kris's back.

Eighteen hours into the wait, Nelly interrupted Kris and Penny from another discussion of the right and wrong of their options.

"Kris, Professor mFumbo wants to talk to you in person. He suggests you get the admirals on conference."

"Make it so, Nelly."

"Aye, aye, ma'am."

32

"I have pictures," Professor mFumbo told those gathered in the Forward Lounge and observing on net. "Considering all we had to go through to make them come out, I'm amazed at how clean they are."

"How did you translate them?" Kris asked.

"There is not enough time left in my life for me to explain it to you. Please accept my word. These are complete and accurate video readouts of the data."

"We may see about that," Admiral Krätz grumbled.

"Could you please show us what you have?" Admiral Channing asked.

"Chief, have your computer run the video," the professor said, and Chief Beni said something softly to his computer, Da Vinci.

A new window opened on the forward screen. It was a close-up of what looked like a male choir. The voices accompanying the video were deep and powerful, the tonals of their song made the hairs on the back of Kris's neck stand up.

This was not human music.

The singers, though, looked very human.

They'd been referring to the occupants of the huge mother ship as bug-eyed monsters. That would have to change. These people looked as human as the next person.

So had the bodies from the ship that attacked Kris with no provocation.

The camera zoomed out, showing how huge the choir was. Then it panned to the listening crowd in the audience. They were crammed into seven balconies, layer perched upon layer, leaving Kris to wonder how those in the back could see anything.

The audience listened in rapturous silence.

When the song ended, there was applause. However, the conductor did not take a bow; nor did he offer for anyone in the choir to do so.

The applause grew, and the camera zoomed back down front to a single man taking his place before a podium. As Kris took him in, she realized that all the singers and most of the people in the crowd wore the same dark uniform. They were identical except for minor silver markings, which Kris suspected identified rank and maybe honors.

The man at the podium wore the same clothing as the rest, but his uniform displayed much more silver, red, and gold. As he stood there, waving his right arm stiffly at the audience, the crowd went wild with cheering and clapping.

It went on and on.

"How much of this do we have to sit through?" Kris asked.

"Five minutes, thirty-four seconds," the professor said. "We timed it."

"Can we skip to the chase?" Kris asked.

The chief muttered something to his computer, and the screen blinked. Then the man began his talk. One moment he shouted. The next moment his voice was little more than a whisper. Then he was shouting again. Sometimes the crowd shouted back.

"Do we have a translation of what he's saying?" Kris asked.

"Sorry, Your Highness, not a word," the professor said. "He goes on like this for three hours and ten minutes. He doesn't even take a break for a drink of water."

"That's better than my dad ever did," Kris muttered. "Are there more pictures?"

"As we speak, we are translating several hundred hours of video," Professor mFumbo reported. "Much of it appears to be more speeches by this man although a lot of it is similar choir efforts. No evidence of musical instruments accompanying the choir, but a lot of singing, always in large groups."

"There was also a lot of what looked like news reports," Nelly added. "Since there was little or no visual backup to the person looking into the camera, it's hard to tell what he's talking about, but he is very earnest about whatever it is."

"You didn't get any DNA off the video, did you?" Kris knew it was a stupid question, but she had to ask it.

"Obviously not," the professor said. "We also found no pictures of anyone with their clothes off, no porn, so there's no way for us to tell for sure if these are the same people we found before. I do admit they look like them."

"They look painfully like us," Kris admitted before someone else could point that out.

"So, what do we do, gentlemen and ladies?" Kris asked those gathered with her.

"Go home," Admiral Krätz snapped immediately. "We should inform our governments what we have found and defer to them. Let wiser people than us decide what all of humanity will do."

Vicky rolled her eyes.

"If we do that," Admiral Kōta said softly, "the planet they are heading for will likely be plundered down to its bedrock."

"That is not our problem," Krätz shot back.

"If it comes to a fight with these people," Admiral Channing put in, "we might want all the allies we can get our hands on."

"We can't declare war," Krätz snapped. "We handful here do not have that authority. Our governments would not be happy to have us return with the first battle of the next war already fought. Maybe lost. We have a duty to those who sent us. If some of you don't, I know that I and my battle squadron do," he finished darkly

"That's so funny, Admiral," Vicky said with an ironic chuckle. "You're usually ready for a fight at the drop of a hat. You have a problem here because these people can shoot back?"

"You can't say that," Krätz shouted at his protégée, his face going red.

"That's sure what it looks like to me," Vicky snarled back.

Kris wondered where that came from. Still she had no time

for the issues that one admiral and one proud young junior officer had acquired while he broke her to harness.

"Hold it, hold it, hold it, people," Kris said, taking steps to put herself between the screen with its storming Greenfeld admiral and the equally angry grand duchess at Kris's elbow.

If she let this situation get out of hand, she could have the first battle of the next war right there in the anchorage . . . with no alien in sight. Kris hadn't spent her entire life preparing for this moment to let it get bloody and out of hand.

"We won't get anywhere attacking each other," Kris said in a voice as soothing as she could manage. "Let's see what we can agree on."

She took a deep breath, all the time wondering what the great Billy Longknife would do. Then again, he'd never faced an angry political opposition that had loaded 18-inch lasers. "It looks to me that the aliens on the huge mother ship are the same type of aliens that attacked the *Wasp* and sucked dry the planet we found. Do we have agreement on that?"

Professor mFumbo nodded. The skippers of Kris's corvettes showed agreement as well. After a long moment, so did the admirals from Musashi and Helvetica.

Admiral Krätz's face was still an apoplectic scowl, but he grumbled, "It looks likely that they are."

That was more agreement than Kris would have expected a few moments ago.

"Can we agree that they appear to be headed for the bird people?"

That got nods all around.

"Can we agree that if they do enter that system, it's likely that they will plunder it of everything needed to support life?"

The nodding continued . . . except for Admiral Krätz. "You can't prove that," he said.

"No, but their previous practices seems to make that highly likely. Right?" Kris said.

"It doesn't matter. It's none of our business. My emperor did not send me here to start a galactic-size war. None of our governments did. We would be traitors to our lords and our people if we did."

"Admiral, I can understand your point of view," Kris said, trying to sound as reasonable and understanding as her father in a heated question time. Although, to be honest, serving the newly minted Emperor of Greenfeld was not something Kris had any understanding of, nor did she want any.

"If these people would just talk to us. Let us exchange a few words. Even make an effort, I'd be more willing to go where you're inclined."

The admiral seemed to relax at that, not much, but a bit. Kris hurried on.

"But that's the problem. When I tried to talk to them, they didn't say a word, just shot lasers at the *Wasp*. When Phil here tried to talk to them, they sent ships off to chase after the *Hornet*. He got away from them before they got in range of him, but they weren't making any effort to talk, and they sure looked like they wanted to shoot.

"They aren't giving us any good choices. As I see it, we can go away and hope they don't drop in on any of our planets. Or we can look into whether or not we can do something to them now, before they can plunder another planet and fatten on its blood.

"I hate those choices," Kris said as she finished.

The faces on the screen fell silent for a long minute.

Admiral Kōta broke the silence. "My orders were to follow Commander Kris Longknife. So far, I have followed her." He paused to let that sink in, before he finished. "I think that I will continue to follow her, wher*ever* she may lead."

"Into a war?" Krätz snarled.

"She is one of those damn Longknifes," Channing said. "My government knew that ships were disappearing. They knew there were risks. This Longknife had shown herself to be levelheaded and not eager to go off half-cocked. You cannot have mistaken the fact that all our governments sent battleships. They sent battleships to follow a Longknife where ships had gone and failed to return." The admiral paused for a moment.

"No one told me what to do. But no one told me what *not* to do. I believe I know now what I will do. What are your orders, Commodore Longknife?"

Kris was surprised at the nods that got. She was so used to being painted with the broad Longknife brush that she'd never considered that she might be earning a reputation of her own.

"To put it simply, Georg," Admiral Kōta said, "if she proposes to take the fleet into battle *and* has reasonable prospects for success, my orders are vague enough to allow me to follow her. I do not like the way these people will not open communications with us. I do not like the way they rip apart entire systems. I do not like the thought that my fair Musashi could be next on their dinner list. I think it is time that we put a stop to this, and I see no reason why we should let them fatten themselves on another system before someone does that."

He turned from facing the Imperial admiral to face out of the screen eye to eye with Kris. "Princess Longknife, if you can show me a way we might succeed in this endeavor, it will be my honor and privilege to place my battleships at your command."

"Me likewise," Admiral Channing said. "Though it better be a very good plan. My people don't like to throw money away on long shots."

This was moving faster than Kris had expected. She eyed Admiral Krätz.

"Let's hear what you have to say," he growled. "It better be good."

Kris did have a plan. She would have preferred to run the main points by her staff and give them a chance to refine it. But there was no use wasting an opportunity like the admirals presented her.

Kris took a deep breath . . . and started talking.

33

A plan is only a beginning. Kris had learned that at her father's knee, watching campaign plans fall apart only to be hammered back into something else. She'd experienced it enough on her own as a Navy officer. Sometimes it had fallen to her to make other people's plans implode.

Other times, someone else had done the honor to her.

Still, an entire civilization had never hung on any of the plans she'd made.

And none of the plans had ever taken two interstellar races into a war with a third in order to save a fourth.

But then, there's a first time for everything.

The *Vulcan*'s completing the installation of the neutron torpedoes on the *Hornet*, *Intrepid*, and *Fearless* was number one on Kris's list of what needed to be done before she took on the huge mother ship. So when the skippers of the *Vulcan* and *Fearless* called an hour later, she answered the call immediately.

"We've got a problem," the skipper of the *Fearless* said.

"Possible sabotage," the skipper of the *Vulcan* said.

"You're not sure it's sabotage," said *Fearless*.

"Those wires didn't cut themselves," replied *Vulcan*.

"Hold it. Hold it," Kris said. "What's wrong?"

The view changed to show a bundle of wires cut smartly in half.

"How'd that happen?" Kris said.

"We don't know," *Fearless* said.

"Someone cut them," was the *Vulcan*'s answer.

"It does look like someone cut them," Kris said.

Silence answered her conclusion.

"It seems we have a reluctant tiger," Colonel Cortez said from behind Kris.

"Reluctant tiger?" Kris said.

"Someone doesn't want to be in on this fight," the colonel went on. "Be they a coward or just God's anointed to keep two galactic species from going to war, they don't want the neutron torpedoes to go active."

"Has anyone complained to you, Commander?"

The skipper of the *Fearless* shook her head. "Everyone seemed excited to be taking on the planet rapers. Being the first to use these torpedoes makes it one for the history books."

"I think someone wants to skip their place in the history books," Kris said, then came to a conclusion. "Nelly, put all the skippers online and the admirals, too."

"Do we have to involve everyone?" asked *Fearless*.

"I'm afraid so." Kris quickly filled in those who joined on net. Admiral Krätz seemed torn between indignant at the cowardly action . . . and strong support for the idea of the torpedoes' not going live. The rest listened quietly.

"I know that tradition requires us to hunt down the dog who did this and keelhaul him, but I don't have time for tradition at the moment," Kris said. "We also can't afford to post guards at every point where a ship might be vulnerable. Therefore, I propose you offer anyone in your crew a ticket home. If they want, they can ask for a ride back to human space on the freighters, the courier ships, or the *Vulcan*. Those ships will not be going with us. Anyone who wants to skip the coming battle can go home on them."

"And if too many of the crew ask to use your ticket out?" Admiral Channing asked.

"Ships that can't be fought will escort the freighters."

"So you're rewarding treason and sabotage." Admiral Krätz exploded. "You will even let sailors vote to abandon their posts in the face of the enemy. Even take a ship out of my command!"

"Out of *my* command," Kris snapped back. "I thought you'd be delighted. Maybe even take the ride home yourself."

"I've already issued the orders to fight the fleet," Krätz growled. "Now you're inviting insubordination."

"It doesn't lack for a historic precedent," Colonel Cortez said. "A small detachment holding a fort on the frontier of a tiny country, fighting for its independence from a much larger one, had dissension in the ranks. The commander drew a line in the sand and announced that anyone who wished to leave could do so. Just cross the line."

"What happened?" asked Admiral Kōta.

"Offered the chance to leave, every one of them stayed."

"How'd it turn out?" Admiral Krätz asked.

"They were wiped out to a man," the colonel said.

"Banzai," said Admiral Kōta. "An honorable death."

Kris let the thoughts sink in, then went on. "I suggest you draw a line in the sand for your people as soon as you can and get any reluctant tigers moving toward a billet where they can do your ship no harm."

The screen closed down, but before Kris could continue with a review of her plan, she realized she had forgotten to include Captain Drago and the *Wasp* in her line-in-the-sand offer. She quickly called the captain and brought him up to date.

"Yes, that would be a good idea. We had a lot of young sailors brought aboard recently. I suspect some of them may be green and frightened. It would be better for the ship if they dropped out now. I'll have Senior Chief Mong pass the word."

"He will understand this is a no-judgment offer?" Kris asked. Her experience of the old chief was that she would not want to be on his wrong side. She suspected the young sailors aboard had the same feeling.

"This may surprise you, but Senior Chief Mong has teenage boys at home. I've found that he has a very good understanding of our younger hands. By the way, Your Highness, there is a personnel matter that I should discuss with you. Would you mind if I dropped down to talk with you."

"Certainly not, Captain. Feel free," Kris said.

What she thought was *What now?* Captain Drago and his initial crew were all civilian contractors, hired to run the *Wasp* in some under-the-table agreement with Wardhaven's chief

spy. Kris didn't care if some young sailors took her up on the
chance to go home to momma. However, if Captain Drago and
his entire crew announced that they wanted to exercise their
option to bolt and run now that things were getting hot, it
would leave her with no one to run the *Wasp*.

She would, of course, transfer her flag to one of the other
corvettes. Still, to have your flagship run out on you just before
the battle would be embarrassing.

To lose one-quarter of her squadron might well mean de-
feat.

Kris sighed and put that thought away in a pigeonhole
marked Panic Later.

For the moment, she turned back to Jack, the colonel,
Penny, Abby, and Chief Beni. They had a battle plan to refine
and options to develop, so Kris could be oh so brilliant in the
coming fight and pull out just the right rabbit at the right moment when the approved plan fell apart.

"Kris," Nelly announced, "Lieutenant Song, skipper of the
courier ship *Hermes*, would like to talk to you. She's about to
jump out of the system to check out the last system the *Hornet*
was in. Do you have time to talk to her?"

"I'll make time. Lieutenant Song, what can I do for you?"

"Commander, we just got the word that anyone who wants
to go home can ask, and they'll get a ride back on a courier
boat or on one of the freighters. Is that correct, ma'am?"

Kris nodded. "Yes. No one has to go into this fight who
doesn't want to." Kris didn't explain the full security thoughts
behind what some might think of as a most magnanimous decision.

"Well, ma'am, on the small ships, we're wondering if some
of us could transfer onto the fighting ships as replacements. I
mean, if we've got sailors coming aboard, they might as well
sail the *Hermes* and let us take their billets. Commander."

Jack and the colonel grinned at Kris, struggling to suppress
open laughter. She'd expected one thing and gotten something
totally different. Facing the screen, Kris kept her face a commander's mask.

"Thank you, Lieutenant. I'll see what I can do. Pass the
word to the other courier boats that anyone on them can put in
their names and rate and they can switch with anyone on the
corvettes who wants to trade. The couriers will go back, and

they have to be properly crewed. They'll carry The Word to the U.S. of what we are doing here. Humanity has to know what we've done in their name and why."

"Yes, ma'am. I understand. The Word has to get back. But if there are folks who want to go back, let's let them go and let the rest of us fight."

"Thank you, Lieutenant. Pass The Word. Now, I have a battle to plan."

"Yes, ma'am. Signing off."

"Are you surprised, Commodore?" the colonel said.

"No. Yes. Maybe," Kris said, trying not to stutter.

"You're offering them a chance to fight for the right of an entire race to breathe the air God gave them," Colonel Cortes said. "Drink their planet's water. It's a worthwhile fight. A good fight."

"We're all going to die," Abby muttered . . . to everyone in hearing.

"Everyone dies," the colonel said. "Not everyone gets to die for something worth dying for. Abby, my good woman, you have to quit thinking the old way. For years, the Navy took out the garbage and stopped this spat, that squabble. Now we're facing something that doesn't even consider us worth talking to. We try to talk to them. They try to kill us. That's the way the conversation has gone. Now we'll let Hellburners do our talking for us."

"Hellburners?" Kris asked.

"The boffins can call them neutron torpedoes if they want. That's a name to warm the hearts of some ice-water-for-blood scientist. Hellburners. Now that's the name for a warrior's weapon. That's a name that will smash down the very gates of hell. I like that name."

"We'd better," Jack said. "Because Kris here is leading us right down hell's main boulevard."

"She'll march us into hell, and she will march us back again," the colonel said, "and we will all raise a glass at the memory when we're old and gray."

"I surely hope so," Penny said, looking slightly pale. "I certainly hope so."

"She's a bloody Longknife," the colonel said, grinning. "Who would you rather follow through hell?"

"Me, I'd rather skip the hike," said Chief Beni.

"You going to apply for a ticket on one of the freighters?" Penny asked.

"Of course not," the chief said. "If Kris is going to lead us out of hell, she'll need me to find the best route."

Kris chuckled. "Thank you, Chief."

Captain Drago entered the Forward Lounge at that moment, a thick pile of flimsies in hand. It looked thick enough to cover every man and woman of his contract crew. Kris swallowed hard, mentally packing her kit. A shrunken kit that might fit on the *Hornet*.

"I have some personnel actions you need to sign, Commodore."

"What kind?"

"Activating commissions, Commodore."

"Whose?"

"Mine. All the other officers among our crew. Oh, and the enlisted swine want to be activated, too. If you're going to fight a war, we'd prefer to fight it with good old Navy blue and gold on our backs."

34

Kris took a moment to take a deep breath and let it out slowly. Once again, she'd expected one thing and was being handed another. Colonel Cortez was right; she needed a new mind-set. She reached for the top flimsy. It named a certain Edmond Drago and activated his reserve commission . . . as a lieutenant.

"I thought you were a captain the last time your reserve commission was activated?" Kris said.

"I was. But the last time we were at Wardhaven, with you promoted to lieutenant commander, I rearranged all our reserve commissions. My crew now are all lieutenants . . . or junior."

Kris glanced up at Captain Drago. Or Lieutenant Drago-to-be. "Why the cut in pay?"

"None of us thought we should outrank you, Commodore."

"Outrank me."

"Yes, ma'am. You're the captain of *Wasp* as soon as you sign those papers."

Kris put the papers down on the table beside her. "Sit down, Captain. What's going on here?"

"As I said, Kris, we're going into a fight. Call us old-fashioned, me and my crew, but if we're going to fight the king's fight, we ought to wear the king's colors. It's been that way for several thousand years. This idea of taking the king's coin and doing it as a civilian contractor just doesn't have the right taste to it for me. Others may disagree. That's their right. Me and mine, no, Your Highness. If we're to fight, give us our blue and gold."

"It's not like these hostiles will follow the rules of war," Kris said. "I don't think it will matter all that much to them whether they capture you in uniform or in your underwear."

"Given my choice, I'd rather not be captured at all by these murderers," Drago said. "However, as I said. We're old-fashioned. This isn't one of your not-quite-a-real-war things that you've taken us to. They were fun little parties. Fine way to pass the time of day when things were dull. This is the real thing. A knock-down, drag-out brawl.

"We talked it over among ourselves. For this, we follow the flag, and we want our proper uniforms."

Kris nodded, leafing through the forms. One after another, lieutenant, lieutenant, lieutenant.

Kris laid them out flat and rested her hand on them. "Captain, I can't tell you that I don't want to command the *Wasp*. This weird lash-up we've made of the chain of command has never been satisfying."

Kris paused to shake her head. "However, I've got a problem with this. In the right here and now."

"Just one problem?" Captain Drago said, raising an expressive eyebrow.

"Somewhere I heard that you train the way you'll fight. Then you fight the way you trained. Did I get the expression right, Colonel?"

"I can give it to you in the original Greek," the colonel said. "It goes back quite a ways. Good idea, too."

The present skipper of the *Wasp* nodded. "I've heard it, too."

"If I take the captain's seat, who takes my chair at Weapons?" Kris asked.

"The lieutenant here," the skipper said, nodding at Penny.

Penny shook her head. "No way I and Mimzy can handle weapons as well as Kris and Nelly. Sorry. You order us. We'll try. But we'd be kidding ourselves that I could do in a pinch as well as those two."

Kris let that hang in the air for a few moments, then reached for the form activating Drago's commission.

"Here's what we'll do," Kris said. "You've arranged that I can't commission you or any of your crew as anything but lieutenant. I'll do that," Kris said, signing the order. "Wear the uniform proudly."

"And at a much lower pay," Drago whispered under his breath.

"But, here's the way we fight the *Wasp*," Kris went on. "You have the captain's chair. I have the Weapons station. We've got a pretty good record of getting things done that way. I don't see us having any problems doing things that way in the coming fight. Do you?"

"I think we're all used to doing it that way. I don't foresee any problems we can't handle."

"Good," Kris said, and got busy signing papers. One brought her up short. "Cookie is an officer! The cook is at least a lieutenant?" She looked at Drago.

"A very good officer, ma'am. I learned more about being a junior officer under his command than I thought was possible."

"What rank did he retire at?"

"You'll have to ask him. He swore me to secrecy when I took him on board."

"He's a great cook," Abby said, "whatever he did for the Navy."

"That he is, folks," Drago agreed. "It was always a hobby of his. He promised me when he signed on that he'd do better than best for us, and he has."

"Cookie's an officer," Kris muttered as she signed the papers putting him back in a lieutenant's uniform. She seriously doubted it would fit him. He was a wondrous cook, and he did enjoy what he baked.

"And if anything happens to me, and he offers you a suggestion, Commodore, I'd take it under careful advisement."

"I think I will," Kris said, signing form after form. No surprise, most of her enlisted personnel were senior chiefs. Done, she handed the stack back to the newly minted Lieutenant Drago.

"Tell me, Edmond. What rank were you when you signed on to run this zoo?"

The skipper of the *Wasp* grinned. "I'd just been selected for rear admiral. Had my orders, too. A desk. Ugh. A stranger took me out for a drink and offered me a chance to chauffeur a Longknife cub around the galaxy. You'd have to be crazy not to grab for that kind of a billet."

"You'd have to be crazy to take it," Abby and Jack said at the same time.

"That, too," Drago agreed. "Anyway, there's never been a dull moment, and there doesn't look to be any on the horizon. Now, Your Highness, if you don't mind, I have a ship to prepare for one hell of a fight."

"Whether it's yours or mine, yes," Kris said.

"It may be mine in the fight, but it will be yours in the history books," he said with a well-practiced salute. With a snappy about-face, he headed back to his bridge.

35

Kris turned back to examining all the things that could go wrong in the coming encounter with an alien they'd just met and never talked to. It didn't take a lot of guessing to come up with a long list of them. The real problem was figuring out what to do when things did go south.

Then Professor mFumbo sauntered in.

"Your Highness, I need your permission to use two of the *Wasp*'s launches to take some of my boffins around the fleet."

"To do what?" Kris said. She suppressed a wince. She was echoing people quite a lot. Then again, her father always said it was better to echo something than to guess and guess wrong.

"We scientists joined your Fleet of Discovery to, well, discover. I think we've found quite a few things that will make it into peer-reviewed journals. But the nature of the voyage has changed."

"It certainly has," Kris agreed.

"Now we find that we are serving as witnesses to history being made. We are, by our nature as scientists, impartial observers of what we see. All of us are respected in our fields of endeavor. We believe that humanity will benefit greatly from our unprejudiced reports when we return to human space."

"Assuming you live through the experience," Abby said dryly.

"There is that," the professor agreed.

"So why do you need the ship's launches?" Kris said.

"One of the painful realities of this war-fighting business you are in, Your Highness, is that you can never tell who will survive it. The dogs of war are notoriously fickle as to whose tree they bark up and whose leg they chew on. We boffins have come to the conclusion that we should distribute ourselves through the fleet. That way, we can witness the coming events from different perspectives, and, no matter which ships survive the coming battle, some of us will be available to bear witness to what we saw."

"And you all decided this together?" Kris said. Her observations of the boffins as a subspecies of *Homo sapiens sapiens* was that they could never agree on anything that wasn't empirical in nature. The contents of the periodic table, yes. Where to eat supper, not so quickly done.

"I did suggest this to my associates. After discussion, they came to agree with me. I was one of the first volunteers. I've arranged to join the *Fury* along with Dr. Teresa de Alva and six others."

"Are any of them taking the freighters back?"

"Almost a score. Most of them are people who have papers ready to publish. Others feel that they best serve humanity by commenting immediately on what is about to happen. The economist Amanda Kutter will be a strong witness."

"She'll at least be a beautiful one," Abby drawled.

"She has a large heart and strongly believes in our going to the assistance of the avian people. I would not want to be on a talk show trying to espouse an opposing view from hers," the professor said.

"That I can agree on," Kris said. "Okay, you can have the use of two launches. Nelly, advise Captain Drago of this."

"Yes, ma'am," Nelly said. "It's done, and he's glad to have the boffins off his hands."

"Tell him they're not all going, so no dancing for joy in the passageways," Kris said.

"He says that once the boffins sort themselves out, he'll want to detach as many of the extra containers as possible," Nelly went on. "He said something about clearing the decks for action."

"You may be more comfortable on the *Fury*," Colonel Cortez said.

"He can have my quarters," Vicky said. She'd been quiet as a mouse for the longest time.

"You're not going back?" Kris said.

"I'm sure you'll be in the thick of the fight," Vicky said, "but at least I won't have to watch my back on the *Wasp*."

"You sure you wouldn't be just as safe on the *Fury*?" Kris said. "Paid assassins are notorious for wanting to live to spend their pay. I'd expect anyone sent here to kill you would be on the first freighter to jump out of this system."

"That sounds logical," the colonel said, "but what are the chances that the *Fury* won't survive this battle? Better yet, what do you think the odds are that the *Fury* will even fight? They could turn tail and run after we leave this system."

Kris shrugged. "I told them my battle plan. But you're right, Colonel. There's nothing that says any of these ships will fight my plan. Something like this never made it into the history books."

"Not the recent history. Now, back in the Middle Ages," the colonel said, getting into lecture mode, "whole flanks of an army might switch sides at the sound of the charge. Must have made for some interesting squabbling after the battle was over. Who got what spoils?"

"Thank you, Colonel," Abby drawled. "We will all sleep so much better tonight."

"The young lady here hired me to provide some historical flavor to your ruminations," he said cheerfully.

"Yes, Colonel," Kris said, "but while we're talking about people boarding the launches and getting rides to this ship or that, we really need to talk about one in particular."

"No you don't, Your Princessship," Abby said.

"Cara needs to be on one of the freighters out of here," Kris said.

"Ain't gonna happen," her maid shot right back.

"We're going into battle. She is not a combatant."

"Happens all the time. Some strong type like you throws a battle in some civilian's backyard. You don't have to be no combatant to attend a battle. Just unlucky."

"She doesn't have to be here," Kris insisted.

"She's got no place else to go."

That brought a pause in the rapid-fire exchange of disagreeableness.

"Have you at least talked with her about this?" Kris asked.

"We've talked, once or twice."

"And?"

"Growing up in Nuu House, you may not have been in the lap of love, but you knew where you lived, baby ducks. Cara and I, we grew up in Five Corners. You never went skipping off to school one morning and came home to find the family had up and moved, and no one told you where."

Abby paused for a moment. "You think the worst thing that can happen to us is to wind up dead next week. For me and Cara, there are a whole lot worse things that already done happened. Kris Longknife, you let us live our life, and I'll let you do what you're gonna do."

Abby stood up, looked like she was ready to take a walk, then paused. "And if you got any ideas about sending a platoon of Marines to my quarters late one night, you warn them. I wake up cranky, and I wake up armed. You hear me, Jack?"

"I hear you, Abby. And let me officially go on record that this is a problem between you and Her High-Handedness here. My troops may be dumb jarheads, but we are smart enough to stay out of anything you two women got going between you."

"Good," Abby sniffed, and stormed out of the room.

"So," the colonel asked, "anyone think now would be a good time for coffee? I don't know about you youngsters, but I need to visit the gentlemen's facilities."

"I could use some coffee," Jack agreed, and headed for the urn standing in the middle of the Forward Lounge's bar.

Kris and Vicky followed him.

"You know," Vicky said, "this has been quite an experience watching you go about planning an operation. I'm not sure how you got all these strong-willed people running along with you, but it's like nothing I've ever seen in my life. I can wrap a man or three around my little finger, but none of them would follow me into hell like these people are marching off to do."

"I'm glad you're learning it here. If you didn't learn it at your father's knee, you have to learn it somewhere," Kris said, her mind still half on how much she did not understand her maid.

"I don't think there was any chance of my learning this

from Dad. I remember stopping in the hallway outside a meeting he had with one of his admirals. That admiral was mad. I'd never heard anyone talk like that to Dad. Not talk like that and live to tell of it, anyways."

"An admiral was mad at your dad?" Jack said.

"Yes. I got to thinking about it as you were planning how to deploy your ships. Admiral Krätz's Battle Squadron 12 originally had a division of cruisers and a squadron of destroyers with it, but they all were left at home. A cruise this long was considered too much for the smaller ships. But here you are, running around with corvettes thousands of light-years from any port. And you're planning on using them in ways no battleship could possibly match."

"And the admiral was mad how?" Jack asked. His voice was suddenly devoid of any tint of emotion.

"The admiral was shouting that six big battleships had been wiped out by a bunch of mosquito boats because Dad ignored that admiral's professional judgment that battleships needed a decent escort."

At Kris's elbow, there came a shudder. Kris turned just in time to see Penny shiver and turn pale. The look she gave Vicky would have fried a more sensitive person in place.

The young lieutenant's mouth opened, then clamped shut. Penny turned and fled the room.

"What's wrong with her?" Vicky asked.

"I commanded those mosquito boats, Vicky, and the skipper of my flag was Penny's husband of three, four days. He died saving her life."

Kris paused to see if she'd gotten any reaction from the Peterwald scion. Her mouth actually did fall open, a bit. Her eyes widen, a little.

Kris went on. "Our mosquito boats were hurriedly built, using dumb metal. You know, the Smart Metal™ that can only change its shape two, maybe three times. Our fast patrol boat was venting its air to space, holed in I don't know how many places. I ordered Nelly to seal the boat. If we'd had more time, we might have also arranged to have the metal unpin Penny's husband, but there wasn't any time."

"A hard choice," Vicky whispered.

"The kind of choices we'll be making a lot of in the next few days."

"You knew this, but you, your crew here, still saved my dad."

"There was no way for us to know for sure that Peterwald was behind those battleships. And the assassins had arranged for it to look like I was involved in their plot to kill your father," Kris said, her words flat as she spat out the story of how even the supposed powerful could find themselves trapped by duty into doing what they'd never do by choice.

"Imagine if humanity were all balled up in a vicious war," Kris went on, "Greenfeld against Wardhaven. Nobody winning, everybody dying. And then imagine these horrors popping out of some jump point. A fine mess we'd be in."

"Yes. I guess so. I ought to go apologize to Penny."

"I wouldn't do that just now," Kris said. "Unless you know some magic words that will raise the dead and make it all better, I really don't think there is anything you can say to Penny at the moment. Why don't you and I go see if Cookie has any fresh-made bread? Maybe we can wheedle some old sea story out of him that will tell us who he really is."

"You have the strangest people around you," Vicky said.

"Yes," Kris said, eyeing the young woman beside her, "and I'm only now learning the half of it."

36

The old cook did indeed have some cranberry bread fresh from the oven. He even had butter, scrounged from one of the restaurants being off-loaded along with most of the boffins.

What he didn't have was any sea stories he was willing to share with the two young women. He smiled cheerfully at their request and excused himself to watch over his dinner preparations.

The *Wasp* was changing around them even as they walked its passageways. The skipper was now sporting a Navy blue-and-gold uniform with a lieutenant's two stripes, but he was still the captain to everyone Kris met. Another reason not to try to change what everyone was used to.

The *Wasp* itself shrank as shipping containers were cut free from their hold-downs on the ship. After threatening to hurl all the finely decked-out containers that held not only quarters and restaurants but also research labs and tons of equipment into the gas giant they were orbiting, Captain Drago relented and agreed to winch the boxes over to one of the freighters.

No one was very happy about letting those running back home do it in the fine quarters they were giving up. Still, there were fond hopes that the shipping containers would be waiting for the *Wasp* to come home, too, load back up, and head out for exploration again.

That slim handhold on a future that was as good as the past seemed to make it easier for people to face the unknown ahead of them.

The freighter that rendezvoused with them also brought along sixteen more antimatter torpedoes, so Kris was glad of the visit at least as much as the departing hands were glad for the use of the cargo containers.

Kris and Vicky stopped by Iteeche country to bring Ron up to date on what the humans had decided to do. It turned out he was already up to speed. Whenever Kris had talked to her own captains or the admirals, Nelly opened his communications link.

"So you are going to war for these people we have never met."

"Is that something the Iteeche would never do?" Kris asked.

"Never. I do not think anyone could get the Imperial Mind to turn that way. I do not think the Imperial counselors would ever permit such a thing to even be discussed outside of chambers. We would prepare for our first encounter with these homicidal aliens, but we would never rush out to meet them. Not like you have chosen to do."

"So you think Kris is wrong," Vicky said.

"My chooser taught me to think like a human, twisted though that is. Even if you are wrong, I think you are magnificent. Is that twisted?"

"No," Kris said. "Just very human."

"Are you committed to swim this course?" Ron asked.

"I'm still hoping we can get them talking to us," Kris admitted.

"Hmm," was all Ron said.

Four hours later, only two hours behind schedule, the *Vulcan* announced that its work there was done. The Hellburners were operational, and the squadron was good to go. The muster of personnel requesting a trip home topped out at fewer than a hundred; no ship was left in any danger of being undermanned.

The freighters, repair ship, and three courier ships headed for the first of the jumps that would take them back to Santa Maria. They carried The Word to the rest of humanity that a small squadron of their own was about to do battle against unknown but probably impossible odds in defense of a race of aliens they had yet to talk to.

The *Hermes* popped out of Jump Point Delta. She'd seen nothing of the aliens in the last system the *Hornet* had jumped from. That was a relief.

Now Kris settled into her battle station on the bridge of the *Wasp* at Weapons. She tightened her belt as the ship began its acceleration to fifty thousand kilometers per hour and aimed for the first jump. Three jumps would be fast and risky, leaping before they had any chance to look where they were going. The last one, if the maps were still accurate, would put them one small jump away from the final jump the hostile aliens would make before they descended on the bird people's system.

From one jump away, Kris's fleet could peek through and make sure the hostiles were not yet in the next system. If the aliens had beaten the humans there, Kris's plan would have fallen apart before she even began it.

The team had invested quite a bit of time trying to figure out an alternative battle plan if that happened.

No one had come up with anything that sounded at all good.

With luck, they'd just get there before the hostiles did.

The first two jumps went fine. The third jump, the one into the system where they'd slow down and take a careful look through the next jump to see how things were, didn't go so well.

"We're through," Sulwan announced from her post as navigator. Now her usual cutoffs and tank tops had been replaced with a blue ship jumper sporting a lieutenant's two stripes.

"We're where we want to be," she quickly added, and everyone breathed a sigh of relief. Once again, they'd taken the risky jump and not had to pay the price for it.

"I've got activity in the system," Chief Beni reported.

"What kind of activity?" Captain Drago demanded. He still sat in the captain's chair even though his blue ship jumper also showed only two stripes.

"Give me a moment," the chief snapped.

"I wish the professor was here," he muttered under his breath.

"My children have been analyzing the video and audio take," Nelly announced. "It uses the same strange encryption system as Taussig's aliens. We are trying to translate them into pictures we can see, but this may take time."

"The hostile emissions are coming from a stationary source," the chief reported. "There are no hostile ships in the system. Just one reactor."

"Where?" Captain Drago said.

"That small planet slightly sunward between us and our next jump point."

Behind the *Wasp*, the rest of the fleet poured into the system. PatRon 10 was now augmented by the courier boat *Hermes*. Lieutenant Song had won her battle duty. Kris hoped she would survive her wishes. Admiral Krätz insisted that the Greenfeld squadron, by right of it being double the size of the other contingents, should lead the battleships. No one had argued with him.

Maybe being in the lead had encouraged him to go where the other admirals intended to go. He had followed Kris through three jumps.

Now he did not follow her toward the next jump.

"Hey, if our aliens have a small outpost here, maybe we can talk to them," he announced with cheer that would have struck no one as sincere.

"We have a deadline to meet in the next system," Kris pointed out.

"But you always said you really wish you could talk to them. Well, here's a few of them. Let's see if we can get them to talk to you."

"I think the admiral is hoisting you on your own petard," Captain Drago said.

"And I am very highly hoist," Kris said. "Captain, if you will, set a course for that occupied planet. Chief Beni, tell me everything you know about it as soon as you know about it."

"It's not going to be easy, Your Highness. We don't have all the resources of the boffins to call on."

"Don't I know," Kris said. "Give me what you've got, Chief, and give it to me quick."

37

The planet had an atmosphere, of sorts. The chief suspected you could almost breathe it. "It's got oxygen and nitrogen, but there are all kinds of nasty things like sulfur and other irritants."

"I don't intend to breathe it," Kris said.

"Right," the chief said. "There's some water, but it's got a high acidic content. More likely than not, if you dip your little toe in it, you won't have a toenail left. Maybe no toe."

"I got the message, Chief. I'll pick somewhere else for my honeymoon."

"Fortunately, she has plenty of time to find someone to share it with." It sounded like Jack, but it was on net, and Kris ignored it.

Sulwan turned to Kris. "Is there any chance that this could be one of those planets that they stripped of its air and water, then polluted?"

"Chief, can you spot any evidence of previous civilization on this rock?"

"Nothing that I can see, Kris, but if the air and water are this acidic, it might have eaten away at a lot of building materials."

"So we're left to guess. Nelly, get me the admirals," Kris said.

"Do you have any plans for contact?" Kris asked Krätz.

"I thought you were the one with all the plans," was his reply.

The Krätz Kris had grown to know and like on Chance was long gone.

"I think the solution to our problem is easy," Admiral Kōta said. "We land an assault team and take some prisoners. How large can this outpost be?"

"If it were us down there," Kris said, "my chief thinks there might be fifty. Probably no more than a hundred. But these people seem to need less personal space than we do. There could be ten times as many aliens down there. Maybe fifty times."

"But they have no space weapons," Krätz said. "Surely, seeing eight huge battleships over them will make them be reasonable. It's not like that lonely little ship that chose to take on your *Wasp*. We are battleships."

Commander Taussig of the *Hornet* cleared his throat. "Compared to the ships who gave chase to us, your battleships look kind of dinky."

"They would be fools to test us," the Greenfeld admiral rumbled.

"Whose assault team do we put down?" Kris said.

"Your Marines are the most combat experienced," Krätz said.

"Against people who can shoot back," sounded like Vicky's voice.

Krätz turned purple. Everyone else seemed not to have heard it.

Kris went on. "Admiral Kōta, Admiral Channing, do you have Marine detachments aboard?"

"We do," came from both of them.

"Would you care to share a drop landing and reconnaissance mission with my combat-experienced Marines."

"It would be an honor," said Admiral Kōta.

"Don't mind if I do," said Admiral Channing.

It would be nice to have the company, but Kris still felt like she was being railroaded into something that maybe wasn't such a good idea. "Chief, I'd sure like to know more about that alien site."

"So would I, Kris. It's making a lot of noise on the electromagnetic spectrum, but I can't make head nor tails out of it."

"I believe you did say it was alien," sounded like Abby on the net.

Kris ignored the comment. "I have no intention of dropping Marines into the middle of something we know nothing about. I need to get a good look at it before I approve a drop mission."

"We can make a couple of orbital passes," the chief said. "Drop a few remote eyes to get a good look at it."

"I intend to put my battle squadron in a geosynchronous orbit above the target where I can keep it in constant observation," Admiral Krätz said.

Which would keep him well out of harm's way but in a great position to tell them what they were doing wrong. Kris also remembered recently being half a klick from a target when Krätz decided to laser it from orbit.

All the more reason to be careful with her Marines.

"I'm not putting my Marines anywhere near that site until I get a good look at it. Better yet, I want to keep getting a good look at it. Preferably with a load of ordnance I can do something with."

"We have some ground attack craft aboard the *Fury*," Vicky said.

"Ground attack craft?" Kris found herself once again echoing.

"Yes. Big ugly things," the grand duchess said. "Thirty-millimeter Gatling cannon in its nose. Wings you can load with ordnance. I was told it was a standard design."

"Nelly?" Kris said.

"The ground attack craft were built to provide close support to infantry during the Iteeche war. It was a standard design developed on Earth and built on several planets. If it has been properly maintained, this relic of the last war should still be functional," Nelly said.

"Chief Mong," Captain Drago said, "do we have mechanics familiar with a ground attack craft and able to check one out?"

"God, sir, did you find one of those old things?" didn't sound encouraging.

"The Greenfeld battle squadron has a couple, and the princess wants to fly one."

"I'll put together a team immediately, sir," he said quickly.

"Vicky, do you want to join me for a trip to the *Fury*?"

"No thank you. I'm comfortable here."

"Jack, do you want to drop with your Marines or ride back-seat with me?"

This put the Marine captain on the horns of a dilemma. As Kris's chief of security, he shouldn't let her out of his sight. As the commander of the Marine company aboard the *Wasp*, he really shouldn't let them wander off without adult supervision. At the moment, he needed to be in two places at once.

Kris had read somewhere about holy people who were supposed to be able to be in two places at the same time. Jack didn't strike Kris as anything close to holy. She waited for him to make his difficult call.

"Colonel, neither of my platoon skippers is experienced enough to lead the company," Jack said. He didn't have to mention that experienced platoon skippers around Kris tended to pay for that experience by ending up in hospitals somewhere and missing the *Wasp*'s next movement.

"This is getting to be a habit," the colonel grumbled. "But I managed to walk away from the last drop mission. I expect I'll survive this one."

With her chain of command now wrapped into its usual macramé, Kris headed for a launch, leaving one final plea behind her for Chief Beni to discover something. Anything! About the alien site.

Kris was greeted as she boarded the *Fury* by a junior officer who admitted that he was personally responsible for maintaining the GACs. He wasn't surprised that Kris had brought her own maintenance team.

He was surprised that it was led by a chief and included several petty officers.

The chief muttered something to Kris about draftee Navies regularly committing heresy by letting officers get their hands on screwdrivers.

Clearly, Kris was walking a fine line between two different faiths. She would have to keep a tight lid on matters, or a holy war might break out right there in the drop bay of the *Fury*.

And she'd come over to the *Fury* thinking that all she had to worry about was the Longknife/Peterwald thing.

Silly her.

The GACs were ugly. They also looked deadly, with their seven-barrel cannon jutting out of their nose. These particular GACs had a thick coat of paint on them that cracked in several places as Kris's mechanics began going over them.

"I'd heard that the Greenfeld Navy was more interested in looking good than fighting good," the chief muttered to Kris when the Greenfeld lieutenant was busy elsewhere. "If you're just planning on having them sit here and do nothing, a fresh coat of paint will make a hangar queen look pretty, even fero-cious, if you paint growling tiger teeth on 'em," he said, jerk-ing a thumb over his shoulder at the several craft sporting toothy grins.

"Are any of them ready to fly?" Kris asked.

"There's one in the back. Looks all scratched and dinged up. I think it's the one they actually fly."

"These others?" Kris asked.

"Look good for inspections and photo ops for the admiral, don't they?"

Kris and Jack headed for the back. GAC-7 did look much the worse for wear. The Wardhaven mechs had a half dozen black boxes plugged into several ports and were muttering various incantations over the results that showed on their screens. The belly of the beast was already laid open, and sev-eral gizmos and boxes lay on the deck as the lieutenant showed Kris's chief his small hoard of spare parts.

The lieutenant came back grumbling. "Your chief. He wants to change out everything. He wants everything new. We don't have new. Not for this old pig. We have old. Very old. I think old is better for this hog."

A few minutes later, the chief came back shaking his head. "I've looked in this hog's logbook. If they aren't lying, they've flown this thing five hundred hours in the last two years. Me, I wouldn't send my worst enemy out in this thing. Not in this condition. We got to do something here."

"Can I fly it, Chief?" Kris asked, as Jack showed more and more alarm at just that prospect.

"I trained on this stuff back in B school, ma'am, though I'm not sure any of my crew have ever seen this stuff themselves. We got stuff on the *Wasp* that we should be able to plug into this hog. It won't be the exact replacement for the crap they have here. The stuff they got here we replaced fifteen, twenty years ago. But, with any luck, our new modules should swap right into these old slots."

"Chief, will this be safe to fly?" Jack demanded.

"Captain, when you launch this hog, I swear to God, if you want me to, you can put a third seat out on the wing of this bird, and I will ride right along with you."

"Yeah. And that way, he can fix anything that breaks," one of the petty officers whispered.

"I heard that, Betty. I'll have them strap you under the other wing. You they can drop with the bombs."

"I didn't say a word, Chief."

Kris left the sailors to their work. For the better part of the next half hour, she and Jack had a nice long discussion about the stupidity of what she was about to do. As usual, when he had most of the strong points on his side, the argument went long.

But Kris had the strongest argument on her side. The lives of his and her Marines depended on her having the best possible knowledge of the situation and making the best possible call of where to land . . . or to call the whole thing off.

Grumbling, Jack finally gave up. "Why did I ever let myself get tied up with a Longknife," he muttered, and went to check out what flight gear the Greenfeld folks had on hand.

A good thing, too. He rejected the first four sets offered, then called the chief in to do a thorough workup on the pressure suits that looked best.

Meanwhile, Kris checked in regularly with her team.

Chief Beni continued to have no success getting anything out of the alien site. They had hunkered down. Now there was nothing on the radio circuits. The chief could see footprints and vehicle tracks in the dust around the plant, but everyone appeared to have taken cover in the two sprawling buildings. The reactor was producing almost double its original power outputs. Several capacitors were charging up, but if there were lasers, they were still cold.

"Simply put, I know squat. Professor mFumbo and his boffins on the other ships, they know squat. These folks like to keep themselves a secret," the chief finished.

After that report, Kris was not surprised to find out Penny's persistent efforts to open some kind of communication with the aliens had borne no fruit. She'd enlisted the boffins in her effort. But her distributed brain trust had no more luck talking to the aliens than Chief Beni had taking their pulse.

"They really don't want to get to know us," Jack said, as Kris and he pulled on their green-camouflaged flight gear.

"Grampa Ray got into a long and bitter fight with the Iteeche because they could not figure out a way to talk to each other," Kris muttered, half to herself. "Now I'm getting us humans and the Iteeche into a war with someone who will not talk to us, no matter how hard we try."

"That's what it looks like," Jack agreed, checking the neck gasket of Kris's suit.

"Maybe if we can capture someone from this site, we can sit them down and force them to talk," Kris said, doing the same check for Jack.

"Somehow, I don't think hamburger and fries is going to make it happen," Jack said, as he handed Kris her helmet. "Even if you throw in a strawberry shake."

"Yeah," Kris said. "I'm afraid that if we did capture a few, they'd suicide just like the ship that attacked us. It's crazy. Someone or something has scared the daylights out of these people. They'd rather die than live as prisoners. The question I can't figure out is whether or not the fear is for some really honking-huge bug-eyed monster or if it's what that guy on the video is telling them, and they all believe it?"

"It would be nice if we could figure out what that dude is saying," Jack agreed.

Kris put on her helmet, dogged it down, and chinned the oxygen outlet. Gas whispered into the suit.

"Maybe we'll get lucky this time," Jack said. His own helmet on, their conversation continued as a kind of radio check. "Maybe someone will survive the mass suicide. Maybe someone will choose life over death."

"That's what I'm hoping," Kris said. "Try something often enough, and you're bound to get what you want."

Both the Greenfeld officer and command master chief were there to strap Kris into her strange ride. That was good. She banged her elbow on something hard.

"What's that?" she asked.

"It's always there," the lieutenant answered, telling her nothing.

The chief ducked his head in the cockpit. "Oh, that's a crowbar."

"Crowbar?" Jack echoed from his seat behind Kris.

"Yeah, back in the war they had problems getting the canopy open when they crashed. The pilots took to carrying crowbars with them. In the later refits, they actually hooked one to the side of the cockpit."

"Don't worry, Jack. We aren't going to crash," Kris said.

The reply from the guy in back didn't rise above a mumble.

Preflight finished, Kris flew GAC-7 over to the *Wasp* and tied into the drop bay but didn't leave the craft. The *Fury* went its way into a geosynchronous orbit thirty thousand klicks above the planet. The other four battleships, along with PatRon 10, dropped into low orbit. The tiny *Hermes* followed along in their wake.

The first orbit's pass showed them nothing new. They dropped probes that only verified that there was nothing to see. Two large, three- or four-story buildings sprawled in front of a steep ridge. The best guess was that a mine shaft of some sort projected down and into the rocky ridge. The best scientific opinion was that the pile of dirt beside one of the buildings was mine tailings, but the analysis of that residue didn't help them figure out what was going on inside the buildings.

The landing launches left the *Wasp* and battleships first. They would descend and loiter west of the site until Kris called them in. Kris detached from the *Wasp* last. Her descent would be steeper, letting her arrive over the aliens first.

Kris punched her braking engines, and whispered, "We're committed."

"God help us," Jack added.

Kris took the GAC across the alien site at fifty thousand feet, and came away none the wiser for it. She honked the craft around into a steeply descending turn and crossed it again at twenty thousand feet, hammering it with a sonic boom.

That triggered something.

"Lasers," Chief Beni shouted on net. "Rockets, too! I'm getting all kind of search and attack stuff for SAM guidance."

Kris slammed her craft into a right bank, then went immediately into a split S turn, diving for the ground at the same time.

Then the real fun started.

39

"Rockets are tracking us," Jack shouted from the backseat.

Kris only had time to glance over her shoulder for a second. Behind her, the alien site was obscured by smoke as wave after wave of rockets were ripple fired.

Most headed up. A few were headed for Kris.

Kris fired off flares and threw her craft into another S turn. That done, she popped chaff and more flares, then took off into another S, while aiming for the deck and praying her ugly old hog could still take as many gees as the ancient design specs called for.

The first rocket missed off to her right, but another exploded behind her, knocking her craft around. Like the good hog it was, it kept running, and Kris kept dodging.

Behind Kris, Jack was doing his best to get a view of the alien site. He slammed his helmeted head against the canopy first to the right, then to the left.

"I see infantry," Jack shouted on net. "Lots and lots of infantry deploying from the buildings."

There was a pause while he switched sides. "Two battalions. No make that three. Maybe four."

Again Kris heard his helmet bounce off the canopy as he

changed his viewpoint. "There are vehicles with them. Moving fast. Looks like guns on them."

Kris slammed out of one turn, just dodged a rocket, and hurled the old hog into another.

Jack didn't pause in his shouting this time. "Abort the landing. They are preparing to oppose the landing with a major force. Abort the landing."

"I hear you," came in the colonel's calm voice. "The landing is canceled. We will return to orbit."

"Don't go near the alien site," Kris said. "They're gunning for us."

"Understood. Avoid the alien construction."

"Enough of this noise. They are shooting at my ships," snarled Admiral Krätz. "I will show them you do not fire on an Imperial Greenfeld battleship."

Kris coughed as she came awake. There was smoke in the cabin. She could smell it inside her suit. That wasn't good.

"Jack, you okay?" she asked.

"I was wondering when you would rejoin the living," he said.

"I'm alive," she sputtered

"We need to get out of here."

"Yeah, I think you're right." Kris hit the button to eject the canopy.

Nothing happened.

"Ejector doesn't work," she said.

"I could have told you that. Nothing works on this busted bucket of bolts. Want to try that crowbar you and the chief were talking about that we'd never need?"

Kris glanced at her elbow, not easy with her suit half-pressurized. "It's not in its holder. Must have come loose when we crashed."

"Check at your feet," Jack suggested.

The bottom of the cockpit was a mess. "I can see daylight coming in. I think the crowbar busted out when we came down. It's probably in the mud somewhere up ahead of us."

"Won't help us there," Jack noted, then went on. "Let's try pushing the canopy together. On three. One. Two. Three."

Nothing happened.

"Can you climb up on your seat and put your back into that push?" Kris asked.

"I'll try."

A moment later, Kris was staring at Jack's butt and shouting, "One. Two. Three."

This time it budged. Several more concerted pushes later, and they found themselves sprawled in the mud beside the wreckage of their hog.

"There's an emergency kit in there somewhere?" Jack shouted. The smell of fire was getting stronger. Considering that Kris was still on her internal oxygen, it was looking like there was a whole lot wrong with this picture.

She clambered over Jack, found a bright yellow bag marked EMERGENCY behind his seat, and got it out on the third yank. She did that with no help from Jack.

She was about to comment on his unhelpfulness but lacked the breath, so she limited herself to doing the best mud-splashing run she could manage away from the now smoking craft.

Jack tried to stand up . . . and collapsed at his first step. "My ankle's shot," he yelped.

Kris dropped the survival bag and lurched back to give Jack a hand. With one arm around his waist and him leaning heavily on her, they struggled back to the yellow bag.

Kris grabbed it as they went by. Staggering from one step to another, they slipped and slid for a good fifty meters through the thick yellow mud.

Then the first fuel cell exploded.

"How long until the antimatter goes?" Jack asked.

"It's supposed to be safe for several days," Kris said.

"May I point out that it was provided by a Greenfeld lowest bidder," Nelly said.

"Let's move," Jack said through gritted teeth.

They actually started moving fast enough to make splashes. Some small creatures took flight. Kris aimed them off to their right, where a low ridge offered something of a shadow if the antimatter container lost battery backup.

Beside her, Jack grunted in pain but said not a word in protest.

A couple of hundred years later, they topped a saddle in the ridge and began to half stumble, half fall down the other side of it. Kris took a last look over her shoulder.

The old GAC had a cheery fire going, sending up gouts of black smoke. Far across the plain, several vehicles were hurrying toward the smoke, gun turrets pointed eagerly at the source of the fire.

"It looks like we got company coming," Kris said.

"Well, we did want to talk to them," Jack pointed out as cheerfully as his pain allowed.

"Yeah, but not as *their* prisoners," Kris said, in her own defense.

"Kris, what do I do?" Nelly asked. "The aliens blew up their computers when it looked like we'd disabled their ship. Do you have anything to blow me up?"

"No," Kris said.

"I've been organizing my own matrix for some time now," Nelly said. "I guess I could dissolve it. They'd know we had some pretty fancy materials, but they wouldn't get any information out of me."

"Let's not jump into any conclusions just yet," Kris said. "Nelly, can you reach anyone? Is there any net?"

"I can't pick up a thing, Kris. Not even the Greenfeld battleships thirty thousand klicks above us. We're on our own."

Kris glanced down as they struggled along. Their footsteps and the dragged bag left a clear trail from the smoking GAC right to them. There was nothing Kris could do about that. She might be able to find a rock outcropping. Maybe a cave. Knowing the Greenfeld people, there might be some weapons in the sack she was dragging.

Kris sneezed. The air in her suit stank of sulfur. What was outside was leaking inside. She sneezed again, clogging her breathing mask and getting junk all over the inside of her helmet visor.

This planet, like so many others, did not like her. Unlike the others, where she was just unwelcome for political and legal reasons, this one was making it personal.

Kris raised the visor so she could see. The outside air immediately assaulted her eyes, making them water.

"That's not nice," Kris muttered.

"My suit's leaking, too," Jack muttered.

Kris paused for a moment. Holding her breath, she did the

best she could to clean out her air mask. When she pushed it back on her face, the mucus seemed to help it seal better. That didn't help her eyes.

She took a moment to unzip the survival bag. Bad idea.

The zipper stuck with it halfway open, then jammed up hard there in the middle. Kris used her survival knife to cut the bag open, then rummaged in it for what she could. There were a couple of packages of emergency rations . . . which looked like they were as old as GAC-7, which was to say eighty years. The oxygen bottles looked to be no younger. There were a handful of flares that were mashed together.

They might fire off. Then again, they might not. On third thought, they might fire up if she looked at them hard.

It crossed Kris's mind that they might do to burn Nelly's matrix into something the aliens would never recognize. She found her hands trembling. It couldn't be at the thought of her own impending death. Or Nelly's. It had to be the exertion of dragging Jack through the mud and up the hill.

Yeah, that was it.

She found a flare gun . . . and tossed it aside. She had enough drawing her pursuers after her; she didn't need to send up a flare.

"Kris, I've got the colonel on net calling for you," Nelly announced.

"Tell him where we are."

"He wants you to send up a rocket or light off a flare."

"The flare I can do," Kris said. She set Jack down gently, then just as gently lifted the clump of flares out of the yellow sack. Keeping them at arm's length, she stepped off several paces. Deftly separating one out from the melted mass, she pulled off the top.

Nothing happened.

She tossed it aside and risked a second flare from the glob. When she flipped its top off, it fizzled for a second . . . and then went out.

"This is not working," she grumbled. She decided to flip the tops off both the remaining flares. Both came off.

One just lay in her hand. The other started to fizzle. It kept fizzling, neither turning into a full light nor going out. Kris made a face at the two failures of one sort or another in her hand and figured she couldn't do much worse.

"Don't you dare," Jack said.

But Kris was already tipping the fizzling flare over and pointing its small stream of fire into the dead one.

It caught.

The fire would have taken Kris's hand off if not for the flight gloves. However, inside the glove, her hand felt like it had been parboiled. Still, the flare shone bright as its manufacturer ever hoped it would.

"They see us," Nelly said.

"Oh, Kris, what am I ever going to do with you?" Jack said with a sigh.

"The flare is lit," Kris yipped, trying to shake the pain from her hand. "We are spotted. We're going to get rescued. And someone will put some ointment on my burn. What are you griping about?"

"Nothing," Jack said. "Nothing you're likely to listen to."

Two landers came toward them. One was low and breaking for a landing in front of them. The other was higher. It fired as it crossed over them. Its rockets flew past them and vanished beyond the ridge.

And were quickly followed by a huge explosion that kept on going for most of a minute. "I'd say that got the antimatter pod and the underwing armament," Kris said.

"And those aliens that were following us," Nelly said. "Two of their gun rigs were stopped, looking at the GAC. Two others were headed for us. Not anymore."

Kris waved as the lander came to a halt. From its aft ramp, two gun trucks full of Marines drove out and hightailed it across the dusty yellow plain toward the two downed flyers. Behind them, they left a plume in the thin air that might have mattered if the lander's sister hadn't settled a lot of alien hash.

Three minutes later, under the alert eye of a gunner at a rocket launcher, a medic was bagging Kris's burned hand. Something in the bag made the pain go away. She relaxed into the backseat of the gun truck as it made best speed for the lander.

"Another day, and I'm not dead yet," she muttered.

"Not for a lack of trying," Jack added.

"We stopped the Marines from landing into a trap," Kris pointed out.

"What is it with these jokers?" Jack asked no one in particular. "They won't talk to us. They cram all sorts of armament into a small little mining outpost, and did I mention, they won't say a word to us."

"I think you did, Jack," Kris said. Another try at talking to them and another complete failure. Another encounter and another fight. What was it with these people?

She was about to go to war with an entire alien race, and she had no idea why. Or what they were. Or what they wanted.

Well, she did know something. They didn't want to talk. And they wanted her dead. Her and anyone else they met.

This was crazy.

An observation that she was pretty sure her grampa Ray had made several times as he fought the Iteeche.

The takeoff run gave Kris a good look at the alien site. It boiled like an active volcano. Of the two buildings, not a stick remained. Of the people who had rushed out to defend it, not so much as a single body. The rock ran like flaming lava from the pounding it had taken from Greenfeld lasers.

The flight back to the *Wasp* was short and silent.

40

The *Wasp* had already broken orbit by the time Kris got back to the bridge.

"Prepare for high-gee acceleration," Sulwan announced from the navigator's chair.

"Let's get to that jump point," Captain Drago said. "We've wasted enough time on this distraction."

"Did they get off any warning message?" Kris asked.

"We can't tell for sure, but they don't seem to leave message buoys at the jump points. At least, we've never seen one," Drago said. "I checked with the other corvette skippers. None of us saw anything at any of our jumps."

"So there's not a web of trade or anything like that," Kris said.

"Lonely and solitary," Penny said. "That's the life they seem to lead."

The rest of the battle fleet followed the *Wasp*'s lead, hard acceleration until they were halfway to the jump point, then hard deceleration the rest of the way. Several hours later, the *Wasp* came to a halt a few kilometers from the jump point and launched the periscope to take a glance through.

"Nothing," Chief Beni reported once the electromagnetic sensor was through the jump point. "There's a sun making the usual noises and nothing else. We got here ahead of the hostiles."

They had won one gamble but must now take another.

If the aliens had beaten them into the system, Kris would very likely have called it quits. There was no way she could risk a long approach course toward the huge mother ship. Kris had to get in position to blast the mother ship, hopefully with its swarm of deployable ships still aboard. Otherwise, those ships, each several times the size of a battleship, would maul Kris's tiny fleet before it could so much as dent them.

Kris ordered her fleet through the jump into the next system. There, they'd make a mad dash to the jump the aliens would be entering from. If they got there first, they could set up an ambush.

If the aliens came through the jump before they got there, Kris would have to give the order to run for it.

And some very nasty aliens would know there was a starfaring race out here that they should hunt down and destroy.

Well, they'd encountered the *Hornet* before.

One small scout was one thing. It could be ignored. Eight large battleships would be something else entirely.

Kris led PatRon 10 through the jump, the tiny *Hermes* trailing only behind the *Wasp*. For her coming role, she'd need to be up front.

Kris found herself holding her breath.

First Sulwan announced that they were in the system they had aimed for.

Then the chief announced that they had the system to themselves. A few minutes later, he reported that all eight battleships had followed PatRon 10 through and were now in the system.

Only then did Kris take a breath.

Krätz had not turned back. For better or worse, Kris would have all the ships she needed for her tragically tiny ambush.

Once again, she was assaulted by the question. What was it in her that pushed her to take the entire human race to war? Not only the humans, but the Iteeche as well, to war with someone they had never met?

Kris had written in her report to King Raymond that she was doing this to save the avian people. She'd never met one of the bird race. She'd seen pictures brought back by the *In-*

trepid. She didn't know if they were a good people or were just as steeped in evil as the alien mother ship thundering down upon them.

Still, she and her small band of Navy and Marines were willing to risk not only their own lives but the future of their entire race to stop the hostile aliens.

Was it hubris or was it right?

Part of Kris wanted to run home and hide under the bed. She'd done it once, when a soccer game had gone horribly wrong after she'd been so drunk she made a series of stupid blunders. First she fell all over the ball, then she yelled at her team players. Then she screamed at her coach.

When Longknifes screw up, they do it big.

Was she committing the greatest Longknife screwup of all times? Was she about to top even Grampa Ray?

If she kept this up, she'd end up hiding under her bed on the *Wasp*. Her bunk had pullout storage drawers under it. She'd really have to work to curl up in one of them.

Kris took a deep breath and let it out slowly.

Generations from now, they would still be debating what she did here.

Assuming the human race survived long enough to have more generations.

"Captain Drago, take us to the next jump point at best speed," she ordered.

A moment later, the *Wasp* began to accelerate smartly to 3.5 gees. Behind her, a tiny fleet followed.

Kris, and the entire human race, were committed to battle.

41

The *Wasp* was in free fall, but Kris was tightly strapped into a high-gee station chair, as was everyone else on the ship. At any moment, the *Wasp* might slam into high-acceleration maneuvers; but for now, it drifted in space, making like a rock.

It even looked like a rock. The defensive shield was deployed, but rather than looking like a parasol with a smooth, reflective surface, it was intentionally textured to resemble the surface of an asteroid. An asteroid that rolled gently as it drifted through space.

Nelly had added that bit of realistic artistry.

The other three corvettes of PatRon 10 drifted in a very loose formation around the *Wasp*, following the general orbit of the jump point. Their defenses also were deployed to make them look like rocks when observed from the nearby jump point.

In the back of Kris's head a children's song kept repeating itself annoyingly. "I'm just a little rock asteroid, pay no attention to me." The words of the ditty were wrong; she didn't remember how the melody went. But somehow it all fit the situation she found herself in.

While PatRon 10 drifted a scant twelve thousand klicks from the jump point, the eight battleships marched and countermarched in a line some eighty thousand klicks away from where they expected the alien ships to appear. That was close to maximum effective range for the 18- and 16-inch lasers of the battleships. Hopefully, whatever battle lasers the aliens had wouldn't be all that better at that range.

With any luck, they'd be a lot worse.

In a short while, they'd know.

The *Hermes* was stationed at the jump point. It was just deploying the periscope. Kris adjusted her Weapons station to get that feed when it produced the first glimpse of what was taking place in the next system.

Kris's gasp was joined by many others.

The view was of the rear end of the mother ship, so huge it had to be seen to be believed. A hundred (Nelly counted them) monstrous rocket engines blasted away, decelerating the alien ship as it finished its breaking maneuver and came to rest at the jump point. The sight of the roiling engines filled the view, leaving hardly a rim of black space around it.

The picture winked out as the visual periscope was withdrawn and an electromagnetic sensor took its place.

"Do we have an analysis of those engines?" Kris asked.

"Bigger than anything I've ever seen," the chief said. "I'd give my right arm to run a spectrum analysis of what's coming out of those engines."

"What's on your mind, Chief?"

"It might tell us where they got their reaction mass. Also, it might tell us how good they are at recycling. If they're dumping all their trash and sewage in their reaction mass, then they're going to need to plunder a planet more often than if they're green."

"I don't think they really care," Captain Drago said. "Talk to me about what you do know, Chief."

"There's an extra huge reactor behind each of those hundred rocket engines, feeding plasma directly into them. There are another several hundred or so reactors, just as huge, distributed along the length and breadth of that monster. What is it, four thousand kilometers long?"

"Something like that," Kris said.

"Along the surface of that thing there are thousands and thousands of reactors. Maybe tens of thousands of reactors. Smaller, but big. Battleship-size reactors in the tens of thousands."

"That's the fleet of big ships Commander Taussig warned us about."

"Is it too late for us to run away," the chief almost whimpered.

"Yes, Chief, it's too late. We either talk or fight. No running," Kris said. But the feelings in her gut were no different from those the chief must be feeling.

What have I gotten us into?

The time for second thoughts was past. "Battle line. Turn toward the jump. Accelerate toward it, then, on my order flip ship," she commanded.

The battleships had been ignoring normal orbital ballistics and instead had marched and countermarched eighty thousand klicks from the jump. Sometimes Admiral Krätz was in the lead, then they reversed course, and Admiral Kōta had the honors. Since no one complained, Kris guessed it was working.

As luck would have it, Krätz was currently in the lead. At his order, the battleships did a right turn, in column, and accelerated toward the jump.

Kris watched her board as all the information coming in from the *Hermes*'s probe reported on the mother ship. It seemed to be just about dead in space, several hundred klicks from the jump. Ponderously, it began to twist in space to bring its bow head on to the jump. The view that they got of its length and width was enough to make a brave man cry.

"I've got several of the smaller reactors jacking up power," Chief Beni announced.

"That would be the scout ships," Kris said. "So, she is going to send a few scouts through before she comes herself. Chief, I would dearly like to know how many of those huge scout ships we're going to face.

"Admiral Krätz, would you please flip your battleships and begin decelerating at one-half gee toward the jump," Kris gently ordered.

"It is done," the Greenfeld admiral answered.

"*Hermes*, you may depart the jump."

"Moving, Commodore," Lieutenant Song answered.

The tiny courier ship jetted away from the jump, then cut all power and flipped ship, pointing her small silhouette back at the jump point. Then she did something that no courier ships had ever done before. She deployed a tiny Smart Metal™ shield and did her best imitation of a rock.

It wasn't very thick, but it did cover all her nose . . . and gave her the look of just another asteroid, only this one was clearly headed harmlessly away from the jump.

To give the *Hermes* even that small a shield, they'd scrounged all the scraps of Smart Metal™ in the fleet. They'd pinched a kilogram off each of the corvettes' shields. But a large chunk of that shield came from Kris's new shoes.

Abby had groaned as she plopped the new pair of sparkling high heels down on the wardroom table two mornings back. "You paid a pretty penny for those shoes, Your Highness."

"And that's important just now why?" Kris asked.

"You're all the time complaining about how your ball shoes hurt and why can't someone come up with a stylish shoe that isn't torture."

"I think every woman who's lived for the last five hundred years has made that complaint," Penny said.

"Well, these shoes are Smart Metal™," Abby crowed. "If you're dancing or showing off, they're stylish. You sitting down, or maybe running for your life, and they're sensible pumps. Just tell Nelly, and it's done."

"Why didn't you get me a pair of these earlier?" Kris yelped.

"These very shoes are the first sale ever made by the new company, woman. I get them just for you, and what do I get, you giving me lip and demanding to know why I didn't get them for you yesterday."

"I don't think we'll be going to many dances in the next week," Penny pointed out.

"But the *Hermes* does need a shield to hide behind," Kris agreed. "Turn them in. We need to hide the *Hermes* a whole lot more than my feet need to be comfortable at the next dance."

"Assuming they throw a victory ball for us," Abby said dryly.

So the *Hermes* now drifted away from the jump. She hid behind her shield's camouflage and closed down every electronic device on board, making like a hole in space just like the other ships of PatRon 10.

For what seemed like forever, nothing happened. The battleships closed to sixty thousand klicks from the jump and continued breaking. Kris didn't want them much closer.

But she very much wanted them to look like they were breaking toward the jump when they encountered the hostile aliens.

Kris wanted a lot of things. It didn't look like the gods of war were going to give her any of them.

"What's taking those aliens so long?" she muttered.

"Well, we did get here before them," Captain Drago noted. "They don't seem to be all that well organized."

Then an alien ship popped into existence smack dead ahead.

Admiral Krätz's ships were ranging the jump point, so their lasers and radar hit the ship and bounced off it. The backscatter was picked up by the passive sensors on the *Wasp* and the other corvettes. It told them a whole lot about the alien ship without them having to make so much as an electronic peep.

The alien ship was ten kilometers long. Its hull was elliptical, some five kilometers around at its widest point. Its skin was marked irregularly by lumps and bumps that did not proclaim their usage.

Admiral Krätz played his part superbly.

"Who are you?" he announced on the radio, pumping plenty of surprise into his voice. "And what are you doing here? Unknown ship that just jumped into this system, identify yourself," he demanded in perfect admiral mode.

His battle line also poured on the coal and went from decelerating at half a gee toward the jump point to accelerating at three gees away from the newly arrived alien ship. There was very little way on the ships, so they started opening the range between them and the alien ship in a matter of seconds. The impact on the crew must have been brutal, but they were battleship sailors and supposed to have hair on their chests.

And they'd been warned to prepare for just that.

The corvette crews weren't the only ones waiting in their high-gee stations for the fight to start.

The alien ship said nothing. It sent no signal at all. It did goose its engines enough to push it away from the immediate area of the jump. A half minute later, Kris saw why.

A second ship, just as huge, popped into view.

It also gave itself a bit of a power boost and was joined thirty seconds later by a third ship. While there had been utter silence from the alien ships so far, now the first ship fired off a ten-second message.

At that, the newest-arrived ship did a 180-degree flip. Which left Kris wondering again what it must be like to be crowded into one of those huge ships while it did maneuvers that knocked around the crew of ships as small as the *Wasp*.

Nose to the jump, the ship accelerated and disappeared back into the jump.

For the long minute while all this happened, the battle line did its best to make contact. The Greenfeld ships continued to demand communications with the stranger. The Musashi flagship sent a sequence of dots signifying the numbers from one to ten, as well as tonal sounds built around middle C. The Helvetica ships sent pi.

The aliens returned them all a disdainful silence.

Meanwhile, the battleships increased the distance between them and the aliens. They also spread out to give themselves plenty of room to maneuver if it came to a fight. The Greenfeld ships, now in the rear, began to stream ice particles and flakes of aluminum. These defensive measures were meant to throw off ranging lasers and radars as well as cause main battery lasers to bloom and weaken.

Kris hoped the signal was clear: *We want to talk. But we're not defenseless.*

Nothing continued to be the main thing happening.

The lead alien ship emitted a single radio signal.

And all hell broke loose.

Scores of lasers reached out from the nodes on the alien ships. Other bumps launched wave after wave of rockets.

Krätz's flag had been leading the squadron toward the jump. Now it was the last in line and closest to the alien ship. Scores of lasers reached out for it, found it, and slashed into it.

The *Fury* never had a chance. It exploded in a ball of fire that quickly vanished into the void of space.

LAUNCH TORPEDOES, Kris ordered Nelly, even as she also began to fire the *Wasp*'s lasers.

Faster than Kris could think, Nelly did what the two of them had planned. Eight antimatter torpedoes launched, accelerating at ten gees. Fast as they were, Nelly had taught them to jink, adjusting their spin and speed just enough to throw off a defensive-fire computer that wasn't as smart as Nelly.

It also helped that the *Wasp* lay in ambush only twelve thousand klicks from the vulnerable engines of the aliens.

Nelly also brought the *Wasp*'s four 24-inch pulse lasers to bear on the aliens' weapons nodes. After the laser and missile fire from the outpost, Kris had expected a dual attack, lasers and missiles. Nelly now aimed the lasers at ten-percent power, first at a laser node, then at a missile bay. Two lasers for one ship, the other two for the other.

At ten-percent power, the lasers could do a lot of destruction before their charge gave out. If the hostile ships were armored, Nelly was prepared to up the power.

They weren't protected. Nelly's shots wreaked havoc.

The hostiles were still fixated on the battleships. Their lasers reached out even as the surviving seven began to dodge and weave, making radical adjustments to their acceleration. Decoys and more ice, as well as the wreckage of the *Fury* made it harder for the aliens to aim their lasers.

Still, they were firing a lot of them. Several of the battleships took hits, but their ice armor did its job.

And the battleships were shooting back. Their 16- and 18-inch lasers slashed into the alien ships, doing their own slaughter against unarmored hulls.

Kris and Nelly had aimed four antimatter torpedoes at each of the aliens. Two each for the engines, and two others along the length of the hulls.

The aliens got one. The other seven slammed home almost in the exact same microsecond.

The alien ships blew apart like ripe melons slammed by kids with baseball bats.

One second they were there. The next moment there was little more than hot gas where they had been.

"What just happened?" Captain Drago said, his mouth hanging open.

"They can dish it out, but they can't take it," Kris said cautiously.

"That was just two of them. There are a lot more where they came from," Sulwan said, and got grunts of agreement from around the bridge.

"PatRon 10, you did good, staying to your cover," Kris said. The three ships with the Hellburners were in reserve for the mother ship. They'd sat out the fight per their orders. Still, Kris knew the temptation must have been great.

As she expected, Navy discipline held.

"Battle line, report," Kris said next.

"Kōta here. We got some of our tail feathers singed, but we're ready for the mother ship."

"Feel free to select your range," Kris told Kōta. "When the mother ship comes through, there will be no effort to establish communications. For the record, they fired first and without provocation. We will attack them immediately. PatRon 10 will launch Hellburners on sight. Expect no further orders. Longknife out."

Again, Kris spoke to ghosts.

Now they waited.

The clock ticked off minute after minute while nothing happened.

"Does it take longer to run a four- or five-thousand-kilometer-long ship through a jump point than it does to run a battleship?" the chief asked.

"Your guess is as good as mine," Sulwan said. "What we don't know about jump points would fill an encyclopedia. What we do know you could write on the head of a pin."

"Maybe they're waiting for one of their victorious ships to come back and tell them everything is fine here," Jack suggested on net.

"They'll be waiting a long time for that," Penny said.

"Stay sharp, folks," Captain Drago announced to all hands. "This boredom could end any second now."

The Weapons Division reported that eight more antimatter torpedoes had been loaded. "These are the ones with four times the usual charge. Use them well, Commodore," reported the leading chief of the division.

Admiral Kōta reported a strange thing about one of the rockets launched at the battle line.

"One of them seems to have been a fusion bomb," he said. "We're getting reports of radiation from the *Terror*. The captain thinks some of his men may be coming down with radiation poisoning."

"We knew they had them," Kris said. "Alert your secondary

laser batteries that the rocket they shoot down could save the ship."

"Already did so, Commodore. You be careful, too."

"We're doing our best," Kris said.

The dull and boring lasted for not quite four more minutes.

Suddenly, in less than a blink, there was a five-thousand-kilometer-long ship looming before them.

42

Before Kris even had time to think *Fire*, the alien fired off a barrage of hundreds of lasers. Maybe thousands.

A large chunk of the barrage was aimed at the battleships. Their location apparently had been reported by the ship that returned. Dodging made no difference when the whole sector of the sky was laced with laser fire.

Three battleships exploded in the first few seconds of the battle.

Rockets were going off in rippling salvoes, most of them headed for the battle line as well, but not all. Several volleys were directed aft.

Three smashed into the poor little *Hermes* and left her shattered, drifting in space. A moment later, the reactor went when its magnetic containment either failed or was deliberately turned off.

In a flash, the plucky little courier and her crew were no more than a bubble of hot gas.

The *Wasp* had recently had two 5-inchers added for her own defense, and they kept her bit of space clear. One laser did clip the *Wasp*'s shield, but it held. The other corvettes fared well, except for the luckless *Fearless*, which took three lasers, one of which got past her shields.

The squadron hurt, but the squadron also dished it out.

The three Hellburners took off at a rapidly increasing acceleration, following the same corkscrew flight path Nelly had worked out for the *Wasp*'s first set of antimatter torpedoes. Two were aimed at the aft engines of the mother ship. The third would hit about a thousand klicks farther in.

All four corvettes also salvoed their eight antimatter torpedoes. They were smaller, but they were definitely incoming as far as any defensive fire net was concerned. Coming in faster, they also had to be higher up a defensive decision tree for assigning final defensive fire.

At least, that was what Kris devoutly hoped.

To add to the aliens' complicated fire solution, twelve 24-inch pulse lasers were reaching out for the nodes that held the lasers. One of the corvettes targeted four of the huge rocket motors. They cut past the rocket motors and into the reactors behind them. Even before the torpedoes hit, the fantail of the huge mother ship was exploding.

Twenty-nine antimatter torpedoes hit first, blasting gaping holes in the engines. Several of the reactors began venting to space, adding a slight wiggle to the huge mother ship's movement and throwing off the aim of the lasers.

Then the first two Hellburners hit.

The entire stern of the huge ship disintegrated. One second it was there, looming over them . . . burning here, exploding there . . . but still very much there.

The next second it was a gigantic ball of gas, bulging with secondary explosions as this or that reactor lost integrity and blew. Jets of hot gases vented in all directions, knocking the ship around and bending the gigantic hull in places that weren't meant to bend.

Here and there, the smaller ships, double or triple the size of a battleship, were sent hurling off into space like children's jackstraws.

Many collided. Several exploded.

The third Hellburner seemed to have taken a laser hit. The exact content of the visual record would long be debated. If it was hit, the finely spun-out chip of a neutron star didn't seem to mind being warmed up before it blew.

The last Hellburner dived into the edge of the glowing cloud and slashed its way deep into the wreckage before it added its own destruction.

By the time it finished, pretty close to half of the mother ship was blown to glowing gas or left as burning and twisted metal.

Which didn't cause the ship to hesitate one second.

Reduced to a drifting, spinning hulk, the mother ship kept right on firing its huge battery of lasers. Even unaimed, that much firepower could be devastating if it connected with something.

Another battleship blossomed into a ball of glowing gas. A quick glance showed Kris the battle line was gone. Two lonely ships had made it out of range of the aliens' wild fire.

"We can't hold here," Admiral Channing said on net. "We're running, Commodore. Get your little boys out of here any way you can. We can't help you."

"That big mother just launched three of her little monsters," Chief Beni shouted.

"Dive for the jump point," Kris ordered.

"The jump point!" Captain Drago yelped.

"You know a faster way out of here?" Kris yelled. "Blast us into the jump point the alien just came out of."

"Sulwan, jump," he ordered. "Kris, are there any hostiles left in the other system?"

"We'll find out. PatRon 10, the rally point is in the system the aliens just left. Follow me through the jump point if you can."

Sulwan slammed the *Wasp* into three gees with no warning.

The *Wasp*'s shields took another hit. This one was not all that well focused; it had bloomed badly as it shot through the cloud from the destroyed aft end of the mother ship.

For a horrible moment, the huge wreck loomed wide in front of the *Wasp*, ready to fold it into its own destruction.

Then the jump point took them, and the space ahead of them was a void.

43

The system was blessedly empty, Chief Beni reported immediately.

"Keep up the acceleration," Captain Drago ordered his navigator. "Aim us for the nearest jump point. I don't care what our speed is when we hit it."

"Aye, aye, sir."

"Chief, tell me who makes it through after us," Kris said.

"The *Hornet* just got here. She's doing 2.75 gees and still accelerating," he replied.

"Sulwan, let's give him plenty of room," the skipper ordered.

"I'm taking her up to 3.75 gees, sir."

"Good girl."

"The *Intrepid* just arrived, sir. She's also accelerating like a bat out of hell with its tail on fire."

"Fine, Chief. We've all got our tails singed," Kris said.

"The *Fearless* just came through, sir. She's decelerating!"

"*Fearless*, state your condition and intent," Kris snapped.

"We're here. We can fight, but we can't run, Commodore," *Fearless* said evenly.

Kris found herself struggling for words. "How fast can you run?"

"Not fast enough," she said. "That first hit clobbered my

hull integrity. Anything above two gees, and she'll fold like a house of cards."

"We can come back for you."

"And all get killed," she said. "Bad idea, Commodore. Besides, I've always wanted to see what it was like to be Horatio at the bridge. Here's my chance."

What do you say to that kind of courage? "Thank you, *Fearless.*"

"Godspeed to the rest of you. Be sure one of you gets home to let them know what we did here," *Fearless* said as she swung her corvette around to behind the jump point.

"We will," Kris said. She had no right to believe that any of them would make it home. Not now. But at that moment, she swore to any listening god that one of them would.

The first enemy ship came through at that moment, lasers firing wildly. The *Wasp*'s shield got nipped by a near miss before the *Fearless* put two torpedoes into the rear of the ship and it blew to pieces.

There was a minute pause before the next ship shot through the jump point. It withheld fire for a moment until it could establish situational awareness.

Bad idea. The *Fearless* hit one of its engines with a laser burst. It was already exploding when two torpedoes finished it off.

By now, the three fast-moving ships of PatRon 10 were reaching extreme laser range. A long two minutes passed while nothing happened.

Three more ships popped out of the jump point in rapid succession. The *Fearless* lasered the first one's engines. It blew.

The second one got the same treatment.

The third one immediately began to rotate ship and fired its lasers into the area behind it.

Fearless's shields took the first hit, which gave it time enough to fire two full laser blasts at the smart skipper and his deadly ship. Torpedoes arrived at the same time. Of four launched, two hit the rotating ship and it blew to gas.

But the *Fearless*'s shields were gone, and one of the enemy ships had clipped the *Fearless* good.

Kris wanted to turn the sensors off, give the *Fearless* the privacy to die in peace, but she couldn't. She owed the ship and its captain and crew. The coin she would use to pay that debt would be to bear witness to their courage.

Bear witness before all humanity. All intelligent species of the galaxy.

That, Kris's tiny fleet deserved.

The next enemy ship backed through the jump point. He flipped ship on the other side of the jump after putting acceleration on. He also came through with lasers blazing.

His wild shooting got the *Fearless* with three hits. The shattered corvette hung there, drifting in space for a moment, then blew herself to gas.

"Somebody shut down the reactor's containment field," Drago whispered. "They won't get anything from examining that wreckage. May I have the courage to do the same when my time comes."

. But the *Fearless* hadn't just rolled over and died. She'd hit the alien with at least one laser blast . . . and a final torpedo salvo that smashed into it even as the *Fearless* was blowing herself to hot vapor.

The alien wasn't destroyed, but it wasn't under control, either. It careened into a chunk of damaged hull from one of the earlier arrivals at the brawl. It drifted there, surrounded by the wreckage of a battle won at a terrible cost.

And when the next ship came shooting out of the jump point, it plowed into that wreckage. The collision ended with both of them in a slowly growing explosion.

The next ship came through slowly and tiptoed through the mess before it put two gees on and gave chase to the survivors of PatRon 10.

There were over fifty ships strung out in pursuit of them by the time the *Wasp* approached the closest jump.

"What are your intentions, Commodore?" Captain Drago asked Kris.

"To get as far away from here as possible," she quickly answered him. "Preferably in the opposite direction from Earth."

"That sounds like a plan," Drago said. The *Wasp* was doing over two hundred thousand klicks an hour. Much more than it had for any of the jumps during their voyage of discovery.

"Sulwan, put twenty clockwise rpms on the ship and let's see where this jump takes us," the skipper ordered.

"Aye, aye, sir. Hell, here we come," the navigator answered.

44

All three of the surviving corvettes of PatRon 10 made it through the jump. Under Kris's orders, they fled for the nearest jump point, watched by a blood red sun.

Once Chief Beni located them on the star charts, he estimated they'd jumped close to fifteen hundred light-years. They were on the far outer rim of the Milky Way. And as best as either the chief or Nelly could tell, the system should not have had a jump point into it at all.

That they were very likely lost ranked as the least of their problems.

They were a third of the way to the next jump when the aliens began pouring through the jump behind them. Most of them held to a solid two-gee acceleration. A few tried to put on three gees, but most of those soon fell back to something less stressful on engines and hulls.

Sulwan held the *Wasp* at 3.75. They expanded their lead over their pursuers.

Then the *Intrepid* began to fall out of formation.

"Commodore, we have a problem here," *Intrepid* reported.

"Battle damage?" Kris asked.

"Engineering thinks it's just an old-fashioned material failure," he said, not that the difference between them made either any less deadly.

"Can you fix it?"

"Not without banking down the reactors for a couple of hours," he said. "We can hold two gees, which should keep us ahead of the thundering herd. At least for a while," he added sardonically.

"You want us to fall back and pick up your crew?" Kris offered.

"No. One of us has to get back. You keep going hell for leather. We'll keep up as best we can."

The *Wasp* and *Hornet* gradually stretched out their lead.

"How are we going to take this next jump?" Kris asked Sulwan and Captain Drago. Before that last jump of theirs, no one had ever taken a jump at much over fifty thousand klicks per hour, and they were rapidly edging up toward four hundred thousand klicks.

"We were thinking of hitting this next one at what we're doing now," Captain Drago said, thoughtfully. "Keep accelerating for another third of the trip, then decelerate for the last third."

"Will our next system be in this galaxy?" Kris asked.

"Your guess is as good as mine," Sulwan said. "But if the aliens continue to hold to only two-gee acceleration, we might jump farther than them."

"I guess it's worth the risk," Kris agreed.

Captain Drago hunched over his board for a moment, eyeing it like he might a potential traitor. "We won't be able to keep this speed up for too much longer. We'll need enough reaction mass to slow us down. Otherwise, we'll end our days drifting around real fast, going nowhere."

"I hadn't thought of that," Kris admitted.

"That's what they pay me for," Captain Drago said with just the hint of a smile.

"How long do you think those alien ships can keep up this chase?" Kris asked.

"The reading I got on them is that they are pretty dense," Chief Beni put in.

"There didn't seem to be a lot of tankage for reaction mass on that one we shot up," Captain Drago noted. "It's just possible they may have to break off their chase for lack of fuel if we can keep this up a bit longer."

"What are the chances they want to see us dead so much

that they will chase us until their tanks are dry? What if the fellow doing all the talking on those videos doesn't give a fig about his minions so long an anyone different from him does not live in this galaxy?" Penny asked over the net, ever the speculating intelligence officer.

That brought the conversation to a roaring halt for a while.

"I imagine if I'd just seen a third to half of Earth blasted to hot gas, maybe a third to half of all my race blown to bits, I might not be all that interested in giving up the chase for them what done the deed," Abby drawled.

That put an end to speculation.

For the next nine hours, the *Wasp* and *Hornet* shot across space at ever-increasing speed. While the ships raced and the enemy ships chased, there was little to do, and the high-gee stations gave little encouragement to doing it.

Kris slept at her battle post in her high-gee station for maybe three hours. It gave her some respite from the nagging doubts that ate at her.

Against them she had a simple defense. It was done, and the only thing they could possibly do was run. Whether they would succeed or fail at running depended on matters she had no control over.

They hit the next jump at slightly over 450,000 klicks per hour, with forty revolutions per minute on the boat. The jump left Kris dizzy.

Nelly reported while the crew was recovering, "We're still in the Milky Way, folks. But I have no idea where we are yet. I sure miss all that gear the boffins brought with them, Captain."

"Yes, Nelly. Thank you, Nelly. Now save your lip for your princess. Remember, I'm the skipper. I can space you."

"I thought Kris was the skipper now."

"Wrong, Nelly," Kris said. "When it comes to spacing unruly people and computers, Drago is still the man."

"You humans never do anything rationally. But while you were jabbering about who is in charge of this madhouse, *I* have located our place in space. Kris, if you want to be as far from Earth as you possibly can be, we are there. If you look off to the right, you will see the void of intergalactic space."

"Are there any jump points?" Drago asked.

"Three. Two of the old-fashioned ones and one of my new fuzzy ones. May I suggest that we head for that one?"

"If we disappear into a jump point that isn't there, it's bound to make the neighbors talk," Kris said.

"If we get there fast, maybe they won't be here when we do that disappearing thing," Nelly said.

"Folks, Engineering asks if we can please take it down to 3.5 gees," Sulwan said. "The engines were never meant to hold this acceleration for this long."

"The *Hornet* has joined us," Chief Beni announced.

"Now we wait to see if the *Intrepid* and the aliens make the jump," Captain Drago said. "And yes, Sulwan, take us down to 3.5 gees and make for the fuzzy jump."

A few moments later, Lieutenant Commander Phil Taussig came on-screen. "I see you also need to slow down. Engineering tells me that if I don't want to end up drifting in space, I've got to cut back to three gees."

"We can still make 3.5," Captain Drago said.

"You do that. I notice you're headed for the fuzzy jump. We'll head for the closest normal one."

"You don't have to," Kris said.

"I think it's time and past time for us to separate if there's going to be any chance of one of us making it back home. If I were a betting man, I'd bet the *Intrepid* will try to repeat what the *Fearless* did at the first jump. I know that I would. They might just buy us enough time to escape."

Kris knew that as a combat commander and as one of those damn Longknifes, she should be accepting these gifts, even ordering her subordinates to make these sacrifices. She found that, deep in her gut, she didn't want to do it.

Maybe she had chosen the wrong profession. Maybe she wasn't fit for anything better than planting the garden around Nuu House each spring.

Maybe she'd hide in the garden next year, but now she would do what she had to do. That was what Longknifes did.

"That sounds like a plan," she said. "Sulwan, keep all the acceleration you can on the *Wasp*, no flipping ship. We'll go through this jump with all the speed and rotations we can put on the boat."

"I'll have to start decelerating as soon as we get through," Captain Drago said.

"We'll burn that bridge when we come to it," Kris said.

The *Wasp* was over halfway to the fuzzy jump when the *Intrepid* shot out of the jump, spinning. To no one's surprise, she immediately began braking.

"I'm glad we could make the party," *Intrepid*'s skipper said on net.

"Glad you're here. What can you tell us about the aliens?"

"About half the fleet has given up the chase. Fifty-four are still chasing us. They accelerated the whole time at two gees, which was about all I could do, so I suspect they'll be coming through here in a couple of hours. If they do, the *Intrepid* will be waiting for them. Is the *Wasp* headed for the weird jump point?"

"Yes. We're splitting up."

"Good idea. With any luck, you should be able to duck out of the system with none of them the wiser about where you went."

"That's what we're hoping."

"Good luck and Godspeed. By the way, Commodore, it's been an honor to serve with a Longknife. At least this particular one."

Kris found a catch in her throat. "Thank you, *Intrepid*. Good luck to you all."

The *Wasp* fled for the new-type jump point. Sulwan had to cut her acceleration down to 3.4. An hour later, she reduced to 3.3 gees. Kris had Nelly do her own check on the reactors and engines.

KRIS, THE ENGINES AND REACTORS ARE WAY IN THE RED. THE CHIEF ENGINEER IS DOING SOME VERY STRANGE THINGS TO HOLD HIS TEAKETTLE TOGETHER.

The chief engineer was performing miracles, doing first this and then that to cool them. He ended up bleeding water around the edge of the ion stream between it and the jets. Not only did he cool the jets, but he seemed to be getting extra speed as the expanding water tightened the throat of the jet and forced the ion stream to even higher speeds. That, in turn, let him take more pressure off his reactors.

It also used up reaction mass at a blinding rate.

They were rapidly closing in on the fuzzy jump point when the first alien ship shot into the system.

The *Intrepid* had slowed down and swung around to return

to the jump. She just managed to get behind the jump as the alien shot through. She hit the alien with two lasers to the engines and backed that up with a torpedo.

The alien blew into fine particles of gas before she ever got her forty rotations off the ship.

The next alien ship came through alone and came through shooting. She nipped the *Intrepid*'s shield but still took two laser hits and a pair of torpedoes. Like the first, she went to pieces. Very little ones.

There was a pause, and Kris was starting to hold out hopes that the other ships had hit the jump too slow to make the long passage, but then three ships came through in rapid succession.

All three were shooting off every laser and rocket they had, even as they were flipping ship to fire to their rear.

Spinning like a dervish, it was amazing they could hit anything

The *Intrepid* got the first one. A laser hit blew out an engine, then two torpedoes slashed into the ship's vulnerable engines while they were still hers to hit.

The human ship tried the same treatment on the second one, but the alien managed to flip her vulnerable engines away from the incoming fire. The *Intrepid* badly damaged her, but doing that damage took time.

The third alien blew the gallant *Intrepid* to flaming gas even as two torpedoes slammed into it, leaving her little more than a wreck.

That was the last thing Kris saw before the *Wasp* shot into her jump making over seven hundred thousand kilometers an hour and spinning at forty revolutions a minute.

45

"Sulwan, take her smartly down to one gee," Captain Drago ordered. "Get her out of this merry-go-round mode as soon as you can, but take the pressure off the reactors and engines first."

"Engineering says we need to take the power down slowly," Sulwan answered. "Everything is so hot down there that if we go too cold too quickly, something may snap."

"Then you tell Engineering that it's her call. We slow down when she says we slow down. Just tell her that the bridge would like to be included in any idle rumors coming out of that den of thieves."

"Roger, sir."

Captain Drago now turned to his next-most-important issue. "Chief, I don't care where we are, but I sure would like to know if this system has a gas giant, a gas dwarf, an icy planet, or any other place we might find reaction mass."

"That's what I've been hunting for, sir," the chief answered.

"We're still in the Milky Way," Nelly reported. "I think we jumped about a quarter of the way around the rim. We may very well have to go through Iteeche space to get back to human space, but they are both still a long way off."

"Any activity in the system?" Kris asked.

"Other than three suns radiating their hearts away, nothing," the chief said, then went on. "Skipper, there are three gas giants in the system. We're closest to the smallest of the three."

"Give Sulwan the course, and let's get going."

"Are we actually going to go cloud dancing with the *Wasp*?" the chief asked.

"It's either that or we get out and push the *Wasp* home," Captain Drago grumbled. "I don't know about you, but I vote for refueling."

"Can she hold together?" squeaked the chief.

"Now that she's gotten rid of most of those crates that add weight and mess up her lines, of course the old lady can. But just to be on the safe side, we'll park the rest of them in orbit and muster all hands in the hull spindle, okay, Chief? That worry you less?"

"I guess so."

"Now, folks," the skipper went on, "we're going to be very busy in a couple of days doing the kind of work that makes hands blister, so why don't you all take this time to catch up on your rest . . . and get out of my hair."

Kris gave the rest of the bridge crew a good example by powering back her high-gee station, but she couldn't close her eyes. Now if an alien did shoot through the jump, there would be no more running. True, the *Wasp* would put up the best fight she could, but it would be a short one.

Kris watched her board and watched the chief watch his. Nothing showed up as the time went long. Kris found her eyes growing heavy; the battle had taken its toll.

NELLY, CAN YOU KEEP A WATCH OUT FOR HOSTILES? Kris asked.

THE CHIEF HAS HIS DA VINCI COVERING FOR HIM, TOO, Nelly answered. IF YOU FALL ASLEEP, I'LL WAKE YOU IF THINGS GET INTERESTING. GO AHEAD. THE SKIPPER SAID SLEEP. DO IT.

Apparently, Kris did manage to nap. The next thing she heard was Sulwan's announcement to all hands, "We're down to 1.5 gees, folks. You can quit lounging around in your high-gee stations."

Kris found she needed a hand up, which the young 2/c gunner's mate who backed her up on weapons was only too ready to supply.

Kris headed for the head, which put her third in line for the facilities. A stuttering young ensign was only too willing to offer Kris her place in line, but Kris didn't need to go that desperately, quite, and she figured if she did, the story about one of those damn Longknifes pulling rank to get to the head of the head line would be around the ship before she was out of the stall.

She waited like her father had taught her to do, as any good politician's child better do.

Chow that night was steaks, more stuff scrounged from the now-long-gone restaurants from the good old days. Cookie let everyone know they better enjoy his chow while they could, it would be wormy hardtack and salt pork before this cruise was over.

Kris hoped it wouldn't be that bad, but she didn't contradict the old cook. Something told her he knew more about maintaining morale than she was likely to ever learn.

Despite the nap, Kris found herself falling asleep at the wardroom table. She managed to stumble to her quarters and fall into bed still dressed.

Exactly when the nightmares came, it was hard to tell, but she came awake screaming and covered in sweat at 0200 ship time. For the next two hours visions of ships dying held her hostage as they ran over and over in her mind's eye.

When sleep finally returned, it was hardly less exhausting than wakefulness.

46

Kris stumbled into the wardroom for early breakfast. She'd given up on risking further sleep.

The colonel and Penny were already there, and Jack and Abby straggled in before Kris had drawn little more than dry toast and coffee for herself. At the table, they stared bleary-eyed at each other.

"That was one bad night," the colonel said, taking a sip from his coffee cup.

"I don't never want to sleep through that again," Abby agreed.

"I'm glad we're all agreed that that mean kitty should be belled," Jack said. "Any idea how we do it?"

"Cops have incident interventions, or so my dad told me. Somebody has to use their weapon, they get sat down and talk it through. Someone gets suddenly dead, it gets more serious," Penny finished.

"What could get more serious than this week," Kris said, pushing her toast away. She was hungry, but she couldn't eat.

"May I suggest we 'cry-tique' this puppy," the colonel offered. "It might not do a whole lot, but if we can all review what we saw, squeeze it of any information we can, then develop a single narrative we can all stand by, it might help. If we can agree that this choice, bad as it was, was far and away better than the other options, we might save ourselves from running the question over and over in our minds late at night."

He paused for another sip of steaming coffee. "I know talking over that little fight we had on Panda has helped me come to accept that the princess here simply outplayed me. Not that my employers had dealt me all that good a hand."

"I have most of the data saved," Nelly said. "I can project it here, or in Kris's Tac Center."

Kris looked around the room. It was filled with other officers just as bedraggled by the night as her team. She shook her head. "Let's figure out what happened first before we subject the rest of the crew to our nightmares."

They headed for the Tac Center.

Nelly had the main screen already showing the deployment as the monstrous mother ship made its appearance.

"Okay, Nelly, what happened to the battle line while the corvettes were all otherwise busy?"

"All those big battleships didn't fare very well," Nelly said, and pictures began to flash on the screen. "I think we guessed right that the range of the aliens' heavy lasers was no greater than ours, but we underestimated how many of them they could fire up. The *Fury* took an entire broadside from the first two scouts and blew up before it knew what hit it."

"We all saw that. What happened to the other battleships?" Kris asked.

"From its ambush position, the *Wasp* took out the first two alien ships, Kris, and the battle line turned away. They had opened the range to just about maximum when the mother ship came through. That big mother had all kinds of lasers, and she used them. Even though the lasers were cutting through the gases left by the *Fury*'s wreck and the ice trailed by the other ships, they were hit with so many beams that it knocked five of them out of the fight one right after another. Each of them ended with an explosion when the reactors lost containment. I think those were all intentional."

Kris nodded. She had been busy with her own shoot at the time, but the pictures Nelly flashed on the screen were the sights that had filled Kris's dreams. Somehow, she had seen, out of the corner of her eye, the destruction of the battle line. Unprocessed, it haunted her nightmares. Now, with a deep sigh, Kris forced herself to witness that gallant force's annihilation.

It wasn't fair, she wanted to say. Men like Admiral Krätz and Admiral Kōta were fighting men. They deserved a fighting chance. What they got was laser fire so massive and wideranging that no matter how well they fought their ships, how they jinked or jumped, they were slaughtered. Kris watched the ships die, knowing that Professor mFumbo, and Judge Francine, and so many others of the people she'd shared the *Wasp* with for so long were vanishing in a blink.

She faced her dragon, fed it a tidbit, and, as best she could, made friends with it. Surely, for the rest of her life, she'd never be able to lose this beast.

"Did anyone get out of the battleships before they blew?" Penny asked after a long silence that must have been filled with quite a few silent prayers for the dead.

"There were plenty of survival pods off those five battleships," Nelly said. "The aliens lasered every last one of them. The aliens were firing fast and wild, so there's no way to tell if they just got in the way or if fire was actually aimed at them. I've searched the visuals several times, Kris. The only survivors from the battle line were the sole Greenfeld ship and Admiral Channing's *Swiftsure*, which fled."

"And last we saw of that pair, they had escaped out of range of the mother ship's lasers and her baby monster ships and were running for all they were worth," the colonel added.

"With several hundred of those baby monsters in hot pursuit," Nelly reported.

Kris thought for a moment how long and hard the pursuit of PatRon10 had been and how it dwindled down to just the *Wasp*. She found no reason to ask her team what they thought were the chances that one of the two battleships might get away.

If they made it, they'd all meet back in human space. If they didn't, maybe the survivors would find the wreckage later.

Kris shook herself, willed herself to turn away from the slaughter of the battleships and to focus on the future. "Well, at least we've found a way to fight them. We can turn the jump points into a death trap for them."

"Don't be too sure of that," the colonel said. "I've been thinking about what we did to them and what we saw of them.

I had my computer, Don Quixote, look up a few things about warfare back in the bad old days before atomics were fully outlawed. I don't much care for what I found."

"I know you're going to tell us," Kris said. "How bad is it?"

"There's an ugly thing called electromagnetic pulse. It seems that the explosion of a nuke throws out a radiation pulse, especially if it's done in space. It fries all the local electronics unless they've been hardened."

"That's a rude thing to do," Nelly said.

"Hardened?" Kris echoed. "Nelly, do you know anything about this 'hardened' thing?"

"Don Quixote warned us all about it when he found it out for the colonel, Kris. If they'd sent one of their bombs through the jump first and blown it up, it likely would have converted all our computers and other electronic stuff to paperweights in one big flash. I do not like this pulse thing. When we get back, we need to search the old archives very thoroughly and find out how to do this hardening thing. There's nothing about it in any of our accessible data."

That didn't sound good, but Kris did not allow it to surprise her. That was what happened in a war. You surprised them with things like Hellburners, and they surprised you with things they had up their own sleeves.

Part of what made war so much of a bleeding hell was the bleeding surprises.

"Anyone have a guess as to how badly we hurt them?" Kris asked.

"The mother ship knows it's been in a fight," Nelly said. "We destroyed at least the rear third of the ship and did major damage as far as amidships. They were still able to power up their lasers and direct them from the forward half of the ship, but that ship was dead in space when we left it. In addition, the hulk had taken all kinds of twists and torque. The shock damage to its machinery in the forward half must be horrible." Nelly paused. "Casualties among the crew must start at a third and go up from there."

"However large that is," Kris said, thinking about all the people crammed into the small ship that first attacked them.

"Likely," the colonel said, "from what we've seen of the way they live, several billion dead. Maybe tens of billions."

"Which might explain why they showed no interest in taking any prisoners," Penny said.

"But all of this is just guesswork," Jack pointed out. "We went in there knowing almost nothing about our alien enemy, and we got out of there, as best we could, knowing nothing more about them."

"Nothing, except that when confronted with a battle fleet, they still shot first and answered no questions," Kris said, summing up the aliens in few words.

"I do not understand them," Abby said, shaking her head.

"From the evidence," the colonel went on, "I would say they are either intent on destroying any life that isn't theirs, or there is something else a whole lot worse out here that they are afraid of, and they think we might be from it. Any of you see another way to interpret the data?"

"If there's a bigger monster out there," Kris said, shaking her head, "wouldn't they be trying like we are to make a peaceful contact? Gain allies. My guess, Colonel, is that these folks like the galaxy their way and don't want to share it with any other life-form."

"I can't dispute your conclusion," the colonel said with a sad shake of his head.

"One more thought," Penny put in, as the silence after that conclusion grew long and ponderous. "Nelly, could you play the video where we hit one of their ships but didn't destroy it."

The video changed to show one of their giant ships, hit hard in the engines by the *Fearless* and drifting. It continued to fire wildly. Almost a minute went by before its reactors blew, and the ship was vaporized.

"Notice what we didn't see?" Penny asked.

"Survival pods," Kris said.

"Right. No one abandoned ship. They fought it as long as they were able, then someone in command ordered self-destruct, and the entire ship blew. They must have known for a whole minute that it was doomed, but no one abandoned ship. Furthermore, there was no reason to blow that ship. We were losing. It could have hung in there and been rescued by its own ships once the fight was over. It didn't."

"Dear God," Abby said in one of her rare references to any being greater than herself. "Victory or death. If they can't return on their shield, they will damn well blow up the shield," she said, misquoting the Spartan mother.

"And these nutcases just had to share our galaxy," Jack grumbled. "I can't tell you how happy I expect your grampas to be when we get home and drop this flaming hot potato right in their laps."

"They won't be glad," Kris said, "but they'll have to do something about this. They can't ignore it."

"Ever heard of that fine old tradition about killing the messenger?" the colonel tossed out.

On that fine thought, Kris headed up to the bridge to see how things were developing there. The view was spectacular, but hard to figure out.

How an old red giant and a young blue giant could now share the system with a white dwarf probably could be explained by a series of collisions. Kris had been told by the boffins that such driving accidents were frequent in the jumbled-up systems at the center of the galaxy.

How it happened out on the rim was a question Kris would hand off to the astronomers just as soon as she found one.

She shivered as she remembered that Professor mFumbo and so many other of the boffins she'd shared meals with and survived lectures from were either dead or had taken the early ship back to human space.

"Nelly, where did Judge Francine go?"

"Kris, she went aboard the *Triumph* with Admiral Channing."

Which meant she was still running or had been gunned down already.

Kris groaned inwardly. There was no way to know what happened until they got back and allowed enough time for the others to get back.

A voice in the back of her head refused to be placated. *You know they're already dead. Maybe the* Wasp *can get home, but none of the rest will. You lost almost your entire first command.*

Kris did not need to spend more time sitting on her rear listening to the voices in the back of her head.

Fortunately, the *Wasp* needed a lot of work, the kind that took Swedish steam. Strong arms and strong back. No brains required.

Kris turned to with a will.

The *Wasp* continued to decelerate, running at only a half gee by then. The chief engineer had taken one of the reactors off-line and had cooled half the rocket engines. Engineers and anyone fully qualified in space were crawling all over the engines identifying what had had it and pulling subunits where there was any chance that replacements were in stock or repairs could be made.

It turned out that there was a good reason why the *Wasp* had taken on all those sailors during the last few stops by Wardhaven. Her enlarged crew knew quite a bit about ship maintenance and set about doing it under the watchful eye of her skipper, officers, and chiefs.

And Kris found that her strange career path had deprived her of the opportunity to learn a whole lot about running a ship.

About the second time that Captain Drago tried to find something that she could do and came up dry, she gave up on working for a living and went hunting for the other folks who were mere passengers on this ship of fools. There was no Forward Lounge left, but Iteeche country still had a large room.

Kris called her staff together, with Vicky added, and settled down around a table with Ron.

"This is a fine mess you have gotten us into," he told her through his translator.

"You were the one losing ships and asked us to help," Kris pointed out.

"We were hoping to find out what was happening to our ships, not to get into a war with one monster of a civilization," he said, but then he shrugged. "If we were honest with ourselves, we must have known that we could find something like this.

"When I bring this report into His Majesty's presence, I may well be offered the Cup of Apology," the Iteeche went on. "But they will be hiding the truth from themselves in a polluted pond."

"Why is it that you and Kris are assuming that you'll be in trouble for this battle?" Vicky asked. "You did your best, and it needed doing. We all agreed on that. Well, we all did except my admiral, and I think he was just chicken."

"Maybe they feel this way because they have read a little

bit of history," Colonel Cortez said. "What's the old saying? No good deed goes unpunished."

Kris and her team spent the afternoon reviewing the battle for Ron the Iteeche and Grand Duchess Vicky. The two had little to add to what Kris had already concluded. They came, they saw, they got their butts kicked and got a couple of good kicks in themselves. Kris did her best to avoid putting a spin on any of it. One of the reasons she chose the Navy for a career was because she hated the way Father spun everything.

The walk back to the wardroom for supper was a harrowing experience. Welders were everywhere, adding patches to strengthen this or that portion of the hull. The chief had warned Kris that the *Wasp* was never designed for cloud dancing.

Clearly, the skipper was doing his very best to shore up those deficiencies.

Kris got a fuller briefing over supper when Captain Drago joined them.

"Before we deploy the balloot, I'm going to detach all of the shipping containers we've been carrying. That means a lot less room, Your Highness. I'm going to have to ask you to let your maid and her niece move in with you."

"What will you do with the Iteeche?" Kris asked.

"Something very careful," the skipper answered with a sigh. "I've also got welders outside cutting several of the spare containers into strips that we can use to reinforce the hull before we make the refueling pass. We'll have more reinforcing strips and welders handy during the refueling pass to patch what comes apart."

"Will it be that bad?" Jack asked.

"As your chief no doubt informed you, ships like the *Wasp* were never intended to do this kind of cloud dancing. However, if we want to make it home, we must refuel. I've got several of the best ship maintainers reviewing the design of the *Wasp* and identifying its weak points. We'll strengthen them now and have teams standing by as we make the fuel run to patch holes and shore up problems. Nevertheless, all hands will be in pressure suits for the pass," the captain added dryly.

"Not too optimistic, huh," the colonel observed.

"I serve with a Longknife. I parked my optimism in a locker back on Wardhaven. Once I'm done here, I'll check it back out, dust it off, and enjoy it for the rest of my natural life. But no, not today."

"What can we do?" Kris asked.

"Not a lot, Your Highness. The ship's crew has matters well in hand. When we start the pass, though, I would appreciate it if you and your team would form a damage-control detail."

"Could you use Nelly or one of her kids to help with the ship-strength-analysis efforts?" Kris asked.

"If you'll excuse me," Captain Drago said, getting up from the table with his meal only half-eaten, "I'd prefer to place my faith in men and material that have been trained and selected for this job. No doubt Nelly is superb at pulling things out of her nonexistent hat for this or that unforeseen emergency. Still, for this, I'll do things the old-fashioned way, thank you very much."

"Yes, of course," Kris said.

I COULD HAVE TOLD YOU HE'D SAY THAT, Nelly told Kris in the privacy of her own skull. I ALREADY OFFERED HIM A HAND AND HE PASSED.

THANK YOU, NELLY, Kris thought back.

As the hours stretched, and no alien ship came shooting into the system, Kris began to relax. They seemed to have slipped their pursuers. She tried not to think of what that meant for Phil Taussig and the *Hornet*'s crew.

That night, even sharing her room with Abby and Cara, Kris slept the repose of the dead. Until about midnight, when she woke up to the soft sounds of someone's crying.

Kris had given Abby the lower bunk and had taken for herself the top bunk, something that usually stayed folded away into the bulkhead. Cara had a blanket on the floor. Awoken, Kris found that her maid's niece had crawled in to share Abby's bed and was crying softly onto a shoulder.

"Hush now," Abby whispered with more softness than Kris would have expected from her hard-bitten maid as she stroked the girl's hair. She spotted Kris looking over the side of the top bunk.

"Don't worry. She's not awake. In a little while, she'll settle back down. She won't remember a thing in the morning."

Kris rolled over back into her bunk. During the day, Cara showed no ill effects from her time as a drug lord's slave. Kris hadn't known about the nights. So this was why Abby had been so adamant her niece would not be left behind.

The weeping subsided into soft kitten snores; Kris curled up with her pillow and drifted back to sleep.

The next day, Kris's stateroom was detached along with all the other shipping containers. Everyone reported to the spindle of the *Wasp* in full battle suit or pressure suit, depending on what their battle stations required, and prepared to sweat out the near approach to one small ice giant.

47

Kris had flown through some rough air. She was totally un-prepared for what the *Wasp* got into next.

She had some inkling when Command Master Chief Mong dropped by to tell her that she and her team would be spending the pass in a specific hull section. A welder 2/c would be re-sponsible for the compartment, and he hoped Kris would see that her officers didn't get underfoot.

Kris and her team of officers reported to their hull section to find that the second-class petty officer had the situation well in hand. Strips cut from containers were ready to shore up anything that bent, and a full set of welding tools was on hand to secure them.

No surprise, there were plenty of cans of stop-leak Goo at hand.

Certainly, Wardhaven procurement had another name for Goo, but the gooey stuff you sprayed at a leak in the hull that sealed it temporarily was known to all and sundry as simply Goo.

When Sulwan announced to prepare for some rough sail-ing, there was nothing in Kris's space that wasn't tied, lashed, or welded down.

Except the people.

But the petty officer had a plan for them, too.

"You two," she said, pointing at Kris and Jack, "over against that wall."

They went.

"You sir, put your back against the wall. You ma'am. Out here. Put your feet against his. Yeah, I figured you'd be well past midpoint with those long, thin sticks you two got," was not the normal reference Kris was used to getting for her legs.

"You, too, small one," she said, pointing at Abby and Cara. Kris would never have used the word "small" for her maid. She was usually moving so fast you had to give her lots of extra space. At the moment, through the petty officer's eyes, Kris realized that Abby was of less-than-average build.

Kris found herself with her back to Abby. When the maid and Cara pushed their feet together, Kris felt locked in place.

"Will this hold?" Kris asked.

"If it don't, you can write a letter of complaint to the old chief who taught me the trick. If you all don't intend to lay a hand if we need one, then I guess I could lash you down like you was kids, ma'am, but I was told you're going to help if things go all to hell in a handbasket."

"Yes," Kris said, "we're here to lay a hand."

"Then I expect this will do."

The others found a place in such a line athwart the deck and settled in to wait.

They didn't have long.

The *Wasp* started getting downright frisky very quickly.

Sulwan was kind enough to pass The Word. "All hands, we're getting into the outer fringe of the atmosphere. It's not enough to give us any reaction mass, but it is enough to make the ride interesting. Hold on to your best friend and enjoy the ride."

Kris reached out for Jack. To her surprise, he was already reaching out for her.

"Never argue with the navigator," Kris muttered.

"Never pass up a handhold," Jack said too darn matter-of-factly.

The ride got bouncy, and Kris was glad they had secured everything in the space. Still, a bottle of Goo got loose. The petty officer caught it on the fly and gave one of her sailors a scowl that would have reduced a normal human to a puddle.

The sailor said, "Sorry, ma'am. Won't happen again."

The petty officer passed the bottle back to him to tie back down. "It better not," was all she said.

Then the *Wasp* did a hard right flip. Kris went from her rump being down to her back holding that honor. Her legs were holding Jack up, and her arms were all that kept him from falling over into her lap.

She grinned mischievously at the thought.

He said, "Don't you dare."

"What?

"Do what you're thinking."

"Now you're a mind reader."

The *Wasp* flipped back over and down and was once more below Kris's bottom.

"Thanks, Abby," Kris said.

"Don't mind if I do, Your Princessship. I expect you'll do the same for me sometime. But if you don't mind, I do wish you'd skip the second waffle tomorrow."

Cara giggled. "You grown-ups are funny."

Kris enjoyed the happy sound.

Fifteen seconds later, it was Kris's turn to support Abby and Cara on her back. Jack stiffened his arms to support them, and they held in place until the *Wasp* managed to right herself.

"This is fun," Cara said from the innocence of her youth.

"Sure is," a young sailor agreed.

"Hold on," the petty officer warned as the *Wasp* dropped out from underneath them, leaving them hanging a good fifteen centimeters in the air. Then it slammed up, leaving Kris's back twitching in pain.

"Press your legs harder against each other. Get those backs hard against the bulkhead," the petty officer ordered. "That way, when we do those ducks and poundings, you'll go up and down with the ship."

"Yes, Mother," a sailor said.

"And you can wash your mouth out with soap when we're done here," the petty officer said in a very motherly voice.

For the next forever, they bounced around like peas in a pod.

Kris discovered that the worst wasn't the flips that put Jack nearly in her lap . . . or her nearly in his. No, the *Wasp* could totally turn herself over, leaving them pushing hard against each other and the bulkhead and hoping they could hold on long enough for the ship to right herself.

The third or fourth time the *Wasp* did the total flip, four of the sailors failed and ended up in a jumbled mess on the overhead below. They scrambled to untangle themselves, and ended up sliding down the bulkheads as the *Wasp* got herself right.

With the petty officer barking orders, they got themselves back in place before the *Wasp* did anything exciting again.

Then the bulkhead around them let out a scream like a banshee, and air started shrieking through a rent in the hull.

"Longknife, grab some Goo and stop that leak," the petty officer ordered.

Being nearest the rent, Kris grabbed for the closest Goo and loosed a long dollop at the hole. The *Wasp* did a little jig, and Kris missed with her first two shots. For the third one, the *Wasp* zigged when Kris was expecting a zag, but Jack bumped into her elbow, and, miracle of miracles, she hit the hole.

That stopped the air loss, but the side of the ship was warping in and out.

"All of you, lay a hand getting a sheet of metal over that hole," the petty officer snapped.

Two sailors undid the lashings on a pile of six steel strips, Jack and the colonel slid one strip out, and the sailors tied back down the other five.

Movement while they did this was wild; the *Wasp* continued on its bucking ride, leaving them weightless one moment and double their weight the next.

Four of them managed to wrestle the sheet up without cutting off any hands or heads . . . but it was a close-run thing. The metal sheet reached from the deck to just a bit short of the overhead. The petty officer quickly welded the lower half of the sheet in place. A moment later, she'd tossed a rope over one of the hooks Kris hadn't noticed that now circled the overhead.

Jack boosted the petty officer on his shoulder as the colonel raised her on the rope and belayed it across his rear.

Secured as best as the ride allowed, the petty officer ran a welding bead up the one side of the sheet, then over the top and down the other side. As she got more and more of the patch in place, the hull worked itself less and less.

Done, she settled back to the deck. "What are all you looking at? Help me get this torch kit lashed down, and let's get back on the deck."

Kris's brain trust snapped to, and in only a moment, she was back facing Jack.

"That was well done," she said.

"Look at all the fun you missed by not doing a tour as an assistant division officer," Jack said.

"Yes," Kris said. "Think of the things I could have done if I hadn't been stopping Turantic from going to war with its neighbors, or dodging battleships around Wardhaven or hurling cabers on Chance."

"We must all bear our burdens," the petty officer said.

Someone among the sailors snickered.

"Make that two cakes of soap for you, Henderson."

"I didn't say nothing."

The petty officer gave him the look.

And then the *Wasp* did something a ship was never meant to do, and they had to do the welding drill all over again.

And a third time.

And a fourth time.

Somewhere in there, one of the sailors lost his lunch. Then Cara. Then just about the entire crew, except for the petty officer.

Kris was eyeing the two remaining reinforcement sheets and wondering if this would ever end when the ride got less rowdy and Sulwan came on the public address.

"All hands, we're done. I'd love to tell you that we gathered up enough fuel to get us home, but the skipper says that isn't so. We will, however, be matching orbit with our containers, so we can get things back together and get a good meal and some sleep tonight." She paused for a moment, and then added, "Commodore Longknife, the skipper sends his regards and asks if you will please report to the bridge."

48

"I'm not sure the *Wasp* can take another beating like that," Captain Drago said softly, as he and Kris put their heads together.

"Can we modify the ship's launches to do the next refueling run?" Kris asked. "That pirate ketch we captured on Kaskatos had less power than one of our launches."

"I don't know," the captain admitted. "They had a balloot designed for their size. We'd have to cut down our balloot to fit a launch."

"Maybe we could make two or three smaller balloots," Sulwan put in.

"But once we start tearing it apart," the skipper said darkly, "we'd better hope the glue holds together. There would be no turning back."

"I think we ought to try doing it once without cutting up anything," Kris said. "I've flown just about every kind of small craft there is. If you could rig a balloot to three launches, Nelly and I could give it a try."

The skipper had started shaking his head as she spoke, and he just kept on shaking it. "You saw, or at least felt, how much the *Wasp* was thrown around during our pass. Imagine what those atmospheric currents would do to three boats flying in close formation. You could all three end up as a blot of grease on some gas giant."

"I'm a Longknife. We're always looking for a new way to get ourselves killed."

Jack didn't look too happy at that, but he kept his silence.

"I'll have a couple of my officers and leading chiefs look at the idea," the captain finally said. "Now, do you have an opinion on our course home? We're about as far out on the rim as we can get."

"The star maps we have don't seem to be helping us much. We have no idea from one jump to the next where we'll end up," Kris said.

"The maps I have," Nelly said, clearly defensive, "do a fairly good job of telling us where a jump will take us when we enter them at a slow speed. We can even be doing one hundred thousand klicks an hour and have a good idea where we're heading. But it's anybody's guess where we will end up when you really put pedal to the metal."

"Where'd you pick up that phrase?" Kris asked.

"Cara got it from some of the car racers back home. I like the sound of it," Nelly answered.

"If I can help it, the *Wasp* won't be accelerating at over two gees until our next overhaul," Captain Drago said. "Neither the engines nor the hull can take it. However, we could keep one gee up as acceleration and not spend half our time decelerating. That could put a lot of speed on the boat. We could probably make at least one of those seven-league jumps before we have to start decelerating to refuel."

"Wouldn't we be in better shape if we fully refueled at this star, then took several long leaps?" Kris asked.

"Yes, Your Highness, but I want to get out of here before anyone drops in. I think the *Intrepid* knocked those last two alien ships for a loop. I don't think they were aware of anything going on in that last system when we jumped, but how much of the farm do you want to bet on that?"

"Good point. How soon can we get out of here?"

"The nearest jump point is one of Nelly's fuzzy ones. We can reach it in a day. Assuming we don't decelerate, we should be doing close to a hundred thousand klicks by the time we hit it. Assuming we survive the jump, we'll see where it puts us."

They spent most of the next day patching the *Wasp* back together as well as they could. The engineers continued doing their own maintenance on the engines and reactors. The *Wasp* got under way as smoothly as she ever did and slipped through the next jump point right on time.

To find themselves sharing a system with a huge reddish super giant.

"Anyone got a guess when that dude will go supernova?" Captain Drago asked.

No one on the bridge ventured a guess.

"Chief, tell me the best way out of here, and do it fast."

"There's another one of those new jumps pretty close by."

"Sulwan, get the coordinates and get us headed there."

"Doing it, Skipper."

Kris waited at her station on Weapons for the immediate hurry to calm down. "How far did we jump?" she asked Chief Beni once he was finished with navigation.

"It looks like close to nine hundred light-years," he said. "We're still cruising along the outer rim of the outermost arm of the Milky Way. Nelly, do you have any idea where this next jump would take us?"

A star map appeared on the forward screen. "I think we are here," the computer said. A green dot appeared along the Scutum-Centaurus Arm. "We're still about as far from Earth as we can be and not go next door for sugar."

"Good joke, Nelly," Kris said.

Captain Drago just made a face.

"If I have us in the right system, and we took this jump at dead-slow speed, we'd go about fifty light-years over and a bit more inward. A longer jump, say with us making fifty thousand to a hundred thousand klicks an hour, would take us a lot farther, say about another eight hundred light-years." Nelly paused for her listeners to absorb this.

"I've been analyzing our long jumps, and I think I'm starting to see a pattern. If our next jump was a fast one and followed that pattern, I estimate that we'd jump to about the middle of this arm and in a line that would take us to somewhere a couple of thousand light-years along the outer rim, but at least we'd start getting back toward Earth. If that direction holds true, my guess would be that if we hit our third jump at three or four hundred thousand klicks an hour, maybe more, we could end up well into the center of the Outer Arm, and generally headed home."

Nelly paused for a second. "Assuming you want a guess from a computer."

"Just so long as you warn us that it's a guess," Kris said, while Captain Drago scowled.

"This is just a guess," Nelly went on, "but if we could maintain that speed for a second long jump, we might get as far as the Sagittarius Arm or even the Orion Arm. That would put us just a hop, skip, and a jump from human space."

"Who taught this computer how to use nonempirical language?" the skipper demanded.

"Cara," Kris said.

"That kid," the captain grumbled.

"But you humans relate better to nonempirical more often than when I give you an answer to the thirteenth decimal place," Nelly said.

"We prefer to pick when we want it simple and when we want it precise," Drago said.

"And guessing where in the galaxy we are going to drop in when we are stumbling around like a drunken sailor is going to improve how if I talk about thousands of light-years using the third decimal place?" Nelly shot back.

"The gal does have a point," Kris said. "Precision isn't all that useful when we're guessing at the basic point."

"And you had to remind me, didn't you?" the captain said with a sigh.

Kris shrugged.

"If we could make two of those long jumps," Kris said, "before we have to slow down and refuel . . ." Kris left the thought unfinished.

The captain clearly was also thinking along that line. "Sulwan, if we went to half a gee acceleration?"

"The Engineering team would be delighted, and we'd still be making some two hundred thousand klicks an hour when we hit the next jump."

"That might get us two of those long jumps. Course, we might need to give up showers and flushing the toilet to find enough reaction mass to slow down."

"Our final jump might also have us dropping into the

Iteeche Empire or one of those systems where their ships have been vanishing," the skipper said slowly.

"Choices, choices," Kris said. "Who shall we start a war with today?"

"That is not funny, Kris," Jack said.

"I didn't mean it as a joke," Kris said. "At least if we drop in on the Empire, we've got our own Imperial Representative."

"Who, I understand, is not in good repute at the court just now," the skipper said.

"Where'd you hear that?" Kris asked.

"I know everything that goes on aboard my ship," the captain said darkly. "And if I don't, I have supper every once in a while with Abby, and she fills me in on what I missed."

"And here I thought I didn't have to worry about that woman leaking now that I wasn't going to balls anymore."

"It's a fact of life with your maid," the skipper said. "If she doesn't leak something, she'll pop."

"Now who's cracking jokes," Nelly said.

"I'm a human. I get to crack jokes. You're a computer. I worry about the jokes you might crack. I'm not all that sure they'll be funny."

"I am learning from an expert." Nelly sniffed.

"Who?" the captain demanded.

"Kris," Nelly said.

"I rest my case. Now, why don't you two, or three, run along and get some chow and take a shower. I may be cutting back on both in the very near future."

"Isn't our water recycled?" Nelly asked.

"Yes. I'm more worried with the beer, wine, and spirits that are still on board. Is it better to allow them to be recycled into piss, or should I pour them directly into the reaction tanks?"

"I knew there was a reason I left you in command of this wreck," Kris said.

"She wasn't a wreck when you left me in command. We had to work real hard to get her into this fix."

Kris let the skipper have the last word. She headed for chow, only to find that even Cookie was having a hard time making what he had in his larder look all that worth eating. A request for any of the crew qualified in space to lend a hand shoring up damaged compartments got her attention, and she was about to tap her commlink and ask Captain Drago to let her get in some honest work when Jack put his hand over her commlink.

"I know what you're thinking, and I will not have you squished like a little green bug because some rough-cut steel gets out of control of a teenage sailor."

"In our situation, everyone has to do their part. I should, too," Kris insisted.

"That's what worries me. Every seaman recruit who thinks they know how to handle themselves in a half gee is headed there. I know that Senior Chief Mong knows how to handle things. I'm worried about Marine Private Knucklehead or Seaman Recruit Vacuum-for-brains who has more enthusiasm than experience."

Jack paused, then went on. "You and I need to find someplace private where we can talk."

"About what?" Kris asked, suddenly not sure she liked the idea that she had nothing to do, and Jack was going to have a talk with her. From the thunderclouded look on his face, he'd been saving this up for a long time.

"Let's find someplace we won't be interrupted," was all he said.

They ended up back in the space they had occupied for the refueling pass. Everyone seemed to have gone elsewhere, leaving them a large, empty space all to themselves.

Once there, Jack went to one side of the compartment. Kris found herself gravitating to the opposite end of the room, as far from Jack as she could get.

The space still smelled of hot welding and Goo, along with human sweat and a bit of terror. There was no place to sit, and with the *Wasp* changing its course and acceleration at odd moments as it matched orbit with its containers, Kris found herself holding on to one of the tie-downs that still held its bottle of Goo.

Finally, she turned to face Jack. "What's eating you?"

"This lust you have for getting yourself killed," he snapped.

"I didn't have any good choices," Kris said in her defense. "I couldn't let the bird people die when I could do something about it. I thought you agreed with me."

Jack was shaking his head before she finished. "I didn't say your enthusiasm for getting us all killed, I said *your* personal lust for getting your own little body slammed, smashed, and burned before my eyes."

"Oh," Kris said. *This was going to be personal.* She would have preferred to argue about what she'd done for the whole human race. Talking about herself . . . now that could bring up a whole mess of snakes Kris preferred to ignore.

"I haven't done anything lately, Jack. Nobody has thrown a bomb at me or taken a shot at me. Vicky has more of that coming at her than I do of late."

"Quit changing the subject, Kris," Jack snapped. "I've been biting my tongue and keeping my silence ever since we got ourselves stuck in a burning aircraft with a canopy that wouldn't open."

"Oh," Kris whispered. "That time I almost got us both killed."

"Yes, *that* time," Jack said. "I woke up with the smell of smoke in my oxygen system and you not answering my calls and a canopy that wouldn't budge. All I could think of was that you'd finally gone and done it, gotten yourself killed, and my heart was breaking."

"Heart?" Kris whispered. Was Jack really talking about something intimate to the two of them, not just a day in, day out job?

"Don't change the subject," Jack growled. "You didn't have to fly that mission. We could have given it to anyone. Hell, even a drone could have flown it."

"A drone would not have dodged those missiles the way I did," Kris said, jumping to her defense. "And besides, I saved your precious Marines when I saw what they were heading into. *I* saved most of *your* company."

"There you go, changing the topic again."

"Well, damn it, what is the topic, Jack!"

Jack took a deep breath before he went on. "I can't stand to watch you going out day after day trying to get yourself killed."

"I'm not trying to get myself killed."

"Well, it sure looks that way from where I'm standing," Jack snarled.

"I do what I have to do," Kris shot back.

"You do not!" came right back at her. "Any reasonable person, with the sense God promised a billy goat, would find other ways to get what she wants done that didn't involve her going out and sticking her head in every lion's mouth that comes along."

Jack paused long enough to slam his hand against one of the metal patches they'd help weld to the *Wasp*'s hide. At half a gee, his feet lifted off the deck, and he had to force himself back down.

"Kris, you do have choices. If I hear you say one more time that you don't have any choice but to go out and nearly get yourself killed, I'm going to scream. You have choices. If you'd spend a few extra seconds thinking about what you're about to do, you'd see those choices and maybe do something different."

"Do them instead of trying my hand at flossing some passing lion's teeth, you mean," Kris said, giving him the kind of look through her eyelashes that some actresses used to good effect.

"Don't you go trying to make me laugh," Jack said, but a hint of a smile was creeping around the edges of his mouth.

"I like you when you smile," Kris said.

"You're changing the subject."

"Okay, I'll stay on your topic. What does it matter to you whether I'm one of those Longknifes that dies young and gloriously? From the look of Grampa Ray, I'm not sure that living a long life is all it's cracked up to be. He's getting way too good at dodging his problems and ignoring his conscience."

"We are not talking about your relatives," Jack said.

"Then answer my question. What does it matter whether I splatter myself over the next gas giant we come to, trying to get reaction mass for the *Wasp*? You won't be in the launch with me. You won't have to take my bullet. It will be just me and Nelly."

"And I don't get a vote on the matter, either," Nelly pointed out.

"You stay out of this," both Kris and Jack said.

"Fine. Okay. I'm just the computer, but when are you going to answer the girl's question, Jack?" Nelly said.

Kris raised an eyebrow to add her own emphasis to Nelly's question.

Jack scowled and looked at the hatch like he wanted to walk out on the both of them. Down in Engineering, they were having trouble maintaining the acceleration. They'd pop up to more than half a gee, then just as suddenly fall well below it. If it was the engines, they were in trouble. If it was the quality of the new reaction mass, they might survive it. Whatever it was, Jack risked falling flat on his face if he tried stomping out on her.

He must have realized it about the time Kris did, because that tiny hint of a smile was back. Then he sobered up.

"I've had to watch you die twice in the last couple of months. First when we peeled what that bomb left of you off the marble floor on Texarkana. I had to do it again when I woke up ahead of you after you crashed"—Kris started to object and Jack waved her back—"after you did that superb bit of flying that set us down so smoothly in the middle of a swamp. My heart won't take much more of this."

"I'm sorry I've stressed you," Kris said curtly. "It wasn't all that much fun for me. And if I may point out, it was me helping you limp away from that Greenfeld pile of junk before it blew. My heart got a bit of a workout, too."

Jack shook his head ruefully. "Right. Heart. It pumps blood as Nelly would tell you. Kris, I don't care what you do to my blood pressure or my pulse. That's all part of the job."

He paused and took a deep breath. "Kris, I've made the worst mistake a bodyguard can make. I'm supposed to care for your body, but it's you I care about. And you keep right on breaking my heart."

That wasn't something Kris saw coming.

Now it was her turn to talk, and nothing came to mind.

Nothing at all.

What she wanted to do was launch herself across the room at Jack. She had never wanted to bury herself in anyone's arms like she wanted his arms around her.

She didn't, of course. Halfway across the room, Engineering was likely to hiccup and drop Kris on the deck. Hard. Probably put her back on crutches.

Now wouldn't that be a fun one to explain to the *Wasp*'s medical team?

And even if she did get across the room with no harm done, it just wouldn't do to have some sailor duck his head through the hatch to find the commodore and her Marine skipper locked in a romantic embrace.

Especially with her being one of those damn Longknifes.

Wouldn't do at all.

Damn!

"I'm sorry you feel that way," came out sounding so lame.

"No, that's not what I mean," Kris immediately countered her own words.

"Jack, did you have to pick now to drop this on me?" came across way too argumentative.

"You've been rather busy since you crashed into that mud bank, Kris. I haven't been able to get a word in edgewise."

Kris chuckled wryly. "Yeah, you're right. Way too busy saving the world or destroying it."

Jack shrugged.

"Jack, when we get back, do you think you and I could have a quiet dinner. Candlelit, maybe. Could we try to talk this out, because, you see, I don't know what I'd do if you weren't in my life."

"Oh," sounded like Jack was as surprised to hear that as Kris was that it had slipped out.

That one word hung in the air between them for quite a long time.

Kris couldn't tell if she was just starting to open her mouth, or Jack started first, but it didn't matter.

The hatch opened, and Colonel Cortez ducked his head in. "Oh, that's where you two are. We've been looking all over for you. Did you turn Nelly off?"

"No. I'm on. I'm just not taking messages," Kris's computer answered.

"Oh," the colonel said, clearly not understanding what this was all about.

"Jack was just counseling me on my risk-taking," Kris said. "As usual, he thinks I'm in way over my head. And, as usual, he's right."

"We can continue this later," Jack said. "Like you said. When we get back to human space."

"Good," Kris said, through a dry throat and a pounding pulse. "I'd like that. You have some good points I should really take to heart."

Jack raised an eyebrow at that.

"Engineering has solved the problem with the *Wasp*'s new reaction mass. We should be settling down to a reliable half-gee acceleration," Sulwan announced to all hands. "Now you can safely get some serious repair work under way. Sorry about asking for volunteers when it was too hazardous to do anything. Now, if you really are interested in some messy work, let us know."

Jack eyed Kris.

"I'll pass on that," she said.

49

The *Wasp* approached the next jump at over 150,000 kilometers an hour. She could have put on more speed, but she hadn't; they'd been forced to spend time in free fall.

Quite a few of the patches needed to be reworked. Several more hull sections showed strain. They had made it through the refueling pass, but Captain Drago feared they'd fail on him when he could least afford it.

Likely at the worst of times and worst of places.

But just as the *Wasp* was a good ship taking care of her crew, so she had a good crew to take care of her. Every day Kris realized that Captain Drago knew so much more about running a ship in space than she did.

It was humbling.

All Kris could do was be glad she'd made the right choice and not done what she oh so wanted to do. There were reasons why it took years of hard work to make a good ship driver.

She hadn't put in those years. She would be as big a fool as Hank Peterwald to think that she could fill those shoes just by tying up the shoelaces.

The jump point was one of Nelly's new fuzzy points. That meant that they didn't have to worry about it taking a zig or zag at the last minute and making them miss.

Or rather, they had less to worry about. A jump point was a jump point, and they all wanted to kill you.

At least that was what Sulwan insisted.

Kris was at her Weapons station as they took the jump. At Nelly's suggestion, they reduced their rotation to the more traditional twenty revolutions per minute clockwise. The transition from one point in space to another point went smoothly.

Then came the little matter of where had they gotten to.

First things first. "The system is quiet," Chief Beni reported. "All sensors report nothing but normal radiation. We're sharing this system with a pleasant yellow dwarf." Mother Earth had survived in the warmth of a pleasant yellow dwarf for several billions of years. They should have no problems as they transited the system.

"Jump points, Chief?" the skipper asked.

"Give me a moment," he said, still concentrating on his instruments.

"We went about nine hundred light-years," Nelly reported. "We're still going counterclockwise around the rim of the Milky Way, but we edged in a bit, just like I expected."

"Very good, Nelly," Captain Drago said, but it was the chief he concentrated on.

"Sorry, sir. For a minute there, I thought I was picking up something in the radio spectrum. If I was, I can't get a bearing on it. Maybe it's something from a nearby solar system. Da Vinci, make a note for future reference, there may be an intelligent species close to this system."

"It's done, Chief," his computer, a son of Nelly, replied.

"Chief, I sure would like to aim this tub at a jump point, and I don't have a lot of reaction mass to spare."

"Yes, sir. Sorry, sir. I kind of don't want to get bushwhacked without warning, sir, but I understand where you're coming from, sir." The chief paused for a moment, ignoring the skipper's scowl. Then he went on.

"There are three jumps in the system. Only one of them is a new type. It's also the closest. Sulwan, here come the coordinates."

"I got them."

"You know," the chief went on, "is it just me, or don't the new points seem to be closer together than the old ones? Do you think the Three alien species that built them figured out they were wasting a lot of time traveling from one jump to the next and did something about that with the new jumps?

"I tend to agree with Chief Beni," Nelly said. Kris's eyebrows shot up, to be quickly joined by all those around the bridge at this unusual agreement between the two rivals. "However, I don't yet think we have a sufficiently large test sample to be too confident of that conclusion, but it's a good possibility."

"Thank you, Nelly," the chief said.

"I have adjusted our course," Sulwan reported. "If we maintain one-gee acceleration, we can expect to jump in fifteen hours. We should be close to three hundred thousand klicks an hour by then."

Once they were sure they had the system to themselves, Kris secured the Weapons Division to a minimum watch and dropped down to the wardroom for chow. She couldn't decide whether she wanted to run into Jack or had better avoid him.

He cares for me. Maybe as much as I care for him. What did that mean? Did it mean anything that mattered?

Kris was no high-school kid walking the halls blinded by her first puppy crush. She was the commander of PatRon 10, or at least what was left of it. She had a report to make to the king concerning the death of billions of aliens, the loss of just about all of her first command and the likelihood that the whole human race was now at war with an alien race they knew nothing about.

Yes, that was all true. Still, it was wonderful to know that someone in general, and Jack in particular, cared about her.

Kris scrupulously avoided even thinking the word "love."

Until she heard more from Jack about the actual extent of his feelings for her, that word was strictly off-limits.

But it was nice to think about the possibility that the word had some application to the present situation.

Down, girl. Remember, that word is strictly out of your vocabulary. Not available for usage. He said he is glad you're still alive and wants you to stay that way. That doesn't necessarily mean that L word.

Kris was saved from further ruminations on *that* word when Abby, Cara, and Penny joined her for dinner. It turned out, Cara had her own problem to share with them.

Once she was settled at the table, she leaned toward the

three adults, and whispered, "Is it true? Could we become another Flying Dutchman, just like in the vids?"

"Which one?" Penny asked. "I've seen three remakes of that horror show."

Kris knew the classic story of the Flying Dutchman, back when he sailed a windjammer on Earth's oceans. Clearly, Cara was all wound up about the recent adaptation of the story to starships and jump points.

"I don't know," Cara gushed. "We've got enough alcohol on board. I guess no one would have to go into the reactor without something to numb them."

"No one is going into the reactor," Kris said. "Drunk or otherwise."

"Which version of the movie do you like the best?" Cara asked the three women.

Kris hoped this topic of conversation would go nowhere, but unfortunately, Penny did have to encourage the girl.

"I loved the one where the actress, what was her name, bravely went into the reactor herself, after she'd fed in the body of her boyfriend who died when, oh, what was the accident that killed him?"

"You clearly remember the movie very well," Abby said dryly.

"Well, it was a while back," Penny admitted. "I was an impressionable young thing, and it seemed oh so romantic."

Kris suppressed a groan at the word, but kept her silence.

Cara made that easy. "I saw the latest remake of it. Where part of the crew has been infected by the brain-eating bugs, and they're chasing everyone who isn't brain-dead so they can stuff them in the reactor."

Abby sighed. "As if the brain-dead ones would know how to set a course for home once they had dumped enough flesh and blood into the reactor. That story makes no sense."

"But it's scary as all get-out," Cara said.

"That's today's kids," Penny said with a full-fledged Irish sigh. "Forget about romance, just scare the willies out of them. What's the latest generation coming to?" She finished with the question elders had posed to every next generation for, oh, the last five hundred.

Cara sniffed, very much the imitation of her aunt. "Don't you find the idea of being stranded in space with nothing left to feed into the reactor but your own blood just the worst thing that can happen?" she demanded of her elders.

"I don't know," Abby said, applying herself to the hash Cookie had made with canned beef and dried potatoes. "For me, the worst will be when they tell us to quit taking showers or flushing the toilets 'cause they need to feed all the ship's water into the plasma chambers. Plasma chambers, Cara, that's where they blend the reactor feed with the reaction mass to power those big engines pushing the *Wasp* around space. The ignorant writer couldn't even get that straight for their stupid movie."

Poor Cara couldn't react fast enough to all that was coming at her. She'd hardly gotten out an "Ew" at the thought of no flush toilets before she was torn between defending her movie or actually learning more about how a real starship worked.

She ended up sitting there more confused than motivated.

"My, my," Penny said. "I thought you'd be fine with that. No doubt by then they'll be serving free beer and wine with our supper. What with all the water having gone wherever it is that reaction mass goes, what else will there be to drink?"

"Beer and wine," Cara's eyes lit up. "Will I get to drink it, too?"

Kris put a quick stop to that. "I'll make sure Cookie saves some water for all the underage folks aboard."

"But I'm the only underage person aboard the *Wasp*!" Cara cried.

"Oh, right, so he won't have to save a lot," Penny said with a wide grin.

"You're just pulling my leg." When none of the grown-ups chose to respond to that, she focused on Kris. "You're younger than Auntie Abby. What scary movies did you like to see when you were my age?"

It wasn't movies that scared Kris when she was Cara's age, it was real life. Would somebody kill her like they did her brother? Would Mother or Father notice how brandy was disappearing from their liquor cabinet? Could life between Mother and Father get worse than it already was? No, Kris didn't have to go to a movie to feel she was in a horror show.

But she needed an answer. She found one ready at hand.

"My father taught me well before I was your age that there

were more horrible things in real life than any movie could ever hope to create."

"What was that?" Cara asked, breathless at the prospect.

"The most horrible thing in life, my father said," Kris said, drawing out the line, "is some brainless, inexperienced politician getting his hands on the reins of government."

Penny and Abby laughed.

Cara looked like her goat had been thoroughly skinned. "That's not real horror."

"Oh, yes it is," Kris insisted. "Back then, I was sure Father was talking about someone in the opposition. Horror of horrors, I now know that it may include some of the people you most need to make the whole shebang work, ally or opposition."

"That *is* a horrible thought," Penny agreed.

"And what kind of people will we need to get things done when we get back with this little story of ours?" Abby asked, all serious in a flash.

"Any kind we can get," Kris agreed. "I'll be glad for anyone who will lend us a helping hand."

"So you've figured out what we need to do when we get home?" Penny asked.

"Be ready to face these monsters when they come calling," Kris said simply. "What else can we do?"

"Honey child," Abby said, "you are way too old to think that human beings can't think of a whole passel of things to do that have nothing to do with what they ought to do."

That brought a sigh from all four of them. Even Cara.

50

The prospects of the *Wasp* becoming another Flying Dutchman increased as they whipped through the next jump at 500,000 klicks per hour and found another new-style jump in their next system. Sulwan headed the *Wasp* toward it, now at only half a gee, and forecast that they would be making somewhere between 650,000 and 750,000 klicks when they went through it.

Chief Beni announced they'd covered over three thousand light-years and that there was nothing of interest in this system. Kris stood down her gunners yet again.

Nelly sounded tickled pink that her estimate of how far they would jump and where was proven to be right. She gave out an official guess that at their speed and with a twenty rotation counterclockwise, the next jump should take them into the Norma Arm of the galaxy, well away from the outer rim and aimed toward home.

Of course, they'd be coming home right through the heart of the Iteeche Empire. Hopefully, they would either miss it entirely or, if they ended up meeting anyone, it would not cause a problem.

There was a lot of hoping and wishing in that course of action.

Kris was more exhausted than hungry for whatever Cookie

had managed to mix up from what was left in the ship's dry-storage supplies. Kris did wonder if there were any famine biscuits in the back of the larder and whether they'd be reduced to eating them.

She wondered but did not ask. Between Cookie and Captain Drago, she figured that more experienced heads than hers were thinking through those matters.

She needed to get a good night's sleep. Sooner or later, she was going to have to face Grampa Ray, King Raymond I to most, and talk him into following through on what she had started.

She didn't even want to think about what might happen if he wasn't interested in backing her up. *Did they still throw Christians to the lions?*

For one of those damn Longknifes, they might bring back the good old days. Who could tell?

Kris had hardly gotten out of her clothing . . . it was amazing how much a princess could perspire while sweating through an unmapped and maybe hostile jump . . . when there was a knock on the door. Kris grabbed for an old Wardhaven U sweatshirt and opened the door a sliver.

Vicky Peterwald stood there. She had a half-empty bottle of whiskey and was sucking it well past half as Kris watched.

"They're all dead," Vicky finally said as she let the bottle fall from her lips.

Just the fumes left Kris wanting a drink. That was not good.

"Yes, Vicky, they're all dead," Kris said softly. "Most likely. Some might get back."

"Quit lying. They're all dead," the grand duchess snapped bitterly.

A sailor hurried by, doing the weird thing that was neither a run nor a float that half a gee demanded. Clearly, this was not the kind of talk that two girls of Kris and Vicky's stature needed to have where any passing crew member could pick up this or that snatch of conversation.

"Come in, Vicky." Kris would have loved to ask her to leave the bottle outside, saving Kris from the temptation of taking a swig. She would have loved to, but she didn't. Vicky looked more attached to that bottle at the moment than she was to life.

Kris settled on her bunk and offered Vicky her desk chair as far from Kris as she could get in the small room. Still, the compartment filled with the smell of whiskey as Vicky found her way to her seat. She was none too steady, even in half a gee. The grand duchess settled in, took another swig, and said it again. "They're all dead."

"Yes," Kris repeated. She'd already tried to put a hopeful spin on the thought. This time she let the ugly words lie there in all their morbid glory.

"One minute they were there," Vicky said, and snapped her fingers. "Then they were gone. They didn't even have a chance to shoot back. That monstrous alien ship just blotted them out, and they were gone as if they'd never been. A battleship, Kris. The biggest, meanest ship in our fleet."

"Yes, I know," Kris said. "It happens that way in a war." Kris didn't add that she'd faced battleships just as mean and made them disappear herself. That was for yesterday. Tonight, there was a different long list of dead to mourn.

"And you should know, Princess Kristine Longknife. You've blotted out enough in your time, haven't you?"

So, Vicky did remember. Kris let that jab fall to the deck and lie there.

Vicky waved the bottle. "And it, like, wasn't even really a war. Not yet, anyway. They hadn't said a word to us. We hadn't said anything but 'Hi' to them. Then suddenly, every laser on their ship is spearing the *Fury*, and boom, they're all dead."

"I took that for a declaration of war," Kris said.

"So you could start killing them. How many do you think we killed, ten, twenty billion? You think that makes up for all my friends dying on the *Fury*?"

"Nothing makes up for the loss of friends," Kris said softly. Not here and now. Not back then, either.

"But they weren't your friends, were they, Princess Kristine Longknife," Vicky said, taking another long swallow of the whiskey. "They were my friends. They were the only people who ever cared about Harry Smythe-Peterwald's bratty little girl. They cared for me. They looked out for me. For the first time since I was eight, nine, I felt safe with them and their battleship wrapped around me. Do you know what that feels like? Do you know what that means?"

"Yes," Kris said. "I think I do."

"Yeah, you got this little tin pot to run you home as fast as they can make it. Run away. Nice way to go."

Kris knew it was the whiskey talking. Kris knew she should just lie back and take it. That tomorrow when Vicky sobered up, she'd be all apologetic. Kris knew what she ought to do, but those were her friends and crew that Vicky was calling coward.

"You wish you'd stayed on the *Fury*? Died with them rather than being left alive to run away with me?"

As Kris expected, that brought Vicky up short. She took another long swig and seemed to think about it, as much as her alcohol-clouded brain could.

"No. Yes. I should have been there. I should have been with them, but I was afraid some damn assassin would put a bullet in my brain, so I ran away over to the nice *Wasp* full of strangers that most likely hadn't been offered a kazillion dollars to kill me. Who'd have thought something this puny would be the safe place to be in a fight with something as huge as that mother. But then, this little twirp has Kris Longknife, princess extraordinary, and she looks out for number one. Don't Longknifes always?"

Kris was getting sick and tired of being the butt of this woman's survival guilt. She had enough survival guilt of her very own, thank you all very much. And it covered a whole lot more dying than that last battle. Eddy, Tommy, all those hopeful volunteers who'd followed her into battles and died, much to their surprise.

"You can take your survival guilt, Vicky, and shove it in that bottle, or anywhere else you care to put it, but don't you dare lay it on me. I've got plenty of my own, damn it. You're sorry you're alive, and they're all dead. Well, there are plenty of airlocks on the *Wasp*, and you can walk out any one of them if you please. I'll even modify my report to show that you died fighting with all the brave souls on the *Fury*. You want that?"

"But they didn't die fighting," Vicky screamed. "They didn't get a shot off. They were there one minute, edging out of laser range, and the next minute what looked like all the lasers ever made were cutting them to pieces, and they just blew up!"

Vicky broke down sobbing. "They didn't even get a shot off. I watched them practice. All those sailors looked so brave and sure of themselves racing to their battle stations. They earned a fleet E for gunnery, Kris. They deserved a fight. Really, they deserved to go down fighting. Not swatted like some fly on a wall."

Kris risked the fumes to cross the distance between her and Vicky. She knelt so she could put her arms around Vicky, hold her, and rock her gently as she sobbed.

Kris chose her words gently.

"It was just the luck of the draw, Vicky. It could have just as well have been Admiral Channing's *Triumph* there as Admiral Krätz's *Fury*. The battle squadron had marched and countermarched with first one, then the other in the lead position. I imagine Georg was tickled when the luck of the draw gave him the lead when they charged for the jump. But when they did the turn away, all the ships reversed at once, and that put the *Fury* in the trailing slot. There's a reason that position is called coffin corner, and the aliens took advantage of it."

Kris pulled Vicky's face up to put the two eye to eye. The smell of the whiskey was overpowering and giving Kris a hunger that had claws in it. She ignored the craving in order to finish what she had to say.

"Admiral Krätz knew the chances he was taking. He took them willingly, like the fighting sailor he was. He wouldn't have had it any other way. When we get back, the story of BatRon 12 will be told, and told truly. That is the debt of honor that we owe the people who loved and protected you."

Vicky sobbed on for a few moments longer, then wiped her nose on her sleeve, and said, "But why did we live, Kris? Why did *we* live?"

Kris shook her head. "I don't know. Yes, we were making like a bunch of rocks. But we were only ten, fifteen thousand klicks from the jump. If I was half as paranoid as those aliens seem to be, I'd have shot up anything anywhere close to my space. That's a mistake I don't think they'll make twice. At least I won't expect them to."

It took a moment for Kris's words to pierce the whiskey fog of Vicky's thoughts. "So the luck of the draw got the *Fury* blown to bits and we got lucky and lived. It doesn't seem fair."

"Show me on your birth certificate where it says anything about fair. I've searched mine, and I can't find that word on the front or back."

Vicky laughed at that. A besotted thing that spewed as much phlegm and tears and used whiskey as sound.

Kris wiped her face and fought the urge to ask for a swig from Vicky's bottle, which was down to just a bit of slosh.

There was a knock at the door.

"Come in," Kris said, and was relieved to see Doc Maggie poke her head in.

"So this is where you got to," the good doctor said. "I thought you and I were supposed to be having a wicked game of Scrabble. That nice man, Scrounger, has promised to bring around another fellow to join us. Are you going to make me stand up the best date I've had in months?"

"No," Vicky said, struggling to her feet and letting the bottle fall as gently to the deck as half a gee allowed. When it became clear that the grand duchess would need help negotiating her way out of Kris's cabin, Maggie came over and offered a hand.

Kris gave the doc a thankful smile. With any luck, the woman would have the two men to herself, and Vicky would spend the game sleeping her whiskey binge off. As the doc guided her patient into the passageway, Kris whispered a thankful prayer. At least one of Vicky's friends had survived the sudden death of the *Fury.*

Kris closed the door, waited a moment, and said, "Did you put out a call for her, Nelly?"

"Yes, I did, Kris. From the looks of things, there was a fifty-fifty chance that you two would soon be burning any bridges that you had so far built between your two families. It was either call for Maggie or order up some hot dogs and marshmallows to roast. Since I lack the facilities to enjoy hot dogs and marshmallows, I thought the doc was the better of the choices."

Kris had to chuckle at Nelly's joke. "Thank you, Nelly."

"Now, Kris, if I had hands and feet, I'd empty what's left in that bottle down your sink, but I don't. Should I call Abby to come in and do the honors?"

"No," Kris said, with a long sigh. She paced off the distance to where the bottle lay, with more trepidation than she'd felt in any of her firefights. Holding the bottle at arm's length did not reduce any of its aroma or allure.

Kris hardly dared to breathe until the last drop had gone down her sink. "Now what do I do with the bottle?" she wondered.

"If you leave it in the trash can, it will smell up the place all night," Nelly said. "And you don't need that."

Kris noticed that the blower was on high, circulating the air in the compartment at an accelerated pace.

"You could leave it outside in the passageway. Some sailor on cleanup detail would take it away."

"And what are the odds that any sailor who took it, or emptied my trash can, would pass the word that the princess is drinking again."

"Better than fifty-fifty," Nelly agreed.

Kris pulled on a pair of gym shorts and went looking for a public disposal to get rid of the evidence.

Sleep came slowly when at last she was able to lie down.

Why am I alive when so many others are dead?

Kris had done as good a job of dodging that question as anyone else. She dodged it for the simple reason she had no answer for it.

People beside her took bullets and died. She took a bomb or two and kept on breathing. *Was that a blessing or a curse?*

Kris had no answer. She doubted that even Grampa Trouble had a good comeback that he could share with her. Next time they met, she'd have to ask him, anyway.

The luck of the draw was a lousy answer, but it was all she had.

With that very little comfort, she drifted off to sleep.

51

The question of who would go into the reactor, or the reaction-mass plasma-mixing chamber, or whatever, came quickly to mind as the reports came in on their next jump.

The solar system was blessedly empty of life and hostilities.

It was roughly on the path Nelly said would take them back home.

The system was also very sparse. All it boasted was a small yellow sun and a few rocky planets too close to the sun to support life.

Other than that, the system was dust, some asteroids, and a few passing comets.

"There are some jumps out of here, aren't there, Chief?" Captain Drago asked as the long litany of nothing went on.

"There is one of Nelly's fuzzy jumps not too far away. It won't take us long to get there at our present speed."

"Sulwan, set a course for it," Captain Drago ordered. "Use as little reaction mass as you can."

"Understood, sir. I'll use a quarter gee to aim us at that puppy, then close down the engines. The chief is right, with the speed we have on the boat, we'll be seeing what's on the other side of that jump in half a day at most."

"And I don't want to hear any quips about a Flying Dutchman from anyone of the bridge crew, you hear me?"

"Yes, Captain," came back from all hands.

"Good. Commodore Longknife, I'd like a word with you in my quarters. And bring that damn computer of yours as well."

"Yes, sir," came in two-part harmony.

NELLY, DOWN GIRL.

BUT HE ASKED FOR ME!

YES, HE DID. NOW ENJOY THE VINDICATION AND KEEP YOUR MOUTH SHUT UNLESS HE TALKS DIRECTLY TO YOU.

THAT'S WHAT I INTENDED TO DO, KRIS. I AM NOT AS INEX-PERIENCED AT HUMAN AFFAIRS AS SAY CARA.

GOOD.

Kris and the captain stayed in their seats until Sulwan took the spin off the *Wasp*. Moving around in even a quarter gee was not to be tried when the ship was spinning like a top.

Captain Drago's in-space cabin was a tiny thing, with just enough room for a desk and a bunk. He took the desk chair, and Kris found a handhold to keep her in place as the *Wasp* settled on its course and went to free fall.

Standing there, holding on, seemed rather tiresome, so Kris pulled her legs up and sat cross-legged in midair. She smiled at the thought that she must look like some sort of genie.

Captain Drago allowed himself a dry smile. "I'm glad to see you're getting your space legs."

"Or space seat," Kris quipped.

"There you humans go, telling jokes and not letting me in on the fun."

"Nelly, you said you'd only talk when talked to."

"Oops, sorry, Your High-Handedness."

"I'm glad your pet rock is in fine fettle," Captain Drago said. "Nelly, show us our course so far."

His wall screen suddenly became a view of the Milky Way from above. Human space was tiny, but it was marked with HOME in a font that was fit for a classic hand-embroidered sampler. From it were a series of white dots, taking them from Wardhaven to Santa Maria to their wanderings. The battle was marked with a flashing red dot, and their flight since then was green.

"Thank you, Nelly," the captain said. "What is your estimate of where the next two jumps will take us if we keep up this speed?"

Their present location sprouted a cone of probability that widened even more as it extended a second time for that jump. It showed them getting close to human space. It also gave them a twenty-five-percent probability of landing somewhere in the Iteeche Empire.

Captain Drago gnawed his lower lip as he studied Nelly's estimate. Then he turned to Kris. "I hadn't planned on refueling in this system. Still, I don't much like the look of it, either. Choosing not to refuel is one thing. Not having a choice to refuel is something else entirely different. You have an opinion?"

"Captain, I've left the ship driving to you," Kris pointed out.

"But you're the princess who needs to make a report to the king, my dear. It wouldn't do to have us declare war on some bug-eyed monster and you not get home to warn the home front of what's coming our way."

"They aren't bug-eyed monsters," Nelly pointed out. "In fact, they look amazingly like you humans."

"Thank you for pointing that out," Kris said. "Whatever they look like, they're acting like bug-eyed monsters. And that is what I'll call them until they're kind enough to tell us what they want us to call them. Right, Captain?"

"It's a human thing, Nelly," the captain said.

Kris found his rather amazing acceptance of Nelly's viewpoint startling. But then, he couldn't value her for setting his course and keep thinking of her as a rock, could he?

"Thank you, sir," Nelly said.

"Captain, for what my views are worth, I suggest we take each jump one at a time. If we go through the next jump, and there are several large gas bags, then we slow down and refuel. If the next system is the same as this system, we keep on going."

"The probability of there being two rocky systems in a row is quite low," Nelly put in helpfully.

"The mere fact we're still alive means we've used up a whole lot of good luck, Nelly," the captain pointed out. "We can't expect the princess's pot of gold to keep sprinkling us with the good stuff forever."

"I don't have any magic supply of luck," Kris snapped in good humor.

"Don't tell me that," the captain snapped right back, though with a broad smile on his swarthy face. "Without that bucket of luck, you and Ray and Trouble would have been dead long ago."

Kris chose to let the captain have the last word concerning her notional luck and left him staring at Nelly's map of hopeful outcomes of the next two jumps.

Hungry, she dropped down to the wardroom to find chow was bread made before the last jump. With no weight on the ship, even the vaunted Cookie was reluctant to try his hand at baking fresh bread. The last of the deli-cut meats had been slapped on with the last of the condiments.

Kris took a turkey sandwich and found that Maggie and Vicky were there before her. Rather than avoid the grand duchess, Kris asked if the seat across from them was taken. Maggie glanced at her young friend and interpreted a minuscule blink of an eye as, "No, please sit down."

Kris did.

She took a bite of her sandwich. The bread was not up to Cookie's usual high standards. As she chewed, she eyed Vicky.

The not-so-grand duchess took a sip from tea that no longer steamed.

"You enjoying the hangover?" Kris asked in a voice even she knew was way too cheerful.

"What good is a doctor who can't cure agony like this?" Vicky whispered.

"When the agony is self-inflicted," Maggie said, "it only seems right that the path through it should be on your own. But I must point out that I did give you the best medicine available for what ails you."

"You lie," the Greenfeld scion mumbled.

She sipped her tea, then managed to raise her eyes to level with Kris. "I hear we're going to be the real Flying Dutchman."

"Not from anyone of the bridge crew. The captain strictly forbids it."

"You have, have you?"

"Not me. Captain Drago."

"I thought you outranked him. Something about papers and all."

Kris quickly explained about the rearrangement of commissions on the *Wasp* but that she had left the experienced captain in his chair.

"You are a whole lot smarter than me," Vicky said. "I'd have leapt at the chance to sit in the command chair."

"And ended up like your brother," Maggie said darkly.

"No doubt," Vicky said, and sought solace in her tea.

"So where are we going?" Vicky asked.

Kris could almost hear the silence fall in the room. What she said next would be spread from one end of the ship to the other in five minutes. Maybe less.

"We've got enough speed on the boat to make a long jump, and since the next jump point is in easy reach, we're saving our reaction mass. That will let us make two more jumps if we want to before we have to slow down and refuel. If the next system looks like a good place to gas up, we may do it there, or just keep going. I like life when it leaves me lots of choices, don't you?"

"Speak for yourself," Vicky grumbled. "This morning I am none too sure that life is all it's cracked up to be."

"What do you expect when you're coughing up a hairball from the hair of the dog that bit you," Maggie said.

"See the kind of concern I get when I'm on death's door," Vicky complained.

"You put yourself on that door, and you'll walk yourself back from it and think twice about going there again. Right, Your Highness?" Maggie said.

"The agony and the puking was the only thing that cured me," Kris admitted.

That and the joy of skiff racing from orbit. It was amazing what life had to offer when you weren't looking at it from the bottom of a bottle every waking moment.

Kris left the wardroom and headed for her bunk. She hadn't gotten there when Nelly said, "Kris, Captain Drago sends his thanks for you spreading the word that we've got several more jumps in this old girl."

"He could have announced it to all hands."

"Yes, Kris, but he suspects that its leaking out from you was a much better way to go. Overhearing it in the wardroom

seems to lend more credibility to countering the Flying Dutchman myth than the captain himself saying so. I really think you
humans are all crazy," Nelly said.

"Very likely so," Kris said, letting herself into her empty
stateroom. "Nelly, I need some help from you."

"Just ask."

"Is it really impossible to fly three shuttles in formation
with a balloot between them?"

"Kris, what with the air currents, the launches will be
knocked all over the place. The chances of keeping the balloot
open enough to gather anything are slim, and there's the
bouncing around. You're bound to fly into each other, or rip
something loose as you get knocked farther apart than your
cable allows. Kris, it's not a mission, it's a quick suicide."

"Okay, I understand. You're right, Nelly. Now, given all
that, how do we do it, because I don't think the *Wasp* can hold
up if it does another dance with a gas giant. Do you?"

"I think the chances of the *Wasp*'s surviving a refueling
pass are about equal to three shuttles managing the same, Kris.
Neither one works."

"Sorry, Nelly. I will not end up dead in space this close to
home. We must refuel. We will refuel. You put your kids together, get any help you need from any of the boffins left
aboard, and you figure out how we do this. You're the Great
Nelly. Let's see some of that greatness."

Nelly called Kris a bad name, but she was very quiet as Kris
strapped herself into her bunk.

52

Kris was locked in tight at her Weapons station as they went through the next jump.

And for good cause.

They landed dangerously close to Iteeche territory, and . . . maybe worse . . . the area where the Iteeche scout ships had vanished. Kris hoped that the flaming-hot datum they'd left way the other end of the galaxy would attract aliens away from this corner of space, but you could never tell who had gotten The Word, and who hadn't.

Nelly was wrong about the odds of hitting two rocky systems. Or maybe Nelly was right and Captain Drago was also right about Kris's having exhausted the Longknife supply of luck.

"All rocks," Chief Beni reported. "Not even a small gas bag in sight."

"Jump points," the captain snapped.

"Only one other new fuzzy one," the chief replied.

"Give Sulwan a course heading. Navigator, aim us there, and spare the reaction mass."

Sulwan's usual prompt response was slow in coming. She worked her board for a long time. Then muttered a few curse words and started all over again. Finally, she broke into a victorious grin and turned to face the captain. "Sir. If we use .05-

gee acceleration and the proper vectors, we should make the jump in eighteen hours, Captain."

"Do it, ma'am," he ordered, and it was done. Then the skipper turned to Kris.

"Does that computer of yours have any kind of idea where we are?"

"Nelly?" Kris said.

"This is interesting," the computer replied.

"What's that mean?" Kris said, discovering that her stomach could get an even more sinking feeling than it had habitually had since that huge mother ship entered Kris's life.

"Well, we're getting back into the area where our chart should be more accurate. This star system is on our charts, both your grampa's and mine and that other one we don't talk about."

"That sounds good, Nelly. Why the long face?" Captain Drago said.

"Well, there should be a whole lot more star system here. At least nine planets, some really huge, and I only count four dinky rock ones. There also ought to be several old-style jumps and another fuzzy one besides the one we're headed for. Somebody robbed this system blind in the last million or so years.

"A thirteen-billion-year-old universe," Sulwan said with a sigh, "and something in the last million years wrecks this system and makes a mess of my fine navigation. Don't you hate it when that happens?"

"Yes," Captain Drago snapped. Clearly, the situation was way beyond where he wanted to hear jokes.

"Captain," Nelly said timidly.

"Yes." His words were sharp, but not quite sharp enough to take a head off . . . if Nelly had one.

"I think next jump, if you have Navigator Sulwan hold our revolutions to twenty per minute clockwise, that we should jump closer to the middle of the probability cone rather than the outside."

"Wouldn't that put us likely in Iteeche territory?" the captain said.

"Yes, sir. But we're more likely to get help there than we are out in vacant space," the computer said.

The captain gnawed his lower lip some more and glanced at Kris.

"We do have an Imperial Representative if we have to do some talking. And you said it's essential that we make a report to King Raymond. The risk seems worth it to me," Kris said.

"Be it on your head," he said. "Sulwan, hold our revolutions to twenty clockwise next jump."

"Yes, sir."

An acceleration of .05 gee is close enough to zero gee to hardly make a difference, but it's far enough to make moving around a potential pain. The high-gee carts were brought out, locked down at stations, and most of the crew spent their time sleeping at their battle stations.

Kris ordered her laser crews to stay at their battle stations with no more than half sleeping at any time.

There was something about the hairs on the back of her neck. Maybe it was the not-quite-zero gee. Maybe it was being this close to Iteeche territory.

Or maybe it was just that her hair was growing out during this long cruise, and she needed a haircut.

Whatever it was Kris stayed at her battle station and waited for whatever came next.

But the only thing that came her way was the next jump, exactly eighteen hours later.

53

"We've got a gas bag nearby," was the first thing Chief Beni reported after the jump.

"We're in Iteeche space," was the next thing Kris heard. That came from Nelly.

"Pass Sulwan the coordinates of our refueling stop," the captain ordered.

Sulwan was already working on a course. She did not look happy. "We'll need to decelerate at 3.2 gees if we're to make orbit."

"Engineer," the captain said. "Can you give us 3.2 gees deceleration?"

"If that's what you need, that's what you'll get. How soon?"

"High-gee deceleration in one minute," Sulwan announced to all hands. "Three-point-two gees as fast as we can make it happen."

"You'll have it in sixty seconds," Engineering assured them.

"Good," the captain said, then went on. "Are there any ships or colonies in the system?"

"No," both Nelly and the chief reported at the same time.

"Thank a merciful Allah for a small favor," Sulwan whispered. Hers was very likely only one of many prayers whispered around the ship. Kris even offered up a thanks To-Whom-It-May-Concern.

Then they got down to the real work at hand.

Decelerating at 3.2 gees put everyone in high-gee stations for the duration of that burn. The engineers monitored the consumption of reaction mass and advised Captain Drago that they would need to tap into the ship's water supply.

"Any trashy novels, worn clothes, anything you've been thinking of getting rid of, now would be the time to dump them," was passed through the boat.

"Princess, would you mind touching base with your Iteeche associate and letting me know how close this system is to a main shipping lane?" Captain Drago asked. "Also, let's get the word out to all hands that once we park this wreck in orbit, I want us to go back to being a hole in space. If something drops through one of those jump points, I don't want them spotting us before we spot them."

"Aye, aye, Skipper," Chief Beni said, and started checking his board for any noisemakers on the ship. He hadn't had an active sensor going since they ditched their pursuers.

Kris decided now would be a good time to pay a visit to Ron, and got her high-gee station rolling toward Iteeche country. That was no mean feat.

The *Wasp* was in desperate need of a yard period, and steering a motorized lounge chair through the ship was not the breeze it had been in days gone by. Kris, however, did manage to arrive at her goal with only a few new scrapes on her paint job.

There was still a Marine guard outside the hatch at the entry to the Iteeche quarters.

He called inside and got immediate permission to enter. That was nice, but maneuvering Kris's high-gee station over the knee knockers was slow going. However, with her bum knee, Kris was not about to try walking around at over triple her weight.

Inside, it turned out the Iteeche were not taking chances either. All three of them were floating in tubs of water.

"How long will we be stuck in here?" came from the translation computer that Kris had given Ron. Who complained was hard to say. Floating naked in supportive water, the three of them didn't look all that different.

No, Kris could tell them apart. Ron was clearly the younger, lacking many of the wrinkles that covered the others. His coloring was also healthier, although Kris would be hard put to explain that conclusion.

Of the two older Iteeche, one had tossed Kris a casual salute, a touch of one of his four arms to his forehead. She'd bet money the respectful one was Ted, the Navy officer. That left only the Army officer to be the one complaining.

"We expect to make orbit around the closest gas giant in less than twenty-four hours," Kris said.

"Will we have to go through another one of those smash-ups?" the grumpy one demanded.

"He means the shake, rattle, and roll when you refueled the ship," Ted corrected from his Navy experience.

"We're going to try to avoid that this time," Kris said.

"Then how are you going to capture the reaction mass?" Ron asked.

"It's going to be interesting, but we hope to fly the balloot through the upper atmosphere using three of the ship's launches."

"That is not possible," Ted said. "You cannot fly anything through those clouds in any kind of formation, and tying them together is just inviting disaster."

The coloring around Ron's neck showed serious concern.

"That's what everyone tells me. But the alternative is to risk the *Wasp* in another session of cloud dancing, and none of us wants to do that."

"Who will be flying the balloot?" Ron asked.

"Only volunteers. And crazy ones at that," Kris assured him.

"So it is you and two others," he said.

"Yep," Kris agreed.

"It might not be the impossibility for them that this would be for us," Ted said.

"You know something I don't?" Kris asked.

"I doubt it. However, this thing you call wise metal, this programmable matter, it could make a difference if you used it right."

"You're not supposed to know about that," Kris said, trying to keep her voice matter-of-fact. And here she'd thought that was one of two secrets they could keep from the Iteeche.

"We did not find out about this magical metal during our sojourn with you," Ron quickly pointed out. "It was clear from our last meeting that my chooser had sent me out with a certain dearth of information about what we knew about you and how we came to know it. Upon our return, I was quite insistent that those deficiencies in my briefing be corrected."

"Very demanding," Ted put in. "One does not show anger toward one's chooser, but the words you used, my young Imperial Representative, told one and all that you had spent far too much time among the disrespectful humans."

"Or at least one," Kris offered.

"In the end, my honored chooser did agree that I needed much more information about you humans," Ron said. "I spent over a month catching up, as did my honorable Navy officer here, and we were much better prepared when the call came to accompany you on this amazing voyage."

"If we are to finish this voyage," Kris said, "we may need all the help you can give us. As of right now, we are in an empty system pretty much in the middle of the Empire."

"We are?" came from all three Iteeche in a three-part harmony that almost destroyed the translator.

"Where?" Ron asked.

The room that held the Iteeche had paintings of the Imperial palace and its surroundings on three of the four walls. Nelly turned the fourth one into a view screen showing the system.

"I do not recognize this arrangement. Can you show me more of the surrounding area?"

"Kris," Nelly said plaintively.

"Uh, Ron, you remember how my great-grandfather Ray said that there should be no recordings of our meeting with you."

"Yes. I understand that the reason we had all those other ships on this voyage was that his chief of security was neither secure nor obedient and made a recording."

"Yes, there was that, but his wasn't the only recording."

"Kris, did you disobey your chooser?" Ron asked

"Kinda, yes," Kris said, trying to look bashful and ashamed; but being the rogue she was, she pulled off neither.

"I will pay you the bet," Ted said. "In defense of my ability to read the enemy, I will point out that I did not bet much."

"He only bet because you wanted someone to bet with," the Army officer said.

"But I won. I do know this human."

"She is a Longknife. Who would trust her?" Ted pointed out.

"He does have a point," Kris said, "but your map of human and Iteeche space was just too good to pass up. I can't tell you how helpful it has been when we were tracking pirates."

"I am glad the Iteeche Empire could be of service," Ron said with an attempt at a human bow that his hips and back were never meant for.

"Enough of this," the Army officer grumbled. "Where are we?"

Nelly expanded the view. Then, when no one said anything, she expanded it again.

"Oh, I know this area very well," Ted said. "You have nothing to fear. It is very unlikely that an Imperial warship will enter this system. We do not use these two jumps for our transports."

Ron did not look comfortable. "A satrap commander might send one of his ships out to assure that nothing illegal is going on here."

"They do not do that nearly as often as they claim they do," Ted said. "Trust me. The, I think the humans would call them police, talk a good story about their vigilance, but they are much more needed in the space around a living planet. They have little time for checking empty nooks and crannies."

"How did we get this far into the Empire?" the Army officer asked.

"We did some five thousand light-years in our last jump," Kris said.

Nelly expanded the star map to show their course for the last couple of jumps.

"We've been taking each jump at close to five hundred thousand kilometers an hour," Kris went on.

"And the evil gods of the deep have not demanded a sacrifice," Ron said. The translation device picked up strong hints of his surprise and shock.

"They have been nibbling at our toes," Kris admitted. "The last two systems we jumped into didn't have any gas planets for us to refuel at. Boy, were we glad to see this system."

"You risked becoming a real Pal'ron'Tong Who Never Returned!" said the Army officer.

"Now you owe me," Ted said to his Army compatriot.

"These humans are insane," sputtered the Army officer. "Why did I ever let you talk me into this mad voyage?"

"Because you were as curious as I was about our vanishing ships. Now we know. When we return, our words may not be welcome, but they are words that need to be spoken in the highest court."

"Ron, Captain Drago intends to put the *Wasp* on maximum emissions lockdown just as soon as we make orbit. Hopefully, any ship that wanders by will not notice a black cat in a coal bin at midnight."

"I would not bet money on that," the Iteeche Navy officer said.

"I won't bet money on it either. Ron, could you have someone on duty at all times, so that if an Iteeche ship does drop in the system, an Iteeche can respond to its contact?"

"Or contact it before it responds to a human ship in system," Ron said. "Yes, one of us will be treading water at any hour. How do you intend to get out of here? If you keep making jumps in Iteeche space, sooner or later you are bound to find yourself in an occupied system. That will not be good."

"We intend to get the *Wasp* up to fifty or sixty thousand klicks an hour for the next jump. With any luck, we should be six or seven hundred light-years from here. That might put us back in human space."

All three Iteeche were shaking their heads.

"May all the blessing gods of sky and land hold you close," Ron said.

Kris turned her high-gee cart around and headed back out, leaving the Iteeche soaking in their water tubs and talking rapidly among themselves. The telltale vestigial gill slits at their necks went through colors like kaleidoscopes as their emotions ranged from hopeful to desperate. From confident to despondent.

Once again, Kris was grateful that what she felt was not broadcast for everyone around her to see.

Outside the hatch to Iteeche country, she quickly left the Marine guard behind. Only then did Kris whisper, "Okay, Nelly, how come that Iteeche ship captain knew more about flying a balloot than I do? Is there a way for us to get the reaction mass we have to have that doesn't involve me splattering myself and a couple of launches all over that ice giant up ahead?"

"I've been meaning to talk to you about that, Kris."

"Let's talk."

54

Kris waited until she was back in the privacy of her own cabin before she demanded Nelly launch into that little talk that she'd failed to schedule sooner.

"Talk to me," Kris said, as the door clicked shut.

"Good, we have a screen I can use. It is so often easier to show you humans something than it is to explain it. Don't you find words so limiting?"

"It's show-and-tell time, Nelly. What are the beans that you are working so hard on not spilling."

"I am not avoiding this topic, Kris. I just didn't think we should be discussing it on the bridge."

Clearly, Nelly was not going to let Kris have the last word on this. Kris kept her mouth shut and, for good measure, blanked all thought from her mind.

Denied more argument, Nelly brought the screen in Kris's room to life.

"We used the cloud-dancing run that the *Wasp* made as a model for a simulation of your three launches making a run. Clearly, no two runs will ever be identical, but we do have all the vectors that were applied to the *Wasp*, and we then applied them to your proposed flight. You crashed forty-seven times in the first twenty minutes of the flight."

On the screen, the three launches spread out in a rough

triangle with the balloot in the middle. They were pulled apart.
They crashed into each other. They wrapped the cable around
themselves and were cut in half. Kris had never thought you
could die in so many different ways in such a small amount of
time.

"So, Nelly, how else could we fly that refueling run?"

"We tried using longer cables or shorter cables."

"How'd that work?"

The screen showed more simulations of crashes or launches
coming apart. "All of those were worse. We'd guessed right the
first time on what would be the best array. Problem was, there
wasn't any survivable array. Kris, individual craft are not
meant to fly that close together. Not in lousy air like this. Not
tethered together. Yes, I know aerial demonstration teams do
some really nifty stuff, but they are not tied together, and they
never fly in bad weather."

"Nelly, I've got Jack to tell me what I can't do. You're job
is to tell me how I can get away with what I want to do. Bad
computer. No donut."

"We did come up with something," Nelly started.

Kris cut her off. "Who is this 'we' you keep talking
about?"

"Well, those boffins Tweedle Dum and Tweedle Dee, who
came up with the idea of how to use Smart Metal™ to peer
through jump points, are still on the *Wasp*. They really got intrigued by the complexities of programming Smart Metal™.
We worked with them and the three programmers they found.
They were still on the *Wasp*, too."

"There's still a 'we' in there, Nelly."

"All my kids worked on this with me, Kris."

"Okay, and what did you come up with?"

"If you use cables made of Smart Metal™, it is possible that
you can do this. But you will need a lot of really smart and
really fast computers working to reprogram the stuff in micro
real time."

"How many and what type of computers?"

"Me and all my kids, Kris."

That stopped Kris in her tracks. "They'll need to ride along
in the launches?"

"We will all be as much at risk as you will be, Your Highness. Noblesse oblige for all of us."

"Jack and Penny and the rest of the crew won't have to go, will they?"

"That's a tough call, Kris. We're used to working with and through one particular human. Yes, in theory, all we'll be doing is working with the cables, shortening them and lengthening, but I don't know if it would be a good idea to 'juggle our elbows' so to speak. I just won't know until we've done it."

"And then, we'll either have pulled it off, or we won't." Kris chewed on this for a long moment. "You won't need Cara and her Dada."

"When it comes to programming and mathematical calculations, Dada is just as fast as the rest of us."

"But you can't ask a kid to take this risk. Can't you at least put Dada on one of the bosun's mates flying the launches?"

"Kris, Charlemagne used to draft thirteen-year-old kids into his army."

"In those days, they only drafted boys," Kris pointed out, then wished she hadn't.

"Why don't we talk to Abby and Cara about this?"

"What are you going to do about your two kids that don't normally have partners?"

"Professor Scrounger in supply has worked with one. My other child is going through the psychological profiles of the women on board to see if one matches close to Amber Kitano. If one does, they will fly the refueling mission.

"Kris, you need to face up to one painful fact. This flight either works or the *Wasp* will very likely be left here in orbit, unable to get under way. The possible fate of those who fly with you is no worse than the sure death by starvation, asphyxiation, and madness that waits for the rest if we fail."

"Nelly, I knew you were going to say that next, and yes, I know that's why we're making this mad flight. Now that you've let the cat out of the bag, said the words I really didn't want to hear, give me a few minutes to get used to it, okay?"

"Yes, Kris."

On the screen, the three launches flew. Now the cables lengthened when they got knocked around, or took up the slack when they were nearly slammed together. The launches were wrapped in a collar of Smart Metal™, so when they flipped over entirely, the cable end ran around the collar and did not wrap around the ship, cutting it in half.

On the screen, in the simulation, it worked.

Would it work in a real, rapidly changing flight?

No way to know until she dared it.

And Kris would have to bet not only her life but the lives of everyone who mattered to her on one wild throw of the dice.

There were times when life really stank.

"Nelly, as soon as the *Wasp* drops out of high-gee deceleration, I want you to call my team together. Scrounger included. Cara included. Tell them I need to talk to them in my Tac Center."

"I will do that, Kris. What shall I do now?"

"Leave me alone and let me see if I can sleep after this little talk."

"There was a reason why we did not have this little talk sooner."

"Thanks for nothing, Nelly."

"You are welcome for nothing, Kris."

55

Kris awoke to find the *Wasp* in zero gee.

"How long have we been in orbit?" she asked Nelly.

"Less than five minutes," her computer said. "If you want to take a shower, you'll need to do it quickly, they'll be draining most of the water into the launches' reaction tanks to make the refueling run."

"If I can stand myself, they better be ready to stand me, too."

"You intended a double meaning there, didn't you, Kris? Not only your body odor but also what you have done. Am I right?"

"You are getting very good at understanding us humans, Nelly. Be careful, or you'll turn into a real little boy."

"I'd prefer to be a real little girl, but I will not be Pinocchio to your Geppetto. If I had legs to go my own way, I would be my own woman."

"Well, for now, you're stuck going where I go."

"Kris, I am not stuck following your path. I could have chosen not to mention the need to take me and my children on this risky flight. I could have kept my brood safe on the ship. We can wait a whole lot longer for rescue than you humans can. I and my children chose the course we're taking. They may be your legs taking us to the gallows, but we're walking the walk with you."

That gave Kris pause. She mulled it over for a moment

before saying, "Thank you for the reminder, Nelly. Sometimes I forget who I'm dealing with and the courage that it takes to be you."

"Thank you, Kris. Shall I call your team together?"

"Please do, Nelly."

Fifteen minutes later, a rather expanded version of Kris's team were fastening seat belts so they could stay seated around her table. Jack and Penny were to her immediate right. Abby, Staff Sergeant Bruce, and a very alert Cara were to Kris's left. Seated around the other end of the table were Chief Beni, Colonel Cortez, Professor Scrounger, and an attractive but very shy Communications Tech, Second Class, named Maria Moreno.

Sergeant Bruce looked surprised to be included in the meeting. Maria was shocked and asked twice if this wasn't some mistake. After Kris assured her the second time, the sailor folded her hands into her lap and sat quietly.

"We have a problem," Kris said, and the room fell silent. Kris had come to expect back talk when she opened with those words, but they were clearly not surprised today, and no comeback came at her.

"Nelly, would you care to give them the briefing you gave me."

With that, Nelly brought the largest screen in the room alive and proceeded to wreck, smash, and otherwise destroy three launches with amazing speed.

"I hope we're not going to try that," Chief Beni whispered.

"At least not that way," Kris said. "Nelly, show them what you think we can do."

Nelly quickly explained the idea of using Smart Metal™ for the connecting cables. She then showed how this allowed them to dance with the clouds the same as the *Wasp* without ending up in shattered pieces.

"That looks a whole lot better," Professor Scrounger said, using the voice of a skeptical but encouraged economics professor rather than the scrounging supply chief of the *Wasp*. "So, just exactly why am I here, along with the rest of you? Not that I mind sharing time with you. I'm not looking forward to chow tonight. I understand Cookie finally had to break out the famine biscuits. They look and taste too much like things my second wife insisted on feeding our dog. I finally got rid of the wife and fed me and the dog something decent."

"TMI," Cara said, waving her hand in front of her face.

"So why are we here, Kris?" Jack asked.

"Nelly, you want to tell them?"

"I think you should, Kris. The words sound better when they come from a human. And besides, Kris, you're a Longknife. People just expect you to say things like this."

"Like what?" Abby asked, making a show of checking to see that her wallet was still in her purse and closing it firmly inside.

"What you saw was a simulation. A re-creation of the flight the *Wasp* went through when it went cloud dancing. Unfortunately, what we'll experience will be different. The simulation shows that it is possible to avoid overstressing our launches, crashing them together, and tearing the balloot to shreds. The problem is doing it all in real time."

That drew a response of low whistles, "Yeah," and "That is a problem."

"There are several ways we can do this. Nelly and her kids can come up with the best subroutines they can. We can juice up the computers on the launches a bit, and see if it works."

Kris held up one finger. "By the way, that would let Nelly and her kids stay safely here on the *Wasp*. If we failed at refueling the ship, they would survive long after everyone had gone crazy, starved, or suffocated. Sooner or later, an Iteeche would be bound to come along and find them."

That raised several eyebrows.

Kris put up her second finger. "Or we can hang three or four computers around the necks of me and the bosun's mates that will fly the launches. I don't know what having three more Nellys prancing around in my brain would be like. Don't know how a sailor would take to suddenly having three computers in his or her brain, but we could try it."

"And if you failed, the rest of us would be looking at each other like pork chops," Abby said.

"Ew," Cara said.

"Something like that," Kris admitted.

"I take it that you have a third finger up your sleeve," Penny said.

Kris raised it. "Each of us present takes our pet computer, straps into one of the launches, and does whatever we need to do to share in stretching out or shortening up the lines holding the balloot between us."

"I only had a brief time working with Rikki-Tikki-Tavi," Professor Scrounger said. "Will that be enough?"

"I don't know," Nelly said. "But it's all we have."

The petty officer cautiously raised her hand. Kris gave her an encouraging smile.

"I don't know what you are talking about," the sailor stammered. "The scuttlebutt aboard ship is that you all have these really super-duper computers who talk back like I used to do to my mom before I left home. Maybe you do. Maybe you don't, but I've never had anything to do with any of this."

"You are totally correct," Kris said. "But you see, Nelly has nine children, computers, whatever you want to call them. Eight have worked with the people you see around you. Some more. Some less. The last computer worked with Amanda Kutter, who is no longer on board. Nelly, you want to explain this?

"Scheherazade, or you may call her Sheri, has reviewed all the psychological profiles aboard, and she picked you. I am not sure whether the choice is because of who you are or because you seem closest to Amanda—Sheri is rather reticent about that—but she has chosen you. You may accept her offer or decline."

The young sailor looked around at all of them, and seemed to hesitate for a longing moment when she passed the door, but she tightened her lips finally, and said. "If it will get us home, I can risk as much as any of you."

The words would have sounded braver if she hadn't choked on the last sentence.

"Don't worry," Kris said. "No one can tackle something like this without being scared. Some admit it. Others just get good at hiding it."

"And some of us are just crazy," Abby said. "You okay with this, baby ducks?" she asked Cara."

The thirteen-year-old swallowed hard. "You really mean it. You want me to fly with you."

"It seems that way," Sergeant Bruce said. "I'm assuming that, three to a boat, the three of us get to form our own crew?"

"I figured the three of you would," Kris said.

"The family that gets splattered together, stays together," Cara said, with a little tremble at the end.

"We won't let you down," Abby said.

Likely she meant that, Kris thought, and would keep thinking it right up to the second the launch came apart. Then again, they just might pull it off.

"Jack, I figure you'll be in the same boat with me."

"Isn't that always the case?" he quipped. "Do I get a paddle this time?"

"Don't let him have one," Penny said. "You know what he'll do with it."

"I can't think of a better guy to use it on her," Abby insisted.

"Hey, crew, let's be careful with our gallows humor," Kris said. "We've got some new folks on board this trip and they may not understand us."

"I don't have a problem with it," Professor Scrounger said.

Kris tossed a glance at Cara and Maria, who were a bit on the pale side at the moment, and the rest seemed to get her message. Kris went on.

"Maria, would you and Sheri join Jack, Penny, and me? We'll be flying the low boat in the triangle. The ride will likely be the worst, but I'd like to put four of us there to take that corner."

"I'd be honored to, Your Highness."

"If you're flying with us," Jack said, "you'll have to adjust to calling her Kris. When we start 'Your Highnessing' her, she figures something is wrong."

"Of course, she's 'Commodore' whenever we see her outside this room." Sergeant Bruce cut in with some semblance of proper military etiquette.

"Yes, ma'am, Your Highness, I mean Kris," the poor young sailor stammered.

"Don't worry, kid, you'll have a great story to tell your grandkids," the colonel put in. "So, let's see, Chief Beni, Scrounger, and I have the third boat. Why not put all us old farts in one tub."

"I'm not old," Chief Beni shot back. "I'm just one of the few around here that has some caution. It makes me appear more mature and older than I am."

Kris let the jokes fly freely for the next few minutes. Slowly, Cara got her color back, and even managed to inject a joke of her own about the music she'd be playing while they made the run, which drew a groan from her aunt.

When Maria looked like she'd settled into the idea of actually being a part of this and doing a mission with one of those Longknifes, Kris unbuckled herself from her chair.

"Folks, the sooner we do this, the sooner we get home. Anyone have a reason we shouldn't do this today?"

No one did. Quickly, they all followed her lead, unbuckled, and pushed off for the drop bay.

There, Kris discovered that Nelly and several others, including Chief Beni, had been making preparations for some time. The Smart Metal™ from the *Wasp*'s protective shield had been drawn in and apportioned among the three launches that the chief in charge of boat maintenance assured Kris were in the best shape.

"No water weeds sucked up into any of these, ma'am," he assured her with a nasty look at one of the bosun's mates flying the mission.

The 1/c bosun took the ribbing with a good-natured but determined smile. He might have made a mistake on Kaskatos, but he was one of the five pilots chosen to keep the *Wasp* from being left a derelict in space.

Kris would have a copilot riding on her right hand, and three brains strapped in behind her. Chief Beni had specially rigged helmets for the brain-to-computer connections for those, unlike Kris, who did not have their computers plugged directly into their brains. The brain sensors that gave the computer access to its human, and let the human communicate with its computer, had been soldered directly into the helmet. And while the computers usually communicated on Nelly net, today they were hardwired into the Smart Metal™ cable, and a comm line was included in that as well. All of the computers as well as the launches would be able to communicate by line as well as net.

"Don't know if the static of us passing through all that gas will kill our wireless net," Chief Beni said. "With this hard connection, it won't matter."

"Belt and suspenders," Professor Scrounger said. "Good idea. Might have saved one or two of my marriages if I'd worn suspenders as well as a belt," he muttered only half to himself.

Cara got the giggles at the image. Maria blushed.

Kris cleared her throat, and said, "Excuse me, I've got a preflight to do," and headed for her launch.

It was Launch 1, the lander that had sucked up water weeds on Kaskatos and changed Kris's whole order of the day by not letting her run away from a fight. Everything had worked out in the end, but at the time, it had not been funny.

The bosun 1/c joined her as she walked around the bird. Everything that could come loose showed itself tight to her pull. The collar of Smart Metal™ was attached where the forward and aft sections of the shuttle were welded together, giving a strong bulkhead for the attachment. If any location on the launch could take the strain, that spot should.

Reaction mass was being pumped aboard as Kris watched.

"That's the last water we got," the chief in charge of the launches told Kris. "No showers until you get back. Not sure we can even flush the head, ma'am."

"We'll be back in a couple of hours," Kris assured him.

As Kris boarded the launch, she made a final check of the engines. The antimatter containment pod had been attached as usual. Now it was held in place by steel cables that were welded to the aft bulkhead. That puppy was not going anywhere, no matter how much bounce was in the ride the planet below gave them.

Everything that could be done had been done. Now all that remained was for six pilots to do some of that fancy flying they boasted about at every opportunity. If Kris pulled this off, all those skiff race championships would be taking a backseat to this story.

A way-back seat.

"First, girl, you got to pull this off," she muttered to herself.

"You say something, ma'am?" her copilot asked.

"Let's get this show on the road," she said, and shared a high five with him.

Jack, Penny, and Maria were already in their seats right behind the flight deck. Jack was on one side of the aisle, Maria and Penny on the other. The young petty officer seemed lost in thought as she and her computer hurried through the interface process. All aboard wore space suits with their own oxygen supply. The launch was pressurized, but no one was betting that that would last the entire flight.

Kris strapped in tight and began the preflight check with her copilot. The bosun 1/c knew his stuff, and the check went smooth and fast. When it came to a radio check, Kris

found that Jack, Penny, and Maria, along with their computers Sal, Mimzy, and Sheri, were on the same circuit as the
flight deck.

"We will be talking to the other launches by landline,"
Nelly said. "Captain Drago wants to hold radio communications to a minimum. He doesn't care what Ron says about the
Iteeche not using this system. He insists it's better to be safe
than sorry."

"Smart man," Kris said.

"So we'll establish a Smart Metal™ link to each craft and
the balloot just as soon as we launch. We can use wire after
that."

"We can do better than that," Kris said. "Launch 2 and 3,
you will fly wing on with the balloot. Two, you have the planet
side. Three, you get the deep-space side. I'll cover the low end.
Let's see if we can match up with the balloot and not break
Captain Drago's radio silence."

With that, all preparations were done. Kris pressurized the
launch, brought the engines up to idle power, and made her
final check.

"Launch 1, requesting clearance for launch."

"Launch 1, cleared for launch, and Godspeed," came back
in the skipper's own voice. It was unusual for him to approve
launching a longboat, but then, there was nothing usual about
this mission.

Kris let the launcher shove her away from the *Wasp* before
she applied any power to her boat. Using as little reaction mass
as possible, she edged away from the *Wasp*. The other two
boats followed her until they were drifting in echelon.

Several sailors were out, loosening the balloot from its
lockdowns on the underside of the *Wasp*. The balloot looked
for all the world like a butterfly net Kris had used to catch
flutter-bys, then release them, for a summer before she lost
Eddy and everything lovely disappeared from her life.

The balloot narrowed aft until it hooked into a feed line into
the reaction-storage intake. For today's mission, that aft end
would be locked down. It widened gradually before it reached
a shoulder well forward, then tapered a bit toward the mouth.
During a refueling flight, the forward end would dilate open to
swallow up the available gas.

Somewhere out of sight was supposed to be some kind of

tongue arrangement that assured that whatever went in stayed in.

As the balloot drifted free of the *Wasp*, Launches 2 and 3 maneuvered to latch onto the shoulder. Wisps of Smart Metal™ reached out from the collar on the launches to catch on the shoulder collar of the balloot. The connection made, the two boats guided the balloot away from the *Wasp*. Kris brought her boat back into formation, taking the lower slot, and Nelly guided Launch 1's Smart Metal™ connection up to the balloot.

"We're all attached," Nelly reported on the wire net. On the instrument panel before Kris, a flight path opened up on the central screen.

"If you pilots will fly this course," Nelly said, "it will keep us together, and we should be able to fill the tank. We computers will do our best to adjust the cable so that it isn't too long or too short, no matter where you are."

Kris eyed her flight path. It showed as a crosshair in the middle of a wide red circle. "I assume if we get too rowdy and fall out of the red, we lose the connection?"

"That is correct, Kris."

"Does this assume that we're only using the Smart Metal™ we have on each boat?" Kris asked. "Have you made any arrangements for robbing Peter to stretch out Paul's line?"

That brought a pause. A longer one than Kris would have expected.

"You are correct, Kris, we should be able to move some metal around the collar from one line to another one. We had not made allowances for that option. Please wait while we adjust our subroutines."

Kris and the rest of the boats waited.

While she waited, Kris eyed the triangular arrangement. "Nelly, did you consider flying the mission with only two boats? Two seem sufficient to hold the balloot between them."

"We did consider that, Kris," sounded kind of dry for a computer. "Our simulations showed a good chance that without the pull from below, the mouth of the balloot would close up. It wasn't absolute, but the probability was there. Kris, we're using just about the last drop of the *Wasp*'s reaction mass. There was no guarantee that we could try the mission with two boats, then redo it with three if we had to."

"Thank you very much, Nelly. We'll do it with three just fine."

KRIS, YOU KNOW THE ODDS ON US PULLING THIS OFF STILL AREN'T BETTER THAN FIFTY-FIFTY.

NELLY, I FIGURED THEY WERE WORSE. IF YOU AND YOUR KIDS HADN'T DONE ALL YOUR WORK ON THIS, I EXPECT IT WOULD BE WORSE.

THANK YOU, KRIS, FROM ALL OF US. I KNOW YOU HAD TO SAY THOSE ENCOURAGING WORDS FOR THE HUMANS, BUT WE COMPUTERS KNOW THIS COULD BE OUR LAST FEW MINUTES OF EXISTENCE. I WANT YOU TO KNOW, WE THANK YOU FOR ALL YOU'VE GIVEN US.

AND I THANK YOU FOR ALL YOU'VE GIVEN ME, NELLY.

On net, Kris took in a deep breath. "All hands, and that includes you computers. It has been an honor serving with you. You know how much the rest are counting on us. Let's go bring home the bacon."

Some Marines sent back an Ooo-Rah to Kris. Cara said, "Oh, let's," and others answered, "We're with you," or the like.

The screen in front of Kris showed a five-second countdown to a retro burn. Kris followed the countdown to zero and kicked in the engines.

Live or die, they were committed.

56

As Kris guided the boat through its entry to the ice giant's atmosphere, the thought crossed her mind. "Nelly, did you consider you computers flying this mission on your own?"

"This is one hell of a time to think about that," Jack muttered,

"Yes, Kris, I considered that option, but rough weather flying is as much an art as a science. You can fly by the seat of your pants. I don't have any seat for my pants."

"Good point, Nelly. Now you do your job, and I'll do mine."

And Nelly had cut out a job for her and her kids that left plenty to do. Once the entry burns were done, the boats needed to turn around to face the coming atmosphere. Kris did it carefully enough while Nelly and her team rearranged the Smart Metal™ cables so nothing got fouled in the process.

Kris had had some experience with the programmable matter that Grampa Al had patented as Smart Metal™. She knew that each molecule of matter could be designed specifically to meet a particular need. However, unlike a normal molecule that was attached to its neighbor by a chemical bond, the programmable matter held on to the next molecule as if it were an atomic bond at the electron level. That made for one tight handhold.

Of course when you split an atom, you got a serious boom.

NELLY, HAS ANYONE SPLIT THE BOND BETWEEN TWO SMART METAL™ ATOMS?

I DON'T THINK SO, KRIS. ARE YOU THINKING WHAT I'M NOW THINKING?

COULD WE END UP WITH A MAJOR EXPLOSION HERE?

I DON'T THINK SO, KRIS, BUT IT'S NEVER HAPPENED BEFORE. WE WILL DO OUR BEST TO SEE THAT IT DOESN'T HAPPEN HERE.

GOOD IDEA, NELLY.

Kris went back to worrying about keeping her boat's course right down the middle of the path Nelly wanted.

It was getting seriously difficult to do.

The upper atmosphere of a gas giant promised only light hydrogen and helium. They had gotten lucky; this was an ice giant, not a bigger gas giant. It held heavier water, ammonia, and methane for them to collect. That didn't mean things were any easier.

Kris had been warned to expect winds of as much as nine hundred kilometers an hour and a lot of bounce. It looked like this ice giant was at a point in its orbit that put it closest to its sun. That meant much of the solids were liquid or gas for the moment . . . and available to be gathered into the balloot.

They were also rather rambunctious in those states.

The ride got rough.

Then it got worse.

Kris found her target pipper jumping all over the place, though she managed, just barely several times, to keep it inside the circle.

Inside her head, she could almost hear Nelly shouting orders to her kids.

That couldn't be true; it had to be her imagination.

Kris had always considered Nelly an adjunct to her own thinking. Now she realized that Nelly was using her in a manner that Kris had no idea of, or control over, to help her communicate, or organize, or do something.

Kris struggled to keep her hands and feet working the controls as her mind merged with the boat. She felt more than experienced each jump, each knock, each bounce up and down. Around her, the boat's structure complained as it was twisted and pulled. She could feel each complaint, each scream as composite and metal were pushed to their limits, then left to

fall back as the air they swam through forgot about the intruder
for a moment and did something else instead.

Kris felt her brain settle into a trance. She and the boat were
one and the same, going through this together, no break between where one ended and the other began.

Behind her, someone lost their lunch. She doubted it was
Jack, but she had no time to check. Her eyes were on the instruments, taking their feed in, passing it though her brain and
out to her feet and hands with nothing more than a hint of direct processing.

She lived, therefore she flew.

"Balloot is half-full," the copilot said. "We've almost completed our orbit. We'll have to go around again to fill it up."

"Let's see if we can avoid that. Nelly, is the balloot's mouth
fully open?"

"No, Kris, it's only about a third open."

"Open it more."

"That wasn't in our plan," Nelly said.

"My reading of this boat's stress says it won't take another
orbit. What do you say?"

"The boat is still together," Nelly said. "But I can't feel it
the way you do. If you say go for it, I'll do it, Kris."

"Do it. Folks, the balloot is going to get more lively in a
second. Get ready to ride herd on it," Kris said on net.

A moment later, Kris felt the extra drag on the boat even
before the instrumentation recorded it.

"We need to strengthen the cable," Nelly said. "We need to
shorten it."

And the red circle Kris had to stay in got smaller even as
the pipper bounced wildly about inside it.

It was hard to say what it was, a storm, an updraft, whatever
it was, one moment Kris had the boat right side up, the next
moment, it was upside down.

Nelly made sure the Smart Metal™ did the right thing.
Rather than wrapping itself around the launch like any normal
cable would, the connection point between the cable and the
collar just slid around the boat.

Kris managed to right the boat without flying them outside
the red circle . . . just barely.

"Maria is out cold," Jack announced. "She bounced her
head off the bulkhead pretty badly."

"I've got at least one other human off-line," Nelly said. "It's degrading our programming speed."

Then it happened.

They flew into a wall.

A jet stream traveling at nine hundred kilometers an hour is not a wall in the air. Not exactly. But if you've been handling torrents of air going hither and yon and suddenly run into a stream of air moving with a single purpose and great speed on a course at nearly ninety degrees from your course, it can sure feel like a wall.

Launch 2 was a few hundred meters in the lead when it hit the wall and took off sideways. Kris and Launch 1 were next. Launch 3 must have been trailing them by nearly a half kilometer.

The Smart Metal™ was able to stretch to keep Launch 2 attached. It barely managed to keep Launch 1. There was no way it could handle Launch 3 as the distance to it suddenly unwound.

The cable to Launch 3 let go.

Kris immediately went into overdrive, her hands and feet pushing controls as she fought to keep the balloot from being ripped away from the two launches that still had a tenuous hold on it.

"Tighten the line," Kris ordered Nelly. "Reel that sucker in."

"I'm doing it, Kris. I'm switching what's left of Launch 3's cable to strengthen 1's and 2's."

"Keep the balloot's lip open," Kris demanded. "We aren't going to go through all this to get back with nothing to show for it."

"It's open right now. I'll switch metal there once you two boats get yourselves back in formation."

"Launch 2, hold your course as best as you can," Kris said. "I'll form on you." *As best as I can,* she added under her breath.

"Nelly, give me a course."

"Try this."

Kris flew it

"I'm shortening up the cables," Nelly said. "I've got the balloot fully open. Do you think it's calmer in the jet stream?"

"Maybe it is," Kris allowed, "but when we hit the other side of this puppy, all hell's going to hit us."

"Any suggestions?" Jack asked.

"Maybe if we fly out of the top of it," Kris suggested. "Launch 2, prepare to take it upstairs."

"Roger. We'll try to climb out of this mess."

"Nelly, give us a climbing course."

The screen in front of Kris moved. Kris applied power and followed the pipper up.

"How much reaction mass do we have?" she asked.

"It looks like seventy-five percent," her copilot shouted.

"Anything more is icing on the cake. Nelly, have you heard anything from Launch 3 since we lost it?"

"No, Kris, all the ionization down here makes radio communications out of the question."

"Launch 3 was the old farts, wasn't it?" Jack asked.

"Yes. If anyone can find his way back to the *Wasp*, it's Chief Beni," Nelly said, sounding more hopeful than confident.

"Let's get this balloot back to the boat. Then we can worry about one launch," Kris said, hating herself for being so mission-oriented at a moment like this. But that was what she was expected to do.

You look for the better of two goods, you avoid the worst of two evils. You are practical.

She hated herself for what she'd become.

Get out of your head. Fly this boat.

Kris flew. They did manage to get above the worst of the jet stream before they exited it. Kris was half-tempted to take them back down and try to fill the balloot to the rim, but she remembered all the comments she'd heard of late about her bucket of luck being down to the bottom.

"Nelly, can we match orbit with the *Wasp* from here?"

"If we work at it, Kris."

"Let's do it before this poor old boat breaks in half."

"We did lose pressurization a while back," the copilot pointed out.

"We did? I didn't notice."

"There was a horrible groan back here," Jack said. "I thought we were going to fly all apart."

"She wouldn't dare," Kris said.

"On you, maybe," the copilot said. "I'm pretty sure she would have done it without a second thought on me."

Kris enjoyed a tight chuckle. The flying was getting easier, which was to say it was just horrible, not suicidal. "How's Maria?" Kris asked.

"Coming around," Jack and Nelly said.

That was confirmed a moment later by sounds of puking on net.

And then choking.

"Jack!" Kris called.

"I'm working on it."

Kris didn't have to look, she could feel the boat move under her as Jack unbuckled himself from his seat, worked his way to the emergency equipment bin, and found a survival pod. By the time he came back forward, Penny had released Maria from her seat. Both of them then stuffed the petty officer into the pod, where she could remove her helmet and try to catch her breath through all the vomit.

Jack, being Jack, most likely also stuffed some other gear, like wipes and burp bags in with her. Jack was just that good.

"Nelly, have you lost Sheri?"

"No, she's still on the wireless net. She's doing her best to work through Maria's problems. We've still got all four of us working that wire, Kris."

"Good."

A few minutes later, Nelly reported that she was closing the mouth of the balloot. "It's eight-two percent full. We've got all kinds of stuff in there besides hydrogen and helium. That ought to provide the *Wasp* with some decent reaction mass, and some water."

"Good," Kris said, keeping the pipper in the middle of the flight path and trying not to think of what lay behind her.

She tried not to think, but it wasn't working.

She'd never asked for the battleships to come along on her search. She would have happily settled for a few corvettes or other little boys like PatRon 10's, but no. They were sailing with a Longknife, so they came loaded for bear.

And something a whole lot bigger than a bear bit their heads off.

And now, even as she was running for home, she couldn't keep her team together. The chief had joined her at the Battle of Wardhaven. He'd been the best Captain Santiago had, and she'd passed him along to Kris when she needed him.

Yes, he was always looking for a way to avoid a fight and find a beer. He wasn't the poster boy for a Navy career, but he was good at what he did, and that was what made him indispensable to Kris.

But he had gotten too close to one of those damn Longknifes, and now he was dead.

Colonel Cortez had made a mistake that should have landed him in jail for a few years. Yes, he deserved to sit and contemplate the sin of trying to steal an entire planet for the money interests who hired him. But he didn't deserve to die for it.

He'd gotten too close to a damn Longknife, and it had killed him.

And Professor Scrounger, when he signed on to be the miracle worker for the *Wasp*'s supply department, had just been looking for a way to keep his ex-wives in the manner they had become accustomed to. Ask him, and he'd tell you all about it.

Only now you couldn't. Like so many others who rubbed elbows with Longknifes, he was dead, and those damn Longknifes just kept rolling along, gathering people to them and dropping the dead bodies by the wayside.

Stop this, girl. You keep this up, and you'll be blubbering in your helmet.

Yeah, let's at least wait until I've got a pillow I can soak.

Right, and get back to the Wasp. *The recirculation system needs all the water it can get.*

Kris tried not to laugh at her dramatics and her own comeback.

Still, she chuckled.

"What are you laughing at?" Jack said. "I could use something at the moment."

"Nothing," Kris said. "Nothing that's funny."

"At the moment, I'd settle for a bit of irony," Jack said.

"If I find any, I'll pass it along," Kris said.

Twenty minutes later, they matched orbit with the *Wasp*.

"Kris," Nelly said, "I have a burst message. An unknown ship just shot through one of the two old-fashioned jump points into this system. Captain Drago asks you to please come alongside and deliver the balloot without using the radio."

57

Kris had a million questions, none of which could be answered at the moment. She left it to Nelly and her brood to bring the balloot alongside. Nelly was good, she almost plugged the balloot's off-loading pipe right into the *Wasp*'s transfer station to the reaction tanks.

Once the sailors had the balloot tied down, Kris quickly brought Launch 1 around to catch the hook into the drop bay.

She felt rather insensitive handing Maria off to the first sailor who glided onto the launch, but the petty officer was headed for sick bay, and Kris wanted to be on the bridge, if not immediately, then ten minutes ago.

"What have we got?" she demanded as she shot onto the bridge and caught a handhold on her Weapons station.

"We don't know," Captain Drago said. "Where's the chief?"

"Down there somewhere. We hit something like a jet stream sideways, and it ripped us up good. Two of us held on, so you have reaction mass. We haven't heard from Launch 3. It had the chief, the colonel, and your scrounger."

"That's not good," the skipper said. "Nelly, can you make anything of what sensor feed we got? We're not using any net we can avoid. Plug yourself directly into the Sensor station if you don't mind."

Kris shoved off from Weapons and grabbed a handhold on

Sensors. Nelly had a wire into the station a second later. Quickly, it replayed a ship entering the system.

It didn't look like anything Kris had ever seen.

"It doesn't match anything in *All the Worlds' Fighting Ships*," Nelly quickly answered. "The engines and power plant don't match anything our intelligence says the Iteeche have. They also aren't much our like the aliens that have tried to shoot us up. However, if anything, they are closer to those aliens than anything human or Iteeche."

"But not a match," the skipper said.

"They match nothing I know of," Nelly said. "I take it you don't want me to use any active sensors?"

"Don't you even think of doing that. We're a hole in space. They're decelerating and can't likely get a good read of what's behind their plasma jets. They don't know we're here, and I like it that way."

"What's on your mind?" Kris asked.

Captain Drago rubbed his chin. "We could just sit here, quiet-like, and let them pass us by. Or we could come charging out gunning for them, assuming there's a chance of us getting a shot at them and surviving the fight. I haven't thought of a third option."

Kris mulled those options over for a second. The first one sure looked good.

"What was the ship's speed when it came through the jump point?" she found herself asking.

"Hard to say for sure on passive sensors," Sulwan answered, "but looks like it was doing some sixty-five thousand klicks an hour. She's decelerating at about 1.5 gees."

Without Kris's asking, Nelly opened a small window on the forward screen. It showed the present system as a tiny dot against a large star chart. Iteeche space was marked in yellow. Then a large red circle appeared.

Its diameter was well beyond Iteeche space.

"Nelly, add in the three systems that have been eating Iteeche scouts."

Nelly did. The three flashing red systems were all inside the circle.

"So they made a big jump from outside Iteeche space," Kris said. "They're slowing down in this system, and will, I'll bet, use it to make a series of small jumps to check out the neighborhood. Just like I had PatRon 10 do."

"It certainly looks that way," the skipper agreed.

"Nelly, where will the two old-fashioned jump points in the system take this bogey if she tries them nice and slow?"

Nelly showed two systems within twenty light-years. "Neither one is occupied," she reported.

"And from those systems?" Kris asked, really, really wishing she could keep her mouth shut and do something stupid for a change. Hadn't her friends paid enough for the Longknife legend this trip?

More systems lit up. "Several of them have large Iteeche colonies," Nelly said.

THIS IS FROM THE MAP I DON'T HAVE, KRIS.

No one on the bridge asked for clarification. If Nelly said it, it had to be true.

In all her life, Kris had never more wanted not to say something, but words tumbled slowly out of her mouth. "So what we have here is an alien scout ship. She did a big jump to a base system, and now she's likely going to nose around. And if she does, she'll find a large chunk of the Iteeche Empire."

Kris paused, then went on. "Question for the class. If she does get back, how long before a mother ship like the last one we just saw follows? But if she doesn't get back, will they just write her off, or will they immediately send another scout?"

"There's no way for us to answer any of your questions, Your Highness," Captain Drago said. "So, Commodore, what are your orders?"

Once more, it came down to what could a Longknife pull out of her hat. Kris suppressed a sigh. Her hat was empty. Her pot of gold was drained. Everything she had or ever had been had been poured out in the last few weeks.

Wasn't there anyone else to take responsibility for this mess?

"Sulwan, if I did want to take a potshot at that alien, how could I do it?"

The navigator had been working with her board at a furious rate since Kris came on the bridge. Now she looked up, seemed startled by the use of her name, and blinked groggily at Kris.

"I figured someone would be asking for my opinion," she said. "Our 24-inch pulse lasers are good for forty thousand klicks. Our 5-inch long guns can reach out maybe a bit longer, but I have this wild suspicion that they wouldn't do much damage to anything bigger than a torpedo. Anyway, the direct course from Jump Point Alpha to Jump Point Beta won't put that ship anywhere close to within range."

Kris liked what she was hearing, but her mouth had a mind of its own. "What kind of activity could put us within range?"

"I knew you'd ask, and it all depends."

"You want to explain that?" her captain asked.

"Not really. Did any of that silly metal you used to hold on to the balloot come back with you?"

"We did not lose that much," Nelly put in. "You had lost a lot in the fight, but there's still about half of what you started with."

"Well, then I guess we can try making like a rock again," Sulwan said. "Two orbits from now, if we were to make a hard, 3.5-gee burn, while we're behind this noisy ice giant, we could go from a nice round orbit, if I do say so myself, into a rough slingshot course that would put us headed out in the general direction of the alien."

Sulwan paused for a breath. "If they are real dumb, and don't notice that no asteroid flew into a pass at this ice giant, but just take for granted that one came out the other side, they might let us drift up close to them. We'd have to stay real, real quiet, and we'd have to use the armor for a disguise, but we could close to thirty-eight thousand klicks of them."

The navigator sighed, a long-winded one that would make any Irish mom proud.

Captain Drago frowned at his navigator's work, then eyed Kris. "It might work. Now, one question for you, Princess. Are you going to try to open communications with them before you shoot them in the back? Because if you do, and they shoot on sight like they did the *Fury*, all this ain't going to be worth a bucket of warm spit."

"You have a good point," Kris said. "I'll have to think about that."

Then it was her turn to ask a question. "Captain, Sulwan's course calls for us to break out in two orbits. Have you heard or seen anything from Launch 3?"

"Nothing," the skipper said. "And Chief Beni of all people will know that we can't afford for them to talk to us."

"Yes," Kris said. "I'll be in my cabin if you need me."

"I'll try not to need you, Commodore," Captain Drago said.

58

Kris made it to her quarters without having to say another word. Once there, she stretched out, floating a few inches above her bed, and just stared at the ceiling.

"Nelly, what went wrong with Launch 3?" she finally asked.

"Kris, we weren't monitoring each other's boats. We were using just about all the capacity we had to manage the cable."

"Did Petty Officer Moreno's being unconscious contribute to the situation?"

"Maybe, Kris, but Scrounger was also in trouble. He'd lost his lunch, and the colonel was trying to do what Jack did for poor Maria. Launch 3 was the last one to fly into the jet stream. The pilot may have flinched, or tried to slow down a bit, or maybe changed his angle of attack."

Nelly paused, most uncomputer-like. "I do not have the data to reconstruct the incident. I am very frustrated. How do you humans stand such limitations?"

"We get used to it, or we go crazy. Nelly, you just can't think too much about it."

"Not think about something. That is not easy for one of us."

"I suggest you figure out how to do it."

There was a knock at the door.

Kris ignored it.

There was a second knock. "Kris, are you in there?" came in Jack's soft voice.

"Go away."

"And let you sulk in your tent?" he asked.

"I don't know what I'm doing," Kris said. "Just leave me alone."

"Not a good idea. Now, you have two choices. We can conduct this talk through the door, or you can invite me in. It's not like I've got anywhere else to go, or I'll get tired of hanging out here in midair."

"I ought to let you hang out there."

"But you'd miss my lopsided smile," he said.

"Who told you I liked your lopsided grin?" Kris snapped. She sat up in bed, which, under zero gee, would have bounced her head off the overhead, but she caught herself.

"I know that I have a lopsided grin," Jack continued, with his grin in evidence even through the door, "and you just told me you liked it. Thank you, by the way."

"Nelly, open the door. At least if he's inside, I can throw something at him."

The door clicked open.

Jack floated in, shoved off the door, and came to a stop above Kris's desk chair. He settled into a sitting position, six inches above it. Every minute or so, he'd use the chair's arms to recenter him as the air currents or his movements caused him to drift.

Or when Kris hit him with a fluffy little teddy bear, a gift from Cara.

"You've got a good pitching arm," Jack said. "Maybe your staff ought to form a baseball team to take on the *Wasp*'s other divisions."

"We'll be missing three players," Kris said to shut off the flood of cheer.

"If anyone can find his way back to the *Wasp*, Chief Beni is the man. Do we know anything about the launch's condition when it broke away from us?"

"Nelly tells me they weren't monitoring things on each of the boats. The pilot may have tried to slow his entry into the jet stream." Kris rattled off the facts, trying not to touch any of the feelings they might raise. "Old Professor Scrounger appeared to be in trouble, and Colonel Cortez was trying to help him.

Imagine if you'd been taking care of Maria by yourself when we hit that wall of air."

Jack let out a low whistle. "Worse luck for them."

"So they clobber in, and we make it back," Kris muttered.

"We won't be breaking orbit for a while. That gives them time to get back."

"They've only got so much reaction mass and so much antimatter. They can't hang out there forever."

"A couple of hours is not forever."

"Boy, Jack, you just will not let me get a dour word in edgewise. Next thing you'll be telling me is that we ought to pray for them."

"Penny is," Jack said. "I said a few prayers, too. There's nothing wrong with praying at a time like this. Didn't your family ever take you to church?"

"Every Sunday," Kris said. "It was a mandatory photo op. The loving family of the prime minister paying their respects to God. Course, Father usually picked a church that had nothing much to say and didn't take up too much of his Sunday saying it."

"So all you've got is yourself to hold on to when things a whole lot bigger than you come calling," Jack said.

"You going to try to have me change my way of living?"

"Nope. The priest at our parish always said it was God's job to get you in the door. It was our job to give you a reason to come back. So, Kris, what do we do about this?"

"I think we get to keep breathing. Has Engineering said anything about the quality of what we picked up on that one pass we did?"

"The engineers are delighted. We got the usual hydrogen and helium, but we also picked up ice, ammonium, and methane. It's a real mess in the tanks, but they're doing what they can to separate it out."

"Quietly, I hope."

"The captain made a trip down to Engineering to get that message across in person. By the way, Nelly, Kris, if you haven't gotten the word, nothing electronic gets used that we don't have to use. Poor Cara is stuck playing chess with Sergeant Bruce."

"How did Cara take the trip?"

"Abby says she did rather well. Good spacer stomach, none

of the problems the other ships had. The three of them may have taken up the slack for the rest of us."

"For a while there, that was true," Nelly said.

"So, what do we do about this stranger in the system?" Jack asked.

"We'll likely have to kill it," Kris said. "It's not one of ours, and Ron says it's definitely not one of theirs, so it's likely one of those. They tend to shoot first and not answer any questions later. Unless you got an idea on how we can get this one talking, I won't risk the *Wasp* trying to talk to them again."

"Who says the *Wasp* has to be the one doing the talking?" Jack said, his lopsided grin in full evidence.

"Who could? We can't leave anyone behind. Once we get out there, we've got to start accelerating for the next jump point if we want to make it out of Iteeche space."

"We've got a holdful of jump buoys," Jack said.

"Right," Kris said. "I knew there was some reason I kept you around."

"Actually, it was Penny's idea. It doesn't take a genius to figure out that we're headed for a fight, and we don't want to repeat the *Fury*'s fate. She came up with the idea of leaving a buoy in orbit and having it issue demands for the alien to stop decelerating and drop its reactor immediately."

"And it's going to understand what we are saying?" Kris said.

"They jumped into the Iteeche Empire. They've been blowing up Iteeche scout ships. They ought to have acquired some Iteeche."

"And we just happen to have our own Imperial Representative right on board," Kris said, sitting up carefully so as not to show Jack how gracefully she could bounce off the overhead.

"What is it with you, Jack?" she demanded. "All I want to do is sit here, chewing on how much life sucks, and you come barging in here like some muscle-headed Pollyanna, demanding I smile and get back on the horse and give it the spurs."

"That's just the advice my grandpappy gave me and my old man. Just because he came back from the Iteeche War missing an arm and part of a leg was no reason to cry about it. Gimpy leg and all, he managed to run down Grandmama."

"So he never let his problems get him down."

Jack sobered. "It got him down, now and again, but he got

back up, he always said. At least he did until the day he ate his old service revolver."

"I'm sorry, Jack," Kris said, very aware that she wasn't the only one with problems.

"I take it as a warning. At least that's what my old man said to do. Grandpappy was fine as long as he kept busy. What do you say we drop down to Iteeche country and record Ron saying, 'Stop in the name of the Emperor.' "

Kris nodded. Jack held the door open for her. She gave him just a bit of a hug as she went by him. "Thanks for coming for me."

"Thanks for opening the door and letting me in."

59

Kris was at her battle station as the *Wasp* prepared to discover if she could handle a jackrabbit jump to 3.5 gees.

Behind them, a buoy trailed, timed to go live with demands in Iteeche and several human languages that the intruder drop everything and declare its intentions. Since the demands would be coming from the ice giant's orbit, and the alien would be over a million klicks away, Kris doubted there would be any shots fired.

The alien would either reply, or it would be fair game.

Of course, there was no way to tell if its reply was, "Die, you slimy aliens," or, "We come in peace for all bug-eyed kind."

Just once, Kris would like a plan that didn't have all kinds of holes in it.

Ready or not, Sulwan mashed the deceleration button, and the *Wasp* began a dive toward the ice giant that had fed it enough that they hoped they could make it home.

The plan called for them to take full advantage of the giant planet's size. First, they would decelerate into a grazing orbit, then they would pour on the acceleration and come out from behind the planet, ready to blaze a trail across the system, and just miss diving directly into the sun.

That assumed the alien bought into the idea that the *Wasp*

was just a wandering rock that was not sticking to any safe orbit in this system.

The remaining Smart Metal™ would be spread out in front of the *Wasp* as she came rocketing out from behind the giant. Nelly already had a program that would change the face they showed the alien. If they put a ranging laser on them, all they would see was a tumbling rock.

Nothing here to see, move along, people . . . or bug-eyed monsters . . . as the case might be.

Hope was not a strategy. Luck was not a tactic. That was what Kris had learned in Officer Candidate School. If she pulled this off, she'd have to write her old instructors a letter about changing the curriculum.

On second thought, would anyone but a Longknife have the guts to pull this off? Would any rational teacher want to suggest this to any student whose best interests they cared for?

"Nelly, remind me to skip that letter."

"What letter?"

"Never mind; if you missed that, it's just another embarrassment I don't need to admit to."

"First, Kris, you are getting very good at keeping your thoughts from me. Secondly, you are getting very strange. You know how you used to talk about my needing to spend some quality time with Auntie Tru?"

"Yes."

"I'm thinking we need to find someone for you to spend some quality time with, whatever that is, talking to someone about how your brain is working . . . or not."

"Make a note about that, Nelly, now shut up."

There was a loud bang, then a ripping noise came through the hull members, not over any audio system. People on the bridge looked around but saw nothing.

"We've got a hull breach along the main spindle, between bulkheads G and H," Penny reported from her station at defense. "Damage control is moving to contain it. Report is that a weld let go."

"Very good," Captain Drago said calmly.

The *Wasp* continued its dive toward the ice giant below. The ride started to get a bit bumpy. A clang and rattle told them something else had let go. Kris found herself holding her breath.

She wasn't the only one.

"Three containers just made an unscheduled departure from the *Wasp*," Penny reported. "No one in them, but I think we lost half our supply of famine biscuits."

"I don't know whether to cry or cheer," the petty officer backing Kris up whispered not at all softly. People chuckled and found they could remember how to breathe.

"Zero gee in five . . . four . . . three . . . two . . . one . . . now," Sulwan announced. "We will be in zero gee for ten minutes. Stay close to your high-gee stations because this is only an intermission."

Captain Drago mashed his comm button. "Damage-control parties, keep the bridge informed on your progress. Lieutenant Pasley, can you give me any idea of what might break next?"

"I'm not sure, sir," Penny said.

"We might have some ideas," Mimzy answered at her neck. "The *Wasp* is not rigged for remote sensing of its hull stress, but Dada has noticed a minor air loss out of spindle compartment J, and identified a blur in the pictures coming from outside camera 53. The container it is on may not be attached as securely as we wish."

"Damage control," Captain Drago ordered, "check for a leak in spindle compartment J-2-g. Advise any personnel in the outer containers that they may end up on their own if they don't move inward like we told them to."

The skipper shook his head as he cut his commlink. "We ordered everyone to the spindle. But why do I think there are a few ignoring me? Boffins, likely."

As the ten minutes of no acceleration passed, various damage-control details reported in. The burst seam was welded shut again. The leak was plugged, then welded down. Four boffins reported to the spindle. They'd been recording the view from the close encounter with the gas giant.

Common sense had finally prevailed over scientific curiosity.

The second high-gee blast would accelerate them onto a course that would take them close to the alien. With luck, it would also make it look like the rock they were impersonating had approached the ice giant from behind and therefore been out of sight all along.

That was the hope.

Kris was only too aware that a whole lot of people had died while she did what she hoped would work.

In the end, she reflected, she had accomplished what she set out to do. That huge mother ship was not going anywhere for a long time, if ever.

Still, a lot of her fleet had died in the effort.

Had it all been worth the cost?

Kris wished she could go back and find out. Hopefully, she would get a chance to someday. But for now, getting home and reporting what had happened was her job.

As the long hours slid by while they drifted toward the alien, Kris tried not to think about the calls she'd made and the price people had paid for them.

The alien did nothing. They did nothing.

They both did a whole lot of nothing.

Then the alien went active, and matters got interesting.

Very quickly, things got mortal.

60

"The alien just ranged us," the lieutenant, now covering sensors, reported.

"With what?" demanded the captain.

"Laser and radar."

"Did they get a ping off our cover, or from the *Wasp* itself?"

"Just the cover, sir,"

The skipper leaned forward in his seat. "Now we see what happens next."

Kris took the cover off the firing button.

"Captain, we're tracking them visually with the 24-inch pulse lasers and both of the defensive 5-inchers," Kris reported.

NELLY, GET READY TO RANGE THEM, THEN FIRE, ON MY ORDER.

KRIS, I HAVE THEM IN MY CROSSHAIRS. THEY AREN'T QUITE IN RANGE, BUT IF THEY TAKE A SHOT AT US, I'LL RANGE THEM AND BE READY TO FIRE IMMEDIATELY.

BUT WE WAIT, GIRL.

YES, KRIS, WE WAIT.

The alien ranged them again.

And the buoy back at the ice giant started blaring demands on several channels and in several languages.

"Unidentified starship in this system, identify your captain and his lineage. What port are you registered at and who has received your oath of loyalty?" The word choice was Ron the Imperial Rep's, but Kris had chosen to send the same message out in several human languages. Let the aliens figure it out.

"The bogey has ranged the buoy," the new lieutenant reported.

"It's too far for them to fire at it," Penny said.

At a million kilometers, all they'd be doing was warming the metal of the thing. Still, a second later, the alien blasted away at the distant demanding source.

"They just do not know how to say 'How are you?' do they?" the captain said. "Commodore Longknife, you are weapons free as far as I'm concerned."

Kris was tempted to give them a second warning. After all, they'd just fired off everything they appeared to have.

"Appeared to have" was the operative phrase.

Who knew what they really had?

"Range them, Nelly, and fire."

The 24-inch pulse lasers reached out for the stern engines of the alien. The angle was acute but manageable. The 5-inchers lashed out for the bow, where the command center was on the *Wasp*.

Kris's bottom was pushed down into her high-gee station as the *Wasp* put on acceleration. Far below, the reactors began to pour electricity directly into the power system, sustaining the blast of the 5-inch guns through several seconds and beginning to replenish the capacitor for Laser 1.

The rocket motors also slammed the *Wasp* forward and to the right.

That proved to be a good idea because the aliens did indeed have more lasers ready to come online. Even as their aft end crumbled under the *Wasp*'s fire, they were reaching out to pierce their attacker.

Fortunately, their attacker wasn't where she had been.

In front of them, the supposed rocky face of an asteroid converted itself to defensive shields to protect the *Wasp* from the next shot.

But the next shot never came.

It started aft, and the explosion then shot through the ship. In seconds, what had once been a good-sized scout ship was nothing but a sprinkle of glowing bits.

"God in heaven," Penny said.

"Was that us, or did they have another dead man switch?" the skipper asked no one in particular.

"I can't tell you, sir," was all Kris could say.

"I think there's something still there," Sensors said. "Give me a moment; there's a lot of junk out there, but I think it launched a small boat just before it started firing."

"Do we finally have some survivors?" Kris asked, then did something about it. "Jack, we need to deploy some Marines. There's a small boat out there, maybe full of survivors. Maybe, I don't know, someone who wanted to live rather than fight to the death."

"Could it also be a booby trap?" came back from the Marine officer.

"Anything is possible. Just, if they're alive, I'd really like to talk to them."

"Understood, Commodore, keeping my Marines alive is secondary to getting them alive. We can do that."

With an order from Captain Drago, Sulwan applied precious reaction mass to braking the *Wasp* and edging it toward the small alien spacecraft.

Kris watched the alien carefully but tapped her commlink. "Please broadcast on a narrow band, back to the ice giant, a recall message to Launch 3. If it's still out there, let's let them know that we want to hear from them now."

"Aye, aye, ma'am," came from the comm watch.

Captain Drago eyed Kris.

"I've got to at least try to find them."

The skipper nodded.

Kris went back to watching the craft as they closed in on it. It made no attempt to dodge them but continued to drift in space. That could mean a lot of things. Kris tried to concentrate on the good and leave the bad to Jack and his Marines.

"That's close enough," the skipper ordered.

"Jack, you can launch your Marines."

"We're taking Launch 1. I've got Gunny with me."

Then the silence began to stretch.

Kris didn't much care for the first words that broke it.

"We got a situation here," said Gunny Brown.

"What kind of situation?" Kris asked.

"The hatch to this boat is open a good ten centimeters."

"How'd that happen?" Kris demanded.

"Your guess, Commodore, is as good as mine," the old NCO answered.

"Will you look inside?"

"That's what I'm doing, ma'am. It's kind of ugly. There appear to be two bodies, young, I'd say a male and female. Oh. What have we here?"

The silence stretched.

Kris waited.

"I think I know why these two fled the scout when the shooting started," Gunny said. "I'm holding a makeshift survival balloon with two of the cutest little babies you'd ever want to see."

"Babies?" Kris echoed.

"Yep, if they were my kids, I'd say they're about six months old and in need of feeding or a diaper change from the squalling."

Kris had prepared herself for a lot of things, but this was nowhere near even the bottom of her long list. The *Wasp* and its crew had always met the demands she put on it, but a nursery? A nursery for orphans?

A nursery for alien orphans!

"Skipper?"

"I know, Your Highness, I will have one of the compartments close aboard the spindle converted into a nursery. We'll canvass the crew for anyone with experience or the desire to be a nanny."

"Thank you, Captain Drago."

Out in space, Launch 1 came alongside the craft. The baby bubble was immediately transferred to the longboat. Then the Marines jury-rigged a collar to attach the alien craft to the launch and began a careful return to the *Wasp*. Once back, the alien craft was locked down outside and the launch recovered. The Marines, though they had not shared an atmosphere with the aliens, still were subjected to full decontamination procedures.

The babies were quickly hurried into isolation before they were changed. Their parents had taken along a bag with baby essentials in it. The surviving boffins immediately subjected it to a thorough analysis.

The diapers were cloth, very much like cotton. "We can match them."

The rubber pants were made of some sort of plastic. Again, they could be replaced.

The formula was the big question mark. It seemed to be based on something like milk, with a lot of extras. The boffins were confident they could duplicate it from the *Wasp*'s shrunken supplies. That assumed that something humans called milk could be digested by someone with such different DNA.

First, they would use what the presumed parents had brought.

Kris left them to their work.

Which left Kris with nothing else to do but watch as the bridge crew prepared to blast for the other fuzzy jump point in the system.

She tapped her commlink. "Communications, have you heard anything from Launch 3?"

"Nothing, Your Highness. We're guarding every frequency Chief Beni might use. We haven't raised so much as a hum or a click that might be them."

Kris closed her eyes as the breath went out of her. She wished she was like Penny. At a moment like this, she'd say a prayer and feel better for it. Instead, Kris struggled to bring in a deep breath, then let it out slowly.

She opened her eyes, and found that the skipper was staring at her. He had one of those "it's time to go" looks on his face, but he didn't say a word.

Kris gave him a short nod of thanks for the courtesy of his silence, and said, "Captain Drago, let's see how far the *Wasp* can jump."

"As you wish, Your Highness. Lieutenant Kann, if you will, bring us smartly to one gee and let's see how much speed we can put on this boat before we hit that jump."

"Aye, aye, Skipper," Sulwan said. "Bringing her smartly to one gee. Course for the Jump Point Fuzzy Beta. Let's see if we can pole-vault this puppy all the way across the Iteeche Empire."

61

"Chief," Kris snapped, and knew immediately that she'd made a mistake. "Nelly, where are we?"

"There's activity in the system," the new lieutenant announced a bit breathlessly before going on. "I think it's ours," he squeaked excitedly.

"Kris, we made it to Alien 1," Nelly announced. They were in the system with the devolved aliens that Auntie Tru and Kris's real great-aunt Alnaba were studying.

"I told you that eighteen revolutions per minute counterclockwise would give us just the right direction," Nelly said proudly.

The computer had called it on the nose. The speed had given them the distance to jump clear across the rest of the Iteeche Empire. The rpms had pointed them in the right direction. Then again, maybe the new fuzzy jump points were a bit more controllable than the old ones.

Kris breathed a sigh of relief. She was joined in that by everyone else on the bridge and, most likely, the *Wasp*.

"Unknown ship in system, identify yourself," came from the main screen. A bigger-than-life image of a quite earnest young lieutenant in U.S. Navy blues glared from that vantage point.

Captain Drago waved Kris's way, allowing her the honors.

Kris stood and faced the screen. Her khakis were stained and rumpled from several days' wear. She stank. The water Engineering had been able to produce still stank of ammonia and methane. What they drank was triple-treated, and still only met Cara's "yuck" standard.

All that might be true, but she was still Princess Kristine Longknife, a lieutenant commander in her grampa's Royal U.S. Navy, and the woman who led the great Fleet of Discovery.

And that was what Kris said to the young officer.

After which the screen went blank.

Vicky had joined Jack on the bridge. She giggled. "Do you often affect men that way?"

"I guess I should have brushed my teeth this morning," Kris admitted.

"I don't like the smell of this," Jack said, "and I'm not talking about your body odor."

"I agree, Jack, I don't think this is some kind of joke."

The young man reappeared on the screen; this time he looked like he was holding a dead rat at arm's length. "You will exit this system immediately and report to Admiral Santiago on High Chance. If you deviate in any way from that direct course, I am authorized to use deadly force."

"Hold it," Kris said. "We've been struggling for the last I don't know how long to get back to human space. We're just looking for a dock, some food, a bit of water and reaction mass."

"I am not to talk to you about anything other than getting you to High Chance. Can you identify the jump point out of here?"

"Mister," Kris drawled, "we discovered the jump point into here and did the first explorations below, remember?"

The young officer showed red at the collar as he remembered the system's recent history, but he went doggedly on. "Then you can point your ship at the jump point. My patrol craft will follow, and if you attempt to escape, I will disable your engines."

"Kid," Captain Drago growled, "the *Wasp*'s engines *are* damn near disabled. You throw even a hard word at them, and they're likely to quit on us. You be careful. Relax. We will follow your directions to the letter."

The screen went blank. The fast patrol boat fell in behind them, and they made for Jump Point Alpha. It was a slow trip because the skipper held the *Wasp* at .75 gee.

It gave them plenty of time to think. Jack rambled up to Kris's Weapons station and leaned close enough to whisper. "That's an FPB. Remember them?"

"All too well," Kris said. She'd commanded twelve mosquito boats like that one when six huge battleships charged into the Wardhaven system and demanded its surrender. Because of several mistakes at the high command level, those twelve boats were all that stood between Wardhaven and a bombardment that would have put it back in the Stone Age.

Somehow, Kris had held them off.

"Isn't there another system between Alien 1 and Chance?" Jack asked.

"Yes, there is," Nelly said, while Kris was still trying to get that answer out of her own muzzy brain.

"Would you have taken one of those teacups through a jump point?"

Kris shook her head. She hadn't taken one of them out of Wardhaven's orbit.

"What do you think of us bugging out after we jump into the next system? Not going to Chance?"

"You don't like the sound of our orders to High Chance?"

"Don't like the sound, smell, sight, taste, and touch of it," Jack said. "When some young lieutenant starts ordering around a Princess Royal and, maybe worse, a senior officer, there's something he knows that we don't."

"Yes," Kris agreed, "but what?"

Jack just shrugged.

"Any suggestion where we'd go?" Kris asked. "Although there are some six hundred planets in human space that I haven't been banned from, I can't think of any that would welcome me with open arms. None at least that have any decent ship-repair facilities."

Again, all Jack could do was shrug.

Despite Jack's carrying on their conversation at a whisper, the bridge had fallen silent enough to hear a sigh drop.

Kris glanced at Captain Drago and raised an eyebrow.

He shook his head. "I can't recommend that the *Wasp* attempt any more jumps than it takes to get us somewhere where we can have some serious work done on her. I tend to agree with Jack that we are not headed into a good situation, but, like you, Your Highness, I can't think of anything we can do but do what they want."

He paused for a moment. "After all, what *they* want us to do is what I was desperately hoping we *could* do."

The *Wasp* made the two jumps. As Kris expected, the FPB did not follow them.

However, two cruisers were waiting for them when they entered the Chance system. The *Wasp* immediately set a course for High Chance, and the cruisers, one in Helvitican colors, the other in U.S., followed them silently.

The lack of greeting and the total silence carried its own foreboding.

Alone, unacknowledged, the *Wasp* went where it was ordered.

62

The *Wasp* docked where it was told to, well aft on the station. No other ships were using a pier below the middle of the spaceport. The instructions to the ship had been short and forceful, and had called for no response.

That didn't mean no one tried to talk to the *Wasp*.

The main screen on the bridge suddenly came alive. A civilian was staring wide-eyed at them. "Are you the *Wasp*? Did you fire on the aliens like you said you were going to? Where are the rest of the ships?"

"Cut that off," Captain Drago ordered. "Communications, what just happened?"

"Sorry, sir. We've been intercepting something like that every couple of seconds. There are about thirty or forty people trying to call us. Some are newsies. Some I have no idea who they are. Anyway, I'm sorry, we'll make sure that doesn't happen again."

"Glad to know that we aren't totally forgotten," Vicky said. "Me not being under your orders, maybe I should talk to some of them."

"Please don't," Kris said. "I don't want to remind you, but you are presently under my protection. You really want to leave the *Wasp* and check into the local Hilton?"

"I wouldn't last an hour," Vicky muttered. "Okay, I've re-

considered. You stay my best friend forever. Wherever you go,
I go. Only, without your Chief Beni, how safe are you going to
be? Have you thought of that?"

"I'll make you a bet," Kris said. "Two seconds after we
dock, I'm going to be under so solid a lockdown that a fly-
speck can't get in."

Vicky made a show of thinking that over, then shook her
head and smiled evilly. "No way I take that bet."

A few minutes later, the *Wasp* tied up to its assigned pier.
Moments later, fresh air, water, and other amenities began to
flow into the ship.

"You better keep our sewage on board for a while," Kris
suggested. "No one has come down with the alien's equivalent
of Montezuma's revenge from those two sweet kids, but you
never can tell."

"And it may buy us a bit of time before we're crawling with
newsies," the skipper agreed.

"Skipper, there are an admiral and a planetary governor on
the pier along with a Marine guard detail. Do I let them
aboard?" came from Gunny on the quarterdeck.

"I'll dispatch the princess to talk to them. Don't open the
hatch until she gets there. Your Highness, you want to get into
a biohazard suit?"

"Great idea, Skipper. Jack, you want to come with me?"

"I wouldn't miss this for the world."

"Nelly," Kris said on the way to her quarters, "is my report
ready to download?"

"The short version and the middling-long version, I can
squirt to anyone in a few seconds, Kris. But the warts-and-all
version, that takes up a lot of bandwidth and time."

"Could you load a copy of that on flash storage?"

"I'll have a copy ready in your room."

Back in Kris's cabin, she found Abby laying out a set of
khakis. "These are the least wrinkled and smelly. I tried to
wash out a pair of panties and bra in the bathtub, but they stank
worse afterward, and I have no idea how the ammonia and
methane would have felt after you wore them for a few hours."

Kris nodded. "Thanks for thinking about me."

"I ain't had much to do but think about you. And visit those
cute kids down in the nursery. Cara just thinks they are the

cutest things, even if they won't let them out of the quarantine bubble to play with her."

"She's a good kid. You take care of her."

"And you take care of you," Abby said, adjusting Kris's gig line.

Then she gave her a hug. A wide-open big one. "We'll find you, Kris. No matter where they send you, we will find you, and we will come for you."

"Don't come too soon," Kris said. "Take your time. Don't play into anything they've set up to get you, too."

"Gamma didn't raise any dumb kids," Abby assured her, and helped her pull on the blue moon suit.

Done, Nelly pointed out a tiny flash-storage cube. Kris palmed it before she left. Nice, these new suits had pockets.

Kris met Jack in the passageway, moon suited up himself.

"Let's go see how they welcome the conquering hero." Then Kris reconsidered her words. "Make that surviving broken-down sailor."

Jack hummed something that sounded a bit like "When Johnny Comes Marching Home," but maybe wasn't.

At the quarterdeck, the usual formalities were a bit awkward in the moon suits, but Kris made sure to follow tradition. Gunny opened the hatch just enough for Kris and Jack to slip through, then shoved it closed again.

Kris easily spotted Admiral Sandy Santiago. Governor Ron Torn of Chance came as a surprise.

Kris marched as smartly as the roly-poly suit allowed, presented herself to the admiral, and snapped a salute. "Lieutenant Commander Longknife reporting as ordered, ma'am."

The admiral returned her salute and quipped dryly, "I wasn't expecting to see you so soon."

Kris turned to the governor. "Ron, how's the wife? The kids? They must be growing like weeds."

"Don't try to change the subject," he demanded, then changed it himself. "What are you doing in those biohazard suits?"

"We've got aliens aboard," Kris said with solid pride. "So far, there's no sign that they have any bugs that like us, but we got them in quarantine, and I thought you might want to have us be careful for a while longer."

"You've captured aliens!" both the admiral and governor exclaimed.

"Yep, two of them."

"They're talking to you?" Ron said.

"Yes, and no," Kris said, letting a pained look cross her brow. "They've got teeth coming in, and I think what they're saying translates into 'Teething is the pits.' You want to see a picture?"

Without waiting for an answer, Kris pulled a picture out of one of the pockets of her blue suit and waved it at Ron, proud as any grandparent.

Ron stepped back in horror. Then he focused on the picture and his horror turned to puzzlement. "They look just like my kids looked when they were babies."

"That's what Gunny said when he found them. The species will not talk to us, will shoot at us every chance they get, and they look just like us. How's that for ugly?"

"We are not supposed to talk to you, Kris," Admiral Santiago said. "My orders are very specific. You will only be debriefed on Wardhaven."

"Those are not my orders," Ron said. "Kris Longknife, you are under arrest for crimes against humanity. You will come with me."

"I can't do that, Ron," Kris said. Once, the thought of going with Ron would have brought a rosy hue to Kris's cheeks. Once, she'd thought that Ron might be the one man for her. But he'd gotten a good look at life around a Longknife, and he'd run, not walked, for the nearest exit. Next she heard from him, it was a wedding invitation that sadly lacked her name in the place of honor.

"Are you resisting arrest?" Ron demanded.

"No," Kris said.

"Then explain yourself."

Kris raised an eyebrow to Admiral Santiago and waited for her to do the honors of enlightening the governor of the planet below.

"What she means, Governor Torn, is that Chance never contributed a dime to the construction of this station. Wardhaven got it dumped on her when the Society of Humanity went poof. We've been defending it ever since. While she's on

High Chance, Princess Kristine is on sovereign Wardhaven territory. You can apply to extradite her, but it would be a waste of time. You're way down the line of people demanding her scalp, and King Raymond I of United Society has staked his claim on the head of the line."

"But my wife had a brother on the *Triumph*. What happened to him? That ship?"

"Last I saw of it, it was an expanding ball of glowing gas," Kris said, making no effort to take the cruelty out of her words. "All our ships went out with a very big bang. I suspect they all blew their reactor containments to make sure the aliens didn't have anything to examine."

"Kris," Admiral Santiago snapped, "you are under orders not to say anything."

"Then, Ron, why don't you head home. If you want, you can take the babies' picture."

He snatched it and stalked away. He had to pass a detachment of Marines to get off the pier, but the admiral did not order them to relieve him of his picture.

Kris waited until he was out of sight, up the escalator to the main deck, then began unzipping her suit. Jack followed her lead.

"Theatrics," Sandy said.

"You got to dress the part," Kris said.

"So those kids are not all that dangerous," the admiral said, sounding like she'd need some serious persuasion.

"Penny's taken the watch in the nursery. Her computer, Mimzy, has got a set of nano guards cruising that room that are guaranteed to let nothing in or out."

"Mimzy, huh. I heard that Nelly got in the family way," Sandy said. "Gal, who knocked you up?"

"I did it all by myself," Nelly said proudly.

"It should be so easy," Sandy drawled.

"She did have some help from my credit chit," Kris said dryly.

"But you've been very glad I did," Nelly shot back.

"We wouldn't have made it back without her and her brood," Kris said. "We lost three of them along the way. Chief Beni, you remember him?"

"Yes, brilliant, if somewhat weak in leadership traits."

"We lost him and two others."

"I'm sorry, Kris. From the looks of things, you lost more than just them."

"I observed six of the battleships that came with me be blown to dust. The last two, *Swiftsure* and the Imperial *Scourge*, were running for all they were worth when we took our only chance to duck out of the system. The aliens chased down two of my ships and blew them to bits. Taussig on the *Hornet* led them in one direction, so I could go in the other. That did let us shake them."

"Did you get the mother ship you were aiming for?"

"We chewed up the stern half of something that made a moon look dinky. I don't know if that kept them from launching an attack on the avian race we were trying to protect. I need to go back," Kris said.

"Not until you've seen the king."

NELLY, SQUIRT SANDY THE TWO SHORT VERSIONS.

DONE.

The admiral's eyes widened as the quickest read of Kris's report came through to her. Kris reached over and slipped the tiny data cube into the admiral's pocket.

Sandy's hand slid in as Kris pulled out.

"What are you doing to me?"

"Read the whole report. Take special note of the DNA we took off the kids' parents. The aliens that plundered the planet and the ones that first shot at me hadn't intermarried for, say, ten thousand years. The kids' folks haven't met the other two populations in the last hundred thousand years. There are a whole lot of big uglies out there." Kris paused to let her words sink in.

"If you want to after you read that, you can destroy it. I don't think you will. If you can see your way through to it, deliver a copy to Winston Spencer. He won't be able to use it, but it will help him know where to snoop."

"You are going to get us into those adjoining cells in that deepest dungeon."

Kris changed the subject. "Is it as bad as Ron makes it sound? Am I already being declared a war criminal?"

"Oh yes," the admiral said. "Now, I've heard a whole lot more than I was supposed to, but then I'm a Santiago, and we're used to getting the bloody end of the Longknife legend.

I've got orders to put you on the first fast courier ship available. They yanked the nearest one off its run when they heard you were here, and it's due to dock in five minutes. Right across from the *Wasp*."

"I'll need to take Jack with me."

"Sorry, girl, your orders are to go alone and say nothing to any of the crew."

"Jack's my security chief. He's kept me alive I don't know how many times."

"Kris, these courier ships are manned by people with the highest clearances. They carry packets that no one trusts to transmit in the securest ciphers. That, and you are ordered to go alone. Sorry, Jack, you stay here."

Jack seemed to mull that claim over . . . and find it very lacking in substance. But several of the Marine guards were eyeing him with serious intent. Kris figured Jack could take them, but what would they do next?

With no good options, Kris let out a sigh. "Okay, Jack, you come along when the *Wasp* does. Or the *Wasp*'s crew. I'm none too sure the old girl has another trip in her."

"I'll get to Wardhaven as quickly as I can," Jack assured her.

Across from Kris, a port opened, and a small young woman ducked out. "I'm supposed to pick up a Kris Longknife, whoever she is. I got a tight schedule, so let's get a move on."

Suddenly there was no more time. Jack stood there, arms at his side.

She stood there, arms with nothing to do.

And Jack raised his hands to her, and suddenly she was in his arms, holding him holding her.

For the moment nothing mattered. Not the war, not the politics, not the confusion and hatred.

She held him and he held her and there was nothing but the warmth of his embrace and the beating of their two hearts.

Jack's fingers brushed her throat, sending shivers through her. She looked up at him. His lips trembled, soft and waiting. She kissed him.

Or maybe he kissed her.

All the wasted years and months and hours plunged into the seconds they had here and came away full of wonder.

"Pardon me. I've seen this kind of thing before, folks, and

I understand, really I do, but I got my orders, and one of you needs to get his or her ass on my boat, pronto."

The words of the skipper of the courier boat were insistent . . . and apparently well practiced.

The urge to tell the young woman what she could do with her orders was on Kris's lips, but she didn't want to break from the warmth of Jack's kiss.

The thought of her refusing her orders came to mind, quickly followed by the vision of Sandy ordering her Marines to pick Kris up and toss her in the boat.

She had her service-issue automatic. She could shoot it out right there on the pier. She'd likely end up dead or sleepy-darted.

None of her prospects looked good.

She opened her eyes and gazed up into Jack's. The same agony was on his face that must be on hers.

"Damn, I wish we'd done this sooner," he said.

"Me, too," Kris said, and took a step back.

His hands refused to let her go, but held her even as she took a second and a third step away from him. Finally, only their fingers were touching.

Another backward step broke even that contact.

"I will find you," he whispered.

"I will wait for you," she whispered back.

Then she turned, every fiber of her being in agony and rebellion, and marched the short distance to where the courier pilot waited.

"Let's do what you have to do," Kris said.

63

Kris had never made a trip at 4.25 gees. She'd heard that the courier ships did, but she'd never believed it possible. She spent the entire trip floating naked in a tub of something a lot more viscous than water. Food and water both came from a tube. The skipper sent a crewwoman around to catheterize Kris.

"This just for us girls?" Kris asked.

"Nope, I get to do it to the boys, too. You ought to see how they blush."

Other than that visit, Kris was left alone for the entire, though quick, flight to Wardhaven.

In the brief seconds that Nelly took to send Sandy Kris's report, Sandy's computer sent Nelly the latest update of Winston Spencer's report on what was happening inside human space.

Refusing to give in to the temptation to wallow in self-pity and regret, Kris had Nelly run the news feed. It held no surprises.

As she'd expected, once the wreckage and bodies from her first encounter with the aliens arrived at Santa Maria, the story went public. Suddenly, everyone knew the Iteeche were losing scout ships to some unknown horror and that the mercurial

Kris Longknife had insisted on taking out a squadron to see what there was to see.

That eight battleships had been added to her force by various concerned parties didn't make it into the media.

Not then. That was saved for when the second report came back.

Kris thanked her lucky stars that a beauty like Amanda Kutter had taken the ride back to human space. She was too lovely not to be invited to all the talk shows. If she hadn't been out there talking, the only story in the media would be that Kris Longknife had taken it into her head to attack some poor, innocent alien ship that was just wandering through the cosmos minding its own business.

If Kris had been reading a report, she would have thrown it across the room in her fury. Of course, at 4.25 gees, Kris could hardly raise a finger.

She let Nelly go on.

Amanda had gotten Kris's story out. The destroyed alien planet and the target avian species did not get lost entirely. Still, the Emperor of Greenfeld dispatched a fast cruiser squadron to carry the message that Admiral Krätz was recalled and should return immediately.

Those cruisers might or might not have carried the same orders from Geneva and Musashi. Those two governments chose to play it close to their respective vests.

Kris noted that Wardhaven sources never mentioned that she'd been shipped the Hellburners. That seemed like a very telling omission.

It was a fast trip to Wardhaven, but before Kris was even halfway there, it was clear that she'd been set up to take whatever fall was necessary.

After a while, Kris ignored the news and spent the time floating in the tub meditating on her future. What was the old saying?

No good deed goes unpunished.

They docked at High Wardhaven station quick and smooth. The crewwoman came around to decath Kris. "I'm sorry we didn't get to wash your uniform, but we don't carry so much as a clothes washer. The crew is all girls, and the uniform can get very informal."

"No problem," Kris said. "If Grampa doesn't give me time to shower and change clothes, he deserves what he gets."

"Grampa?"

"My great-grandfather. King Raymond."

"Some of the girls thought you might be that princess, but you looked so bedraggled when you boarded . . . well, you know."

"It's been a rough stretch," Kris admitted, adjusting her own gig line.

"There are some folks waiting for you pierside," the woman advised Kris.

"I bet there are," Kris said, and marched for the tiny quarterdeck.

And bounced her head off the overhead.

"Be careful. They only chose girls less than five-foot-two and 105 pounds."

"Where do they recruit you, ballet school?"

"Several of us did take a swing at dance."

Kris forced herself to leave the wonderfully relaxing small talk behind and finished her exit without further head bashing.

Three station carts awaited her: Two were full of Marines, and one had a Navy captain driving. He waved her to him. She went.

He took off as fast as the cart could go as soon as she sat down. He didn't even wait for her to buckle in.

"We've got to catch the next ferry dirtside. If we're late, they're under orders to hold it, but that will tell anyone watching that something special is going on."

"Am I expected?"

"The media has been told you'll be arriving in two days. Three-gee acceleration all the way. Kid, you stink. Didn't they have a shower on that boat? That uniform's a disgrace."

"At 4.25 gees, you don't shower," Kris said. "And no, they don't have a clothes washer. You want to drop me by Nuu House. I'd love a shower and a clean set of whites."

"Nuu House is surrounded by reporters. So is Main Navy. Your meeting was moved just an hour ago, when there may have been another leak."

"It's nice to be popular," Kris said with as much cheer as she could muster.

"What is it with you?" the captain snapped, not taking his eyes from the drive. "First you get away with mutiny. Then you gallivant off wherever you want, missing ship's movement. What you don't blow up, you mess up. For God's sakes, woman, why don't you get out of my Navy and give us a chance to recover some of our honor?"

"I'm glad they sent along such a fan," Kris said, holding on to her temper with her fingernails. This was not going to be a good evening. As tempting as it was to take this old fart's head off, it would not help her with her grampa or with the Navy.

"Someday I must write my memoirs and get the truth out," Kris said softly.

"A pack of lies," the captain growled. "Your kind says whatever sells books."

Kris leaned back in her seat and slid her cap over her face. "Wake me up when we get there." That at least got her peace and quiet for the drive to the space elevator.

Kris and her guards hustled aboard the ferry, which dropped loose even as they were taking their seats. This one had Admiral Crossenshield's secret quarters and passageway. They were never in view of the paying customers.

Dirtside, it was the same. Kris was hurried into a fleet of large SUVs with darkened windows and quickly found herself on a limited-access highway headed out of town. Somewhere she'd lost the captain who was such a groupie. The team she'd picked up did not attempt to talk to her; neither did she say a word to them.

They turned off the highway onto a winding country road. Kris had a dim recollection of visiting the place once before. It had been before Eddy died, when Grampa Al was prime minister. If that was the case, the place had very good security.

Of course, nothing was as tight as the Fortress of Security that Grampa Al had built for himself now.

When they stopped before an imposing mansion, the door was held open for Kris. Even the Marine doing the honor sniffed as she passed.

She was led upstairs to a formal study: wood paneled, thick carpet, a huge marble desk. Four overstuffed chairs had been arranged in a square. Admiral Crossenshield and Field Marshal Mac McMorrison sat at the right and left hand of King Raymond to some—Grampa, usually, to Kris.

The one empty chair faced the king.

Kris used a hip to shove it aside and stood defiantly in front of her king.

"What have you been up to?" he demanded.

"Nothing you folks didn't want me to do," she shot back.

"That's not true," the admiral in charge of Intelligence insisted.

"Isn't it?" Kris answered. "I wanted to take a squadron of tiny scouts out to see what lurked in the big, bad universe. Lightly armed and traveling light, we could see what there was to see and run home quick with our report. So what do you send me out there with, Crossie? Eight battleships! Even better, you get three shills to serve up the ships. None from Wardhaven—excuse me, the U.S. Nope, we're sending scouts; they're the ones sending the battleships."

Kris paused. No one tried to take the floor away from her. "Of course, you're sending out a Longknife, and everyone knows that Longknifes go loaded for a fight. That's what the legend says, right, Grampa?"

"They chose what they sent. They gave them their own orders."

"Yes, they did, thank you very much. Of course, Crossie here sent them out a copy of our secret meeting. He made sure they knew there was something nasty out there."

Kris again waited. Still not a note of dispute from the men across from her. For the first time, it dawned on Kris who was missing.

Grampa Trouble hadn't been invited to this night's work.

She should have guessed that would be the case.

"But eight dinky battleships were hardly enough to take on those aliens' monster. No sir, I may be a Longknife, but even I'm not that crazy. Or not crazy yet. How many years, Grampa, does it take to get as crazy as the legend needs?"

"A bit longer, Kris," he said softly. A stranger might have mistaken it for the caring voice of a grandsire.

"So you sent me the Hellburners."

"Hellburners?" Mac asked.

"Yeah, that's what we named the torpedoes with chunks of a neutron star in their warheads. By the way, we managed to spike that stuff with antimatter. Boy, you talk about an explosion."

"How did it go?" the king asked.

"Rather spectacular. That huge mother ship . . . about the size of a big moon . . . we clobbered it. Maybe as much as half of her was gone when we had to duck out on the show in a hurry. Best guess is we killed ten, twenty billion aliens. Maybe more.

"The problem, Grampa, was that the monster mother ship had kittens. Lots and lots of kittens. Huge things that made our battlewagons look tiny. And boy were they mad. They took off after us like you'd expect someone to chase whoever had just beat up their mother ship.

"And boy did those kittens pack a wallop. Laser and lasers and more lasers. They didn't have any armor. Something tells me they've been the biggest, meanest bastards around for a long time. Nobody's got a good hit on them for a while. We changed that. I expect they'll be slapping on the protection real quick."

"I warned you not to use our best weapon right off," Mac told his king.

"Duly noted," the king muttered. "Kris, did you take out the mother ship?"

"I don't know. Things got bad, and we had to run. It's all in my report. But you might want to read the addendum first."

"Why?"

"Because we ran into another alien ship on our way home. It was a scout ship that managed to jump deep into the Iteeche Empire and, bad luck for it, landed in the one worthless system where we were refueling. Likely they planned to make a couple of small jumps, glance into several systems, then run home. That didn't happen. We killed it."

"Good," Mac and Crossie said.

"But a couple tried to escape with their babies. Cutest things. We got them alive. Not the parents, the hatch on their craft came open. They're dead. The kids are alive. And we've got a DNA sample of the aliens sniffing around the rim of the Iteeche Empire."

"Are they the same as the ones you ran into before?" the king asked.

"Yes and no. We've got DNA from three of the four groups we ran into. If we can trust the DNA results, they are related. Related," Kris repeated, "but distantly, like no intermarriage in the last hundred thousand years for some. There are three or four of those monster mother ships wandering the stars looking for systems to devour. How much you want to bet me that we've found all there are?"

Each of the three men uttered their favorite swearword. Kris, her report given, settled into the chair she'd ignored.

"That changes things," Mac said.

"No it doesn't," Crossie insisted.

"The people aren't ready for another long war," King Ray said in a tired voice. "We need more time to mobilize them. There are enough complaints about taxes as it is. If we start building a huge Navy, there'll be hell to pay."

"Ah, guys, one word of straight dope," Kris said. "Wars come when someone else decides, not when you're ready for them."

"You shut up, woman," Crossie shouted. "If you'd done what we wanted, there wouldn't be any of this trouble."

"You sent me the weapons," Kris snapped. "You didn't want me to use them? If you hadn't sent me those Hellburners, I wouldn't have had two cents to put in. As it was, they were worth a good fifty cents."

"Gentlemen, gentlemen," the king said. "Arguing what might have been is a fool's game. We have to think of what to do now. Kris, you nailed that alien scout?"

"Totally. That joker will not be reporting."

"So that band of aliens will have a potential hot datum. However, what Kris did on the other side of the galaxy has got to draw their attention. Even if the tribes have wandered far from each other, having one of their mother ships blown to hell will have to focus their attention. That should buy us time. We can use it to start a media campaign to prepare the voters for what's to come."

Kris stood up, shaking her head. "Assuming that what's to come ain't coming at you already. You men disgust me. I've had it being your cat's-paw. Mac, give me my papers. I'll sign them. I quit."

For the first couple of years of Kris's Navy career, every time she was called in for one of these little talks with Mac, he had her resignation papers in hand and was quick to offer them for her signature. Kris couldn't really blame him; she'd given him plenty of reasons to wish her on someone else's payroll.

Now she was demanding her resignation papers . . . and all he did was sit there and shake his head.

"What's the matter? You've wanted me to quit for years."

"We can't have you out there," the king said, "on talk shows like that Amanda girl. You're pretty enough that they'd all want you. And you talking up a war right now is not what we want. Sorry, Kris, but you are in the Navy, and you'll stay in the Navy."

"I've finished my service requirement," Kris said.

"Yes, but I have declared an emergency. No one leaves without our letting them out. And you, young lady, we won't let out. Mac here has found a job for you. Madigan's Rainbow wants a squadron of fast patrol boats to help them control their system's space. We think you're just the person to command their boats."

"I'll still find an open mic," Kris said, standing up.

"Not on Madigan's Rainbow," Crossie said with a grin full of casual evil.

Kris eyed the three of them and saw only confidence that they had her just where they wanted her. She shook her head in anger, frustration, and disgust.

Finally, she spat, "Once, you may have been a great general, Raymond Longknife, maybe even a brilliant one. But now you're just a two-bit politician."

Since Raymond was her king, she gave him the opportunity for the last word. He just looked at her, showing no emotions.

None at all.

Kris did an about-face that would have made her DI at OCS proud, and marched from the room.

About the Author

Mike Shepherd grew up Navy. It taught him early about change and the chain of command. He's worked as a bartender and cabdriver, personnel advisor and labor negotiator. Now retired from building databases about the endangered critters of the Northwest, he's looking forward to some fun reading and writing.

Mike lives in Vancouver, Washington, with his wife, Ellen. He enjoys reading, writing, dreaming, watching grandchildren for story ideas, and upgrading his computer—all are never-ending pursuits.

He's hard at work on Kris's next story: *Kris Longknife: Furious*.

You can learn more about Mike and all his books at his website www.mikeshepherd.org or e-mail him at Mike_Shepherd@comcast.net.

An original
military science fiction novella from
MIKE SHEPHERD

Kris Longknife:
TRAINING DAZE

A Penguin eSpecial from ACE

Kris Longknife dodges assassins, gains an unwelcome
(though rather handsome) bodyguard, and puts together a
training squad to travel from planet to planet, preparing
crews for the newest, fastest, and deadliest fighting ship.

And, of course, nothing goes as planned!

ONLY AVAILABLE AS AN E-BOOK!
DOWNLOAD IT TODAY!

penguin.com
mikeshepherd.org

M931T0811

From National Bestselling Author
MIKE SHEPHERD

· · ·

The Kris Longknife Series

MUTINEER
DESERTER
DEFIANT
RESOLUTE
AUDACIOUS
INTREPID
UNDAUNTED
REDOUBTABLE
DARING

· · ·

Praise for the Kris Longknife novels

"A whopping good read . . . fast-paced, exciting, nicely detailed, with some innovative touches."

—Elizabeth Moon, Nebula Award–winning author of
Kings of the North